Oh My GOD *My Heart!!!*

IT IS THE PURSUIT THAT MATTERS

BY
APRIL D. METZLER

Scripture quotations taken from the New American Standard Bible® (NASB), Copyright © 1960, 1962, 1963, 1968, 1971, 1972, 1973, 1975, 1977, 1995 by The Lockman Foundation Used by permission. www.Lockman.org

All supporting/secondary characters in this book are fictitious and created from a combination of character traits witnessed through real encounters of many people from the author's true life experiences. Some scenes are depicted in full transparency and completely factual, others have been created in a more generalized context to reach a wider audience of readers in hopes they would be more relatable for general daily applications. This book is fictional and based on real stories.

Quotations chosen to accompany this book pre-date the 1924 year specified as of January 1, 2020 per Public Domain guidelines.

ISBN/SKU: Print - 978-0-578-72120-0
Cover Art created by April D. Metzler © 2020
Photo used is an original, royalty free, Creative Commons Photo by Adrianna Calvo available via https://www.pexels.com/@adriannaca

CONTENTS

Introduction

Dear Heart,

There is a pursuit happening *Right Now* - a pursuit of the heart. It is not a pursuit of just any heart, though. No, indeed! This pursuit is *of* **Your** heart! God is pursuing *Your* heart with a fervent, unending, unfailing **Love** of the greatest kind! **His Love** endures *forever* and reaches from *everlasting* to *everlasting*! It does not change. It does not leave. It does not falter or break. It is always there! It is never anymore but a breath away, waiting for *Your* heart to see it, to know it! Can you imagine **that** kind of love!? Can you fathom what that love feels like, what it looks like, what it must be like to experience on the daily?! If you are like me, you cannot begin to imagine, cannot begin to fathom the extent of such a pursuit as the one God has for *Your* heart. Oh, to know fully and completely the depth, the width, the height, and the length of the vastness of His Great Love for me! What a day that will truly be! May the eyes of my heart be enlightened to the all in all of the fullness of God's Love for me! This is what I pray.

If you are like me, you know that there is another pursuit happening *Right Now*, as well! It is also not a pursuit of just any heart – It is a pursuit of God's heart *by* **You**. Once you have even simply glimpsed such a Love as God's for *Your* heart – *that's it*! Nothing else can satisfy. Nothing else compares! And so, the pursuit begins! The closer God draws you in, the more your heart desires to pursue Him… to know Him… to seek Him… and to Love Him more!

Like a lot of folks I know, you may be saying, "Alright, April. I get it. God Loves me. **BUT** where are all the details?! What does that look like in action? What does that sound like in the way that I think and communicate? How does that work, exactly?! What happens when things go South? What do I do on those silent days or boring days, busy days or stressful days? How does this whole pursuing God thing work, on the daily?" I hear you! When I first accepted my Daughtership from my Heavenly Father, it was all a foreign language to me. *MANY* years later,

Introduction

I am here writing this story for you and for encouragement of my own heart, even, to help answer those questions and more!

Based loosely but deep-to-the-heart-of-the-matter on my life experiences, trials, struggles, truths, and more - Join me as I walk you through life's adventure seen through the eyes of one woman who is pursuing God on the daily… at least trying to! You will get to read about her deepest desires, her inner thoughts, her relationship with her Father God, and all the in-betweens are explored as she pursues God in her days. You get the inside view of what is going on in her mind and her heart, what her soul struggles with right in the middle of these circumstances, and example after example of God's provision in and through it. Each new day is a gift, she knows that – **BUT** what she *doesn't know* is what is coming in each of those new days! Is she prepared? Is her heart ready for what comes next?!

As a mother, as a wife, as a business owner…and simply – a woman and daughter of the King, you see her heart and soul completely unveiled and vulnerable with glimpses of 30 minutes here, an hour there, a morning here, and a day's recounting there. She even takes you down memory lane a few times to as she considers and thinks upon God's Provision even before she knew Him! Whether she is faced with a weakness or a strength, this one woman is doing her best to *walk the walk* and *talk the talk* now, but is it Good enough? Have you ever wondered that, too? She sure has! Yet, what does God say about that? You can see what her reaction to this is, as well! Also, find out *with* her as she strives to find the answer within all the moments that we each ask during this pursuit our hearts are called to for Him: What do I do now…What do I do right now, in this very moment to honor God and glorify Him?

It is the Pursuit that matters,
for in the pursuit you find who you are called to be!
We are Daughters and Sons of the Father –
Yes, you are a Child of God!
And <u>**Your Father Loves You So Very Much**</u>!

Opening Prayer

Father,

Thank You for this day and thank You for Your provision in and through every moment! Father, let this book bless the heart and strengthen the resolve of the reader that comes before You with me today in prayer to walk with You, Dad, in all that is chosen to do, to say, and to think - yes, indeed, in all ways! I thank You, Lord, for blessing this book to be an encouragement to set our eyes upon the Lord Almighty - First. Yes, let it be a sharpening tool, a comforting tool, and a tool for the heart to know You are with us! Finally, I stand in agreement in prayer with Paul, just as he prayed over the church at Ephesus, for the reader - Lord, thank You for hearing this prayer over Your child, today! Dear Reader - I pray *"that the God of our Lord Jesus Christ, the Father of glory, may give to you a spirit of wisdom and of revelation in the knowledge of Him. I pray that the eyes of your heart may be enlightened, so that you will know what is the hope of His calling, what are the riches of the glory of His inheritance in the saints, and what is the surpassing greatness of His power toward us who believe."* Thank You, Father, for all You do and all You are every single day - my all in all - my life - my heart, is Yours. Your will be done in this day & always.

Your Daughter,
April D. Metzler

ACKNOWLEDGMENTS

To God I give all the glory and honor. His will be done. I would like to thank my husband and daughter who have supported, encouraged, and prayed with me, day in and day out, through the course of creating this book. Thank you, both, for this last year of endurance and perseverance in this writing journey! I love you both very much! To my mother and stepfather, thank you both for your love and support, prayers and encouragement in and through this! To my father and stepmother, thank you, as well! To all my church family, sisters and brothers in Christ, family and friends - you are loved so very much and your encouragement has been so very appreciated, dearly.
And another grateful heart Thank You to all of the *beta readers* who participated in their candid feedback of reading this book! You have been such an encouragement to my heart! I appreciate the time you invested in reading and all of your wonderful thoughts to help improve this from the reader's viewpoint.

All those involved in this process, whether big or small, have been such a blessing to my heart and I would like to sincerely say to your heart from mine,

"THANK YOU!

~And please, dear heart, remember always~

God Loves You So Very Much!"

Chapter One

The Talk

> *Glory in His holy name;*
> *Let the heart of those*
> *who seek the Lord be glad.*
> *Seek the Lord and His strength;*
> *Seek His face continually.*
>
> 1 Chronicles 16:10-11

Oh, how chilling the night air seemed to be on my skin! It had seemed so timid throughout the day. Yet, it had turned from that slight and bashful breeze to a persistent fan of frigid wind. The chill of it caused me to begin shivering. The goosebumps and hair standing up and down my arms reminded me tonight that my body knew this feeling, oh so well! My skin shouted through the shivers that it simply was not an advocate of it, in the slightest! I stepped inside the welcoming shelter of my home just long enough to quickly grab the burgundy sweater on the back of the chair. I had nonchalantly tossed it there as I went through the living room earlier that day. The sun's warmth and the lack of consistency with the breeze did not warrant such a covering then, but this night air sure did! As quickly as I had entered the house, I returned to the beckoning arms of the night. "Why was I out here again?" I asked myself as I considered the chill, my body's blatant defiance of the cold and its avid desire for warmth. "Oh, yes. That is right. I was going to have *The Talk* again," responding to myself as if I really needed a reply. I chided myself for falling into that old trap of having a two-sided conversation with...myself.

It had been a few months now since I had set aside this special time to really, genuinely, intimately have *The Talk* with God. This 'set aside' time had somehow managed to be 'tossed to the wayside', instead. Whether accidentally or absentmindedly, it just had. I thought about this for a bit longer with a shake of my head. Visiting with my Heavenly Father was a priority, but more importantly, it was something I longed for deeply. I desired to share my heart before Him. There was an intimacy in our *Talks* that I could not find anywhere else! I knew that. Yet, here I was with months behind me and no steps taken to ensure that I had quality time to share with God. I could feel my heart sadden at the thought, growing heavier with every passing breath as the realization came upon me that I had missed Him vastly! Like a child that sees her father sitting at the table, I felt my heart's desire to run up to the Father with that same measure of great urgency! Yes, like a child would leap to her father's lap to join him at that very same table, I too desired to leap up into my rightful sitting place with God at this figurative table for that special time of our *Talk* tonight!

I knew that this missing time was not because I did not care, of course. It was nothing at all like that - quite the contrary, actually! I had just…been busy. "Yes, that is right," I agreed with my own thoughts on the matter. I had been busy. Life had been busy. There had been

- appointments and schedules to keep
- family gatherings we were expected to participate in
- holidays and birthdays to recognize
- events that my little family had been excitedly waiting to attend
- work and church throughout the week
- responsibilities and duties that had to be done
- daily chores, of course
- meetings to be at that could not wait
- and the list goes on...

I could not and did not want to remind myself of them all! In hopes of preventing myself from being too overwhelmed at recalling all the many things, I resigned from the thought process with the simple summation that It had just been busy. I settled with the insufficient list I had unwittingly allowed to begin.

There was a lot to do. There seemed to be many people who needed me. I merely had not been able to get free until now. "So, have I been too busy, then?" I countered in conversation to myself. "No, of course not! I could never be too busy to have *The Talk*, right? …...Or could I?" I immediately defended myself in thought. "Oh, this is just nonsense! Stop it!" surprising myself by speaking out loud. The words came with a sting and stern sharpness that shocked me somewhat. I was right, though.

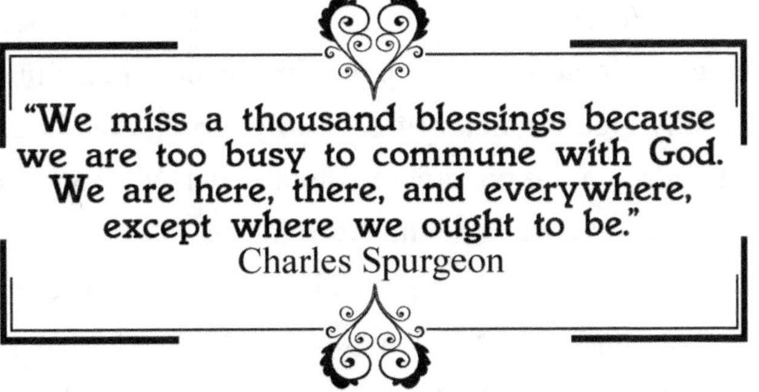

It was nonsense. If anything, I had allowed other things to pull me away from focusing on one of the higher priorities in my life: what I fondly referred to as *The Talk*. I had been distracted by things that could have been placed on hold. Some, I could have chosen to say no to, all together. They had redirected my focus from what was important. "So, what was I waiting for?" I asked, encouragingly, while simultaneously reprimanding myself. I took a hesitant step forward, breathed the chilly night air deeply in, and began.

The next morning had been full of rushing around. Our only child had a sleepover with friends the night before. They were all excellent and well-behaved teenage girls. Not much oversight needed at this stage beyond telling them to go to bed…multiple times… with a hidden smile upon my lips. I recalled the many nights that I, myself, stayed up way beyond a reasonable hour at that age with visiting friends. I paused and thought, "Well, that is the girls' night thing to do, right?!" There were having a blast and that is all that mattered. My own night was focused on *The Talk*. I had spent a few hours outside, eventually making a warm fire in our little portable fire pit. It was a convenient little contraption that we could drag from the front to the back porch and on trips, out-and-about. It was not super-hot, but warm enough to cut through the chill.

Afterwards consisted mostly of lying awake in bed - hoping and praying the girls would go to sleep. Unfortunately, their failed attempts at whispering and the silly giggling that drifted loudly through the house and echoed off the walls to our bedroom did not quickly quiet down. My hope was that they would eventually find their way into a restful sleep for the sake of us all. I knew full-well that it was a slim possibility, yet I still hoped. I could only imagine what my parents experienced in those nights like last night. A new sense of appreciation hit me deeply as I recalled the many nights I was allowed to have friends over and how that must have impacted my parents. The morning's rush consisted of getting the same late-night kiddos around and ready for the new day - their breakfast made, clothes on, shoes tied, hair and teeth brushed. I marched them through the usual routine. "That routine continues, sometimes, until their late teens and early twenties!" I said to myself with a hint of comical exasperation. It never seems to fail that one of those darlings drops the ball on one or more of those essential tasks. Amidst the rush they place themselves in - whether due to drowsiness or far too many outfit changes – they always miss something, it seems, that needs a gentle reminder to do.

When any of our daughter's friends come over, responsibilities do not get shucked. It is a rule and understood expectation at our house. Chores still exist, and they do not magically disappear when friends come over. On the contrary, friends are incentivized to pitch in and give our daughter a hand from day 1. Now, that does not mean our home is fun exempt. Fun and silliness are always encouraged in our home. I am not the evil dragon queen, or some other mean, ole character. "They can have fun and make sure work is done, too." I said to myself. Yes, that *work hard, play hard* motto is jokingly referenced, from time to time. Agreeing again, I said, "It works for my little family and definitely explains our environment!" In addition to making sure the girls got around, I had to make sure the chores were not overlooked, as well.

With the excitement and fluttering around that comes with the abnormal routine of friends visiting, it could have been easily overlooked. However, I did not need the girls starving any animals today. No matter how hard I have tried, the oversight responsibilities never seem to fade as a Commanding Officer parent. Otherwise, the ship takes on water and sinks. As the only adult on site this morning, it was *my* responsibility to make sure

> "All your children will be taught of the Lord; & the well-being of your children will be great."
> The Lord

they maintained *their* responsibility. My daughter had a few things to do before we left: feeding & watering the cats, dogs, and our 5 little chickens we had raised from baby hatchlings. "Girls...go get chores done so we can head out," I said sternly. "You don't wanna miss any of the action, do you?" I asked, already knowing their answer would most certainly be No. They jumped up and scurried to do the tasks. Considering the chickens, I thought, "Of course, those little chickens are not so little anymore, but I still like to fondly refer to them in that way, for cuteness's sake." In my memory, they are still those small balls of fluff that we brought home the year before last - wide-eyed and cute as buttons! I stuck to my guns with the girls doing the chores. Slackin' wasn't happenin'. Nope! Not today! As sure as the day is long, the animals were all tended to fairly quickly.

By the time the first hour of the day was up, I was already worn down from all the activities. It is nice to have a bit of extra energy on days like these. The rush and weight that comes from getting kiddos and myself around, all at the same time, making sure the household responsibilities are taken care of, and tending to all the animals can be quite the achievement! It definitely was when only going on a few hours of sleep! "To think, it is all done before even having the option to step one foot out of the door. Amazing!" I said.

So, when I don't have that extra energy, coffee is my go-to. Yes, on these days, if the coffee had a name, it would be something like Mr. Bounce for all that bouncing around one does, sometimes. Or maybe Mr. Boxer for all those moments that follow of fists a-blazing, ready to go, and *Let me at 'em*. That's what role coffee has in those days. The days that I have been deprived of sleep, and energy is nowhere to be found! The days where energy did some disappearing trick during the middle of the night like the famous Houdini – there one moment; and 'POOF!', just like that, gone the next! Those days that you can say 'Goodbye' to energy, because it left, stating defiantly, "I am never coming back. No! Never!" In those 'no-energy' days, I tell the day to say 'Hello' to its combatant. I kindly introduce it to my swirling-with-wispy-smoke, nice-and-hot morning cup of Joe that fills the air with its aroma. As the steam floated above the rim, I thought to myself, "It looks like the heavy, dense fog covering the hills of the Ozarks after a Spring rain. What a lovely image!"

I took a moment to myself. Just as an expert thief would swiftly remove fresh produce from the open market stand, I prayed that my moment would go undetected, also. I looked around and evaluated my surroundings. I immediately realized the girls were their very own distractions for one another. I did my best to catch the sigh of relief that was upon my lips, but it escaped. As if I might be captured any minute, I quickly looked around before sinking down into the kitchen chair that was calling my name with the cup that the coffee machine had finished preparing for me. The minutes it took seemed like forever as the machine had stoutly brewed the wonderful liquid energy. I was looking forward to having its assistance to get through the next few hours that had been highly anticipated by the girls. As I sipped the first drink, my mind drifted back to my initial question from *The Talk* last night. "Was I too busy?" I asked myself. I had somehow been sucked into this world of far too many irons in the fire.

Task after Task. Duty after Duty. Responsibility after Responsibility. Chore after Chore. Errand after Errand. Commitment after Commitment. Meeting after Meeting. Volunteer Effort after Volunteer Effort. Help after Help. Job after Job. Call after Call. List after List after List, and it seemed unending, at times! "There is so much meaning to the phrase, *there is not enough time in the day*," I thought to myself. In complete contradiction of the more profound point that rested heavily upon my heart, I countered it with, "But is

it not all just *striving after wind*?" Solomon sure thought so! He spent much time analyzing and working through what it meant to be human in this world. God had blessed him with a special gift – a deep and overflowing well of wisdom, just as he had requested. And with all the God-gifted wisdom that was bestowed on him, Solomon could surmise it all down to a few lines of what it meant to be human in this world. "*Vanity of vanities, all is vanity*," he had written. He had noted that it was all just *striving after wind*, several times…changing from this phrasing to that of *chasing the wind* throughout his lengthy considerations.

This thought struck a chord in me. For, it did seem to be such routine, such vain things, indeed, that absorbed my time and seemed to suck me dry. Those very same things would leave me feeling exhausted and lifeless in those attempts to *catch the wind*! As if one could ever catch such a thing! As is my usual response to such ideas, I ventured down the road of looking into this further. My curiosity had pulled me toward the first word - *Vanity*. It seemed odd to me in that passage to use such a harsh term. After all, *Vanity* was not used in a kind manner at all, that I knew of. In my experience, it meant the opposite. It was a rather shallow way of being that was only surface deep. So, it begged the question: "What Hebrew word was used before it was translated into this odd English word that just did not seem to fit?" Intrigued more at the thought, I flipped through the book I had pulled from the dusty shelf of my office. "Goodness! It looks like the dust has come back to mock me again! Another time, my old nemesis…another time…" my thoughts drifted quickly back to what I was searching for. The promise of future cleaning said to the dust upon the shelf seemed unimportant and minuscule in comparison to the task at hand.

I found my chair and prepared to investigate. I had many of these books for research that lined the dusty shelves of my office to appease my learning and curious heart and mind. It was something of a heart's desire of mine to learn more. Like a sponge soaking up every drop of water it can; I, too, found such a sense of fulfillment in learning and growing. Soon, I had found the target of my research - the word *Vanity* was initially written as *Hebel*.

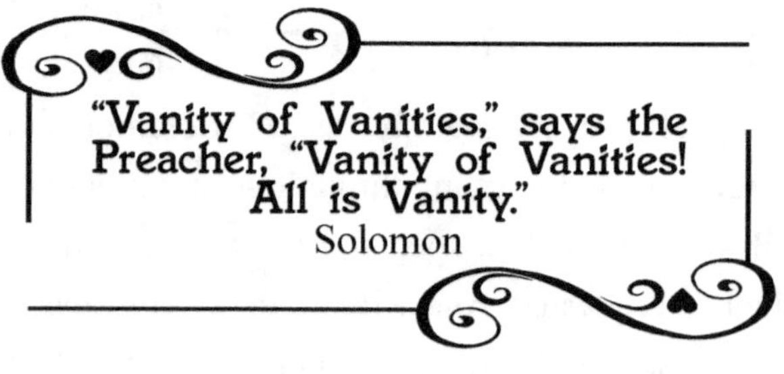

"Really?" I thought to myself. It was an even stranger sounding word than *Vanity*! Taking a moment to soak it in, I read the many references and root word meanings.

Overall, it meant *to act with futility or be futile - like a vapor…a mist…a breath, it was there one minute and gone the next - such a fleeting thing*! "Well! Was that not ever so true!? Life, itself, is so fleeting," I thought as I found myself dwelling on the profound restatement of what *Hebel* meant. I pictured the fog, again, that I had imagined against the hills when the aroma from my cup of coffee had filled the room just minutes ago. What a thing to see! Such a beautiful added adornment to an already stunning landscape. And, yet, who could capture the fog with their bare hands?! It would merely change its form, no longer this beautiful, cloudy covering of vapors floating through, across, and in-between the many trees that befall such a view as this! No. It would simply no longer be itself. It would be gone. Here one moment and gone the next. It was ever so fleeting!

"Moooommm!! We are ready. Where are you?" came the questioning call from the other room, piercing my momentarily found solitude with a sudden blast of unexpected noise. It pulled me abruptly out of the depth of the thoughtful reflection I was in. As quickly as I had snuck out of my parental duties, I was immediately pulled back into them – setting off to enjoy the day's events with a car full of girls. "Shall we, young ladies?" I asked. Their shouts of joy, exclamations, giggles, and instant chatter followed. And, so, I led them - finally able to step one foot, and then another - out the door.

MEMORY VERSE

*"Then you will call upon Me
and come and pray to Me,
and I will listen to you.
You will seek Me and find Me
when you search for Me with all your heart.
I will be found by you," declares the Lord.*
Jeremiah 29:12-14a

Chapter Two

In the Silence

My soul waits in silence for God only;
from Him is my salvation.
He only is my rock and my salvation,
my stronghold; I shall not be greatly shaken.

Psalm 62:1

The next day, I found myself in a place I don't find myself very often. The environment around me was still. A strange thing was this lack of sound - this silence. My morning had been busy, of course. It had been filled with various routine tasks that I did not care to recount within my newfound silent atmosphere. I did not dare to have this stillness shattered with such intrusive thoughts of previous busy behavior. I proceeded with care as if I was handling some kind of fragile item like a tiny, beloved glass ornament handed down from my great-grandparents. With the same level of considerate and thoughtful attentiveness, I gently unwrapped this moment to behold its beauty, as well.

My husband had a busy day ahead of him that required his departure time from our home to be roughly 5:15 a.m. It was well before the chickens even considering daring to venture outside of their nesting box, let alone cluck and crow to let us know it was morning. In-kind, neither had the sun given a single thought to its professional responsibility to show up in all its brilliance to splash beauty upon the sky in a beautiful array of colors. For, it was not anywhere near time for its cue of entry to be called. It was not ready to appear from behind the curtain of darkness that was still ever-present on the far-too-early morning stage.

With such an early start, his day at work would be a long one, but he would come home to me soon enough. He would be full of stories of the day when he returned. He would share about the many tedious areas he had to get through, unexpected twists and turns he had to navigate, and disappointments or successes he had, amidst it all. With his day being one of the longer ones - setting out so early that day and likely working late - I knew his endurance level would need to be great! So, I had taken the time that morning to pray for his over-all well-being and God's provision to be ever-present, every step of the way on this long day for him.

There are days that I invest time in prayer for my husband, and there are days that I invest deep time in prayer for my husband. This deeper caliber of prayer time for him meant that I focused my efforts on all areas of the day that my husband would encounter. I intended to cover them all! I found scriptures to ground my prayers in. Thinking about this, I said to myself, "Yes! It is super important to stand firmly upon the Word of God and His promises when interceding in prayer!" I definitely wanted to do so on behalf of my husband for this long day before him. During this time of petitioning for him, I asked and thanked God for His love, His grace, His mercy, and His faithfulness to be surrounding my husband on all sides throughout the day ahead. I know God always provides for our family. He always meets the needs of each of us as individuals as we go about our day. So, I rested in that knowledge and stood firmly in that understanding on behalf of my husband. He was still on my mind and heart as I was intently pondering on my quiet surroundings, sitting there in the kitchen, and drinking my boldly brewed morning coffee.

Prayer for protection is always a must when it comes to my husband's work industry. Money motivates and temptations lurk around every corner like a serial killer waiting to prey on its next victim as it stalks its prey like a calculating predator. Protection was very much needed, daily! And, just as the need came to my heart, in turn, scriptures to intercede and help him fight that battle came. I bowed my head. Standing firmly in His Word, I declared victory

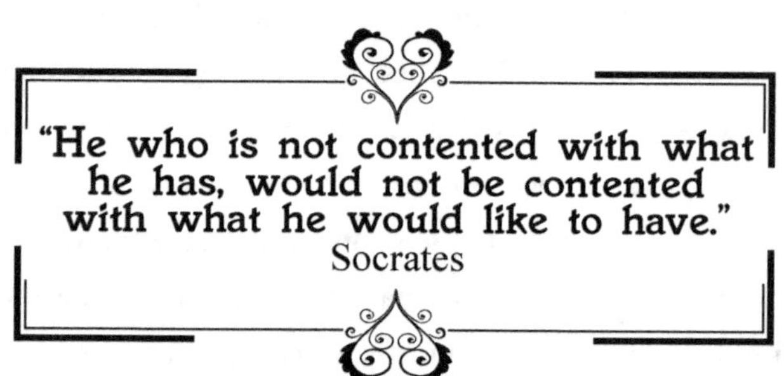

over those things that would attempt to come against my husband in this very long day. A half-hour had passed before I opened my eyes again. With that confidently spoken, I stood up - wiping away the metaphorical drudge of the muddy trenches from my armor-covered knees. "He is Yours, God, and so is this day," I said, "Thank You for taking care of him today."

After praying over my husband's day, my mind had shifted to the day ahead for our daughter. She had decided to hang out with one of the girls who had visited for yesterday's group adventures. All throughout the morning, she had been very intent upon helping with whatever she could around the house. I could see her excitement growing with each half-hour, it seemed. I recalled her excitedly saying, "I am ready to go spend some one-on-one time with one of my besties, Mom!" After a full day of events and activities, one would think that those girls would be worn-smooth-slick-out! Organizing yesterday's teenage itinerary required me to put my best foot forward to achieve the high hopes of my daughter wanting to be able to say "my-mom-is-the-best-planner-ever" for her and her friends.

We started the day with a trip to the mall. The last few weeks had been injected with perpetual requests for them to do so. So, of course, that was first on our list. After a couple hours of giggling, browsing, chatting, and a quick laughter-filled stop in a photo booth, we went to our next destination: The Art Museum. I had come across a fancy-schmancy little scavenger hunt paper that the museum puts out for its younger crowd on our last visit. So, yesterday, was the test drive for that adventure through history and art. The girls loved it! Some parts were even a bit challenging because they used hints and riddles throughout that you had to guess before finding the item.

However, that was not all we did at the museum. No, the museum was a two-fold part of our itinerary. The building, itself, rests upon about 20 acres that have been maintained pristinely over time. A luscious array of expansive, beautiful adornments scattered across the acreage in intricate details comprises the museum's well-renowned botanical gardens. So, needless to say, this little group of girls had 20 acres to explore after our lunch on the veranda of the little cafe/bistro provided by the museum. I was so grateful to remember to bring the sunscreen! Two of the girls, one being my daughter, have very fair skin and would've surely burnt to a crispy critter had it not been for those extra applications of SPF protection! Hours in the sun will do that to the fairer in skin. Sunburns were not a fun experience to endure through, no matter the age! Thankfully, I was reminded to grab it before heading out for the day.

After our museum and garden time, it was off to the races...well, for them, that is. They could do all the racing around they wanted within the confines of the roller-skating rink. My primary mission there was to relax! And, boy, did I ever need a break by that time! My back ached, my legs were telling me, "Please, no more!" and I was ready to chill, mentally, for a bit.

At some point yesterday, I remember asking myself why in the world I agreed to do all this stuff in the first place. I knew why, though. I was doing so as a favor to all the other mamas. I knew a couple of them were going through some tough patches, one in her marriage, and the other with work. So, I offered to make weekend arrangements for their girls with my daughter. However, that offer came with a contingency. I told them both I would do so as long as they made sure to make arrangements for the other little ones so they could have the day to relax. They both had agreed wholeheartedly. Thankfully, they each had a relative that answered the request. It worked out beautifully with God's provision behind it every step of the way! God knew I was quite capable of handling a weekend of activities to keep teenage girls busy, or He wouldn't have placed it on my heart to do so. I had to remind myself of that fact and encourage myself with the *I can do all things through Christ who strengthens me* passage a few times. The Holy Spirit also encouraged me to continue in His joy by reminding me with the 'why' behind my teenage entertainment crusades a number of times. Yes, their giggles are contagious, but their little moments of yacking back and forth with cattiness when they

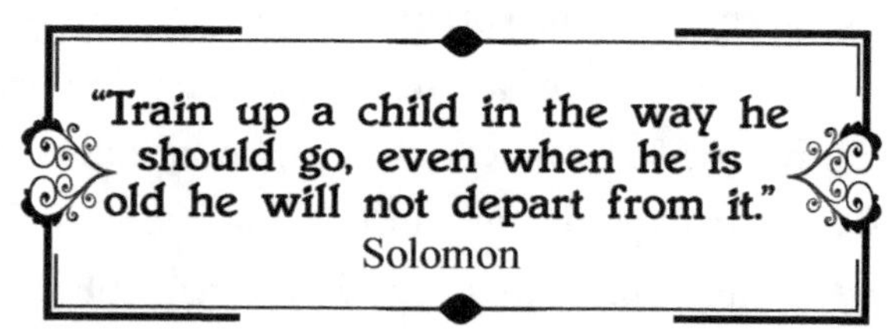

do not agree, I could most assuredly do without, especially when my body was aching to sit down toward the end of the day. Thinking about it now, I said, "Thank You, Lord, for the roller-rink-break!"

Dinner and a rented movie to take back to the house for the early evening were the last two items on the list. By the time parents came by to pick up their kiddos - I was kaput. Sucked dry of all the energy, my bed called my name in desperation! Yes, I would have thought the girls would have been just as exhausted as me the next day! However, that was not the case. It was not the case at all! On the contrary, they were both ready for another full day of adventure! Their plans would have made a worthy adversary for our jam-packed day yesterday. If the two days were likened to two resilient boxers attempting to wear the other out in the ring by dealing strike after strike, it would be accurate. I imagined each fighter dealing blows with great fortitude and strength, persisting on as each strives to be the victor, neither giving up. Yes, a worthy adversary this day would be to yesterday! "Oh, but didn't yesterday feel like that all by itself, too!?" I thought. Such a day of activities had me exhausted and ready to recharge my battery for, at least, one day. All boxed out and drained of all the fortitude and strength needed to conquer yesterday's master schedule of events, I was done…stick a fork in me… serve me with a glass of milk, because all you were getting from me was "cake" as my daughter would say. Yes, just the easy stuff today was it.

My daughter was ready to go and bursting with such energy, though! With that thought, I felt much admiration for her ability to continue. Her level of endurance with such a busy schedule was astounding! I gave credit where credit was due and commended God for renewing her strength and her health. "In all His mastery, He plans my whole life and hers, too," I said with a fond smile. Agreeing, I said, "Yes, *from before we are born*, until after we have left this earth, You Know it all, Father. Any given age and the stages of life we walk through are both parts of that masterful plan of Yours. It is all by Your beautiful design, Lord." He blessed her with such exuberant energy at the stage she is in now, *according to His purpose*. My heart was happy that she was happy and healthy and full of life.

A sparkle probably illuminated my eyes as I smiled, adoringly, at the thought of the blessing of a child God entrusted to me. He has gifted me with one of the most precious gifts - a child - and I will always be forever thankful for His grace to bestow such a gift as she! With thoughts of her on my grateful heart, I had lifted her day up in prayer, as well. I said, "I pray her needs are met in great ways! Please let her day overflow with Your love and joy. I ask for the Holy Spirit to direct her steps and caution her against any dangers that may be laid before her. Thank You for protecting her throughout the day and for Your provisions for her, Lord." A sigh departed my lips. I continued to thank God for all His many promises and His great love for her. She was His child, and He had entrusted her to me as a mother. I was so very grateful! "She is Yours, God, and so is this day," I said, "Thank You for taking care of her today."

Returning my focus to this new silent state of existence, I opened the back door. As I stepped outside, the air was so clean and fresh! I was immediately distracted by the wind and all the many colors that caught my eye. It seemed I glided down the steps that flowed so smoothly to the patio at the base of the stairs. The air welcomed me with a wave in the wind. A brief gust pushed my hair out of my face to lay gently down behind me upon my back. I said aloud, "It is a beauty of a day outside, Lord!" The temperatures were mild and refreshing. The brilliance of it all brought to my remembrance a sweet passage, *The Lord your God is in your midst, A victorious warrior. He will exult over you with joy, He will be quiet in His love, He will rejoice over you with shouts of joy.* I replied gently, "Yes, Father. You are here. In this soft quietness I hear Your sweet love. Thank you."

The weather had reported earlier that morning that there was to be no rain today. I eased over to the edge of the patio floor to verify the weatherman's report. I inched just under the cusp of the roof that covered the entire area with pleasant shade as if to not fall off some tall building. Sure enough, not one rain cloud lingered in the sky or on the distant horizon that could be viewed. The sky was a fantastically vibrant blue and quite clear of rain! It was filled with light that beamed bright enough to cause many a squint as it came in line at just the right angle with my view. The sky was populated with huge, fluffy clouds that morphed from moment-to-moment in a gazillion different dance routines. They reminded me of some type of massive production of art. I imagined a few scenarios as I stared at the clouds. In one, there was an entire symphony of music orchestrated to perfection that overtakes its audience. In another, a stupendous Broadway play production that ascends to the crescendo of excellence! And in another, an elaborate ballet of a hundred dancers that results in a magnificent standing ovation! It was Beautiful!

Just as the clouds danced upon the sky, my imagination danced about for some time. I was in awe and wonder at the ever-changing painting that was before me now, only for this day - never to return or be copied. I may have stood there longer, were it not for the two chattering birds that flew suddenly up into the bows of the roofing structure just above me. Before their chatter, I was stunned by the beauty. I was as frozen and speechless as the marble statue that I pass in the town square on my way through.

The birds left quite the impression on my thoughts. With their chatter, the Holy Spirit brought to my remembrance one of my favorite passages in the book of Matthew. It was a lengthy passage, but I had read it so many times that I had it memorized! It was written on the tablet of my heart and I rejoiced over reciting it now.

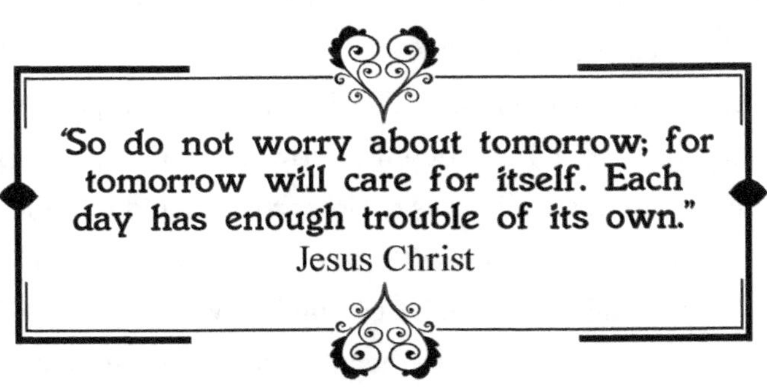

"Look at the birds of the air, that they do not sow, nor reap nor gather into barns, and yet your heavenly Father feeds them. Are you not worth much more than they? And who of you by being worried can add a single hour to his life? And why are you worried about clothing? Observe how the lilies of the field grow; they do not toil nor do they spin, yet I say to you that not even Solomon in all his glory clothed himself like one of these. But if God so clothes the grass of the field, which is alive today and tomorrow is thrown into the furnace, will He not

much more clothe you? You of little faith! Do not worry then, saying, 'What will we eat?' or 'What will we drink?' or 'What will we wear for clothing?' For the Gentiles eagerly seek all these things; for your heavenly Father knows that you need all these things. But seek first His kingdom and His righteousness, and all these things will be added to you. So do not worry about tomorrow; for tomorrow will care for itself. Each day has enough trouble of its own."

Each time I thought about this section of God's Word, it would bring such peace! Going about my days, I would simply remind myself with the instruction: *Consider the Lilies* or *Look at the birds*. Immediately, my worry would evaporate into the air!

If it was a bit more difficult of an attack, I would also remind myself of one of the subtle themes sprinkling the book of James. He expressed the importance of focusing on this day, as well. I would say to myself, "I only have this very day. That is all. I just have this day. God will take care of it all. *The Lord will fight for me, I need only to be still*!" That theme in James coupled with the passage found in the book of Exodus is my go-to when anxiety, doubts, and worry come. I *breathe in* His peace and *breathe out* the stress of the world that weighs upon my mind. I briefly thought about how this simple technique works every time for me. My heart fluttered at the thought of how awesome and helpful God's Word was in my times of need such as these. Times that I could not do it on *my own*. "He is always faithful," I said. "Any battle that comes against me has nothing on God! Not one of them stands a chance," I concluded with great confidence in Him.

I gazed upon the beauty around me to soak it in more. "I relish these moments, though! The ones that take me by surprise - that I am not looking for, but they seem to find me, anyway!" I thought with a beaming smile of pure joy. "They are glorious!" I affirmed. I was just checking the sky for rain clouds and BAM!!! There it is, in all its wonder, God's glory and beauty before me - unexpected and astounding! "You would think I would not be so surprised by it all the time and have come to expect it," I thought to myself. "Yes, but it is new and different every single day! There is no way you could derive a level of expectation that is certain, because He never does it the same way twice, silly," I retorted with encouragement and correction. I continued to expand and wrap up my retort to myself, "He is, after all, the Greatest Artist, always intricately painting the sky new just like He intricately paints all the details of our lives. With every single day, He brings

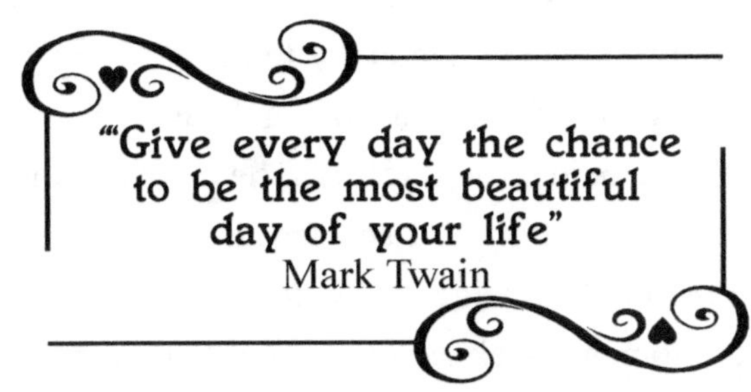

a new depth and understanding of His love that was not experienced within the confinements of the preceding day's lessons." I dwelled upon the words and concluded with a nod, "Yes. He is the Greatest Artist!"

I walked over to the hammock chair that we had drudged out of storage the week before in preparation for the late Spring season that was upon us. The early months of Spring are always filled with storms that had heavy winds and torrential rains, at times. Those storms were not exactly *hammock-friendly*. The stormy weather months had passed us by, finally. Thinking on them now, it seemed as quick as a blink almost. Gone were the childhood days in my life in which time seemed to pass so very slowly. Months no longer drug on for years and years; or, at least, my youthful mind exaggeratively thought they did as a child. Time had a tendency to pass quickly, now. The torrential rains had transitioned from their cooking level of boiling water to that of a simmer. The winds had finally become tolerable and moderate enough to be deemed safe for hammock setup. "It is so nice today!" I thought to myself.

The hammock chair rocked me back and forth. I lifted my feet off the ground after a gentle push back to begin the relaxing sway through the fresh air. I breathed in, deeply through my nose. I felt my chest rise and shoulders curl as my back arched with the deep breathing motion. I held my breath, momentarily, as I intently focused upon my surroundings. I was adamantly trying to capture and tune into the depth of awareness that I so longed for. Yes, I thirsted to witness more of my gift of stillness in this day. As I slowly exhaled through my mouth, my chest and my shoulders gradually fell as if to say they were done working and ready to relax, if only for the time being. In agreement, I thought to myself, "Yes, if only for the time being, I will relax." The moment was beautiful.

The time had seemed to momentarily come to a halt as I was drenched in the light of being still with God. There was always a thirst in the background for moments such as these. That thirst never was quite satisfied by anything else and seemed to continue to need a refilling of such. It was as if someone had taken one of our rickety old buckets and pin-pricked it a billion tiny times so that the water that filled it would trickle out, slowly and unnoticed. Then that very same water-stealing culprit had cunningly placed it at just the right angle for the bucket to *appear* to be full. It wasn't until the time came for further inspection that it was found to be low, or sometimes, altogether empty! The desire to use the water would come to the forefront to motivate such an inspection. "I don't ever want to lose the desire, Lord," I said.

> "The water that I will give him will become in him a well of water springing up to eternal life."
> Jesus Christ

The analogy of the bucket that ran through my imagination made me think of the woman at the well. Jesus had said to her, *"Everyone who drinks of this water will thirst again; but whoever drinks of the water that I will give him shall never thirst; but the water that I will give him will become in him a well of water springing up to eternal life."* Of course, I did not want the water of the world, just as she did not. My thirst was something different than this passage. When I use the words *thirst* and *hunger*, they are synonymous with the word *desire*. I agreed in my thoughts, saying, "They are simply other words that I use to describe my *desire for more* of Jesus, God, & the Holy Spirit. When I am thirsty and hungry my body does everything in its power so that call can be answered. Lord, I desire to answer Your call, every time!"

With that clarified in my mind, I asked, "When was the last time I have been still in Your presence, Lord?" I didn't need an answer, though. I knew it had been quite a while. Instead, I asked, "Prompt me to check the bucket more often, please?" An utterly empty bucket was an even worse conclusion to the mischievous efforts behind the billion tiny holes than just a low water level bucket! "No one wants an empty bucket of beautiful moments, especially not me!" I exclaimed. That thirst for God's beauty comes from somewhere deep in my bones. I can feel it with every fiber of my being! "Yes, Lord, please prompt me to check the bucket!" I likened that longing desire within me to that of a heart being pursued by a lover. The longer the time passed between, the deeper the desire. The deeper the desire, the more thirst prevailed.

Yes, the call to my heart was like that of a beckoning lover, coaxing me gently. I could hear the words being spoken now in the silence. They were reassuring and full of love. He said, "Come closer. Draw near to Me. Get to *Know* Me. It's safe to be vulnerable with Me. I will hold you close and reassure you as I protect your heart from any and all harm. I will capture every tear and count them as precious. I will keep your heart safe, for it is highly prized, fervently desired, and greatly wanted. *Just Be* here with Me. Cherish this moment with Me as I cherish the time you give *to Be* here in this moment. You are so beautiful to Me! Come learn more about the many ways I love you. *Oh, how I love thee*!! Come sit with Me and let Me count the ways that I do! Your value is *more precious than jewels*; Your worth is *far above rubies or pearls* and *more than diamonds*!! Come closer and let Me love you. Lean into Me and let Me be your *refuge in the storms*. Trust Me when I say it will be ok, for it is always ok with Me. You have nothing to fear in this perfect love of Mine. Learn more about Me and I will show you so much - about Me and about you. You are so very loved! Grow in this *Knowledge* and wisdom of the great love I have for you, until you feel it in the depths of your soul and can recount all the ways from the memory of your heart. Share with Me your deepest thoughts. Share your most intense feelings, fears and doubts, greatest hopes, biggest dreams, most passionate desires, most severe disappointments, cruelest experienced heartaches, and every last broken piece! Share it all with Me and let Me show you what it means to be

Truly
Intimately
Completely
Deeply Accepted and Loved, My Love."

That is what I feel when the thirst is refilled - Love. A love story that surpasses that of the greatest tales in history! A true and intimate romance with the *Lover of my Heart*: One that beckons sweetly to the soul. It is within these rare, still moments of silence that I can genuinely and intimately dwell upon the longing desire that is in my heart and the call that is ever-present to it. In them, I find rest in His presence, fully aware of His great love for me. It is in these times that I can feel His blessed restoration throughout my whole entire being. In the quiet hush of times like these, I am keenly attuned to His grace and mercy. His incredible peace, His overwhelming love, and His far-reaching beauty are everywhere! He surrounds me and encompasses my heart, my mind, and my soul – leaving my body to do nothing more and nothing less than *to Be* in a state of easy & blissful rest in Him. Oh, how I cherish the stillness! How I love these moments to *Be Still*." Yes. So much is heard within the silence if I practice being a good listener!" I thought. With a smile, I breathed in and closed my eyes in hopes for the moment to continue.

The Holy Spirit ushered in the Word to my memory. He said, *"Be still, and know that I am God; I will be exalted among the nations, I will be exalted in the earth."* I thought about my admittance of having too many irons in the fire. I agreed with the scripture, saying, "Even in the toughest battles, I just need to be still. Thank you for this reminder, God." *Too many irons* can be such a battle! I recalled another Psalm that is one of my favorites for battle. It is written a bit like a pep talk to the soul which makes me smile. The passage in chapter 62 always reminds me of how I tend to give myself pep talks in difficult times. David wrote: *"My soul, wait in silence for God only, for my hope is from Him. He only is my rock and my salvation, my stronghold; I shall not be shaken. On God my salvation and my glory rest; The rock of my strength, my refuge is in God."* Yes, there is greatness to be found in the silence with God!

<u>MEMORY VERSE</u>

*Therefore, having been justified by faith,
we have peace with God through our Lord Jesus Christ,
through whom also we have obtained our introduction by faith
into this grace in which we stand;
and we exult in hope of the glory of God.*
Romans 5:1-2

Chapter Three

Thinking Straight

> *Therefore if you have been*
> *raised up with Christ,*
> *keep seeking the things above,*
> *where Christ is seated at the right hand of God.*
> *Set your mind on the things above, not on*
> *the things that are on earth. For you have died*
> *and your life is hidden with Christ in God.*
> *When Christ, who is our life, is revealed,*
> *then you also will be revealed*
> *with Him in glory.*
> Colossians 3:1-4

Monday and Tuesday had all but disappeared with a blink. Activities were bursting at the seams of those last 2 days. Today was no different. Even my stillness in the morning a few days before had ended with much time invested in errands. There were higher priority household items that really could not bear to wait for another day! Before I knew it, the time had swiftly disappeared into thin air like the resulting mist that arises from the crash of the water at the base of a little waterfall. The pressure of the water crashing sent it upward with such force, only to dissipate into the atmosphere into nothingness. There it was, already 5:00 p.m. and time for Wednesday night Church soon. It was time to wrap up all those tasks and put them on the shelf of To-Do's that awaited me another day. They were not finished, but they would have to wait. I had more critical family stuff to focus on than all this unending, will-still-be-there-tomorrow-and-the-next-day, monotonous, and tedious work. Work is not a priority over my family time. It never has been, and I wasn't going to start allowing it to be now.

We were sharing our evening supper with our Church family. Bible study would follow after. The opportunity to fellowship was of high value to me. There was a sharpening that came with the Word of God during these times. "I dearly appreciate fellowshipping with our brothers and sisters in Christ every Wednesday, for sure!" I often said. One of the best parts about sharing dinner with our Church family was more than just the food. It was the real talk backed up by God's Word that permeated through the conversations. Yes, I looked forward to being sharpened and encouraged tonight. One of my favorite passages concerning fellowship is in 1 John. I thought about it now with thoughts of dinner ahead. John writes boldly, *"If we say that we have fellowship with Him and yet walk in the darkness, we lie and do not practice the truth; but if we walk in the Light as He Himself is in the Light, we have fellowship with one another, and the blood of Jesus His Son cleanses us from all sin."*

I easily dismissed the worldly weight associated with work. "Work will be there tomorrow. It is never finished, anyway," I thought. As soon as I made that focus-shift, my shoulders felt tremendously lighter. The worry and stress lifted. I had a bit of excitement sneak its way up to my lips, forming into a smile that lit up my eyes. It was time to have time for the good stuff – sharing losses and victories of the week with our brothers and sisters in Christ. "There is so much edification when we get to visit with others about God and the application of His Word!" I thought with delight. My husband asked why I was smiling so brightly. I replied, "It is Wednesday and I am elated at the opportunity to share with our family at Church. I love to fellowship with them and build one another up in the Word!" He smiled and said with a wink, "Me too! Love me some Wednesday!" Agreeing with his response, I said resolutely, "Oh! Plus, it will be nice to have a moment to climb out of these trenches for a break. I need to clean off this battle armor, anyway. Gotta get prepared for the next week to come, God willing!" He nodded. Our daughter added her 2 cents in with her own take, saying, "And I get to hang out with my friends *while* learning about Jesus, too! That's pretty cool! I am not a fan of eating around a bunch of people…or some of the food on the menu sometimes…but I am a fan of fellowship, too! It's fun!"

"Let us consider how to stimulate one another to love & good deeds." book of Hebrews

Wednesday night Bible study turned out to be an engaging message from the book of Philippians about our thoughts. Our teacher for the evening started the class with the main verse: *Finally, brethren, whatever is true, whatever is honorable, whatever is right, whatever is pure, whatever is lovely, whatever is of good repute, if there is any excellence and if anything worthy of praise, dwell on these things.* If they only knew all the thoughts that made up just one of my days… I know they would surely be worn out trying to review them if they did! Thankfully, my thoughts were privately held between God and me. "Phew! I am so thankful that You are literally the beginning and end, God, and all-powerful," I thought to myself. "It would take Your kind of power and strength to handle understanding and unraveling the depths of these thoughts of mine and what they mean. I most assuredly need You when it comes to my thoughts, Lord. 100%!" I chuckled to myself at the absurdity of being left to my own devices. "Oh, No! God forbid that!" the pleading thought followed.

I was exceptionally grateful for how much He cared, how much more He knew that I didn't even know about myself, and how little I had to explain myself to Him when it came to my *Thought Life*. Well, was that not a profound label to make of it all – my *Thought Life*? "It is quite capable of bringing into shape a life of its own, sometimes, for sure!!" I said, pondering the truth of it. How many times had I had thoughts of fear that seemed to grow bigger and bigger with every single one that came at me? I likened it to a firework bursting in the sky! The fuse would be lit and would sizzle down the tube to the inevitable KAPOW! Off it would go, flying up into the air! Just like the giant explosion across the night sky, those fears

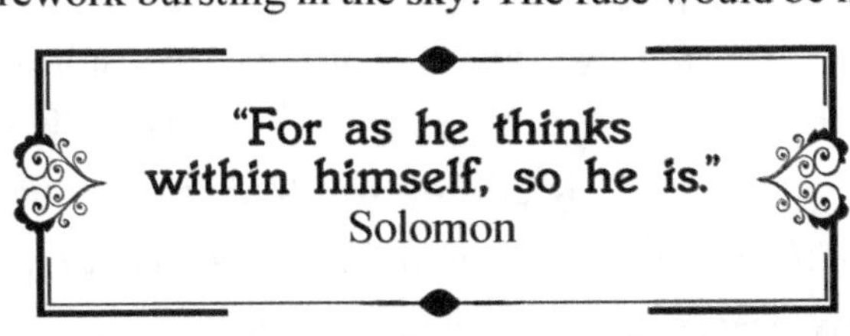

would become such a massive mountain of a thing before me! At times, they had even seemed as if they were my current state of reality! The thoughts would breathe out lie after lie, deception after deception, and half-truth after half-truth. They would come at me until I believed they were a real, live monster-of-fact that I thought I needed to…yes, fear. "And yet, My God is bigger than those fears, no matter how much they figuratively form into a giant monster against me," I said.

Fear was one of the tougher ones to battle for me. Other thoughts of attack would come against me as well. Some were just as difficult, others not so much. The enemy was highly skilled at using thoughts tied to many things, actually. Quite the extensive list came to mind with this thought. *Doubts, insecurities, confusion, worries, anxieties, shame, envy, resentment, unforgiveness, guilt, condemnation, depression, despair, anger and frustration, self-pity, jealousy, lust of the eyes, lust of the flesh, hate, stealing, greed, self-righteousness, pride…*and all the other temptations that could be listed here. I am quick to remind myself that none of these things are *mine* when these attacks do come. It isn't *my* fear – It is *the attack* *of* fear from the enemy. It isn't *my* anxiety – It is *the attack of* anxiety that is coming against *my* mind, *my* heart, *my* spirit, *my* flesh...and so on. They were all and each in their own right, a scheme - the enemy's tactics.

I was quite cautious with my words when it came to battling these devices meant for my harm. "There is power in the words I choose to speak and claim over myself, indeed!" I added in thought. I could accept the lies as my truth, or I could choose to accept His truth - as my truth. I knew this. Confirming my thought, I said, "Yes, the scripture is very clear about this. I am *Your* child, created in *Your* image – not the enemy's." I had a choice in these times of attacks. I could choose to speak life or death over myself – accept His truth or the enemy's truth of ill-intent for me. The Holy Spirit echoed this understanding with His Word. He brought to my remembrance my go-to Proverb of faith in this, *"Death and life are in the power of the tongue, and those who love it will eat its fruit."* God had impressed it upon my heart many years ago to begin practicing words of life and truth, alone. Boy, had it EVER made a HUGE difference when it came to battling the enemy in these tactical arenas, for sure!

The enemy was well-versed, indeed, at using thoughts to gain ground in my life. I had encountered many of his tactics throughout my life. "Yes, *Thought Life* is an accurate label. A thought is, indeed, something able to be brought to life if I allow it to have breath to breathe and exist," I pondered for a moment and concluded, "Yes. You name it, and I have probably thought about it, at least once, and done it twice, probably, with some of those thoughts!" The truth of that fell smartly and loudly out in the open. It visibly laid upon the ground at my feet. Like a loud thud, I momentarily feared it would be heard for miles away - but it did not. The thought may have been booming in meaning, but thankfully, it was kept within the confinement of my mind. I concluded, "Yes, and those thoughts lead to speaking words of acceptance of those very same lies spoken straight from the devil's mouth." I paused for a moment and lightly brushed it off with a simple, "Not today, satan. In the name of Jesus, you will not have your way. It's God's way for me – all the way!"

There was a time in my walk that such a dooming conclusion about how I let the enemy get away with deceiving me would have brought about a tremendous amount of heaviness. That heaviness would be followed very quickly by condemning thoughts that would bring about a horrible sense of shame and guilt. Those, in turn, would lead to other thoughts that directly impacted my view of my self – my worth, my value, and…well, just Me. I would be target *Number 1* for the arsenal of thoughts that would flood in. They would bombard my mind and damage my heart, even more so, with each attack! With one fiery dart after another, the thoughts would be flung my way with one intent and one intent, only – to hurt and to hurt deeply, tempting me to do something against God. It wasn't until farther along in my walk that I was trained in the understanding that thoughts are not always our own. Through study, prayer, and seeking sound counsel from those spiritually older than me, I was able to distinguish between my thoughts, the Holy Spirit's instruction & leading, and the enemy's temptations and lies. There was a difference - A HUGE difference!

There was a fundamental scripture that I was advised to begin using early on. It did not make a bit of sense when I first heard it, and it did not make a bit of sense when I first started attempting to apply it. However, the more and more I practiced it and studied God's Word on the subject – the more sense it made. My understanding of the battlefield of this *Thought Life* increased, gradually, over time. Paul was an apostle and well-known author of many of the books in the Bible. He discusses the struggle between our flesh and spirit in his letter written to the Corinthians. He wrote, *"We are destroying speculations, and every lofty thing raised up against the knowledge of God, and we are taking every thought captive to the obedience of Christ, and we are ready to punish all disobedience, whenever your obedience is complete."* Now, the only part of that lengthy passage that I was given was the importance of *taking every thought captive to the obedience of Christ.*

My first response was, "What in the world does that mean?!" Of course, I did not venture to say that out loud to the 3 ladies that had provided me with sound counsel - but I sure thought it! First of all, how does someone even begin to *capture a thought*?! It was absurd and made absolutely no sense to me. A thought was not a material item that someone could hold or grasp. It may as well be in the same exact category as trying *to catch the wind,* let alone *take it captive!* "What is this…some random hostage situation?! Do I need to go recruit a Swat team for this attempt? And how in the world is a Swat team going to knock down the doors of my brain and retrieve thoughts as they come?" I had thought to myself. I concluded in question to myself, muttering and shaking my head, "How can anyone succeed at *taking thoughts captive*?!" At the time, the concept was not something easily understood in my worldly way of thinking as a new Christian. Little did I know, though, that would soon *not* be the case! "Oh, how devastating to the enemy that change must be, now!" I thought to myself with a sense of completion lingering.

Through many failed attempts of understanding in my own efforts, I had finally come to a very straightforward conclusion to all this *Thought Life* stuff — It wasn't *in* me. I mean, it wasn't *in* me that I would find understanding. It was through leaning in and trusting God: allowing Him to teach me what that meant through the Holy Spirit and His Word. It was in trusting that *His ways are higher than mine, His thoughts are higher than mine. My* dependence upon myself, *my* knowledge, and *my* understanding was, literally, causing me to *not* understand and *not* know what that passage meant. Crazy, right?! And yet, there it was — the truth of the matter. Once that moment of awareness hit, it was a downhill breeze, sort of. Compared to the treacherous rocky mountain of a landscape I had been previously attempting to climb on my own and failing, often and miserably — it was a breeze.

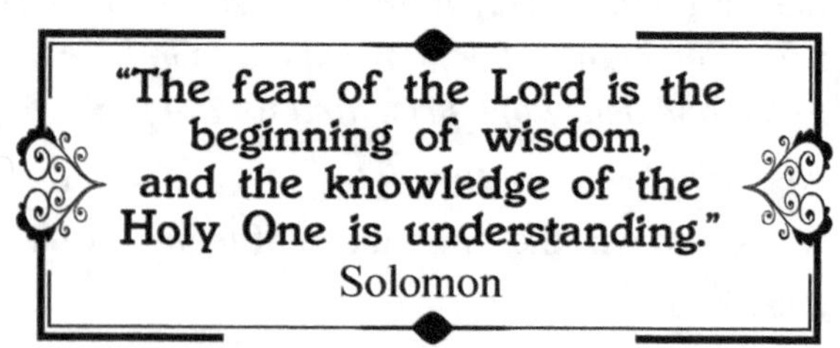

As quickly as I had given up on figuring out what it meant to *take thoughts captive to the obedience of Christ* within *my own* strength and ability through *my own* intellect – His understanding came. I surrendered with a white flag waving and did not desire to continue the struggle to figure it out on *my own*. That's when He showed up! Just like that! The moment I checked my pride and self-dependence at the door, He was able to work it out and show me what it meant! "I was fascinated during the moment!" I said, remembering it fondly. "Your *lightbulb moments* are far more brilliant in brightness than anything I can muster on *my own*, God!" I told Him.

Now, I call those *growing seasons*. Those are the moments that trigger a time in which God calls me to *grow* deeper in my understanding of Him. He draws me in deeper to learn all the many things He has made available for me to learn about, in His perfect timing. It is in those *seasons* that God draws me closer to Him. And, Oh, the great and gentle patience He has with me during those times! "Thank God for His long-suffering level of patience, especially with me!" I exclaimed at the thought. How much patience it must take when I get sucked into the tendency to be stubborn and do it all by myself! I took a moment to agree in confirmation with my previous thought, in a note-to-self manner, "To have such patience and gentleness is, most assuredly, a thing to strive for in this life!"

These growing seasons are filled with abundant mercy & grace that He overflows my cup with. I stumble around, blindly, and struggle to undo myself, layer by layer, to get to the bottom of it all. Only to find it is not the bottom, at all! Instead, I discover a *newness* in those areas that I have never known before. It is just like tediously working toward unwrapping a present that has been duct-taped, tied up with twine, and quadruple wrapped in box after box. When I finally come to the end of those long-invested times of unwrapping, I am elated and overwhelmed with joy at the precious thing which I finally find! The *new* present at the end of all my endeavors of work is unexpected and received in thankfulness! The gift of *So Much More* is precisely that, *So Much More* to look forward to!

Growing seasons were like opening a hidden door at the back of a big room. There is an even bigger room beyond it! One second, I think that is all there is, but wait on it………….No! No, it wasn't the end, at all! It was just the beginning! Yes, it's an unexpected *newness* to walk in with God! At the thought, I replied, "Need I say more?!" Gratefulness interrupted the imagery of my thoughts, and I said, "From everlasting to everlasting. Your love is unending, dear Lord! Oh, how I do love how

> **"Therefore we have been buried with Him through baptism into death, so that as Christ was raised from the dead through the glory of the Father, so we too might walk in newness of life."**
> Apostle Paul

You love me and teach me about Your heart toward me! Sometimes it's gently and sometimes it's sternly. I just love how it is always *more and more* every day, though! Thank You, my Abba, Father!"

It was quite a solid moment of humility & joy for me to think upon those seasons of deeper time with God. Yes, I thought upon those things on our way back from Church that evening. I thought about the many things which He has brought me to and through so that I may *grow* closer to Him. I pondered to myself, "Wow! If only I would dare to seek it more and dare to intentionally work through these growing seasons He brings me to - no matter how difficult or painful! There is so much of an opportunity for deeper healing! There is so much of an opportunity to *unroot* things that I did not even know existed! Before those seasons, I thought I was doing well. Yet, in each of them He draws me closer again! I think I am close, already. Yet, there is still *So Much More* waiting on the other side! Each time that I seek Him more like that, He does so! There is so much potential for breaking down walls that may be hindering or even blocking me from a deeper walk with God that I can get rid of! The great worth and valuable treasure found within the growing seasons He has given to me, so far, are fascinating! If only I would get out of my own way!" I thought. I paused in my reflections of my own chastising encouragement to myself as we pulled into our driveway. The long day was coming to an end and would soon be behind our little family. My heart felt renewed. My mind was even more set and determined at seeking after more of these growing seasons in Him.

It had been a long day and not one for the faint of heart. Suddenly, one of those sneaky thoughts tried to come in with the *fear of the unknown*. It stayed for a bit as my mind thought of all the undoing and fortitude that seeking after such tasks of more growing would entail. I thought about the potential for heartache, tears, anger, avoidance, suffering, persecution, frustration, and all the other ways that I had already endured. Events from previous growing seasons came flooding over me like a crashing tsunami. With the authority that God had taught me, though, I immediately told it, "No! That is not true! There is nothing to fear. God's *perfect love casts out fear.* The Word of God is truth, and His Word says to *not let my heart be troubled, believing in God and Jesus Christ. In Him, I find and will have Peace. In this world, I will have trials and tribulations,* and there will be troubles; but I have no need to fear and can be of good courage, for *Jesus Christ has conquered and overcome the world*! His promises are true! Victory is already His, and I can place my complete trust in Him, for He *will never leave me nor forsake or abandon me. I will be content with what I have in Him.* He is my fortress and strong tower. *No weapon formed against me shall stand*, because He is the maker of the enemy that forms the weapon. God is in control. Not the enemy. He fights my battle on my behalf. It doesn't matter what I know or what I don't know. God knows it all, and I place my trust in Him! His truth for me is what I accept. Not yours, satan! Fear, you are not welcome here. You must leave in the name of Jesus!" With that affirmed, I discredited the sneaky thought of *fear of the unknown* and dismissed it out of my mind. That declaration of prayer and affirmation of my thoughts aligned my focus to God's goodness and victory and truth. I concluded in thought, "Each of those characteristics of His are found in the growing seasons He brings about.

That is what matters! Only what God is doing in and through those seasons…That is what I choose to focus on. The real estate of my mind is not for sale! Nope! Not today! The years before me aren't looking good either, devil!"

Battling like this is necessary. I stand firm against the enemy when he tries to come at me to twist things around and make me stumble. There is no way I am going to allow it to linger! The enemy's attempt to sneak his way into my *Thought Life* had been stopped tonight. The lies he was spewing were not going to be accepted as truth by the rest of the gang of my mind! Nope! Not Today! I had, after all, just received thorough teaching in Philippians on what to focus on and direct my thoughts to at Church. With much gratitude, I said to God, "Reminders of Your Word are so very essential when it comes to my *Thought Life*. They are a great encouragement to my heart to continue the *Good Fight* that You have set before me. Thank You, God, for Your Word that was shared tonight. Thank You for guiding the speech of the teacher through the Holy Spirit!" I was not about to let another day pass by with sneaky thoughts of fear getting a foothold in my mind! I, most definitely, was not going to allow it to sink down into my heart! No, sirree or ma'am! Nope. Not at all! Not today and not ever!

We had all come inside from the garage, by this time. I had recounted and affirmed in prayer all these truths as I made my way in and started the settling in for the evening routine. I Invested a bit of time visiting with my daughter before making sure she went to bed. Her and I agreed in prayer for the requests she had on her heart. She snuggled under the covers and said with a yawn, "Amen. Good night, Mom." I replied, "Good night, Sweetheart. See you in the morning, kiddo." Walking to my bedroom, I whispered aloud, "Thank you, God, for the time of reflection this evening. I needed that." I felt an immediate warmth over me and knew it was Him telling me, "You are welcome, My child," with a reassuring embrace of His presence. I could not help but smile.

My husband commented on my smile, telling me how much he loves to see it. Just like a cat who curiously investigates an unknown object on the floor, he curiously investigated further by asking me what it was I was smiling so fondly about. Of course, I was not about to go into the immense detail of reflection that I had just experienced! That would simply be overwhelming to him and a lot of information to absorb. I know this because it was overwhelming to me and a lot of information for me to absorb, and I am the one who is doing the reflecting!! Although my heart and soul desired to bubble over in excitement and pour out to share all this terrific heart enlightenment of God's goodness with my husband, I didn't do that. Instead, I chose to keep my response simple and be considerate.

We were both ready for the evening to end. I knew my husband had experienced a trying and wearing day. I could hear the pillows calling his name just by looking into his eyes. He slowly eased his body down to sit at the edge. He expectantly waited for my response, but he was tired. I already knew how mentally exhausting and strenuous his day had been. I could clearly tell that any more thoughts would just burden his mind more with effort that did not need to be invested right this second. "My poor tired husband!" I thought to myself. I watched his shoulders slowly relax as the weight of his body was relieved by the soft mattress top. "You know, my dear, there are days we have blessed moments, and there are days we learn something new because God makes us aware of them. Today was one of those days that I had both. I was able to reflect on God's goodness even more than normal because of that. I felt a lot of love, today, in His presence, and it made me smile." I responded with a mixture of obscurity and detail that hinted at the heaviness and sincerity shared with God. "You just happened to catch me in that smile after I had told Him, *Thank You*." I said to him, teasingly. With that, he smiled and simply said, "That's good, Babe. I like catching you in smiles. It's one of the most beautiful things I get to see in my days." His compliment brought another smile to me as our eyes rested upon one another. He laid his head down, wearily – soon, exchanging our gaze for that of rest.

As was his norm on the more tedious days, he was able to find sleep within a few minutes. He was prone to find it much more swiftly than me on any day, really. I fondly rested my gaze upon him, still, as he lay there sleeping - breathing in and out, his chest rising and falling in a peaceful rhythm. His smile had lingered on even until after the *good night's* and *I love you's* had passed. It was nice to see him at rest like this. Agreeing with this, I added, "Yes, it is nice to see him without the weight of the world of work and toil on his shoulders." I rolled over to gaze up at the ceiling. White popcorn spackling of a gazillion bumps and bubbles were spread out across the entire space above me. "It looks just like a gazillion stars in the sky! I am not about to try to count those!" I jokingly said to myself. "Besides, You know exactly how many there are, just like all the stars in the sky, Lord! I don't have to know. You know and that's good enough for me," I said to Him softly. The Holy Spirit added in agreement, saying, "Yes, *He counts the number of the stars; He gives names to all of them. Great is our Lord and abundant in strength; His understanding is infinite!* The same God that created the stars and knows them each by name...He knows your name, too, and calls you His child. He is here with you now.*"* I smiled from His reminder to my heart. Ignoring the temptation to count away and waste the sleep that was very much needed, I shifted my focus.

"Relaxing is what I need to do," I softly said to myself, with my head on the pillow. I closed my eyes and began to *Focus* on the *Relaxation* of the many parts of my body. I relaxed my neck and shoulders. I let the tension from my closed grip fall to that of open hands resting across my stomach. I felt my breath come in slowly and gently. I felt my chest rise and fall with

> *"How precious* also are Your thoughts to me, O God! How vast is the sum of them! If I should count them, they would outnumber the sand. When I awake, I am still with You."
>
> King David

each exchange of oxygen. I released the tightness of my back and felt my body sink further into the mattress. I had placed a pillow under my legs, earlier, but had not rested them on it, yet. Slowly, I let my knees drop and extend across the top, resting the weight of them on the pillow's softness. My feet were the last thing to go in this handy *Relaxation* exercise. I had come across it a few years back, and it was quite helpful when my mind was scattered; or when it was over-stimulated and fatigued like tonight! Tension in my calves from the day's exertion left a mild aching in them. However, with the extension of my legs, a sharp pain pulled my mind away from the *Relaxation* effort suddenly. I opened my eyes, blankly looking at the dark-adjusted view. I wasn't about to go down rabbit holes tonight. "Lord, I need some of Your kind of rest, tonight, please!" I asked. I was tired and ready to be in a peaceful state, just as my husband was in. The Holy Spirit answered, reminding me, *"Meditate in your heart upon your bed and be still. Trust in the Lord. In peace you will both lie down and sleep. For God alone, makes you dwell in safety."* I thought about this. "Yes, I will be still and trust in You, Lord." Then, I said to myself, "Today was a good day, and I am thankful for the moments I was given to be in it. Thank You, God. I love You very much! Good Night." I took a breath and started the sensory *Relaxation* process again. The Holy Spirit added to my final thoughts with one of my favorite scriptures. I smiled as He recounted it to my heart. He said, "God says, *Come to Me, all who are weary and heavy-laden, and I will give you rest. Take My yoke upon you and learn from Me, for I am gentle and humble in heart, and YOU WILL FIND REST FOR YOUR SOULS. For My yoke is easy and My burden is light."* Thankfully, the very-much-needed sleep for all of us was found quickly that night. I never even made it back down to my feet! For me, that is amazing!

MEMORY VERSE

My child, let them not vanish from your sight;
Keep sound wisdom and discretion,
So they will be life to your soul
And adornment to your neck.
Then you will walk in your way securely
And your foot will not stumble.
When you lie down, you will not be afraid;
When you lie down, your sleep will be sweet.
Do not be afraid of sudden fear
Nor of the onslaught of the wicked when it comes;
For the Lord will be your confidence
And will keep your foot from being caught.
Proverbs 3:21-26

Chapter Four

Long-Term Commitment

*That their hearts may be encouraged,
having been knit together in love,
and attaining to all the wealth that comes
from the full assurance of understanding,
resulting in a true knowledge of God's mystery,
that is, Christ Himself,
in whom are hidden all the treasures
of wisdom and knowledge.*
Colossians 2:2-3

A disturbing noise pierced through the peaceful silence of what could have possibly been the best rest I had experienced in quite some time. At first, it reminded me of the shattering blast of noise bouncing off the kitchen floor a few weeks back. I had accidentally dropped the drinking glass I held in my hand. The alarm shocked me now, just like the bursting glass shocked me then. I shot out from the comfort of the pleasantly warm sheets of our bed like a rocket taking flight! I was on high alert and ready to take on whatever intruder had just invaded my safe-haven environment of blissful sleep. I frantically tried to gather my bearings and come to some sort of understanding of what was going on. It took quite the focus! Alas, the only intruder to be found was the obnoxious alarm on the side table.

The dream I had been involved in was a full-scale production - live and in an array of colors. It felt real enough that it was difficult to wrap my mind around why I was in a bedroom, suddenly. After all, just moments ago, I was in the middle of an emerald green field with a stream heard running softly nearby, although I could not see it. I was awe-struck from the beauty! I was watching the colorful flowers twirl and dance at the sound of the wind. Their vast companions of grass blades dressed in their vibrant green glory attire were all swaying in perfect *Unison*. The tempo was dance-worthy and seemed to be weaving in and out around them like notes upon the sky. There was such *Unity* as every bit of nature arose to play its part, flawlessly on cue! I was blessed with my very own reserved front row seats to a most astounding show! Such grace and tranquility were abounding all around me! "What a dream! What a way to be - to exist! Boy, oh boy, what a place!" I exclaimed in thought to myself this morning.

However, I realized, soon enough, that I had returned to the reality of life. In addition to the alarm, the cat had much to do with this jerk-back-into-reality. Our morning wakeup call from the cat on the other side of the bedroom door was not a welcome noise, either. Every morning…without fail…that cat meows at the door. The cat is a borderline stalker, in my opinion. My husband agrees. She waits to hear the slightest of sounds, then she meows as if to say, "Ok, you are up. Time to pay attention to me. Come open the door." Maybe the label of stalker is a bit too harsh to describe her. Perhaps she is simply clingy some days more than others. "Or is it more days, rather than some?!" I thought. I dismissed the thought with a simple, "Who knows?" Regardless of labels, there she was again at the door this morning. She was meowing in her innocent-sounding, conversational voice. "Those attempts to coax me into opening the door are about to be very successful, but not in the way she wants, I bet!" I thought. "Water bottle it is," I mumbled to myself – the irritation falling off my lips with the words. My bed was beckoning my body back to it and I, flat-out, *did not* desire to part ways with it, yet.

To return to that dream and be surrounded with such harmony and peace would have been phenomenal, but it would not be today, unfortunately. I was already awake. The cat was definitely not about to allow me to get away with making so much noise. Yes, our dear, sweet cat was making sure I heard all about her feline-sharp awareness that I was awake. The water bottle would, at least, pause her noise for me to acclimate to my surroundings. Our cats are trained with a simple tool – the water bottle. One-shot and done is usually all it takes. Sometimes, I have only to shake the bottle. Between the sloshing of the water inside and my firm tone in my voice, they know they are in trouble. It is quite an intriguing thing, a cat's behavior, when it knows it is busted. Typically, ours take off like a dart to the nearest hidey-hole and then slink around the corner to see if the coast is clear just to do it all over again. They are like addicted little robbers hungry for their next heist. "Silly creatures, very silly, indeed!" I said as I bent down to pick up the water bottle. Suddenly, I remembered what lay ahead of me for the day. I thought to myself, "Yes, I remember why that silly alarm is set for this early." Begrudgingly, I put the bottle back down and backed away slowly.

I shifted my focus to the day. "Before I do anything, I need to get my head on straight. This attitude will not do," I told myself. "Reset, yourself," I sternly directed. I forced myself to sit still and close my eyes. I took a slow breath in and released it out slowly. "Alright, Lord. I submit. I will seek and receive what You have for me. I'm ready to trade out my thoughts for Yours, my ways for Yours," I thought with a sigh. I pictured myself releasing my grasp of the frustration that had already managed to slink itself into my day.

"With such a good rest, the day's start should mirror it. It should be just as peaceful, right?" I asked myself. That was not the case, though. "Armor is very much needed. The trenches are already forming. Time to get prepared. Let's do this thing!" I encouraged myself with battle preparation thoughts to gear up for the day ahead of me. I placed piece after piece of God's Armor on me. I put on my *belt of truth, breastplate of righteousness, shield of faith, helmet of salvation*. I grabbed my *sword of the Spirit* and *shod my feet with the Gospel of peace*. I cautiously looked over at my husband and was grateful to find that he was still sound asleep.

All the commotion of my preparation and spiritual gearing up in my mind seemed exceptionally loud to me. For a moment, I was worried I had woken him. Inward imagery of all the noisy clanking around I was doing was precisely that – inward imagery, nothing more. However, in my mind, it was like the pans clanking around when I put the clean dishes back in the cabinet. In reality, it had not broken the silence in the bedroom any more than a pin dropping on a plush carpet would have. I was relieved.

> "Therefore, prepare your minds for action, keep sober in spirit, fix your hope completely on the grace to be brought to you at the revelation of Jesus Christ."
>
> Apostle Peter

Usually, my husband is a light sleeper. I knew from last night's weariness that this abnormally heavy sleep was easily explained away by the weight of the first part of the week for him. Actually, it had been a full week for all of us, and it was only Thursday! I countered the temptation to be overwhelmed by saying, quickly, "Thank You, God, for all of Your abundant provision and grace through it all, though!" My husband had been tossing back and forth that evening enough to awaken me with his restlessness more than a few times. I quickly drifted back to sleep, though, and seemed to pick up my adventures right where I left them last! The evidence of his tossing was prevalent this morning. It had caused much disarray of the covers to where he was half-in and half-out of them. I pulled the covers up around him with loving gentleness fueled by concern the chill of the cold air may cause him to wake up too early. He needed as much rest as he could get! A smidgeon of a dimple appeared on his face from the fade of a smile. He curled up even more within the newly acquired warmth and rolled to his side. "Phew! I am glad I did not wake him. That was close," I thought to myself.

I tip-toed over to the dresser, then to the closet to gather the items I would need for the day. By this time, I was wide awake and in ninja-stealth mode! I was not about to let anything, let alone myself, be the culprit behind stealing my husband's time of rest. Thankfully, I managed to get around and ready that morning without any hitch in that plan. "Everything went smoothly, and I pulled it off with flying colors!" I thought to myself as I sat at the kitchen table. I shook my head at this, of course. I couldn't possibly pat myself on the back any harder with such a thought! I replied, immediately, saying, "You were not that stealthy. Ninjas don't bust their toe on the door jamb as they go out and make a bunch of racket in the process." With a bit of reluctance, I received the correction of my inaccurate boast. As a replacement, I said, "I am full of gratefulness to You, Father, for having my back this morning, already. Thank You!" I began eating my breakfast of oatmeal, toast, & coffee. My mind was redirected to those innumerable *Thank You, God* caliber of moments. With God's assistance, I had managed to get myself around and wake up our daughter without any animals making a ruckus…and my husband remaining asleep. That was, most assuredly, something to be grateful for!

Our daughter was busy getting around while she ate her bowl of oatmeal. She felt the urgency, just as I did, and was quite talented at figuring out how to balance those morning skills. "Hopefully, she finishes the oatmeal before she tries to also brush her teeth. That would taste disgusting! Minty oatmeal does not sound good to me at all!" I thought. I felt I was in a bit of a rush, by the time breakfast came around, as well. I decided I had to be a little bit of a multi-tasker this morning, too. That way, I would not go without reading today. To one side of my bowl, I had placed my notebook. To the other side of my bowl, my Bible. I was reading 2 Corinthians in chapter 5 and had been there for the last 3 days! There was just something about this particular passage at this particular time in my life. It seemed to be too much to read all at once! As I thought about the last 3 days, I recalled a conversation with one of the ladies at Church. I had said to her, "It has been like trying to eat a whole, entire *Extra-Large* pizza by myself when I have been fasting from solid foods and sticking to a liquids-only diet for two weeks! It is not doable right now, for whatever reason."

I had been working on reading the Bible from one end to the other for a while now. The tally of time was rounding up on a couple of years. Of course, this was not just your typical front-to-back reading. Nope, this was my *Study* Bible. It was jam-packed with commentary and cross-references and keywords to study. I was reading the whole thing! As one can imagine, it was taking a bit longer than the customary *Read the Bible in a Year* plans available. "A year! Yeah, right?! Not doing *this kind* of reading will I finish in a year!" I remember thinking early on. It was a thought that rang true today as I sat there looking at 2 Corinthians...*yet again.*

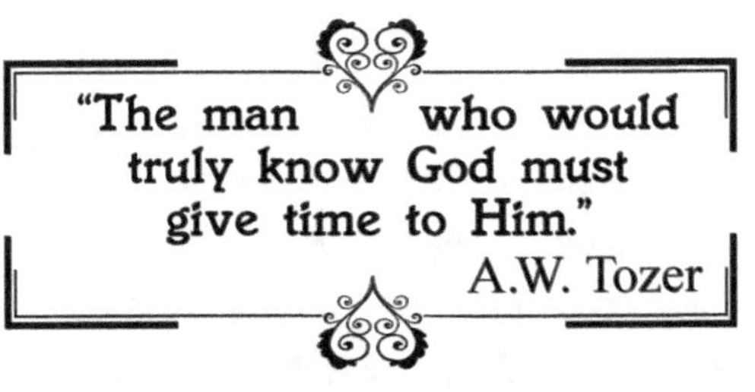

My research tendencies to dive deep and become more rooted in words and history played a role in the time that had passed, as well. I liked to look up the history, traditions, culture, practices, and stuff that went along with what was going on during that time. I had the *Strong's Exhaustive Concordance*, an *Interlinear Hebrew & Greek Bible*, & a couple of dictionaries that went with the concordance: *Vine's Complete Expository & AMG's Annotated Strong's Dictionary*. Those were just a few of the tools lining the shelves of my office. I would read one word that hit me in the spirit, and off I would go into research mode so I could better understand the passage. I desired to know how it pertained to the book in its full context.

One of my favorites to research was how the word *Know* was used in reference to *Knowing* God. "Chills! That is what *that* particular understanding gave me! I remember! Chills!" I lovingly recounted. It was a good one and one of many reasons why my commitment had turned into a very *Long-Term Commitment*. The definitions for just the word *know* in the *Vine's Dictionary* covered two and a half pages! *Knowing* is a full, complete union with Him through an all-encompassing awareness of Him. It is a filling up of all-things-empty through a deep, intimate, vulnerable relationship with Him. It means to be privy to the secret things of God through a deep personal connection found in abiding in Him. It is used in an absolute form of fullness and completeness in understanding the spiritual truth of His love as it pertains to me. It is a *Knowledge* that perfectly *Unites* the subject with the object through the discovery of more of Him. "Yes, I want to *Know* Him more! I want to *Know* everything about Him!" I said as I recalled the vastness of the definition I had studied. Thinking about this, I flipped over to 1 John chapter 2 and read this passage: *By this we know that we have come to know Him, if we keep His commandments…but whoever keeps His word, in him the love of God has truly been perfected. By this we know that we are in Him: the one who says he abides in Him ought himself to walk in the same manner as He walked.* I paused and concluded, "Yes, I desire to have the love of God perfected in me, for sure!" The entire book of 1 John is full of references to the word *Know*. Direct and to-the-point with a matter-of-fact tone, it was one of my favorites to read!

Oh, I had read individual books of the Bible like 1 John, yes. Some, even many times over! I could venture to say that I had probably already read the Bible completely. That is, *IF* I would actually

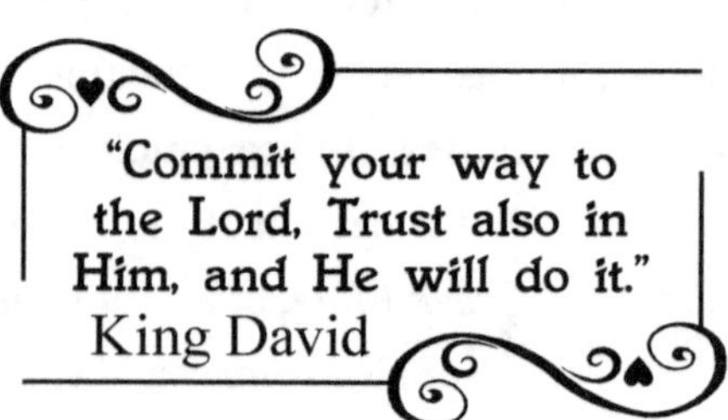

sit down to take the time to consider all the books that I had already read over the last 20 years of my life. However, I could not say that I had ever read it, from one end to the next, like someone reads an ordinary book. If I was asked, "Have you ever read the *entire* Bible cover-to-cover?" I wanted to be able to answer that question with complete certainty and a smile and say, "Why, Yes, I have!" So, I had made up my mind and made that commitment. And, wouldn't you know it – once I started making plans like this and investing time in God's Word, here came the many attempts of the enemy to distract from that very thing! At least, that is what my experience has been, so far. Interruptions, distractions, emergencies, temptations, avoidance of specific subjects, etc. – you name the category, and I probably have an example in that category. Come to think of it, I probably have *a bunch* of examples to put in there! Two years had already passed since I made that commitment, but I was still chugging along up the hill - ever so slowly, *BUT* surely!

I am bound and determined to accomplish this goal, no matter how long it may take! "I am not about to give up now!" I affirmed out loud. So, continue, I must. Some days, like today, are a bit more challenging to keep that *read-once-a-day, no matter how little* self-imposed goal of mine. There were other days - too many to keep track of, or that I did not want to acknowledge to keep track of them - that I did not even get around to reading. After the first 3 months of going through the process, I found that the easiest way for me to make sure I read a little bit was to do so first thing in the morning. Otherwise, there was no telling if I would do so at all that day!

It is not that I do not want to read. It is not that, at all! There are simply a few things that I need, so I can *read to comprehend* - not just *read to be reading*. You see, I do not only want to go through the motions of reading it. I want to understand what I read. I want to truly, deeply *Know* what I read in God's Word. I want to have it well enough in my mind to be able to consider it, thoroughly, from many angles. I wanted to think upon it, consistently, throughout the day, as well. I desired to figure out ways to apply it to my daily walk through that meditation. When the opportunity from God presented itself, I wanted to practice that application. Yes, I wanted to have it written on my heart, deeply. I desired to keep it fresh in my mind to speak to the Word and share it with others, when He prompted me to do so.

Reading the Word had become so very important to me. "Yep, I desire to learn the Word of God…for keeps...to truly *Know* it in my heart!" I reinforced to myself. With this thought, the Holy Spirit brought an interesting scriptural connection to my heart. First, He said, "You are intentionally working on personal relationship building when you sit down and read God's Word." I sat there and considered this for a moment. I was intrigued at the thought. He continued, "Connect and reconcile these verses together,

- *Jesus said to God, "Sanctify them in the truth, Your Word is truth… I do not ask on behalf of these alone, but for those also who believe in Me through their word; that they may all be one; even as You, Father, are in Me and I in You, that they also may be in Us, so that the world may believe that You sent Me."*
- *Jesus said, "I am the way, the truth, and the life. No one comes to the Father except through Me."*
- *In the beginning was the Word, the Word was with God, and the Word was God.*
- *Jesus said, "If you continue in My word, then you are truly disciples of Mine; and you will know the truth, and the truth will make you free."*
- *Jesus answered, "You know neither Me nor My Father; if you knew Me, you would know My Father also."*
- *Jesus said, "It is the Spirit who gives life; the flesh profits nothing; the words that I have spoken to you are spirit and are life."*

I pondered these for some time as I sat at the kitchen table. A string of connections came to me. I thought, "Lord this interesting, help me connect these…

- Jesus is the truth…the Word is truth…they are one in the same…
- Jesus is the life…the Word is spirit and life…they are both life…
- The Word was in the beginning with God and was God…Jesus is in the Father and the Father is in Him…they are one in the same…

- No one comes to the Father but through Jesus…there is relationship with the Father to be found in Jesus…If Jesus and the Word are one in the same, then reading His Word is coming to the Father…
- To continue in the Word means to know the truth…so, continuing in the Word means to know Jesus…because Jesus is the truth…if I know the truth, then I know Jesus…If I know Jesus, then I know the Father also…reading His Word intentionally builds a deeper relationship with God…

… wow!" I exclaimed in awe. Wrapping my mind around the scriptures and the connection was quite the task! I definitely wanted to invest time intentionally to building a closer relationship with Him! "Yes, Lord! I desire to *Know* You more! Sounds like I have some intentional relationship building to do! Reading Your Word is absolutely the way to *Know* You more, for sure! Thank You for sharing this *Knowledge* through Your Holy Spirit, Father," I concluded.

However, as excited as I was to read more after this, I wanted to do so efficiently. I knew myself well enough to know that I needed a few things before this efficiency-goal is achievable. One of the things that I need is *sufficient time*. Without sufficient time, I have dealt with feeling rushed and flustered, and, in turn, nothing I read will stick. "Talk about frustrating!" I thought to myself. I pondered the times of frustration I had experienced from this. I would read the same thing 10 different times and just give up for lack of understanding of what I was reading. "It is just not efficient," I concluded in my thoughts. Another thing I need when I sit down to read is *quiet*. The best time to find that quiet has been when it is just me in the early hours of the morning. It is before the house echoes with the sound of my husband and daughter preparing for their days. In the quiet, I am *even* able to read out loud! There is no concern about bothering or interrupting someone else's activities in the quiet of my *just-me* mornings. Those are exceptional days because I not only get to *read* the Word, but I also get to *hear* the Word. This morning, I was uncertain. I wasn't sure if my attempt to read would be successful. I didn't have either of those to focus on the 2 Corinthians passage staring me in the face. It loomed at me with no forward progress. God had other plans, it seemed. He had already given me many scriptures to dwell upon in this day! I reassured myself and said, "Even if I am not able to digest the passage on my To-Do, God has provided sufficiently, as He always does!"

I thought about why it was so important for me to have *sufficient time* and *quiet*. "Ideally, I want to hear His Word, too," I replied to the consideration in my thoughts. In the letter to the Romans, Paul explains to the church the importance of sharing the gospel of faith in full belief, because it brings about salvation in Jesus Christ to those who believe the *Message*. He says to them, almost in summary of his point, "*Now, Faith comes from hearing and hearing from the Word of Christ.*" When I read out loud, I think about this scripture passage. Just like my generation and those before me were taught to *read it, say it, & write it* in order to thoroughly *learn it* – Similarly, I also prefer to study in 3 parts, if the environment allows for it. I can do that with *sufficient time*

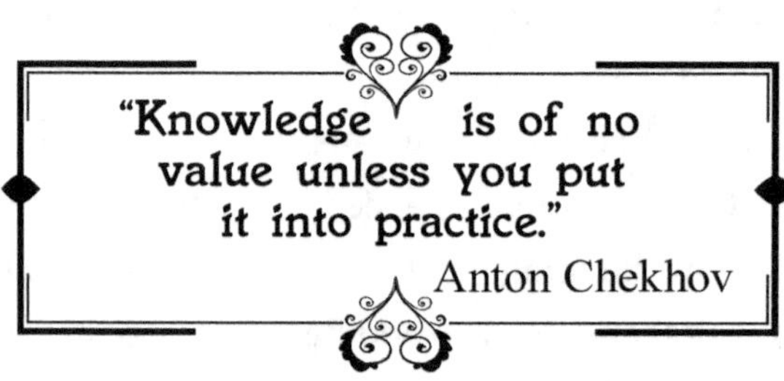

in the only-me *quiet* mornings. Between *hearing it, reading it, and writing it* down – more times than not, I get it memorized. Thankfully, oh, so thankfully, it is not just within *my own* strength and dependent upon *only me* to learn the Bible. "Nope, nope, nope – it isn't! Not at all!" I thought gratefully. I seek God's wisdom and guidance through the Holy Spirit *as I read* through His Word. "It is only with His assistance and teaching. It is only *in Him*, not in *my own* understanding, at all!" I agreed firmly and humbly in thought. He had already guided me through scriptures of His choosing. I knew this to be true! It didn't help me make a dent in my plans to reread 2 Corinthians 5 again. However, it did make a huge impact on my heart! "That is what is important as I study my Bible anyway – the heart impact of it all!" I said with great certainty and joy in my heart.

I must admit, there are some books in the Old Testament that I chose to just listen to through the audio Bible I have. I did not venture into praying about those before I studied them because I didn't really study them. After all, I knew that I had to get through the long lists within them before I fell asleep from boredom! "Lord, please forgive my bluntness in this perception!" I countered quickly. All the *so & so* begot *so & so*. This *such & such* law was written in adherence to the observance of *such & such* feast. That feast is to be done on *such & such* day of the year with *such & such* ritual to take part in. I am sure, when I am a bit more spiritually mature for that type of more in-depth historical study, God will lead me through those, too. A few of them provoked my interest enough to research a bit of history tied to them. However, it was just a few. Right now, though, I am still one of those *fall asleep while reading that kind of book* students. Some of those Old Testament books are like that for me at this time in my walk. They just are. I don't feel discouraged by that, and God understands exactly where I am at. He meets me there, exactly where I am in my learning – not at some long-winded, mono-tone professor's level of enjoyment in reading such things. "Thank goodness for His overflowing grace and endless compassion for His children!" I responded. I knew they were important, yet God had not placed that new desire in my heart to delve into those kinds of scriptures. "Nope. Not yet," I confirmed, "but He will. Of this, I am confident."

Of course, I am quite well aware of the passage concerning God's Word being profitable. Paul writes in his 2nd letter to Timothy, *"All Scripture is inspired by God and profitable for teaching, for reproof, for correction, for training in righteousness; so that children of God may be adequate, equipped for every good work."* I get it. All those hum-drum-to-me-right-now scriptures are *profitable*. The flesh in me, though, didn't find enjoyment from it and would end up in a mid-day siesta if I allowed it. I said, "Yes, I know His ways and thoughts are higher than mine." I shook my head at the flesh in me. Then, humorously added, *"His* reasonings to include those are just really, really far beyond *my own* reasonings right now!" In my walk, I am currently learning from the passage just before that. The 2 Timothy passage where it says: *You, however, continue in the things you have learned and become convinced of, knowing from whom you have learned them, and that from childhood you have known the sacred writings which are able to give you the wisdom that leads to salvation through faith which is in Christ Jesus.* I agreed with the passage that came to mind. I said, "Yes. I am *continuing in the things I have learned.* I am working on *becoming convinced* deep in my heart of all of them." In my days, I desire for them to resound through my mind in preparation for times that they are needed. I want to be ready for those times that God divinely establishes opportunities for me to share His Word with others. I desire to do my best and be a helper to those around me, whatever His purpose may be in it. "By my best, I mean all in for Jesus, of course," I acknowledged. My heart beat quickly at the thought. I knew my desire was for His fullness to be complete in me. I wanted that same fullness of His love to overflow to others in my submission to His leading. It didn't matter what He called me to do. I desired to do it. It could be to encourage others and lift them up. Other times, it could be to help build up one another *in the Word of Christ to build Faith.* It may simply be for the purpose of being a comfort to those who need comforted in a time of need. On the more difficult side, though, it could also be to admonish with love my other sisters and brothers through sharing the Word. Regardless of knowing what His purpose in it was, I wanted to serve Him. Learning His Word and writing it upon the table of my heart was a part of the sanctification, renewal, and transformation processes. I affirmed this in thought to myself, "When God is beckoning my heart to do something, no matter what it is, I want to do it." I responded with a simple admonishment, "Yes, that's all good and well - but I cannot follow Him, *obediently,* if I do not prepare myself with the Word of God in me. Whether I enjoy reading it or not, it still must be done." And, so, I had read those hum-drum passages, whether my flesh liked it or not.

As I sat there for a moment, I smiled. My mind rested in fond reflection of all the time I had already invested in this reading endeavor. I had accomplished quite a bit of what I started out to do and was excited to reach the goal of finishing.

"This Bible reading commitment of mine, no matter how long it may take me, is going to be completed. Lord, You put it on my heart to do, and I am going to do it!" I said, excitedly. As if to add to my confirming thoughts, I rhetorically asked myself, "How can I possibly expect to *do my best* and be all in for Him if I do not prepare and learn about *what* I am doing or talking about in His Word?" However, I already knew the answer. It was just like when a person is supposed to prepare for a test; but, instead, chooses to goof off and not take it seriously. That person fails the test, of course. If I wasn't going to invest

"For in Him all the fullness of Deity dwells in bodily form, & in Him you have been made complete, & He is the head over all rule and authority." Apostle Paul

the time and learn how to live to the fullness that God has called me to live, as His Child, then I could not expect to do anything but fumble around, blindly and ill-prepared. I, too, would fail the figurative 'test' of truly *Knowing* Him. I had made up my mind and set my heart upon it. I confirmed to myself, "Whatever He calls me to do - I desire to be ready and prepared. I intend to invest time into learning and *Knowing* all I can about God, His love for me, and the purpose He has called me to in this life. Yes, I have made up my mind, and that is the end of it! There is no further conversation needed. That's all there is to it!"

I reestablished my focus to the task at hand. "Now, then, where was I?" I pondered for a moment. "Oh, yes. That's right! 2 Corinthians," I answered. My oatmeal was only half-way finished and my notebook page was half-empty. Interrupting myself, I asked, "Or is it half-full?!" Regardless, I was *all the way* in and ready to conquer the next few passages in front of me! I bowed my head and asked God to protect and *guard my heart and mind in Christ Jesus* as I welcomed His Holy Spirit into my presence. I asked Him to guide me and teach me in all that I was about to read. I try to remember to pray the *Spiritual Wisdom Prayer* each time I read. It is found in Chapter 1 of Ephesians. It says this: *that the God of my Lord Jesus Christ, the Father of glory, would give to me a spirit of wisdom and of revelation in the knowledge of Him and for the eyes of my heart to be enlightened so that I will know what is the hope of His calling, what are the riches of the glory of His inheritance in the saints, and what is the surpassing greatness of His power toward me, who believes.* Closing the prayer, I began my reading and listened, intently, for the Holy Spirit's beckoning upon my heart as I spoke the words out loud. Before long, the next page of my notebook had been overtaken with words that leapt off the pages in 2nd Corinthians. I knew I needed to look up the original Hebrew word to understand the full context and meaning of some of them. There were a few different scriptures that the Holy Spirit had given me to look up and meditate on throughout the rest of my busy day ahead, too. I did so and wrote them down on a post-it to take with me.

With a quick, unladylike slurp of the last spoonful of my oatmeal, I got up out of my seat from the table. I closed my Bible and zipped up the case to take with me, just in case. I also closed my notebook and placed it on the counter. Then, I put away all the dishes I had used that morning. My daughter was ready to go and waiting on me. She stood there in the frame of the door. She had her daily devotional book in hand for us to read on the way into town. We were both on the same page of urgency and I was ever-so-thankful for that! I asked her, rhetorically, with a bit of a teasing smile, "Ya ready to go, kiddo?" She smiled back and replied, "Yes, ma'am – I was born for this kind of day! We've got this!" Her energy brought an unexpected laugh, which I immediately had to stifle before entering my bedroom.

I walked into our room to kiss my husband goodbye for the day. He was sleeping, peacefully. I did not want to wake him up, although I knew his alarm would be going off within the next 15 minutes or so. He would have been disappointed if I did not tell him goodbye for the day. With that, I gently kissed his forehead. I told him we were heading out and I would let him know when we arrived safely to our destination. He smiled and said, "I love you too, Babe," and slowly rolled over, falling abruptly back to sleep. I shook my head and thought to myself, "He didn't comprehend a word of that!" At that, another chuckle of fondness escaped me; but I caught it, quickly enough. I slipped quietly out of the bedroom.

The rest of the day was an adventure waiting to unfold. "I am excited to see what God does in this day!" I said enthusiastically to my daughter as we walked outside to the car. My excitement must have been contagious because she didn't even hesitate when she said, "Me too!" Then, as quickly as she said that, her face had an inquisitive look on it. She curiously pondered out loud, "I wonder if it's gonna be something cool…" Sitting in the car, I thought about her words for a moment; and, then, confirmed my hope for the same, "I sure hope so, Honey. We will see!" A brief silence between us settled in as the garage door made its racket in opening. I concluded, "Regardless of what is in store, the Word tells us to Rejoice in the Lord *Always*." Before I could finish the verse, she piped up and sang, "And again I say Rejoice!" Her reply made us both laugh as we left for our day and whatever He had planned for us in it.

MEMORY VERSE

So that Christ may dwell in your hearts through faith;
and that you, being rooted and grounded in love,
may be able to comprehend with all the saints
what is the breadth and length and height and depth,
and to know the love of Christ which surpasses knowledge,
that you may be filled up to all the fullness of God.
Ephesians 3:17-19

Chapter Five

Triggered

> *And put on the new self,*
> *which in the likeness of God has been*
> *created in righteousness and holiness*
> *of the truth. Therefore, laying aside falsehood,*
> *speak truth each one of you with his neighbor,*
> *for we are members of one another.*
> *Be angry, and yet do not sin;*
> *do not let the sun go down on your anger,*
> *and do not give the devil an opportunity.*
> Ephesians 4:24-27

"That's it!" I thought to myself, fuming with anger. "I've had enough!" I was like one of those frog legs that Grandma had forgotten to take the tendons out of. When she would cook them, the oil would splatter everywhere in that super-hot frying pan! Those lively legs would hop up in the air and slam back down in the pan. Yes, like them, I was *hopping* mad! Losing my temper is not a regular thing. It does not happen very often, but when it does – watch out! It is like ice - cracking and breaking apart - as it falls from the very top of a 50-foot glacier. The tippy-top piece comes crashing down, breaking off more and more parts of the iceberg as it descends! Finally, falling into the pit of below-freezing water that surrounds the base, it sinks, evermore, into the darkness of the depths of the sea. "I am exaggerating just a bit." I admitted. The imagery was definitely an exaggeration! However, that is also one of the surface symptoms of me when I am this angry. Melodramatic descriptions from my imagination usually come quickly after. I bet I would be exceptionally embarrassed if ever God provided me with a *rewind and replay* edition of my exaggerated angry patterns of thought. I agreed with this, saying, "Yes, I would be *quite* embarrassed, indeed!"

In this moment, though, it does not matter! "Nothing matters in this moment, but my feelings and I am beyond mad right now!!" I shouted, indignantly, to myself in my thoughts. "Oh, Buddy! When I get ahold of them! They better find Jesus quickly!" My thoughts were racing, and there was no stopping them! I could just imagine the steam that was rolling above my head and up to the sky as my cartoon character edition of myself turned the bright, vibrant, angry color of red. The steam was starting at my feet and escalating to the top of my head – just like one of those mercury thermostats Mom would use to check my temperature when I complained of being sick. "Speaking of being sick…" I thought. I felt a sick feeling in the pit of my stomach and found myself becoming light-headed. "I have to sit down," I told myself. Thoughts were whirling through my mind. "All the work I have done…" I said. "All that I have lost almost instantly!" I added in horror. It was overwhelming! I had spent hours upon hours upon hours, and days upon days upon days that turned into weeks of work on a side project for one of my clients, and it was all gone! It was *Nowhere* to be found!

We had let my in-laws stay the evening on their way back from the city as a rest-stop, of sorts. Before they left, they had shown their appreciation by cleaning around the house before heading out. "Or, so I thought!" I remarked indignantly. They had to leave early this morning around 3:00 a.m. to make it home in time for plans they had made. The house was *picked up*. Most of the random items that were strewn around had been put away. They could have won a trophy for *Cleaning with Stealth,* given we were not disturbed while we slept. "That is a bit of an exaggeration. You were pretty tired," I told myself as I acknowledged another reason we did not wake up. I was exceptionally grateful and excited to call them, at first. I was going to do so, as soon as it was a decent hour, to tell them how thoughtful and kind it was, but then … I entered the office. The piles of papers that I had been tediously working on were gone! Vanished into thin air! Vamoosh!

> "But we have renounced the things hidden because of shame, not walking in craftiness or adulterating the word of God, but by the manifestation of truth commending ourselves to every man's conscience in the sight of God."
> Apostle Paul

At first, it was no big deal. I didn't react or over-react. I simply responded. I thought to myself, "Surely, my in-laws just relocated the papers somewhere." I looked in the cabinets. *Nothing.* I looked in the drawers. *Nothing.* I looked on the shelves. *Nothing.* I continued calmly. "Maybe they just decided to be helpful and put them out of the way somewhere else, for now. After all, you always have extra totes out in the garage, right?" I asked myself, as I consider the other places that a tote of papers may be. I looked in the rooms of the house. *Nothing.* I looked in all the closets. *Nothing.* I went to the garage and looked through the totes. I looked in the ones that were stacked on the shelf and those that were to the side. *Nothing*. I could feel anxiety creeping in. Just like a thief stealing a precious jewel, I felt my hope being taken right out from under my nose as I was standing there. I felt helpless and was in a state of shock. At this point, I had looked everywhere! Immediately, I transitioned from *search-and-rescue* mode to *total-freak-out* mode! Not only were all of the papers missing *BUT*, Oh, the thoughts of anxiety that came crashing in around me!

What am I going to do?
How am I going to explain this?
There is no way they will believe that I lost that much work!!...
...it is just as lame as saying my dog ate it!
I am, surely, never going to be asked to do another project like this again!
All that time invested...
What were they thinking?!
Why wouldn't they ask before taking something to make sure it wasn't important?
What is wrong with those people!?!
I would never do something like that to them!
What can I possibly do now?
It is ruined! The whole client/provider relationship is ruined!
Oh, No! But This client isn't just any client – it is a BIG client...
...a client with many, many connections to my other clients...
...What if word gets out that I botched this project?!...
...What if I lose ALL my clients because of this!?

There were so many thoughts that came flooding in as I tried, frantically, to find a place to rest from the overwhelming amount of them all! I couldn't stand the thoughts. They were so distressing, so heavy, so dooming! In my state of dismay, I asked, "What *IF* they are true?!"

In the course of what seemed a lifetime but was only a mere half-hour of my time, so far, that morning – I had gone from *peaceful bliss and thankfulness* to *utter despair*. Now, I had transitioned into being in the middle of an intense amount of *anger*. The unexpected flow of my morning was not an easy one to handle. It had come out of nowhere, it seemed! I recounted the steps now. Yes, my morning of *peace & quiet* had led to *thankfulness*. That was a nice place to be – in thankfulness. Then, *thankfulness* led to *mild concern* that was still covered by *hope-for-truth*. Then, my *hope-for-truth* led to attacks of *moderate anxiety*. That *anxiety* escalated with every found *Nothing*. Then, after the last *Nothing*, my emotions leaped into a *complete panic-attack*. This, in turn, led into a *woe is me, I will never recover from this* devastating state of *utter despair*. "This morning is horrible!" I finished.

I found my state of existence rooted in what would easily be labeled as a *fuming mad* emotional state. I felt betrayed and unappreciated! I believed I was not taken into consideration by the choices of others being made that impacted me directly! "They did not even have the decency to think to include me in making such decisions!" I said with much irritation in my voice. "I am, literally, the victim of someone else's irresponsible choice!" I said with even more frustration. I had no idea how I was going to climb out of the giant hole that was dug from under me by two other people. I could understand if it was something of *my own* doing that caused this. *BUT* it was something done by others! *AND* it only impacted me! *It was crazy!* I was speechless. I felt trapped and bound up. *It was all out of my control!* "There is nothing at all that I can even do besides sit here and watch it unravel," I said in great despondence. Yes, all that was left to do was for me to fall apart at what had been done.

Initially, I was at a loss for words to articulate how I felt. There were so many feelings and thoughts rushing through my mind, hitting my heart, and crippling my ability to even speak, let alone move! I was paralyzed by the *fear of the unknown* that befell and surrounded me this morning. I said, "I cannot fathom how anyone could be so rash with someone else's lively hood and work!" I added, questioning, "How could someone *not think* about how this would affect me?" I could not fathom how someone would not even take a said person (me) into consideration as they took actions and made decisions that devastated another person (me, again) in such a way as this! Bewilderment and disbelief confounded me and encircled my every thought. Most of all, though, so did the anger. I was so passionately upset that I had found myself becoming sick to my stomach. Another lifetime seemed to pass, although it had only been a mere half-hour, yet again. "Why is time moving so slowly?" I whined to myself, as I pleadingly looked at the clock to check if it was a decent hour to call them, yet. *It wasn't.*

   I tried to wrap my mind around how to calm down. With everything inside of me, I held myself back from running into the bedroom and shaking my husband awake. I wanted, so desperately, to demand that he handle his family and tend to this, immediately! I shook my head,

> **"For every minute you remain angry, you give up sixty seconds of peace of mind."**
> Ralph Waldo Emerson

though, at the thought. "How absurd I would look if I did! How unreasonable I would seem, in his eyes," I stated. Even if my feelings were 100 percent founded in truth and completely and totally valid... Even if I had every right under the sun to be as distraught as I was... I would still not wake him up like that! I asked myself, "Can you imagine, being woke up by an angry, hysterical person?" Almost immediately, I responded to myself, "No. That would be *way* too much to deal with so early in the morning; and, probably, negatively impact my entire day! *No way*! That would suck!" I had to take a step back from this *riddled-with-betrayal-and-despair-and-anger* thought process and figure out a way to calm down. There was no way in this world I would be able to do so on *my own*! In *my own* self and in *my own* head, I was a mess. I felt like one of those stretchy toys that my brother had received as a gift one year. He used to wrap it around all sorts of things. Just like that toy - I felt wrapped up in total disarray around every which way! I felt twisted up and stretched out to the max and in all crazy sorts of directions that I was not be able to untie. No, not alone…not on *my own*. "That is the kicker, right there! I cannot do this on *my own*. No, not alone," I confirmed to myself as I repeated the thought.

Like a light bulb flipping on suddenly to shatter the darkness around it with its brilliant illumination of all things hidden, so was that simple thought! By this time, though, the legs that I had rested upon had become tingly and were now asleep. I had failed to find a decent seat to sink into. Instead, I had resigned myself to a pitiful mess on the floor. Sitting on my legs in all this despair and anger. Had caused them to become numb. I had to sit, though, from all the sick, light-headedness that had followed. "So much for standing up quickly," I said. I was irritated with the state of my numb legs. "That's what happens when you don't focus on God. You get into a state

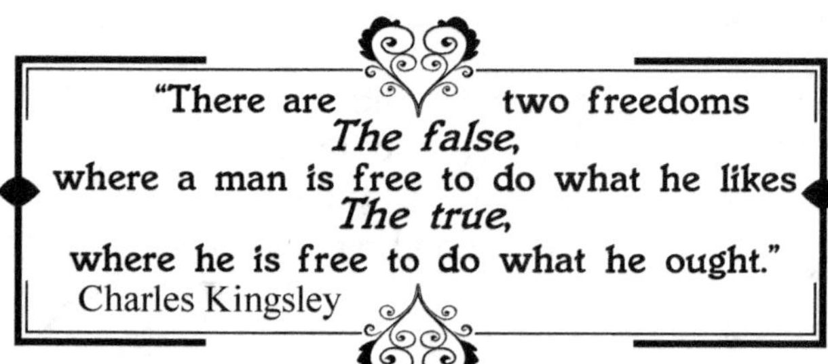

of numbness, and you cannot stand firm. Scripture says we *do not sleep as others do but stay awake and sober.*" I chided myself with this comment as I slowly stood up, shaking the sleep from my legs.

It was time to hold myself accountable for my *Thought Life* and emotional state. I even began elaborating with a question and answer to myself, "*Awake,* meaning what? *Alert,* right? Yes. The Word says to *Be of sober spirit, be on the alert. Your adversary, the devil, prowls around like a roaring lion, seeking someone to devour.* It also says, *for our struggle is not against flesh and blood, but against the rulers, against the powers, against the world forces of this darkness, against the spiritual forces of wickedness in the heavenly places.* Know the real enemy! Use proper discernment," I instructed myself.

Another question and answer followed, "*Sober* in what? *Sober-minded & of Sober Spirit,* right? Yes. The Word says, *and do not be conformed to this world, but be transformed by the renewing of your mind, so that you may prove what the will of God is, that which is good and acceptable and perfect.*" I built upon this accountability through another Q&A. I followed this with, "What else does it say about sobriety of spirit, though?" I answered with the scripture, "*Therefore, prepare your minds for action, keep sober in spirit, fix your hope completely on the grace to be brought to you at the revelation of Jesus Christ.*" Then, I asked myself and responded, "The *Armor of God* is needed in battles such as these, right? Yes. The Word says….," the thought lingered. I didn't know the scripture completely to recount it in my memory. "What are you waiting for, then? Go get your Bible!" I sternly commanded myself. I was still in rebellion and battling the fleshly desire to stay upset. I slowly sulked my way to the table that held my Bible. If I was a child, I presume I would have been on the edge of a tantrum, in that moment. All it would have taken would have been one thought let loose

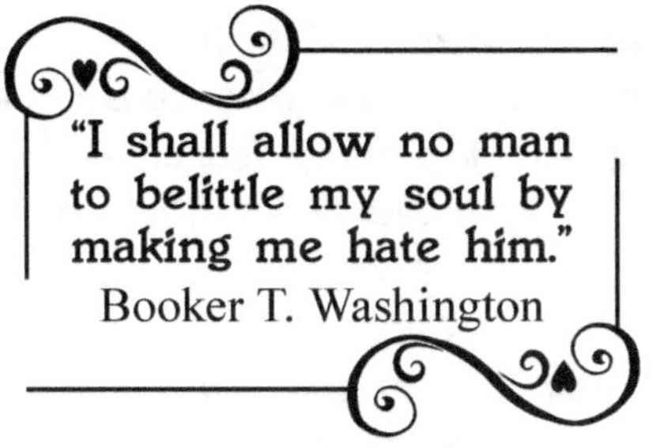

again. One thought and I would be right back into that pile of despair all over. "No. You've got to stay focused on Me. You know that," came the gentle guidance.

Thankfully, the Holy Spirit is with me, always. He helped me passed that tantrum-tempting moment to get to His Word. I said to myself, "Ephesians 6 is where it is located at. I know that much, at least." I also knew it was a rather lengthy passage to memorize. Only recently, I had intentionally sought to study the *Armor of God* - along with all the pieces and what they meant. I had yet to delve into memorizing the full scripture to have them ready when battles arose. Mainly, it was because of the length. It was intimidating enough that I had been avoiding it and practicing avid procrastination. I admitted this, now, saying, "It is quite intimidating! That's a lot of words to memorize like that!" In this particular moment, there was much disdain for the taste of truth the words held. I responded to the thought, saying, "It has been easier to simply *do it later*…i.e., that has meant *never*, apparently."

I felt a sense of a bit more fortitude and motivation beginning to creep up. It was a direct response to this undesirable matter of fact. I was being lazy about reading and studying this particular passage. I had been putting off. I said, "Well. Now is as good a time as any, I suppose." I was still quite irritated and not desiring to cooperate. "Read it out loud. You need to hear it, too!" I commanded myself. And, so, I did. The words struck my heart with certain, unequivocal aim. I began reading aloud in the quiet of the devastating, empty, early-morning living room: "*Finally, be strong in the Lord and in the strength of His might. Put on the full armor of God, so that you will be able to stand firm against the schemes of the devil. For our struggle is not against flesh and blood, but against the rulers, against the powers, against the world forces of this darkness, against the spiritual forces of wickedness in the heavenly places. Therefore, take up the whole armor of God, that you may be able to withstand in the evil day, and having done all, to stand. Stand therefore, having girded your waist with truth, having put on the breastplate of righteousness, and having shod your feet with the preparation of the gospel of peace; above all, taking the shield of faith with which you will be able to quench all the fiery darts of the wicked one. And take the helmet of salvation, and the sword of the Spirit, which is the word of God; praying always with all prayer and supplication in the Spirit, being watchful to this end with all perseverance and supplication for all the saints - and for me, that utterance may be given to me, that I may open my mouth boldly to make known the mystery of the gospel, for which I am an ambassador in chains; that in it I may speak boldly, as I ought to speak.*" I had to let all that sink in.

It was a lot and not what I would call *light reading*, by any stretch of the imagination! My mind was still clouded with frustration. It made it difficult to focus entirely on the words in front of me. The static from the emotions flowing again made it even more so! "Breathe," I told myself. "Just breathe and find your focus," I repeated. Sitting there with my Bible still open on my lap, I closed my eyes. I, intentionally, focused on slow, deep breathing in…and…slow, deep breathing out. As I did so, I began to, purposefully, focus my mind on *feeling* the movements of my body as I breathed. I *felt* the fabric on my shirt sleeve move as I moved. My right hand was resting under the Bible. I could *feel* the texture of the leather on my fingers and palm. There was air coming from the ceiling fan that made the hair on my arms tingle. I *felt* that, as well. Then, I focused on *hearing* the sounds around me. I could *hear* birds singing outside. With difficulty, I tried to *listen* closer. I caught the faint sounds of the train passing in the distance. I imagined that it was probably able to be *heard* from miles around! The wind was blowing the trees against the top of the roof. I could *hear* that, too. The tension in my shoulders was slowly releasing. I shifted my focus to the *smells* of the morning. There was a *smell* like linen with a hint of lemon. The fresh laundry basket was on the coffee table in front of me. I knew that was where the linen *smell* came from. The lemon could have been from two places. Lemon was in the cleaning spray I had used earlier that morning. It was also in the glass of lemon water I had made. "Maybe it was coming from my lips after drinking some!" I thought to myself, inquisitively considering the *smell* of lemon. As I focused more, a new *scent* was recognized. Flowers with a touch of freshness. I raised my hand to my nose. I *smelled* the inside of my wrist. "Yes. I was right! It is my perfume!" I said with a sense of accomplishment from identifying the *smell*. A few more long breaths and I opened my eyes. Focusing on *sight* was my next step in this process. I concentrated on *looking* at a few specific objects in the room around me. I thought about their physical descriptions. I *saw* the brightness of a candle that I had lit earlier. My eyes *watched* the flame dance and move with great gentleness and grace. Then, they shifted to *looking* at the bookcase. 4 shelves high, it was full of books. "Have I even read all of them yet?!" I asked myself as my *gaze* rested on them. "That's a lot of books!" I thought. As I *looked* at it, I noticed that there were many shapes and sizes with

> "God never hurries. There are no deadlines against which He must work.
> Only to know this is to quiet our spirits & relax our nerves."
>
> A.W. Tozer

different colors throughout the bookcase. I could tell that most of the frustration had subsided by this time. I didn't care too much for doing the final focus exercise of *taste*, so I moved on in my thoughts. I felt a bit more settled than I was before.

I commented in confirmation, "Yes, I feel a little more like my sane self instead of my hysterical self, for sure!"

"Ok, then. Now, pray first," I instructed myself. I took a moment to ask the Holy Spirit to guide me with wisdom and understanding in the passages I had already read through. "Reread them," was the simple instruction that came to me as I prayed. So, I did. I began to read them again. This time, the words came out so much clearer! Not that I was amazed, by any means. Any time I willingly lean into the Holy Spirit, reading His Word comes easily. However, it did help me to realize how unclear my thought process and emotions were. I reflected on the scripture

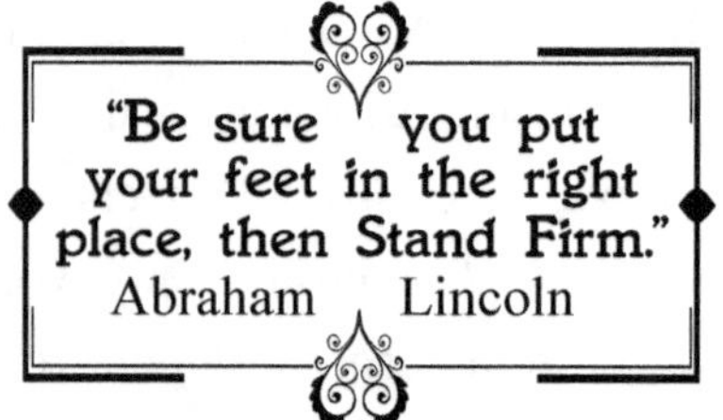

again. I observed, "The word *Standing* is repeated so many times in just the first few lines!" When God's Word echoes something over and over again, I know in my spirit that it is truth that is essential. There is a reason. Funny that the word *Standing* would be what His Spirit would point out to me. Literally, moments ago, I couldn't stand due to my legs thinking they needed to take a nap mid-morning because of my state of despair. *Standing Firm* was even more profound than merely physically *Standing*, though. "Yes, it means to hold my ground against the enemy. Do not allow the enemy to advance forward. *Stand* strong and firm. Do not waver. *Resist the enemy, and he will flee from me*, is what it means. He must flee in this very moment!" I exclaimed to myself, wincing at the conviction that quickly followed. I was not *Standing Firm*, at all!

My final Q&A to refocus was sprinkled with its own dose of scripture. It complimented that conviction quite well, indeed! "The Word says in many ways to *diligently keep focused on Jesus*, not this world – not these circumstances, but *on Jesus Christ*, Who has *overcome this world*, right?" I asked myself. I responded to my accountability question, "Yes, that is all correct, all of it! My focus does not need to be on these things. It needs to be on God and what He is doing in and through these circumstances. There is always a reason for what I must endure. Even if that which I endure is not of my choosing." It was with a tinge of a frustrated, begrudging tone that I answered these in my head to myself.

I *Knew* the words were right. I *Knew* they were truth. Yet, *Knowing* that did not change the circumstances that were surrounding me. It did not alter the tremendous amount of anger that was being held at bay, for the time being. At any mention of the thoughts that had run rampant an hour earlier, that anger was waiting to come rushing back in. My flesh did not desire to submit. My circumstances were still flaming the passionately volatile emotions just underneath the surface. Those emotions were hindering my submission. I *Knew* that I needed to submit, though. However, the flesh in me did not want to. My reluctance to let go of all the fleshly things driving my emotions was evident in my face as I looked up.

I was facing myself, now, as I gazed into the reflection of the mirror in front of me. I had stepped inside the bathroom to splash some sense into myself, hopefully, with the sudden shock of cold water! I had to reset. I just had to! "You *know your tongue is not easily tamed, and no man alone can tame the tongue. It is that which burns and destroys, kills, and damages if left unbridled.* The only One that can tame that crazy thing is God. Don't you dare speak until you seek Him!" I, sternly, commanded myself. I was still looking into the mirror as I spoke. Again, I felt the impact of the crisp water splashing upon my face. I rested my eyes upon my hands as I watched the water run over the top of them and fall into the porcelain sink below. With ease, it found its way to the drain to disappear from my sight. "I wish my anger would disappear that easily!" I commented.

> "Therefore humble yourselves under the mighty hand of God, that He may exalt you at the proper time, casting all your anxiety on Him, because He cares for you."
>
> Apostle Peter

I paused for a moment and considered this. Looking at the water flowing was soothing. I breathed in and sighed, hoping that some of the frustration would depart with the breath. "Visualize it leaving. Let it go. Give it to Me, child," said the Holy Spirit. As the water vanished from sight, I visualized the anger and emotions dripping off my fingertips. They flowed down the inside of the sink and into the drain to disappear, as well. I took a deep breath, again, and let go of the anger.

Looking myself in the eyes, I stared boldly and directly into the mirror. It was a challenging sight! I couldn't very well beat my stubbornness into submission. However, that look might have just done it! "I don't even know how something like that would play out!" I thought incredulously. Yet, here I was in a similar state of a visual standoff. My flesh and my spirit were at war with one another. I imagined the reflection of myself being on one side, the real me on the other. We were one in the same in the battle for leadership that ensued. "Lord, I need You. I need Your help in this." I said, not breaking my gaze on myself. Coming in like a cool breeze, I began to feel a sense of strength and fortitude welling up from my heart. I could see it seeping out through the depths of my eyes. "I can do this! With You, God, I can do this! *I can do all things through Christ who strengthens me*! Lord, I want to *learn to be content in whatever circumstances I am*. God, You are mightier than *EVERYTHING*!" I said, with boldness. "Enough! Submit! Now!" I commanded to the reflection before me. With a sigh of submission to His will, not my own, I let it go. I could feel the driving force of my flesh coming to a halt. It was like a dissipating Oklahoma tornado. It had finished inflicting all its damaging attacks and had twisted its way back up into the clouds, out of sight. I reminded myself, "I've got this. I'm not going to lose sight of Him. He will make a way for me. *When I acknowledge Him in all my ways, He will make my path straight as I keep on Trusting in Him with all my heart and not my own understanding*." With one last, firm look in the mirror, I lifted my eyes up and said, "Thank You, Father. I can't do this without You. I'm gonna need Your help. I don't *Know* how...I don't *Know* when...I don't *Know* why, or who, or what...but I *Know* that You *Know*. And that is enough for me. Forgive me and help me unroot seeds of unbelief sown by the enemy in times such as these, Lord. Amen."

<u>MEMORY VERSE</u>

*Blessed be the Lord,
because He has heard the voice of my supplication.
The Lord is my strength and my shield;
my heart trusts in Him, and I am helped;
therefore my heart exults,
and with my song I shall thank Him.*
Psalm 28:6-7

Chapter Six

Beneficial Confrontation

> *Seek the Lord while He may be found;*
> *Call upon Him while He is near. Let the wicked*
> *forsake his way & the unrighteous man his*
> *thoughts; And let him return to the Lord, and*
> *He will have compassion on him, and to our God,*
> *for He will abundantly pardon.*
> *"For My thoughts are not your thoughts, nor are*
> *your ways My ways," declares the Lord.*
> *"For as the heavens are higher than the earth,*
> *so are My ways higher than your ways*
> *and My thoughts than your thoughts."*
> Isaiah 55:6-9

Mid-morning the next day, I desired the day to be over with, already. "Wow, aren't you just being ungrateful, today?" I asked myself in utter amazement at this desire for ending my Saturday so early on. I knew that was not the way to be walking around thinking, by any means. "Each day is a gift, and we are not promised tomorrow." I reminded myself. Yes, I knew better. However, a sense of dread came over me at the remembrance of the unavoidable conversation. My husband and I agreed to have a little chat with the in-laws. We had waited until today to do so. I wasn't putting it off, though. No, my husband and I had a lengthy discussion of the situation. He was exceptionally irritated with his family for me. It was all I could do to convince him Not to do something about it, right then and there when we discussed it yesterday afternoon! He was furious with them, even more so than I was. That, of course, did not seem possible to me. I was beyond agitated, myself. A brief shot of adrenaline hit my heart as I quickly remembered the sickening feeling that had brought me to a slumped over, pitiful pile on the floor Friday morning.

However, here we were, again. At least it was us together now, instead of me by myself in my misery. He was doing his best to deal with his response to the entire situation. I had managed to talk him down to a calm state, just as I did with myself the day before. Both attempts were ridiculously trying and hard to get through – each, in their own right! We had agreed to sleep on it and visit with them on the phone…tomorrow. That would allow for sufficient time to cool off, or, at least, we thought it would. Unfortunately, in between here and there, the frustration had come back to the forefront for my husband. I believe it only stayed under the surface of the volcano eruption we were dealing with because he was called into work. There was an emergency. So, he had to shift his focus to it, instead of the unraveling of the events at hand.

Yesterday was everyone's day off at his office due to an internal holiday. A few years back, the company decided to make a special holiday in remembrance of the founder's passing. Unfortunately for my husband, that special holiday did not apply to his position. No holiday did, ever…and neither did vacation time, personal leave, sick days, or even funerals. I remember one year, he had only been at the funeral service for his uncle for about 30 minutes before receiving an emergency request from a customer through email, text, and voicemail. He had only said "Hello" to his aunt and cousin before, regretfully, having to excuse himself. He drove clear across town on something that ended up not even being an emergency and was fixed within ten minutes. It is the nature of his industry, and there is nothing that he can do to change it, but he sure wanted to! I try my best to be understanding and support him in this. I lean into God to take care of him in his days, especially the days he gets pulled away from family events like that. On the more trying days that his work puts a strain on our marriage, I ask for God to guard my mouth, my heart, & my mind in Christ Jesus. " Thankfully, You provide those guards," I said with a smile, "You Know I need them, desperately. My mouth has a foot in it quite often!"

If anything, I was irritated on behalf of my husband about this company he worked for. I felt sad & frustrated for him. Daily, he had to endure through all the added stress and frustration that this company created in his life. It made me sad, sometimes, frustrated, other times. However, I had already Learned that speaking in support of him against a workplace did not go very far. Even if I was holding the role of his cheerleader and emotional defender/helpmate in that arena…fighting for him, advocating for his side, etc., etc. it was lost in translation…somewhere… somehow. His reply was a 50/50 shot. One day, he didn't see it that way. Another day, he did see it that way. I had decided, a while ago, to only listen to him; instead of being upset at the company with him. I am the type that would have a friend's back if stuff got real; so, this was a bit of a learning curve for me in our marriage. "It must simply be a man thing," I said, trying to explain it away with that old ridiculous stereotype. I laughed at the thought that a stereotype of any kind would ever be 100% accurate, though. "That's just absurd!" I exclaimed in my mind.

I did not know what it was about that kind of in-your-corner support not being well-received, because I am simply that kind of woman. I am the type that would fight for her man. I would be by his side in battle, in peace, in war, in bliss, and in all things. All of the above and the in-between – that is me, by his side. Thankfully, God knows the reasons behind the hit-and-miss responses from my husband. If that advocacy part of me is something He deems as needing to be molded into a better way, so be it. If not, God would mold my husband to receive that caliber of support from me, consistently and positively. Better yet, He may just mold us both, at the same time: My husband to be more receptive to my support and Me to take the advocacy banner down a notch. I summarized in my thoughts, "Regardless of who needs molding in that area, God knows best, always. I will do my best to submit to His will in all things and in all my ways. His ways are way better than mine will ever be, and His picture of my story is 100 times better than I could ever paint!"

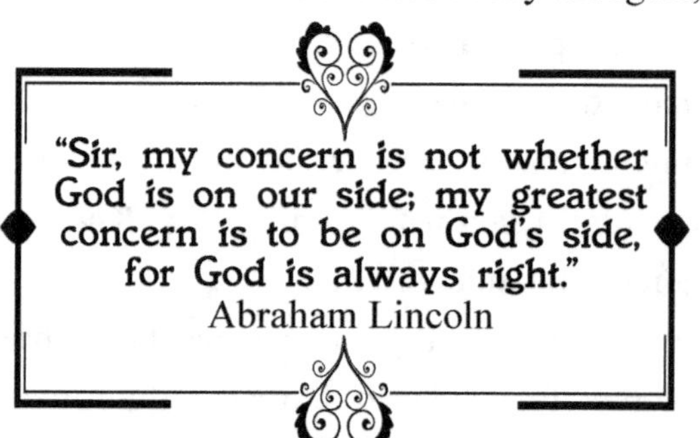

The cold, hard truth of the matter was simple: There wasn't anything my husband could do about how the industry worked. Sure, he could try to influence those around him and cultivate a change, but it would be quite the task in that industry. It had been uncompromising and uncaring since inception. The mighty bottom dollar was the only priority, and that was the way it was going to stay. My husband would jokingly refer to his work as feeding the machine. It never seemed to be full or enough. They just stayed in that state of wanting more. Short of one of God's miracles, I knew that it would stay that way simply because it was one of the world's industries. It was a worldly industry with a temporal focus. It bothered me how taxing it was on my husband, though. I could see it in the way his face would look relieved upon the entrance into our home and finally getting to see our daughter and me. I could see it in the way his broad, tense shoulders would relax as he sunk down into the living room chair to take off his boots. I could hear it in his voice the instant after he was finished recounting his tedious day, and he would shift the topic to something else. My heart broke for what he endured on the daily. Many times, when I prayed for him in his days, I would weep. I knew he wasn't fulfilled, spiritually, there. There was no edification like there would be if he were surrounded by men of God. It was hard. He was surrounded by men of the world, and that wasn't going to change. It hurt my heart, but my husband was definitely a trooper!

It was a temporal environment full of temptations of the flesh, and he endured it like a champ! I knew it was difficult, every day, to work in such a place. "But such is the world," he would say. Yes. It is a place that money rules, sin continues, and all things of self are idolized. It just is. He was right. It didn't stop me from my heart feeling the pain of that for him, though. A few years ago, I had learned the depth of being one with my husband after marriage. As the scripture goes, "for this reason a man shall leave his father and mother and shall be joined to his wife, and the two shall become one flesh." Over the years, that awareness had grown quite keen! When he hurt, I hurt. When he was dealing with stuff, I felt the weight of it, too. That was just a part of our marriage. Yes, this marriage of ours has taught me and my husband to understand the

"Where there is unity there is always victory."
Publilius Syrus

whole two become one thing, intimately, with each passing day. I thought of the scripture from Genesis. It read, *"For this reason a man shall leave his father and his mother, and be joined to his wife; and they shall become one flesh."* We both take it very seriously. My mind pondered on the growth of that knowledge between my husband and me briefly. "It is sweet and tender to reflect on such things!" I said, feeling a closeness to my other half with the words.

Shaking my head, I redirected back to the topic of the world. I thought, "There is nothing that anyone can do about the nature of the world any more than we can turn back the hands of time and talk some sense into Adam & Eve." For a moment, I entertained what that conversation might consist of.

Eve could have seriously used some training on:
how not to be deceived by the enemy
how to continue to trust in God's Word to be Truth
how to thwart any attacks of the enemy
how to be submissive to the leadership & order established by God

Adam could have used some major discipline in:
how to stand up against the enemy
how to intercede on behalf of his mate to stop the deception
how to stand firm in the Word God had spoken to him as Truth
how not to be a passive man, but a true leader in - the heart, the mind, the body, and the soul

Of course, both could have used a bit of training in good ole obedience. Dwelling on such things of the past did not change the present state and was not fruitful for the mind. I knew that. Especially, an event as far back as the first sin of the world scenario. The past was the past. With that awareness, I snapped back to the present. This discussion we were going to have with the in-laws weighed heavily in the air...still. "Neither does dwelling on past mistakes of others or yours, for that matter," I told myself.

Today, my husband was all about being my vindicator and restorer of all things good and right. It did not matter who it was on the other side of the problem. "He is walking in the protection aspect of *Husbands, love your wives, just as Christ also loved the church and gave Himself up for her,* for sure today," I thought to myself. His demeanor was a powerful and impressive display of us against the world. I had to admit, I liked the security, unity, and protection he was providing through it. His initial response and attempted actions at calling them to demand they explain

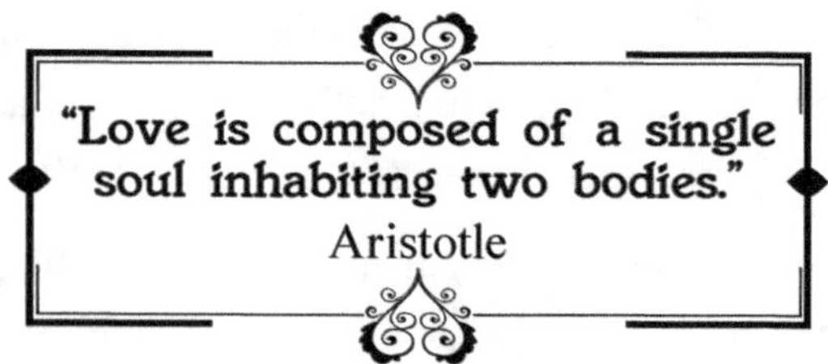

themselves and make it right by me and us was something like you would see in a fairy tale. He was handsomely playing the role of the knight in shining armor coming to my rescue. And, boy, was I ever a damsel in distress, after yesterday! "At least, I sure felt like one," I said to myself, as I recalled my totally out of control state of despair that wound me up on the floor. "What kind of man does that, anymore? After-all, chivalry may as well be as dead as a doornail in this world," I pondered to myself. "It's not every day you see a man actually stand up for his wife - no matter what is going on or who is involved," I continued in thought. I appreciated his response to having my back, completely, and caring so very much about all the work and time I invest in what I do. Even though I didn't like the circumstances I was in, this was a positive to it. It was quite flattering to see this side of my husband! With a little reluctance after the realization, I acknowledged, "Without those circumstances, I probably would not have seen this side of him." A seemingly out-of-place sense of gratitude for the dismay I had endured came over me. "Gratefulness for dismay," I said to myself, "Who would've thought!?"

A part of me was super-excited that he felt so passionately about defending me, protecting my efforts, and supporting what I had put so much dedication and hard work toward. It was thrilling and intriguing to see him demonstrate through such actions and express such desires in his choices. Hearing words that hinted at the possibility that this was the case was not the same as seeing this display. Even if he was firing words their direction, it wasn't equivalent to taking action for something. Yes, words may sound good, but they don't *Do* anything. They do not *Show* anyone anything. It has been some time since my husband has demonstrated where he stands...in such a way as this! "No. It hasn't just been some time or a long while. It has been a long never," my corrective voice chimed in, eager to make the distinction that this was, in fact, a first for my husband to stand up for me. We really had not encountered too many trials that tested the resilience of our union. When we did, his choice was not to confront it. This, of course, was in direct opposition to my preference to confront it. "The past is the past," I stated to myself, again. Nine times out of ten, those smaller things had worked themselves out without confrontation. We both knew, however, that this one was not going to simply work itself out. Confrontation was needed. It didn't have to be a negative thing. Another scripture had come to heart as I considered this. God's word was clear on how to address one another in the letter to the Ephesians. Paul teaches the importance of how to *walk in a manner worthy of the calling - with all humility and gentleness, with patience, showing tolerance for one another in love, being diligent to preserve the unity of the Spirit in the bond of peace.* Applying it to the subject of confrontation, I said, "Yes, confrontation is a good thing if done correctly, this way."

My mind returned to my husband, though. Even through this, there was something wonderful to be witnessed. I wanted to soak up as much of this chivalrous response of his that I could! I was mystified and had this strange desire to have this moment continue for as long as he would remain in it. Although there was potential for backlash from my in-laws, I sort of didn't really care how they reacted to it all. It felt good to see him willing to *advocate* on my behalf and petition for justice for my sake…I mean, "for our sake," as he had said. My husband was willing to put even a close-ish family relationship to the test in his chivalrous attempts to *honor* and *cherish* his wife. "Think of the possibilities of where this kind of response from him would lead him…What if he did this all the time…Demonstrating to me and everyone else on the planet that he has that *no holds barred kind* of love for me… that he is that *don't mess with my woman kind* of man… *I will do anything for her kind* of husband… *change the whole world for her kind* of friend… *cross oceans in a paddleboat and deserts in barefoot for her kind* of companion…" the descriptive list of titles continued in my mind. I entertained these imaginary scenarios like something out of a storybook for the next 10 minutes. I said to myself, "If he keeps this up, I may just have to tell him how attractive it is!" Imagery of all sorts fell into my thoughts as pictures of a fantastic love story were allowed to flow freely in those moments. A love that would not only stand the test of time but also promote change throughout the world in the way husbands actively demonstrated their commitment and love to their wives. "Wouldn't that be something?!" I asked myself in summation. "My husband is a great leader, after all! He could easily lead such a massive amount of change, for sure!" I affirmed with significant confidence in my words. "He could totally do that!" I could feel my cheeks turning red from the blush that followed. My response to his response was that of fascination. He was so dashing as my advocate in this. He was, indeed, putting on love for me as his ambition. At the thought, I was reminded of the scripture of unity in Colossians, *Beyond all these things put on love, which is the perfect bond of unity.* Yes, maintaining the unity in the spirit in our marriage and keeping the peace with others, as intentional peacemakers, was important.

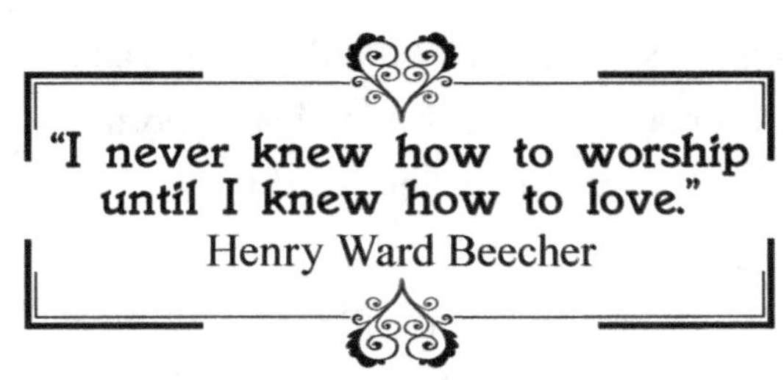

My fascination with my husband's response still lingered. It was not that I wanted him to be some crazy dude that went out and around town beating people up and being some kind of barbarian at every injustice he thought was served to his wife. It was not that, at all! On the contrary, I had much confidence in my husband's diplomatic abilities to handle any situation; while, simultaneously, being very blunt about how he stands by his wife's side. I also had complete trust in the Holy Spirit within him to be able to guide him and direct his actions to advocate on my behalf and that of our marriage. Advocacy is Jesus' wheelhouse. My husband knew that. And, I knew he understood the importance and necessity to submit to the authority of Jesus Christ in all he would or would not do. In some cases, it would be difficult, but I was quite confident he would not allow the flesh and self to dictate his actions and would choose to seek God in what he did, on the daily.

I thought about the strong belief I had in my husband's abilities to handle himself in other areas, too. I also had confidence that he desired as much as I did to protect our union from doubts, insecurities, and fears. We had both closed any doors with the opposite sex looooong ago. He would say, "Babe, you are what matters to me, most. None of those attacks can get in if there isn't an opportunity given to the devil for them to do so." He had respectfully closed the doors of his past, and I had done so, as well. He knew the complete story behind every single male on all of my email accounts, work stuff, social media outlets, phone, etc. I laughed at remembering a few of those interactions when we had first started out. I remember telling him jokingly but quite seriously, "If you question 'em, I'm disconnecting 'em." I didn't see then and still don't see now why there would ever be a reason to give the devil an opportunity into our marriage like that. Of course, I was of the firm belief that if there is an easy solution, do it. It was pretty cut and dry with me.

80% of the people we both weeded through that we still had connections of some sort with were ancient history, anyway. Some of them, neither of us had talked to in over 2 decades!! We didn't even know those people anymore!

Do they have kids?
Are they married?
What is their spouse's name?
Where do they work?
What are some of their hobbies now?
Do they have any pets?
Where do they live?
What are the names of their parents?
Are their parents still alive??!!

We didn't have answers to any of those questions. It made it very simple to quickly remove the enemy's ability to weasel his way into our marriage through people of the opposite sex. We simply removed it altogether. We didn't even crack the door open for temptation to attack our marriage or each other with those caliber of doubts, insecurities, and fears. Shaking my head and rolling my eyes, I thought to myself, "I don't want to stay connected with guys that find me attractive and want more, anyway! I am committed – in it for the long-haul – and I want it to always be crystal clear to the man I chose to marry that he has absolutely nothing to be concerned with! I'm not even going to allow the devil the opportunity to do anything." Like my husband says, "you can't have a concern if there is no one there to be concerned about." That was true, so very true! I had found his willing eagerness to choose me over any woman of his past very attractive. It had promoted a strong bond of trust between us, right out of the gate! Thinking about it now made me smile. "He's pretty awesome, that man of mine," I said.

I pulled my attention back to his initial reaction yesterday. It wasn't the anger in his demeanor, frustration in his words, or chaotic solution-seeking pacing that appealed to me, either. Those were more of a turn-off than anything. Actually, I wasn't a fan of anger in myself, either. I did my best to stay away from it. Although a healthy enough emotion when held in a righteous state, anger was still a fickle thing that bordered too closely to the edge of temptations to sin - more so than other emotions, in my experience. "What about the scriptures tied to what a man thinks not being accurate or able to depend on as truth," I thought to

"When you are offended at any man's fault, turn to yourself & study your own failings. Then you will forget your anger."
Epictetus

myself. "People may think of anger as righteous in their own eyes and justify it. Yet, I bet about 95% of the time, they are walking the wrong way in the sin that follows holding on to anger," I surmised. In response to this, I said, "I wonder how significant the percentage is of times that this is from self-deception?" From my own experience, I could establish that deception of one's self is learned over the years by adverse life experiences that aren't true. "The long game played by the enemy to chip away the truth by inserting lies that distort reality is definitely disheartening to think about," I said, shaking my head sadly. With that, I cautioned myself, "If I don't turn to the Word of God to learn the difference, I can wind up sinning against my brother/sister in Christ, myself, or, worse…sinning against

God! I definitely don't wanna do that!" To me, playing with anger is like playing with fire: It is only a matter of time before someone gets burned. No. It definitely wasn't my husband's angry response on my behalf that interested me in all this.

The most intriguing part of his response was that he was *Actively Choosing* me. It warmed my heart to see my husband's passion & desire to care about something that impacted me. Yesterday, he was taking me into such intentional consideration as he spoke of his heart hurting for me that I had to choke back tears! He was actively demonstrating that he desired to be the stand-up-for-my-wife caliber of husband. I was taken aback by the strength I saw in his response, the conviction and protective nature, and, most of all, his heart for me in it. I felt cherished. I felt important to him. I felt like I was his top priority, directly under God. I felt wanted. I felt protected & safe. I felt lots of things from the prompting that this little glimpse of the potential for a new season and depth of love with him gave me. "Even more intimacy with the man I call my husband? Yes! Please!" was the enthusiastic response of the wife in me. I really did not know where this new energy from him had come from, but I sure did enjoy seeing it! "That's it! It is the potential that I see to grow closer with my husband in our intimacy together in all fullness. That is what is so appealing!" A blushed sigh and a nod followed this affirmation.

> "If God has made your cup sweet, drink it with grace; if He has made it bitter, drink it in communion with Him."
> Oswald Chambers

It was quite tempting to stay in this state of thoughtful imagination of all the *What Ifs* I could daydream about. Thinking about our future together on the battlefield of life was something I found great delight in. However, that was brought to a screeching halt at the thought of the in-laws, again. I knew that the discussion with them needed to occur soon. I had no idea what was going to unfold in the conversation, nor how it would end. I only knew it was something that needed to be done. I was being attacked with fear. It was not that I was afraid of our in-laws. The fear that was lurking was the fear of the unknown. It was doing its best to mess with my mind and emotions again. All night, I had gone over scenarios in my head.

"How do I say this correctly?"
"How do I say that correctly?"
"What do I respond with if they say, this or that?"

As it stood, right now, I had about a hundred different simulations of conversations with them all practiced out. On top of that, I was going on about 2 hours of sleep. That was only found after sleep deprivation finally beat me! I had gone through, in-depth, all those silly, useless scenarios - to no avail! It was not the fault of our in-laws, of course. No. I was the one responsible for my lack of sleep. I had chosen to allow the thoughts to be entertained that came my way. I chased them around like silly, little butterflies in a forest of uncatchable, imaginary things. One rabbit-hole after the next, I would dive in, until I found myself utterly exhausted from the unrewarding chase. It was a chase of the invisible - a race of the unwinnable. Yet, I still participated. I was tired.

Nothing that I could say would change the reality that this conversation had to happen. I banked on the fact that not one of those scenarios would be the real one; because the actual situation was unpredictable and in the future. Still, I tossed and turned as I was visited, over and over again, by fear and its sidekick cousins – doubt, anxiety, insecurities, and worry. Anything could happen between here and there! Plus, I did not even know the full story of where in the world all the papers disappeared to!! That was the main objective of this whole thing. Find the papers.

The problem: The papers were missing. *The solution:* Talk to the in-laws who moved the papers from their original location to find the papers.
Additional objective: Somehow manage to thank them for being so kind to lightly tidy up the office, kitchen, & living room before they left…no matter how upset I was with them.

Politeness and consideration of others were not things to dismiss. Kindness, gentleness, goodness, and other acts of love were not to be diminished - regardless of circumstances. They were to be appreciated and practiced. I was, definitely, going to need to focus and pray for God's wisdom and the guidance of the Holy Spirit before I spoke a word or even picked up the phone to dial their number.

It didn't matter what type of discussion I was going to have with them. If I left out the basics of being understanding then I would have not done as I should, on my part. Listening to understand & empathize; desiring to relate & be reasonable; showing them compassion & love; working toward hearing their side, completely; going into the conversation with a forgiving heart; and seeking unity & mutual consideration throughout it all were each important parts of that process. "I am responsible for my choices, my words, my thoughts, and my actions. Regardless of what they have chosen, choose, or will choose to do/say to me, I am still responsible for me," I said to myself, in personal reflection. In a moment of a reminder of my own responsibility to maintain personal accountability, I thought to myself, "Those are between God and me. One way or the other, I am accountable for what I choose." I paused for a moment, then asked, "So, what will it be this time?" I knew what my answer was. I was choosing to make peace, as best as I could.

I had walked into the office and saw the printed off list from my old training manual. The header read: *Active Listening Training*. It was a tool that I learned from years ago in a highly customer-support-driven job. We were trained, in-depth, that it was imperative for success! There were many steps to the process flow that this company used. Today, I know many companies that practice *Active Listening* in one fashion or another. However, not many people practice it, personally. I, for one, found it quite useful in my everyday life application! The key points they highlighted on the list were:

- Ask about the problem
- Clarify: Restate sentences for clarification

- Be Polite: Do not interrupt the customer
- Ask further open-ended questions to gather more details about the issue
- Reflect & Relate: speak about the problem with sincerity of understanding
- Express Empathy & Compassion for the problem they are experiencing
- Apologize for the inconveniences that the problem has caused
- Escalation Prevention: Use 'I' statements to Focus on the issue & solution. Don't blame-shift to the customer
- Refocus: If the customer gets off track in conversation, bring the focus back to the problem
- Do not patronize, antagonize, advise, or preach
- Try to add in comfortable silences throughout the communication to allow the customer to think through the options & not feel the pressure of the problem
- Do all this *while* listening - intently & intentionally - to achieve a thorough understanding & comprehend the problem completely

Being there was the biggest thing, I think. Intentionally choosing to be present. Staying in the moment made all the difference in the success or failure of the communication. I remember my mentor, who trained me, would tell us repeatedly, "*Active Listening* training is not to *wait and tell*. We don't just *wait* for the opportunity to talk so we can turn around *and tell* people what to do, or what to think, or how much they messed up." No. He had made it clear. The purpose of that training was two-fold: *to establish a good rapport with the customers,* and *to decrease the number of repeat callbacks by solving the problem(s) at the root, not just the symptoms.*

Yes, a correct and crystal-clear diagnosis was instrumental in understanding how to correct the situation in its entirety, not just at the surface. That was the goal in the company I used to work for. It was also going to be the goal in this conversation with the in-laws. *Active Listening* was the solution. It was important enough for every single tech to be required to go through the training every quarter as a refresher and for quality control standards to be met. That company, like others, felt it was necessary to learn. It was a primary way to ensure quality customer communication was provided. It worked then, like a charm. So, that was how I was going to address the conversation with the in-laws, as well. Years of training and etiquette in handling high-pressure, stressful situations was something I was well-versed in. I had every intention of pulling this off like a champ, too. I continued

talking myself up, by saying, "Yea! If I can get promoted twice within the first 3 months on the job due to those quality communication skills, I can handle this conversation. Plus, now, I have God!"

> "There is in every true woman's heart, a spark of heavenly fire, which lies dormant in the broad daylight of prosperity, but which kindles up & beams & blazes in the dark hour of adversity."
> Washington Irving

Back then, I was just barely scraping by in the God's Word arena. The Bible I had at that time was covered in ten times the dust my shelves in the office were! "Walking with You sure makes my outlook better on confrontations like this, Lord," I said, with a hopeful smile. As I was thinking about the impending confrontation, The Holy Spirit hit my heart with one of my favorite chapters in the first letter to the Corinthians. Paul writes to the church telling them, "without love, you have nothing…it is all for naught. No matter what great things you achieve or do, it is worthless without love weaved into the very fibers of those great things." That is my quick summation, of course, in the initial lines of chapter 13. It reads, *"If I speak with the tongues of men and of angels, but do not have love, I have become a noisy gong or a clanging cymbal. If I have the gift of prophecy, and know all mysteries and all knowledge; and if I have all faith, so as to remove mountains, but do not have love, I am nothing. And if I give all my possessions to feed the poor, and if I surrender my body to be burned, but do not have love, it profits me nothing. Love is patient, love is kind and is not jealous; love does not brag and is not arrogant, does not act unbecomingly; it does not seek its own, is not provoked, does not take into account a wrong suffered, does not rejoice in unrighteousness, but rejoices with the truth; bears all things, believes all things, hopes all things, endures all things. Love never fails; but if there are gifts of prophecy, they will be done away; if there are tongues, they will cease; if there is knowledge, it will be done away. For we know in part and we prophesy in part; but when the perfect comes, the partial will be done away. When I was a child, I used to speak like a child, think like a child, reason like a child; when I became a man, I did away with childish things. For now we see in a mirror dimly, but then face to face; now I know in part, but then I will know fully just as I also have been fully known. But now faith, hope, love, abide these three; but the greatest of these is love."*

There is an unshakable nature about God that I can rely on during times like this that I need and desire. I know my heavenly Father will make sure I am taken care of before it, during it, and after it. His Great Love will provide for every last bit of it all! With His definition of love articulated by Paul fresh on my mind, I humbly admitted to myself, "It isn't confidence in myself that gives me the courage to make this call. No, it is confidence in Jesus Christ within me that gives me the strength to do so." I looked over at my husband who looked like a panther in stealth mode ready to pounce at the word *Go*. He was on high alert and I could tell. So, I told him with intentional gentleness in my words, "I am not sure about dealing with this…alone. But I am sure about dealing with this...with God and you both backing me today. Thank you so much, Babe!"

His frustrated apprehension melted away at the appreciation. His stature shifted to one of fortitude – his stance was tall and his shoulders broad. His eyes were beaming with a newfound strength. I could see that my knight was ready to take up arms for his fair maiden. I felt my face flush and quickly turned away so he wouldn't see the redness that came upon my cheeks. He was very dashing in this moment, and I was quite the enamored wife! I breathed in sharply, to gather my focus back to where it was supposed to be – the phone call. With a sigh, I picked up the phone to dial the number to this confrontation. "Here goes…whatever this is, God…It is Yours; I submit to You. Thank You for guiding my words and guarding my mouth, my heart, and my mind through it and after it, in Jesus Christ," I thought to myself. "Amen," I said out loud, surprising my husband and myself. He didn't miss a step, though, and echoed, "Amen, I agree, Babe."

MEMORY VERSE

*For as the rain and the snow come down from heaven,
and do not return there without watering the earth
and making it bear and sprout,
and furnishing seed to the sower and bread to the eater;
So will My word be which goes forth from My mouth;
it will not return to Me empty,
without accomplishing what I desire,
and without succeeding in the matter for which I sent it.*
Isaiah 55:10-11

Chapter Seven
Part One

Let's Talk:
The Fruit of the Matter

*Delight yourself in the Lord; He will
give you the desires of your heart.
Commit your way to the Lord,
trust also in Him, and He will do it.
He will bring forth your righteousness
as the light and your judgment as the noonday.
Rest in the Lord and wait patiently for Him;
do not fret because of him who prospers in
his way, because of the man who carries out
wicked schemes. Cease from anger & forsake
wrath; do not fret; it leads only to evildoing.*
Psalm 37:4-8

It was the *Day of Rest* for the week already. It had seemed that Sunday had only just left us a few days ago. Yet, here it was again! My mind really was too worn out. I was not about to wrap it around the thought of how or why it had been so abrupt. The speed of traveling through this week had zipped right on by! I allowed my mind to linger on the contemplation only briefly before moving on as I got up out of the comfortable bed. I was getting up earlier than usual. I needed to. I did not pay any attention to the crankiness my bones and muscles were demonstrating. I ignored the soreness and stiff areas that rebelled at my early morning movements. My body had its own sound effects, built right in! It felt like I was making tons of noises with the pops and cracks that came from it. Regardless, I was going to get up. I stealthily attempted to drag myself from the bedroom to the living room without my husband noticing. "Success!" I tiredly thought to myself with as much excitement at the small victory as I could gather. I gently closed the door behind me.

Getting up early was an intentional choice I had made the evening before to ensure I had quality time with God before anyone in the house woke up. I needed to spend some time resting. Not in the physical sense, mind you. If that were the case, I would have stayed in bed and slept in... for a looooong, comfortable time. No, it was in the spiritual sense that I needed rest. The week had been full of unexpected twists and turns. There had been some of those crazy loop-the-loops like on the roller coaster rides, too. Somewhere, some structural engineers decided it would be fantastic for all the thrill-seekers to experience their world turned upside down and back around, super quickly! Like some of those thrill-seeking roller coaster riders, I, too, had my stomach turned by the immediate, unexpected flip upside down of my business world. My spirit had been run down in the battles that came with every turn. Rest was, most assuredly, needed!

It had all come out of nowhere! One minute everything was peachy, the next a disaster! It dropped out of the sky like a tornado on a stormy Spring day. The weight of destructive forces it brought could have, easily, devastated me for a long time. "Oh, and how long it would have taken me to rebuild!" I thought to myself. It had knocked the wind right out of my sails, Friday. My mind shot back to the pitiful state of despair it had brought me to. It took the breath right outta me and made me sick at the thoughts that came against me. I shook my head as if to reel it back to the moment. Between the already busy schedule of the preceding week and the bubble-bursting explosion that happened Friday, I was worn out. Not to mention how all the plates I was attempting to juggle came crashing down around me, slamming on the floor and shattering to a gazillion tiny pieces with the disappearance of the papers. Yes, indeed! I was worn out! I had endured, yes. I had persevered, yes. I was alive, yes. I was still breathing, yes. But I was tired in the drained and plumb exhausted sense deep down in my spirit. I found myself to be quite the happy camper, though, interestingly enough, on this early morning. "At least, in comparison to what I was Friday, for sure!" I said.

Yesterday's phone call had been a tough one to even make, let alone speak during. Yet, today, it was in the past. A super recent past, but in the past, nonetheless. It was completed and over with. Although it had been very challenging, it was still successful. Actually, it had succeeded more-so than I had initially thought! It took a lot of strength to accomplish the feat of holding my tongue and waiting during the conversation. There were a few times I, literally, had to bite my tongue to remind myself not to speak. It was so very tempting to lash out with all the frustration. Venting to them about all the stress their actions had caused was knocking on the door of my mind.

"They need to understand how they made me feel,"
I had thought to myself amid the daunting and trying conversation. Throughout some of it, I had to fight the words from coming out of my mouth.

"They need to make it right and fix this and apologize..."
"They need to act like they care and show some respect and consideration for other people's property and situations..."
"They need to say they are sorry and mean it and...and...and..."

My thoughts had been those of wanting justice and a sincere apology for the wrong done to me. However, those were my thoughts in the flesh, not in the Spirit. I had to, continuously, remind myself that walking in the Spirit left no room for any of those things. Yes, what had happened was central to the situation, and my feelings mattered; but I could not force them to care about me or my feelings. I could not force them to want to relate or understand how their choice had impacted me. I couldn't control their desire to practice compassion. I could not make them look at it from my perspective and place themselves into the circumstances that I had endured and experienced. Neither could I direct their desire to want to empathize further to feel every aching and stressful moment I had went through. "No one can force another person to be empathetic and compassionate - me included. Either care is there, or it is not. Consideration for someone else is either present or it is not," I said in summation. I knew that. I also knew that the only reason my flesh wanted those things was because of the motivations tied to pride and self I was entertaining. *There is a way that seems right to man - but, in the end, only leads to death* is what the book of Proverbs says, and rightfully so it is! I knew that, too.

Jesus said, do not resist an evil person; but whoever slaps you on your right cheek, turn the other to him also. If anyone wants to sue you and take your shirt, let him have your coat also. Whoever forces you to go one mile, go with him two. Give to him who asks of you, and do not turn away from him who wants to borrow from you. Not to say that my in-laws were evil people. That really was not my place to pass judgment concerning such matters. Only God knows a person's heart condition. Not me. Not now. Not ever would I be called to that role!

> "You cannot do a kindness too soon, for you never know when it will be too late."
> Ralph Waldo Emerson

No, I was only judging the fruit of their choices, their behavior, and their words. And, boy oh boy, did they sure slap me across the cheek with a massive dose of *I am not taking you into consideration with this choice I am about to make* caliber of decision! It stung, but it was just my pride that was injured at the thought. Well, to be completely thorough, it was damaged at that initial thought and others like it that had soon followed like a flood. It was the flood of thoughts that came against me amidst the realization that all my hard work was gone that had caused the most damage. They, momentarily, left me paralyzed and in shambles from the nuclear reactor size of the crazy mixture of emotions that hit from them. Those emotions only sought self-oriented means of restoral. That was the fact I was faced with, though. Those two people did not care about talking to me before doing something that would impact only me. They just did it. My flesh was seeking their sincere apology with their clearly conveyed understanding of my feelings and how their actions had impacted me on those very similar grounds of reasoning. My flesh wanted *full accountability*! The apology would serve as the band-aid to cover the injury their actions had made against their apparent poor calculation of my worth. At least, in my mind, it made sense that way, at the time. I was in an offended state. "Of course, it makes sense!" I remembered thinking. I had thought about all the many ways my emotional needs should be met by the perpetrators of such injustice. There were many, believe you me. After the emotions subsided, though, clarity came. "Offense is just a symptom of my pride," I said to myself.

> "for all have sinned & fall short of the glory of God, being justified as a gift by His grace through the redemption which is in Christ Jesus."
> Apostle Paul

I checked my pride at the door yesterday. On the phone, I was more concerned with keeping the peace and finding a solution. That was my priority after the reality hit me of the weighted conviction the Holy Spirit placed on my heart. It knocked some much-needed foundational sense into my momentarily blurred by emotions thought process.

My thoughts shifted to two things:

God's Mercy, Grace, & Forgiveness
My own sinfully imperfect, mistake-prone nature

I considered them thoroughly. As a result, I had forgiven them before I had even gotten on the phone! I had to. Otherwise, that conversation would have been like one of those *Shoot the Star* BB gun games at a carnival. Holes would be blown out everywhere on the paper, without any success of winning the prize of restoral. The only thing remaining would be a horribly damaged, flimsy piece of paper relationship, barely hanging from a string. I could visualize the Star parts that make up that very relationship almost eradicated and unable to be glued back together from all the shooting. How much damage I would have caused from all the firing away of emotions and the blatant disregard for others!! What a great mess acting out of offense would have made! No, I did not need any apology to forgive them first. No matter how much my flesh was arguing that I did, I was going to forgive first anyway.

It would have helped, of course. "Doesn't receiving a sincere, deeply meant, fully repenting apology always make forgiving someone so much easier!!??" I thought to myself. "Yes, it would have made it less challenging," I readily admitted to myself. However, the two people I was talking to did not have compassion, like that. They did not desire to relate and understand, empathize, or even really care. There was no way I was getting an apology from either of them. I knew that. Yes, it would have made the conversation a more comfortable one if they were the type to practice *Active Listening*.

It would have been great, actually! Yes, it would have made it quite the effortless talk if they valued a relationship with me and sought the same level of restoral I did. That would have been terrific! It

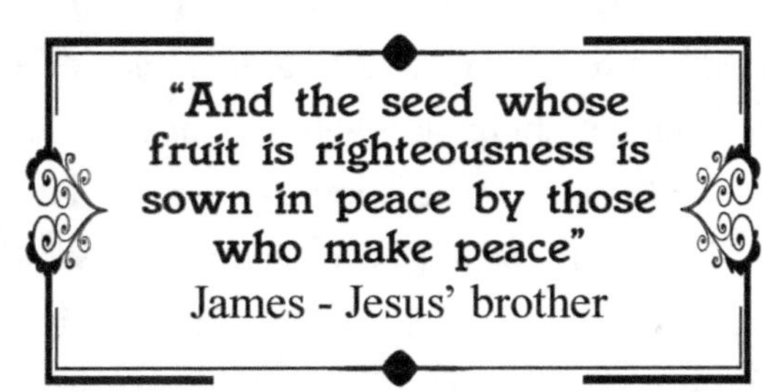

would have been rather trouble-free if I had received that caliber of consideration for them to seek forgiveness and make amends. That would have made things super simple! However, this particular set of in-laws was not in *that* category of folks.

I had known that, though, since the first month that I was married to my husband. I had my first healthy dose of their self-serving personalities, early on. At the remembrance of that first dose, my flesh got the best of me. The haughty, indignant thought hit me hard! The culmination of all my many negative experiences and encounters with these two was a bit upsetting. "The fresh wounds are probably to blame for my reaction. They are definitely made for each other!" I said. The thought escaped before I could capture it. I felt the Holy Spirit's gentle correction concerning it and quickly apologized before returning to my recollecting. Many upon many times, their actions and choices had clearly demonstrated a very *self-serving, prideful, desiring-to-be-right* pattern of behavior.... It was the constant, no matter the resulting cost toward the relationships around them. "When it comes to considering people who seek after things of the world, *Trust* does not hold a good connotation," I said, shaking my head. I considered the character that was and is still held by those two. The truth that I could *trust* in with these two individuals was just that – they would be contrary. Yes, I could *trust* that they would be a certain way – selfish, prideful, and fleshly-driven. Those were only a few worldly character traits they both held. "I don't want to dwell on the full gamut of these traits," I said with determination to not linger on the extent of worldly fruit.

My mind thought back to a recent teaching I had read in Matthew chapter seven. I agreed, "Yes, *Testing the Fruits* of a person's character is a part of proper discernment. Judging whether fruit is good or bad is part of the process, and it definitely helps me to know how to intercede in prayer!" I paused and said, "Yes, but it all still goes back to reading the Word, though. That requires wisdom and knowledge in Christ, always!" As I said this, my mind went back to the couple I had confronted and their fruits I could trust in. *Testing Fruits* was not a thing to enter into lightly. Before I could catch it, the thoughts escaped my grasp! The husband was the first to come to mind. I knew him to be consistent in his choice to refuse to hear what others had to say. He tried to talk over, interrupt, or jump in with his 2 cents at the first opportunity he could find in his conversations with other people. It did not matter who the person was. Although, it was more-so prevalent…dare I say, worse…when he spoke to women. It was like he was there, but he wasn't. After years of observing his same paths of action, my best guess was this: He was the type whose wheels were turning regularly to figure out what his next reply was…yes, the type that only listens so he can speak. He did not really care what words were being spoken by the other party. As a matter of fact, he often forgot what others shared with him!

He was also the type to one-up others. Someone would be telling him about an experience he/she had, and here he would come with his story that was even worse, better, or "just like that!" he would say. His attempts to steal the show or steal the glory always left this horrible taste in my mouth any time I witnessed it. I wanted to shout out to him, "For goodness sakes, just listen to her, Man! Let her tell her story already. It's not about you today!" Even that kind of outburst, I felt, would not phase the man in his current state of self-servanthood practice. He was very much, center- focused on Number 1, and Number 1 was definitely not God, unfortunately. In his eyes, he was Number 1. There were more apparent fruits demonstrated that I could discern about his character. They were simple enough. He was walking in pride, selfishness, jealousy, some impatience, lack of self-control of mouth and mind, a bit of greed, and a tinge of envy. Most of it, though, I could see originated with underlying insecurities, which are, inevitably, rooted in fear and doubt from belief in lies and rejection of God.

It was apparent, though - His flesh needed the attention. I thought for a moment, then said to myself, "You know, it is probably from a hurt experienced from way back in the day…maybe even as a child from his mother…Or, his father… maybe…actually, they were both pretty disinterested parents from what I've been told. Neither of those kids were paid much attention. Fending for themselves most of the time…" my words trailed off in the silence of the morning. I could empathize with him most days when my own flesh wasn't getting frustrated with his actions and choices to be unkind in this way or that. He was quite talented at tap-dancing on those nerves, intentionally and with full vigor.

My husband struggled with similar awareness and eventual frustration at his family member's disregard for people. He once put the man on the spot by asking him to repeat what was just asked of him from one of our friends. Of course, the man wasn't listening or retaining what was said. He was in the middle of answering our friend, and he couldn't even say what the question was that he was answering! I remember thinking to myself, in disbelief, "How does someone even answer a question they don't hear??!!" That act of my husband's to call him out, of course, just ended without success. Agreeing with my husband, I said, "Yep! That man is a smooth operator, for sure!" He had managed to redirect that conversation to a completely different topic, seamlessly! Our sweet friend was none-the-wiser on how the discussion even ended up in the new subject it was in! A smooth operator of manipulation was that man, indeed!

Seeing him in action was definitely hard to swallow, sometimes. I felt so terrible for the poor people he would victimize. So many people were just completely oblivious. Another fruit displayed was this kind of word twisting and manipulation - deceitfulness. Most people he engaged with in conversation never could catch on to what was going on right in front of them, let alone hold him accountable for what he was doing. He was like some theatre show magician of manipulation: Now you see him, now you don't. I would see him in action and think, "He is certainly never going to get the locks off!" or, "He will definitely drown in the water of lies he poured over himself this time...Surely!" However, all of a sudden, there he would appear! He would be standing way over on the left side of the stage, without a scratch! He was just sitting pretty and free from the chains his words had wrapped around him. I would probably be a bit amazed and envious of his expertise at getting his way all the time. However, my understanding of how heartless and inconsiderate and abusive such behavior was to others kept that in check. "Envy isn't a good thing, anyway," came another gentle, corrective reminder from the Holy Spirit. I agreed and corrected myself with a shake of my head. "What is hidden in the darkness *will be* revealed in the Light," the Spirit concluded. I thought of the passage in Luke. I knew it well and prayed for it often over my husband's work environment. I said it out loud, as if to confirm to Him in agreement I knew it, *"For nothing is hidden that will not become evident, nor anything secret that will not be known and come to light.* You are right, Lord." I moved on with my thoughts to that of his partner in crime.

The wife…well…what to say about the wife? She was almost identical in personality. She, too, loved the sound of her own voice. She also loved to hear others talking about her or talking with her about her. Any other subjects, though, and she would just walk off! If she did stay - which wasn't too often - she was disengaged throughout the conversation. During those times, she would find a way to busy herself with a task that had nothing to do with paying attention to the other party speaking. She would fill the air with courtesy words that gave the appearance as if she were listening and hearing the words like:

'Uh-huh', 'Oh, really?!', 'Wow', 'Hmmmmm'…and so on…

When the other person paused for a response, her classic go-to was

'Well…that is interesting, isn't it?'

That, of course, was her way of redirecting the conversation back to the person speaking. They would answer with the typical, "Yes," and continue along with their story. It was quite the art of manipulation in its own right.

Countless times I witnessed these exchanges, and it would always baffle me to no end! I just couldn't wrap my mind around how, like her husband, she got away with it, too. "Are people really that oblivious, or was she just really that good at distracting people from her obvious lack of care or *true invested* engagement?" I often wondered. Her idea of investing quality time was simply her presence. That's it. It seemed she felt it was enough, and she had accomplished her job by merely being there. If she graced a person with her presence, she was doing her part. No effort needed. No honest engagement or interest was necessary. No depth of sincerity required. Just her physical appearance.

Thankfully, I did not have to live with either of them. I had wondered how two people could live with one another and manage to get along, being of such a similar character. Maybe they did not. Idle time at gatherings was usually when I allowed a thought or two of this curious kind to be considered. Otherwise, it really did not make much difference to me. It just made me sad to think of how much friction could potentially exist. No giving and a lot of taking. No comfort offered to one another. Of course, only God knows the inner workings of their day-to-day. We had only been privy to a glimpse of it. In that glimpse, it wasn't a positive experience.

A few months back, my husband and I had spent an entire two-week vacation with them. Thinking upon it now, I said, "Man! That was a looooong... looooong two weeks! Enough to last me a lifetime!" It had been a healthy dose of a refresher to these fruits of theirs. Neither one of them desired to know anything about God. We knew this because they had said precisely that on numerous occasions! My husband and I had tried to share with them over the years, in little ways and significant ways, the love of Jesus Christ and the gospel. We had attempted to do so, as a couple and as individuals during this particular vacation. Me to her and my husband to him. It had been to no avail. Their response has been the same for years. My heart hurt for them, quite often. I prayed for them, often. My husband did, as well. We included them in our prayers together. Of course, we both knew that it did not have to be through us that God reached their hearts. No, it never did. We just desired for them to experience what we shared in Jesus Christ. The love of God is beautiful, and we wanted *Beautiful* for them. "Well, not just for them," I replied to myself, interrupting this thought. Continuing I said, "No, we want *Beautiful* for everyone, just as God desires the same reconciliation back to Him." I recalled my husband and me in our prayers, asking, "Lord, if not heard by or through our sharing, then send someone else, please." That was our agreement in prayer for my husband's family members.

We prayed for them and prayed for them and prayed for them. Yet, my impatient flesh knew quite well that it still had been many years with no hint at a possible path-change. There was no sign of a *Heart-Healing* in progress. There was no demonstration of a desire for reconciliation back to God expressed in word or in deed - neither witnessed by us nor any mutual friends or family members of ours. Nada! "It's discouraging, I know, but continue to pray, we will," I thought to myself as I recounted the many attempts and hours upon hours of petitioning in prayer for those two.

After years of marriage, I had gradually learned more about their history. That knowledge gained had helped me to be more understanding than I would have been without their back-stories. It was easy for me and my husband to see now. Most of the fruits they were demonstrating through these choices and actions were because they had been hurt. They had been molded into the world's way of doing things. They were surviving as best as they knew how. Unfortunately, because of those hurts, they both had a lot of walls. "A heart grows cold behind walls from the lack of sun allowed in," I acknowledged. "They are as we were.... before we found Jesus." I told myself. It was true. They were without the Love of God in their hearts...without the Love of Jesus Christ...without the Love of the Holy Spirit.

I had very much desired to see them find a sweet church family that would wrap them up with love. It would be terrific to see our brothers and sisters in Christ come alongside them and care for them! Then, they could work toward understanding what God's love looked like, threefold through the Father, the Son, & the Helper. With God as their focus, everything else will fall into place and healing could begin in all those areas of damaging choices. Yes, my prayers consistently included them, especially for divine appointments of people to minister to their hearts about God's love. When they were unkind to me or attacking my husband, I made it a point to pray for them. When they attacked our relationship with their choices of cruel words, snarky remarks, manipulating behaviors, or deceitful twists that they would try to use to wedge a gap between my husband and me, I made it a point to pray for them, again.

> "But I say, walk by the Spirit, & you will not carry out the desire of the flesh."
> Apostle Paul

"Unfortunately, they are not friendly people to be around," I said to myself. "Lord, You know it makes it a bit more challenging to pray for them, but I do because I know You love them, too," I admitted. His voice spoke to my heart with scripture, saying, "You are doing as I have told you to do. *Loving your enemy and praying for those who persecute you.* Continue in this. Let Me take care of the rest." I nodded in agreement and obedience. "You are God and I will let You be God. Your will be done in this, Lord," I said in humility.

Suddenly, a bit of frustration came to the forefront of my thoughts, though. I flash of memories hit me. I recalled how the wife had tried many times to make it sound as if or look as if my husband and her had some elusive-to-the-light, sexually charged, hidden past that only they knew about. Even in front of her own husband, of all things! As a result, I could not bring myself to believe a word that came out of her mouth. Abruptly, I reminded myself, "Hate the sin, Love the sinner is what Pastor said Sunday before last." It was an excellent reminder to block any footholds of irritation when thinking about this woman. "With this woman, I need plenty of spiritual guards and blockades against attacks," I affirmed.

She was the spitting image of one of those controlling manipulators you hear about on television that gaslight others. Her attempts to gaslight were not successful with her husband. Neither were they with my husband and me. We both recognized it. However, she was successful with her poor sister-in-law. Her husband's little sister was an easy target for her. That poor young woman was at the point that just the other day she second-guessed herself 10 different times when we were speaking! She said to me, "I think so, but you know my brother's wife said this, this, and this…and now I just don't know. From talking to her, I think I might be going crazy. Everything I do is wrong! It's really all my fault. She said I was just too sensitive…maybe I am. I mess up all the time when I am over there." I could hear the sadness and defeated confidence in her voice. It hurt my heart to listen to her like this. She was such a sweet, gentle soul. I lost track of how many times she apologized in that conversation, alone! "Dear thing! She is being attacked and doesn't even know it!" I thought to myself. I had asked her if she would mind if I prayed for her. She agreed, but with uncertainty riddling her tone. I prayed for strength, discernment, and encouragement. I also prayed for her to understand that her confidence is not found in people or things of this world – it is found in Jesus Christ. As I recalled the conversation, I lifted her up in prayer this morning again. "God please intercede on behalf of this young woman. Continue to fight this battle for her and protect her, in the name of Jesus." I sent her home with a book and workbook combo that day called "Search for Significance" and simply said, "Just read it. It may do your heart good, even if you just glean one thing from it. It will be worth it." She had responded with a nod of curiosity as she turned to walk out the door after our brief goodbye embrace.

Yes, regrettably, that in-law of my husband's was highly skilled at manipulation tactics! On my weaker days, it made it quite difficult to separate from the fleshly response I had toward her abusive behavior. I had to, though, to be able to lift her up in prayer with the right heart and mindset. In my own life experience, I was quite familiar with that character of person. I had a history of dealing with people choosing a path of this behavior. A few previous friends, a few former boyfriends, and a few family members were on that historical list. "It does not matter the face of the person. It is easy to identify that particular type of character in someone when I have had personal experience with such abuse," I said to myself. With a bit of reluctance to admit, I responded, "Yes. Experience does help in identifying that." I likened it to seeing a person decide to chase after addictions. Even if a person is a high-functioning addict, the signs are still there. The addiction signs, symptoms, and outcomes are always prevalent. It is evident and super-easy to spot to those of us who have had the unfortunate and un-prized experience in life with dealing with such choices of addiction by people we have known. It was not fun. It was not joyous. It was not an easy thing to endure. Addiction was its own battle, not just for the addict – but the damage the addict causes to those around. "It's heartbreaking," I said with the thought. A bit of sadness crept up on my heart as I recounted the many difficult years that I had witnessed this, first-hand. "Unfortunately, interacting with people practicing abuse and addictions are quite similar, in my experience," I said, still a bit disheartened. "Thank You, God, for Your grace being sufficient for all circumstances. You have sustained me through very trying times, indeed! I thank You that *Your strength is made perfect in weaknesses such as these*," I told Him. I shifted my focus back to the young woman who I was praying for. "That is the past I have dealt with, but she is enduring this now. That precious, naive girl," I thought to myself.

I heard on a documentary show, one time, that gaslighting can lead to the victim's complete dependency on the gaslighter. The show said that it is just like the effect of Stockholm Syndrome on hostages with their captors. The receiving party actually embraces the gaslighter due to co-dependent tendencies and the slow demise of self-worth that

> "Do not fear, for I am with you; Do not anxiously look about you, for I am your God. I will strengthen you, surely I will help you, Surely I will uphold you with My righteous right hand."
> God

occurs. At first, I thought to myself, "Surely not!" Yet, with a tinge of reluctance, I took a moment to consider my own personal experience. As I begrudgingly recounted my own state of mind back then, I sighed. "Yes, I could have fallen smack-dab in the middle of that very description!" I admitted. I had, indeed, been effectively swayed and was very dependent upon the predator. Yes, unsuspecting prey – that, I was! I allowed my mind to rewind again.

When I have shared such experiences, I use words like *Surreal* to describe my perception of the world within those circumstances. I did not care to dwell on those memories much nowadays. It was like a whole other world…an unrealistic and crazy…unfathomable-to-the-me-now kind of world. I've had people ask,

"Why did it take you so long to leave?"

or respond with something to the extent of,

"I would never have dealt with that for so long!"

I used to have this haughty attitude run through my thoughts as a result. I would be quite upset and think to myself,

*"Take me so long…You have the nerve to ask why it took me so long??…
…Oh, You would never, huh??"*

Years later, after I had worked through those touchier subjects, the sensitivity had numbed. I remember the first time the Holy Spirit made me more aware. He gently pointed out to me, "Those, who ask such questions, do not know." I had responded immediately by saying, "And I thank God that they do not! I would not wish that upon anyone!" I interrupted my train of reflection to praise Him, again, for such mercy and grace shown to those who did not know. It was a good thing to be inexperienced in such matters. I had chosen to share my story with them for a reason. Most were struggling to find healing from pain, even if some responded this way. I said to myself, "It is a testament to what God has brought me out of. There is hope and healing after such circumstances. That's why I share it. Maybe, just maybe it will help someone." My mind thought of those who, unfortunately, did know, as I did; and my heart ached for them.

"It has been amazing to see God's hand, though, in what He has done with that experience, after the fact," I acknowledged with a smile to myself. His hand had masterfully worked those events into an arena for me to minister to others who had experienced the same, if not more, levels of abuse and manipulation – whether it be from an addictive personality or not. It was not God who had brought me to those circumstances, though. No, indeed! I owned that responsibility 100%, for sure! No, I had ended up in those circumstances on my own, in my own choices, in my own acts and words of the flesh. I, too, had been lost and without any forward movement toward God, in that season of my life. Oh, of course…at the time, I had this veil of self-deception that made it seem to me as if I had my eyes set on Him, and I was moving forward in Him. However, it was not the case. I mean,

> I was going to church at the time…
> …when I could and it didn't start some dramatic fight...
> I would read my Bible…
> …every once in a great while...
> I was baptized in front of everyone like I am supposed to…
> …I think…
> I knew of and about God…His Son…and the Holy Spirit...
> I knew all the stories…
> …I mean, all the stories that the preacher had shared at least, because I wasn't reading it for myself...
> I would even say Prayer after Prayer…

…but those prayers weren't exactly Word-focused or God-focused. They were more along the lines of:

> *"Poor me"*
> *"Save me"*
> *"Why don't You fix this, God"*
> *"Why don't You do something for me in all this, God"*
> *"Me…me…me…I…I…I"*

Yes, I *knew of* God but didn't *know* God. I knew of His stories, but I had not *Made His Story My Story*. I was selfish and full of desires that had nothing to do with God and everything to do with me…me…poor me. Yet, I called myself a Christian. "HA!" I exclaimed. "A young and dumb Christian, maybe…." the spoken words of reflection lingered for a moment. "Be gentle to yourself, not so harsh in this remembering, little one," came the words of encouragement following soon after from within, to my heart of hearts. "I know, God. I know. Hindsight is 20/20 perfect vision, right?" I responded, rhetorically, not really needing an answer. I knew it to be true. "It's definitely easier to look back and point out the obvious than it is to see it from within the moments of the circumstances themselves," I stated. "Of course, You know far better than I do, in all things," I told Him. Continuing, I said, "I am so grateful for Your Holy Spirit, God. You sent Him to help me learn how to pray, too." I looked over to the inscription on my bookmark that was beside my daughter's devotional. It had the scripture from Romans 8 on it. I had found it at a little bookstore in the city and given it to her for her birthday last year. It was meant as a sweet token of a reminder for her to lean into the Holy Spirit to learn how to pray. I read it now to remind myself of this. *"In the same way the Spirit also helps our weakness; for we do not know how to pray as we should, but the Spirit Himself intercedes for us with groanings too deep for words; and He who searches the hearts Knows what the mind of the Spirit is, because He intercedes for the saints according to the will of God."* Thinking about it now, I said with much confidence, "Yes, you

"Those whom I love, I reprove and discipline; therefore be zealous and repent."
God

have taught me well in this prayer life unto You, Lord. Thank You, Father, for showing me Your way and bringing to Your blessed light the ways of my own that are not in Your will. Your corrections are so sweet to my soul!" Another scripture came to my remembrance through the Holy Spirit. He said, *"Now may the God of hope fill you with all joy and peace in believing, so that you will abound in hope by the power of the Holy Spirit."* I thought to myself in full agreement, "Yes, Lord! Fill me up so that I will abound in hope by the power of the Holy Spirit! Amen!"

<u>MEMORY VERSE</u>

O love the Lord, all you His godly ones!
The Lord preserves the faithful
and fully recompenses the proud doer.
Be strong and let your heart take courage,
all you who hope in the Lord.
Psalm 31:23-24

Chapter Seven
Part Two

Let's Talk:
Humble Encounters, Gratefulness Abounds

Behold, I stand at the door & knock; if anyone hears My voice & opens the door, I will come in to him & will dine with him, & he with Me. He who overcomes, I will grant to him to sit down with Me on My throne, as I also overcame & sat down with My Father on His throne.
Revelations 3:20-21

This thought process about my in-laws and this young woman had developed into quite the demanding recollection of accounts. I walked out onto the back porch for a bit of fresh air. My thought was that it would be soothing to my heavy heart to do so. "This life has sent me through the ringer a time or two... or fifty," I confessed. "Without You, it was horrible!" I said to the sky. "My heart was not fully Yours, back then. I had not even come to the point in my life that I felt I needed anything else, let alone You, Lord," I humbly admitted. "But, you eventually did come to Me, kiddo." I heard the encouraging reply that swiftly followed. "You remember the moment. You remember the peace that followed that I gave you with the moment. You remember how I showed you the many times I have provided and protected you. Even now, you can see My Hand working in your life more than you did before," came the continued strengthening words. "Yes, I do. You gave me and continue to give me everything that I need. I really do not understand, looking in hindsight, why it took me so long to surrender to Your will instead of my own, in the first place. If I knew then what I do now...If I knew all the many, many, many unending ways that You fill my heart...Lord, You care about my days; You invest Your time in me, and You love me in so many ways!!! If I knew then…I would have come to You sooner, so I could love You longer, God. Truly, Truly! I would have!"

I stood there in the solitude of the morning in a state of tenderness. I cherished precious moments like these with my Father. I affirmed my love to God in almost a pleading fashion. Yes, a pleading in hope that He would believe me more with the outwardly spoken words shared from my heart. Although I know He knows my heart better than even I know it, I still declare to Him that I love Him. These acknowledgments of devotion often occur when I share *The Talk* with my heavenly Father. He has a way of breaking down the walls that shield my vulnerable heart and make it safe to share everything. "Yes, Lord – You have a way about You that surrounds me with this safeness I've not ever known in this life. A safeness that reassures me I will be accepted by You, in all my faults and brokenness," I said to Him. I needed that. "Oh, my heart! How much breaking it has been through!" I acknowledged. I could not recount all the many times I, too, would break in His presence. There were too many! "Yes, Father…Oh, how I need You!" I declared.

Tears I had attempted to hold back were now slowly streaming down my cheeks and neck to find their ending rest upon the white and blue threads of the

collar of my shirt. I felt the chill of them with the wind that blew upon the salty proof of the current state of my heart. "There are so many times I mess up. There are so many times I fall short, Lord. Even now. Yes, even now, I cannot get it right;

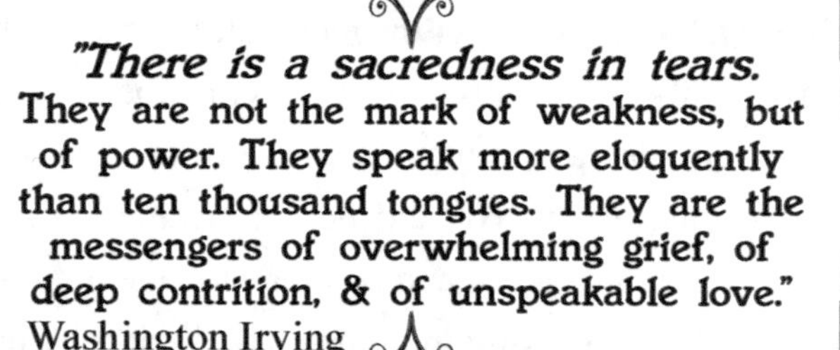

yet, there You are. Again and again, there You are, just as You always have been and always will be, Father. I cannot begin to seek Your forgiveness for the many ways my performance falls short. Thank You, God, that my performance is not calculated into this equation of my salvation! If it were, there would be no end in sight to the immense upset I would be causing, on the daily, as Your child…. always failing, never quite measuring up, still having to fix or work on what I totally bombed…I would be exhausted! That would be the most tedious endeavor I could even fathom attempting!! All for naught, though! It would be all for naught! It's impossible through any means of my own accord, in my own strength, in my own mind, in my own heart to try to earn or deserve or gain or win Your love. On my own, it is seriously pointless, Lord. I know this…now."

I took a moment to reflect on this truth. I lifted my hand and gently wiped away another stream of tears. However, it did not damper the flow. My heart was in a vulnerable place with God and my eyes were simply the vessel of outward demonstration of such a sweet place. I looked up at the sky with great adoration. The sun's light was hidden behind a giant cumulonimbus cloud. The storms on the morning horizon were much like the reflections that had emerged in my *Thought Life* today. They both had slowly grown into quite the display - welcomed or not. Regardless of how they had started, I was grateful for where they had ended up. These sweet times with my Father are good for my soul and counted as precious beyond measure to me. "I am always grateful for these, Lord," I said tenderly.

My heart returned my attention to His love over the years. I gently admitted, "Yes, You loved me before I knew You. You knew me before I was born. You loved me when I was still a sinner, wholly separated from You. I know that it is not through any act of mine that I will ever measure up to the perfection that is found in Your Son. Jesus made me right with You. I did not. He reconciled me back to You. He did what I could not. It is because of Him that nothing can ever separate me from the love You give to me that is found in Christ Jesus." The Holy Spirit spoke to my heart in reply to this accolade to Him, saying, "Read the rest of Romans 8, kiddo." I nodded and returned into the house to retrieve my Bible. I sat down and began to flip the pages until I found the chapter. The first part of the chapter was titled *Deliverance from Bondage*. Skimming down to the bottom, I read the second title. It read *Our Victory in Christ*. "That is exactly what I have in Him! Victory," I said. I felt my heart quicken in joy with the words. I continued to read the passage, as I was instructed, "*And we know that God causes all things to work together for good to those who love God, to those who are called according to His purpose. For those whom He foreknew, He also predestined to become conformed to the image of His Son, so that He would be the firstborn among many brethren; and these whom He predestined, He also called; and these whom He called, He also justified; and these whom He justified, He also glorified. What then shall we say to these things? If God is for us, who is against us? He who did not spare His own Son, but delivered Him over for us all, how will He not also with Him freely give us all things? Who will bring a charge against God's elect? God is the one who justifies; who is the one who condemns? Christ Jesus is He who died, yes, rather who was raised, who is at the right hand of God, who also intercedes for us. Who will separate us from the love of Christ? Will tribulation, or distress, or persecution, or famine, or nakedness, or peril, or sword? Just as it is written, 'For Your sake we are being put to death all day long; We were considered as sheep to be slaughtered.' But in all these things we overwhelmingly conquer through Him who loved us. For I am convinced that neither death, nor life, nor angels, nor principalities, nor things present, nor things to come, nor powers, nor height, nor depth, nor any other created thing, will be able to separate us from the love of God, which is in Christ Jesus our Lord."*

I smiled at the encouragement that this passage brought. In the warmth of His presence, I conceded, "Your love was poured out through that victorious act that You've taught me is agape love. Yes, I know that…now. Then, however, oh, how much of an *I've got everything under control*, and *I can handle this on my own* kind of person I was! The absurdity of it, looking back, is quite the thing. In that season of my life, though, no wonder I fell apart when things or plans would fall apart!" My mind paused at the simplicity of this share, mid-conversation. It was quite the obvious thing now. Yet, I knew that it was not anywhere near obvious when I was in the middle of those circumstances. It was difficult. It was hard. It was a struggle, more times than not, to get out of bed. Depression and despair and fear riddled my days from all the uncertainty and instability in my environment without God. I thought about the young woman I had prayed for earlier, and the struggle she was going through. Again, my heart ached for her, and I lifted her up in prayer. The abuse I had endured had been in a previous marriage. I was grateful for her that she was not in that type of environment, day in and day out. "No! I do not desire to ever be in the middle of those circumstances again. No way!" I stated at the thought. Thankfully, she was single, and the person abusing

> "You have taken account
> of my wanderings;
> Put my tears in Your bottle.
> Are they not in Your book?"
> King David

her could be avoided, somewhat. In my empathy for her, I thought back to my own experience.

Second-guessing became my way of life and thinking I was losing my mind…well, that was the constant. Dealing with abuse for a decade is not a path I ever intentionally chose. It was familiar to me, though, and that was what had drawn me in. "Lord, I didn't know any different at such a young age, coming from such a similar background. Those familiar spirits were attractive. It was the norm that I was accustomed to. I thought it was supposed to be that way," I recounted to Him, apologetically wanting to explain it all away. I knew it wasn't God's Best for me…and…I knew I wasn't even on the same frequency to have *The Talk* with Him back then. I was in the flesh. I would have sought Him before I chose to marry, had I known Him like I do now. "That one is definitely all on me, Lord," I confessed with a shake of my head. "Yes, it was familiar; and, therefore, attractive," I thought to myself with a tinge of disappointment.

Interrupting the spiral of unproductive reminiscing that I was traveling down, came the voice of the Helper again, "Gentle. I said to be gentle, child. My children know what they know when they know it. You did not know then what you do now." He continued with the words I was so fond of from chapter 13 in the first letter to the Corinthians about knowing His love, *"Then, you saw, dimly…and you still do see, dimly. For now, you see in a mirror, dimly, but then - face to face. Still, now, you know, in part; then you shall know, fully, even as you have been fully known by Me*, little one." Solemnly, I nodded. He was right. I sat still. My focus shifted from that of concern to that of waiting and listening. I desired to hear more of what He spoke to my heart. "There is no need to go through these *I told you so* scenarios to yourself. You did not know to be able to *tell you so*, then. You still do not know to *tell you so*, now, as much as I do. That is ok. You will learn, more and more, as you come closer to Me. Remember this: as you are learning, it is ok to not know all the many things I am doing…All the many ways I am doing them…All the many things that I know. *Peace I leave with you and My peace I give to you; but, not as the world gives, do I give to you.* This peace is *a peace that surpasses everyone's understanding*, My child. Everyone's, not just yours. So, *let not your heart be troubled* about this and *do not fear* the mistakes that you surely will make. *The Perfect One has come* already. My Son, whom I sent, has covered all by being the One Gift that was needed for you and everyone. The One and Only Gift that could restore you and everyone back to Me. *You are not alone* in this. *I will never leave you alone* in this. *My peace will guard your heart and mind in Christ Jesus.*" His words washed over my tired mind and re-broken heart that had come from empathizing with the young woman. I began to recall the many, many…many, many, many…mistakes and screw-ups I had made over the years of this life. Adding this to the longer road of thoughts I had already traveled down made me weary. "This new and renewed life that God has given me is precious," I said. I focused on that, finding rest in the minutes that followed.

I looked up at the clock on the wall. "I traveled that road rather quickly considering the many topics my mind covered this morning. Time is such an elusive thing!" I thought to myself. "It is rather sneaky, isn't it?" I replied. "The enemy is sneaky, too!" I said as I looked out the window. "Yes, he can sneak in and twist things around, Lord. I

"The cleverest ruse of the devil is to persuade you he does not exist!"
Charles Baudelaire

know this. Still, his trickery is successful, sometimes. There are so many ways that he uses to take Your wonderful, gentle, sweet conviction and try to turn it into condemnation, with guilt and shame abounding! This knowledgeable awareness of sin that You have taught me is good for edification and growth. Yet, that twisted blade of condemnation he uses makes it hurt so very deeply, doesn't it…that is… if I allow it in. It's just like a heated knife jabbed in the middle of a healed and vanishing scar line. Those jabs of his can make the blood flow so rapidly and painfully out of, yet another, freshly opened wound. It makes it seem as if it never healed! The enemy's attacks sure are tricky and conniving, aren't they, God? I mean, he has been at his game of deception and lies for how long, now?!" I left the words suspended in the air briefly before continuing. I answered, "2,000 plus years is a long time to hone a craft, no matter how vicious and dark the craft might be! I am so very thankful that You, Father, are *All-Powerful and All-Knowing*! I am so very thankful that You are the Creator of even *the enemy who fashions the weapon that is formed against me*, and THAT is precisely why *it will not stand*! You are Who I place my hope in and Who I will listen to, alone," I said to Him, with a heart renewed in gratefulness and hope.

As I spoke these things, His blessed Holy Spirit brought to my remembrance His Word, again. He said, "Read about how My Word is truth. This will strengthen and comfort your heart today." Obediently, I did so. I turned my body sideways and rested my feet upon the length of the couch. Leaning back, half on the arm, and half on the cushion, I snuggled into a reclined position that seemed to me to be the most restful for my still tired body…at least, for the time being.

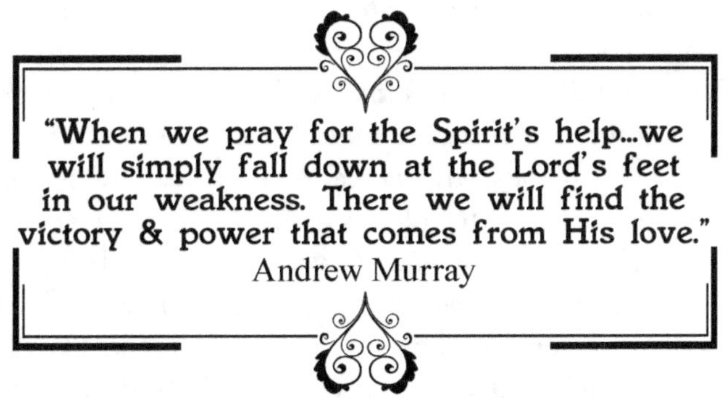

After a quick search online for the scripture reference, I opened my Bible to John 17. It is where the passage that contains the phrase *My Word is Truth* is found.

Much to my surprise, what I found was Jesus' prayer conversation with God! Of all things that I could have had the Holy Spirit put on my heart to read - it was *The Talk* with God that Jesus, himself, had! "What a good thing to read! What a wonderful way to learn more about sharing *The Talk* with Him than by a conversation with His only begotten Son!" I thought to myself. "Thank You for this intimate direction to You, Lord!" And, so, I began to read the following passage out loud so that I could not only see but also hear the words of Jesus to His Father. My heart longed to practice this just as a real conversation would be heard. I made sure to add emphasis and intonation on my words and used active modulation in my voice, just as if I was delivering a highly engaging speech to an audience. Although, in this instance, I was the audience being engaged by my own speech. (Yes, I was talking to myself in reenactment fashion…out loud…but it was very much needed!)

I said: *Jesus spoke these things; and lifting up His eyes to heaven, He said, "Father, the hour has come; glorify Your Son, that the Son may glorify You, even as You gave Him authority over all flesh, that to all whom You have given Him, He may give eternal life. This is eternal life, that they may know You, the only true God, and Jesus Christ whom You have sent. I glorified You on the earth, having accomplished the work which You have given Me to do. Now, Father, glorify Me together with Yourself, with the glory which I had with You before the world was. I have manifested Your name to the men whom You gave Me out of the world; they were Yours and You gave them to Me, and they have kept Your word.*

Now they have come to know that everything You have given Me is from You; for the words which You gave Me I have given to them; and they received them and truly understood that I came forth from You, and they believed that You sent Me. I ask on their behalf; I do not ask on behalf of the world, but of those whom You have given Me; for they are Yours; and all things that are Mine are Yours, and Yours are Mine; and I have been glorified in them. I am no longer in the world; and yet they themselves are in the world, and I come to You.

Holy Father, keep them in Your name, the name which You have given Me, that they may be one even as We are. While I was with them, I was keeping them in Your name which You have given Me; and I guarded them and not one of them perished but the son of perdition, so that the Scripture would be fulfilled. But now I come to You; and these things I speak in the world so that they may have My joy made full in themselves.

I have given them Your word; and the world has hated them, because they are not of the world, even as I am not of the world. I do not ask You to take them out of the world, but to keep them from the evil one. They are not of the world, even as I am not of the world. Sanctify them in the truth; Your word is truth. As You sent

Me into the world, I also have sent them into the world. For their sakes I sanctify Myself, that they themselves also may be sanctified in truth.

I do not ask on behalf of these alone, but for those also who believe in Me through their word; that they may all be one; even as You, Father, are in Me and I in You, that they also may be in Us, so that the world may believe that You sent Me. The glory which You have given Me I have given to them, that they may be one, just as We are one; I in them and You in Me, that they may be perfected in unity, so that the world may know that You sent Me, and loved them, even as You have loved Me.

Father, I desire that they also, whom You have given Me, be with Me where I am, so that they may see My glory which You have given Me, for You loved Me before the foundation of the world. O righteous Father, although the world has not known You, yet I have known You; and these have known that You sent Me; and I have made Your name known to them, and will make it known, so that the love with which You loved Me may be in them, and I in them."

I paused between verses, taking in the words that were so very spiritually heavy. It was a deep conversation of petitioning and interceding by Jesus to His Father. It was quite similar to the intercessory prayers of petitioning that my husband and I had been doing for his family members…Quite similar to the intercessory prayers I had been praying on behalf of the young woman…Quite similar to the lengthy, in-depth conversations I would have with God as we shared in times of *The Talk*. I thought of God's goodness despite what the world had tried to throw at me this last week. I sat there, reflecting on Jesus' conversation with His Dad.

> "each man's work will become evident; for the day will show it because it is to be revealed with fire, and the fire itself will test the quality of each man's work."
>
> Apostle Paul

I reminded myself, "God takes that caliber of circumstances that I find myself in and brings forth His goodness. Even when I am choosing to walk in the flesh - giving into temptations of despair, condemnation, depression, fear, shame, and the like, He does!" I paused for a moment and considered the times He had opened up introductions to people going through difficulties. I said, "He always somehow manages to create these divine appointments with others going through similar circumstances for me to be a comfort for in their time of need, too." The Holy Spirit brought the scripture of truth to my remembrance, saying, "Remember reading the second letter to the Corinthians at the beginning when Paul speaks of the God of all comfort who comforts us? He wrote that *God's comfort is given in all of our afflictions.* This is so *we will be able to comfort those who are in any affliction with the comfort with which we, ourselves, are comforted by God.* That kind of comfort is what you are called to give to others, child, *just as He comforted you* in your trials." With that last teaching moment, I sighed a deep sigh of relief. The weight of this conversation with God was heavy. I needed the pause to soak it all in.

Maybe it was the fact that some of the subjects hit far too close to home. Perhaps it was the deep empathy I felt for the young woman in her struggles. Whatever it was, this time, *The Talk* I was sharing with my Father felt exceptionally deep and laid heavy upon my heart. I felt saturated in His wisdom. "There is a lot of potential in a lot of areas in all of this, Lord. You've shown me a great deal, today!" I said. "You lifted plenty from my shoulders with that last bit of training about comfort, too!" I commended. I rested in His presence for the next half hour. Then, I nodded solemnly, and said in reverence, "Thank You, Father, for Your time and Your love. In Your Son's name, I share this time of *Our Talk.* Ame-…Oh yeah! …and, Thank You for Your guidance and comfort through the many crazy obstacles in this life that You have blessed me another day in. I praise You for Your goodness that is in all things and in all circumstances, God! I will continue to praise You in the good and the bad - even in the trenches I will thank You & shout Your praise! I may not always know what you are doing, but I will continue to trust that Your way is best and blessed for me and mine! I will look to You for the strength I most assuredly need so I can endure! Thank You for all of my weaknesses so I can learn to trust You more! Thank You for sending the Helper to lead me in proper discernment. If it were not for the Holy Spirit, I would not know how to test the fruits and intercede for others in prayer to You, Lord. Thank You for all You do and all You are, God, everyday! Amen." With that I closed my prayer and began the day with a renewed strength and confidence in Jesus Christ. My weariness faded away into the background until seen and felt no more – the Joy of the Lord was my new strength! "I am ready to rejoice in You, Father," I said with a smile of gratefulness from the comfort He was providing to the hidden from the world parts of my heart.

MEMORY VERSE

But now, thus says the Lord, your Creator,
O Jacob, and He who formed you, O Israel,
"Do not fear, for I have redeemed you;
I have called you by name; you are Mine!
When you pass through the waters, I will be with you;
and through the rivers, they will not overflow you.
When you walk through the fire, you will not be scorched,
nor will the flame burn you."
Isaiah 43:1-2

Chapter Eight

Continuing in Prayer

*These things I have written to you who believe
in the name of the Son of God, so that
you may know that you have eternal life.
This is the confidence which we have before Him,
that, if we ask anything according to His will, He
hears us. And if we know that He hears
us in whatever we ask, we know that we have
the requests which we have asked from Him.*
1 John 5:13-15

"Monday, Monday…Oh dreary, foggy Monday...What ever have you done with the sun this morning?!" I asked in my most melodramatic attempt at a humdrum and sing-songy voice. Truth be known, though, I had really not succeeded at all on my vocal drama this morning. I've had better performances. I was a bit tired, though. That was probably the reason why it wasn't nearly as successful, in my view. Nevertheless, my daughter thought it to be quite well done and had burst out laughing at my silliness. She was unusually wide-awake for this early hour and ready to conquer the day. Usually, the sun would have barely been tipping its hat to crest the edge of the horizon at this time. However, with the dense fog and drizzly rain that had snuck in overnight, I struggled to see the lights of its rays.

The sky's dark gray cover meant that the clock was the only way to determine the actual time. Looking at the clock, it was far too soon for her to join me in my day, compared to her regular schedule. Curiosity got the best of me, and I inquired of her what the reasoning was for the early time, saying, "What has you up and going so early, kiddo?" Without skipping a beat, she said, "God woke me up this way! Isn't it cool!?" I replied, "Why, Yes! Yes, it is. Of course!" She rushed over and gave me a tight squeeze of a hug that was unexpectedly strong, leaving me relieved when her arms released. "Thanks, kiddo, I love you that much, too," I told her. As if she had suddenly remembered something paramount, she exclaimed, "Oh my goodness! I gotta get ready!!" With a vibrant, beaming smile, she dashed back into her room as quickly as she had come out. I was left in the kitchen, holding my almost spilled glass of milk and pondering what it must be that was behind my daughter's newfound excitement. I set the glass down, relieved at the fact there was not another mess to clean up. I wrapped up cleaning the rest of the morning dishes I had been tending to. Then, I made my way to the couch to read some scripture before investing some time in much-needed prayer.

My husband was venturing out into the direction of my in-laws today. They had agreed to meet him half-way between their house and ours. Yes, he was meeting those same in-laws who had wreaked havoc on my life just last week. Long-story-short, they still possessed all the papers of my clients, including the documents of the critical project I had been working on. I just remember sighing with such great relief when they had brought that to light in the conversation, finally. "Never again will I work strictly in paper without making some kind of backup and, possibly, hiding it from the sight of my in-laws!!" I vowed to myself. Prayer had worked. Turning to Him had worked. Relying entirely on God amid some really crazy and unexpected circumstances that were totally out of my control had worked. Giving Him all my concerns and letting Him take care of it and fight that battle for me had worked. God had worked in that situation all the way around! He even helped me to guard my mouth and practice self-control of my thoughts and emotions during that struggle of suffering. As a result, I was definitely in an over-flowingly thankful mindset as I settled into the couch to read and study His Word.

"Holy Spirit, I invite You into my morning and seek Your wisdom and guidance through the scriptures that I am about to read. I don't know all of what they mean, but You do. Please teach me. *Enlighten the eyes of my heart to the knowledge and wisdom of God* that is found within these pages. Thank You for Your help in learning and thank You for Your help to apply these lessons and *write them on the tablet of my heart* in my days God grants me. It is in Jesus' precious Name; I humbly ask this. Amen," I closed the prayer and opened my Bible. Prayer was still weighing heavy on my heart. I was so drawn to it that I began pouring over the scriptures listed from my concordance on words like it, such as: *Petition, Meditate, Intercede, Authority, Supplication, Praise, Thanksgiving, Counsel, Prostrate*, and *Prayer*, of course. Instead of my typical chapter study time, I was avidly enthralled in studying the meaning of words in His Word. My research-mode was set to 100 degrees focus!

"Mom, are you ready?!" came the silence-piercing request from my daughter. Somehow, she had managed to sneak up right beside me without me even noticing! I jumped – very startled at her young, sharp voice that shattered my quiet study time. "Ready for what, might I ask?" I questioned, after regaining my composure from my shocked-back-into-reality state. She giggled at the reactions she was receiving from me. "I've got to go to the Community Center for the rehearsal of our play, remember? We have to be there before ten this morning." I was slightly humored by her barely contained enthusiasm at her day's scheduled event. I said, "Yes, Honey, but it is only six in the morning, right now. We still have, roughly, about two and a half hours before we need to leave, kiddo."

A surprised look ran across her face. It was followed by a momentary wrinkled forehead from what seemed to be slight concern or confusion. With that, her energy-driven vibrancy returned as her smile appeared. It lit up her eyes and spread swiftly to her raised cheeks and upward turned corners of her mouth. "Ok!! Sounds good!! I will be in my room," she cheerfully said. She skipped back to her room in an even more joyful way than she did when she was getting ready! Laughing softly to myself and shaking my head, I said to myself, "That silly girl." I returned to my study to finish the last three words that I had been drawn to cross-reference in the scriptures. It was good. All of it was just really good! With every word studied, I felt my heart being brought in, closer and closer to Him, this morning. It was just so excellent! "Well with my soul. It is well with my soul," I told myself in confirmation.

I rose from the couch and walked into the other room to visit with my daughter. She was already on another adventure. She was setting her focus on finishing the art piece she had been working on this last week. "Mom! I can finish this painting, probably, before we leave! Ya know, if I hook it up, like you say all the time, of course." She was busy mixing colors on her palette. "Honey, the best pieces you have made so far have just come naturally, in their own time. So, by all means, shoot for the goal of getting done before we leave; however, don't rush it. If it doesn't flow, it's not time. Whatever you do, don't force it." She laid her paintbrush down to listen. I continued in my share to her, saying, "It's just like how God works. He makes so much beauty in our lives that is all around us every day! Yet, not one piece of art He creates is rushed! It is done intentionally and with great care. Even when He made the masterpiece that is you, kiddo! You know you are one of His masterpieces, right?" At that last question, her eyes grew serious. She stopped what she was doing, abruptly. She asked, "Didn't we read something like that yesterday in my devotional?" I nodded. She walked over to the nightstand and flipped the pages until she found then entry. She said, "Yep! It's right here! It says it is in Ephesians 2:10. *For we are His workmanship, created in Christ Jesus for good works, which God prepared beforehand so that we would walk in them."* Her face was quite determined now. "Mom, you're right. Beauty takes time. No need to rush. I'm gonna save this for later when I have time to be...what was the word you used?... Oh, yeah! Intentional!" Her sudden switch to quite the serious tone almost made me laugh, but I was able to stifle my humored response long enough to quickly say, "Sounds good, I will leave you to it, then." I stepped around the corner to allow the smile to cross my lips and a little bit of a suppressed chuckle to depart as I heard her grateful voice say, "Thanks, Mom!" Regaining my composure, I replied, "You're welcome, Honey. I will be in my room praying if you need me. Ok?" "Yes, Ma'am," she said.

My prayer time in the mornings was a time for me to prepare for the day, of course. However, it was much more than that. It was a gift I gave to God — something that I could never get back…gone forever, once given. I intentionally invest my time in prayer. Time is a precious commodity to me, and there is no way to acquire more of it. God had taught me that, firmly. Once it's gone, it's gone. After all, I had invested plenty of time that I will never get back in things of this world. "Why not invest my time in something good?" I had asked myself. I smiled as I recalled one of my favorite Psalm passages: *"So teach us to number our days, that we may present to You a heart of wisdom."* I smiled again and said, "Yes, Lord, please continue to teach me to number my days. I want to demonstrate to You a renewed heart of wisdom."

Those old investments I would like to forget, of course, but not my prayer time investments. They were quite valuable to me! When I was a bit too harsh in my thoughts toward my past choices, I would refer to old investments quite negatively. They were in the bucket of stupid, unintelligent, or a frivolous waste of time. Learning how to be gentle with myself for my trespasses against myself was one of the more difficult growing seasons I had been through in this walk with God. "How do I show myself mercy and grace and forgiveness?" I would sometimes wonder. Usually, this wondering was during my prayer time. I would seek His wisdom and guidance on just how I was supposed to go about that, exactly. It was difficult. It was even more complicated when I was choosing to listen to the lies of the enemy. Needless to say, my prayer time was also a way to sort through the mess in the many parts of my mind: Those parts that were not yet renewed into His way of thinking took quite the investment!

> "But if any of you lacks wisdom, let him ask of God, who gives to all generously & without reproach, & it will be given to him. But he must ask in faith without any doubting."
> James - Jesus' brother

Of course, listening to the lies would result, again, in me being difficult toward myself. Little pieces of my past or how I was raised would creep up in my mind. I would venture down those old familiar roads like I was on some adventure through the woods, down to the riverbanks. Before I knew it, I would be drifting quickly down this unending river on a raft that I had no business being on at all. Those sneaky little thoughts of the days of history tempted me to recollect them. They lured me to choose the old ways of processing information and coping through them. Some days I could easily dismiss them with a response back to the enemy of, "Why on God's green earth would I possibly choose to go gallivanting through those old woods when they are dead and gone?! No! Depart from me in the name of Jesus!"

And, yet, other days when I was on the weaker side of my mind, I would entertain the thoughts as if they were a comforting, old friend I had not seen in such a long time and was so relieved to see! "The devil is sure sneaky, Father," I said, speaking the words out loud. I was quite aware that God already knew what I was dwelling on in my pondering. However, I spoke the words anyway. "The enemy has a way of making everything that he tempts us with appear as if it is shiny, new, and appealing. It is appealing...to the flesh...in so many ways, but it is definitely not new!" I couldn't recount how many times I would get sucked back into old, familiar patterns of thought! I admitted, "It is difficult to deal with repeated refreshers of emotional wounds that have long since healed. The memories he brings about to tempt me into dwelling on are conniving, to say the least! They seem to have nothing to do with the wound and then BAM! There it is, Father, slapping me in the face with the reality of it all! The hurtful ends, the shame, the damage to others, and other similar results all come back to the surface," I continued my conversation with Him about the nonsense of battling the spiritual attacks in the arena of my mind and emotional heart.

The temptations to think about the appealing moments experienced before or after the wound were hard to resist. They had nothing to do with the wounds, at first thought, but they would lead me right back to them! Once thought upon – that passenger train of thought would take me down the same familiar tracks, and I would wind up thinking about those same old things. Yes, they had been quite appealing, and I used to give into them quite often! Yet, these days, they were becoming less and less effective in achieving the goals of the enemy. It was becoming easier to quickly process through and dismiss, even if he was successful with the initial attempt to bait me to walk down the familiar rabbit trails. No matter the ill-intended reason the enemy wanted to bring it back up and attempt to throw it in my face all over again, he was going to have to find a new tactic on a different battlefield. This battlefield was on its way to being entirely renewed by my Father. "Yes, and Amen!" I proclaimed in agreement with my thoughts. Again, I spoke them out loud. It felt good to speak against the enemy like this.

I had grown tired of the condemnation attacks of shame and guilt that led to depression and self-contempt, thoughts of failure, and feelings of just not being enough. I was done with feeling like I wasn't able to measure up to whatever unrealistic standard that had been programmed in my head from life experiences and this world's influence. I had grown tired of them and had given them to my Father to take care of. "In my weakness, You are my strength and my shield, Abba." I recalled how Paul had written to the Corinthians about the thorn in his flesh. This type of spiritual attack had been a thorn in my flesh for far too long. I was done with it. I didn't want it anymore. Although I prayed for the removal of condemnation, those prayers were self- focused. I focused on the self-serving benefits I would have if only these attacks would simply be put to bed and taken away, freeing me from such things. Those me, me, me prayers didn't really amount to much. They only served to wind me up right back into being easily baited.

> "Now to Him who is able to do far more abundantly beyond all that we ask or think, according to the power that works within us, to Him be the glory in the church & in Christ Jesus to all generations forever & ever. Amen."
> Apostle Paul

I didn't really understand why I was spinning my wheels, going nowhere super fast! However, my Father did.

Finally, I had experienced one of those "AHA!" moments of teaching in one of *The Talk*s with Him. It brought me to my knees in repentance very quickly. It was the realization that my selfish prayers did not glorify Him. Of course, He didn't say it that bluntly. When the Holy Spirit impressed this realization on my heart, He said, "Who does a prayer like this glorify, child? Does it glorify your Heavenly Father, or does it only glorify you?" I appreciated those kinds of accountability training *Talks*. They always hit straight to the point and got me lined out very quickly with what God's Word says. I knew from that gentle inquiry that my prayer focus had to *grow up* a bit. He gave me this question to reflect on and find the answer within His Word. So, I focused on *maturing* in my prayer time and studying about what that meant in action.

For the last couple of years, I had begun to focus more and more on Him in my prayer time. Thanking Him for what He was or would do through the circumstances that came against me. Praising Him for all things, bad or good. I noticed a huge difference after only about a month! As I recalled this, I agreed, "No matter what I want to see happen, I am going to choose to actively and intentionally surrender and submit to Him. I do not choose my will, my wants, and my desires for the outcome. I choose His ways and His thoughts on the matter so that only His will is done, regardless of how it may impact me." I paused in this thought, then continued. "Even if it makes matters seem even worse or become worse for me, I am willing to let Him have control of it all!" With a tinge of hesitance, I admitted, "It is difficult still, to do that, sometimes." Then, exclaiming in thought to myself, "It definitely takes tons of effort to get out of myself and out of my own way so that God is glorified, even still! There are some things I flat out refuse to surrender on, but I am doing better. All it takes is practice and practice and practice." I sighed and conceded, "Yes, *Practice makes Permanent.*"

I thought about the day I had finally decided to give control over to Him to take care of these things. At the time, I was meditating on the passages found in chapter 12 of Paul's 2nd letter to the Corinthians. Up until that very moment, I was still operating in the fleshly understanding that showing any sign of weakness meant

> "No temptation has overtaken you but such as is common to man; & God is faithful, Who will not allow you to be tempted beyond what you are able, but with the temptation will provide the way of escape also, so that you will be able to endure it."
> — Apostle Paul

catastrophe. I was under the worldly impression that it would lead to my utter demise! "Admitting that you can't do something is weakness, right? That's a bad thing!" I recall saying to people I once knew. It was my old way of thinking and theirs as well. It was another web of lies that the worldly education of my raising had built. It was a wall that discouraged the surrender needed to gain my freedom from those attacks of self-dependence.

I had to get to the point that I understood that it was not me, but Jesus Christ in me, that would achieve this victory on my behalf. I had to admit that I was weak. I just had to so I could move forward...So I could grow. "At the start of my walk with You, Lord, that was a crazy thought process! I had no idea what people were talking about when they said or referred to such things! My heart and mind and body had been wrapped up in layers upon layers. Safety shields, buffers, fences, and walls with vines of thorns encompassing them to discourage close vicinity with others were everywhere! You *know* that, Father." I thought about the many barriers that had been broken by God in His Pursuit of my heart. He had busted right through some of them!

I continued *The Talk* with Him, saying, "It was difficult enough to get to the point of simply *Being Here* and *Being Still to Know that You are God*, let alone trusting that the Creator of the universe cared about little, ole me! It has taken quite the time investment to learn that You love me like You do, God!" My past did not warrant that understanding, though. It just did not mesh well to think that such unbelievable love is bestowed on me, as His Word promises. It definitely didn't mesh to believe that I was a child of His! "Thank God for growing, though!" I said. With a thankful heart, I thought of what He has taught me about His love. "I know His love is a love that can be trusted, ultimately. It is a love that is always faithful and was, is, and always will be true. His love is my truth and trustworthy. It is safe to lean into Him for everything. Yes, His Great Love has taught me that," I acknowledged.

With my life experiences, though, this was difficult teaching to learn. "I see that now. Although I do still have days that I would rather be the driver instead of the passenger on the racetrack, I see that now, Lord." Learning that whole trusting Him with it all bit has been interesting, to say the least. My own negative, damaging experiences in life said differently. The lies I had known as my old, familiar truth went more like this: "Trusting someone is about the most stupid thing I can do!" ... "Vulnerability is the worst possible mistake I can make!" ... "I am an idiot if I believe him as far as I can throw him!" ... "The only thing getting close to someone is good for is Pain: Self-Inflicted Pain, at that!" I thought about these for a moment and concluded, "Yes, let's just say it has taken a bit to heal from those lies." I had brought my Bible into my room just in case a scripture came to mind during my quiet prayer time with the Lord. I flipped to the passage in Corinthians to remind myself of the strength found in God. It was more so to encourage my heart and edify my spirit with reading and speaking the Word of God out loud. It was one of the ways I used as a defense tactic to guard my heart and mind against the enemy's sneaky tendencies when deceitful thoughts such as these old truths came about.

The Word was my answer against anxiety, worry, doubts, fears, confusion, temptations, lies, and the like. It was my go-to, both defensively and offensively, in my spiritual walk with God. "There it is!" I said as my eyes found the passages in chapter 12, verses 8 through 10. *"Concerning this I implored the Lord three times that it might leave me. And He has said to me, "My grace is sufficient for you, for power is perfected in weakness." Most gladly, therefore, I will rather boast about my weaknesses, so that the power of Christ may dwell in me. Therefore, I am well content with weaknesses, with insults, with distresses, with persecutions, with difficulties, for Christ's sake; for when I am weak, then I am strong."* The passage spoke of the sustaining grace that God provides. "Such GOOD encouragement, Father!! Thank You! Yes! In my weaknesses, I will shout for joy! I will sing Your praise, Lord God! For, *I know that I know that I know* that within those very moments of weaknesses, the very moment I turn to You and admit such weakness - You are there! I know the very moment I admit my ever-present need of You to fight that battle for me

> "I'm not afraid of storms, for I'm learning to sail my ship."
> Luisa May Alcott

- You swoop in! I know You have already claimed the victory for my good because ONLY You know what is best for me in that which You have called me to do!" The excitement of this admittance was fueled by hope in Him. I continued, saying, "I will continue to surrender my heart, my mind, my soul, and my body to You in all humility forever - with the understanding that Your grace is sufficient! Not my will, not my understanding, not my thoughts, not my ways, BUT in all things and in all ways - You, Lord! I deeply desire to seek Your will and Your goodness! I choose You. You supply for all of my needs according to Your riches and glory in Christ Jesus!" I spoke these words with authority and claimed them as my truth. They are truth…Yes, my truth.

I did not take reading the Bible lightly. Early on, I would get distracted like a little squirrel seeing a shiny, sparkly object in the distance as it was gathering nuts for the winter, bouncing off into that very same distance to investigate. More times than not, I would get distracted when I did not take time to pray beforehand. However, that was not the majority of the time now. After practicing it over the years, distractions had altogether disappeared. My norm, now, is to make it a point to invest in prayer time while reading. I welcome the Holy Spirit into my presence and intentionally chose to submit my focus to His leading through the Word of God. My time this morning was a combination of study and prayer.

I had the scriptures open in front of me. The Holy Spirit laid upon my heart specific passages as I studied. I would lift those up in petition to the Father for understanding. I consistently turned to the Holy Spirit for guidance on how to study and how to pray. I remembered the passage I had read yesterday. "The Word says that the Holy Spirit knows what we are to pray about and for," I said. I turned to the page again to read it once more. It read: *"In the same way the Spirit also helps our weakness; for we do not know how to pray as we should, but the Spirit Himself intercedes for us with groanings too deep for words; and He who searches the hearts knows what the mind of the Spirit is, because He intercedes for the saints according to the will of God."* Every time I read that passage my heart feels such encouragement! With that, a memory came to mind. Once before, I had proclaimed aloud with such an outpouring of thanksgiving after reading it. I had exclaimed in gratitude, "It is such a good thing to have the Helper with me, God! Sometimes, I have no idea what to pray for or how to go about it at all in the utter mess I find myself in! Thank You, God! Thank You for sending the Helper, the Holy Spirit, the Holy Ghost, the Counselor, the Advocate, and all the many names Your Spirit has been called!!" As the thought came back to me at this moment of praise, I agreed with it wholeheartedly.

"Yes, it is so good to have the wonderful Counselor here with me as I walk through my days for You, God. Look at last week's events! I had no idea what to pray for or how to get a handle on my emotions, but the Holy Spirit sure did! He talked some good sense, I mean, God-sense into me, thankfully, because I was ….and always find myself in shambles without You when I lean on only my own devices, for sure! 100%! Oh, was that ever a moment of weakness!?" I acknowledged. Actually, it was a bunch of moments swarming around together, with my own fleshliness running rampant *all up in* that situation! I was completely enveloped by it all!

"Goodness! Thank You for Your long-suffering and forbearance with me and Your amazing, unrelenting love toward me, Father!" I said. My thoughts had quickly recapped the problematic circumstances and many upsetting events of last week. I lifted that up in gratefulness and praise for God's glory and honor in all He had done through it. It had been a time of weakness…a time of need. He had provided everything, above and beyond anything I could have managed on my own, and I was a grateful daughter. I couldn't just skip passed thanking Him and definitely did not want to miss an opportunity to

"In the days of His flesh, He offered up both prayers and supplications…to the One able to save Him from death… although He was a Son, He learned obedience from the things which He suffered." - book of Hebrews

praise His name. "No way! I love You too much, Father!" I agreed.

My thoughts turned back to my prayer time. I had a few things I wanted to pray about, but with all this focus on submission and surrender, I decided to let the Holy Spirit do my petitioning this morning. I took this time to submit to God. I put down my ways and my thoughts on what to lift up in prayer and picked up His, instead. I bowed my head and closed my eyes. This is a physical practice that I do mainly to keep my brain from having squirrel moments of distraction while I pray. It helps me to block out the visual interruptions and set my mind only on God. My gesture of bowing my head is also a way that I choose to show reverence and respect for my Heavenly Father. It is a physical submission to His leadership as I come to Him in prayer. I knew that God was here with me, and His presence was present. I agreed with my thought, intimately, "In my heart of hearts, I just know He is here. How else would I dare be but humbly submissive and bowing before the King of Kings!?" I pushed my thoughts to the side and focused on clearing my mind.

"Silence is needed, child," He instructed. I listened and obeyed. A peaceful calm came upon me, and the room fell silent. My mind was alert, yet still. I heard from my lips the words that came. Not words, of course, that my mind had any clue about, but my spirit did. With every Spiritual word of prayer spoken, my soul was built up and encouraged. The room was filled with such love, and my heart could feel the draw of Him pulling me in as I prayed in the Spirit. God had a way about Him in these times of prayer of filling my heart until it overflowed. There was an awareness of His presence that I could not come to in any other way or action. He was real. He was here. He heard all that I needed to pray that even I, myself, was not aware needed to be prayed for. This Spirit-filled time with Him always amazed me. I sat quietly in a compassionate state of existence. I knew the prayer I had just prayed had been about others, and my heart hurt for those I had lifted up. They needed strength and protection from the enemy during this time. I had no idea why. I had no idea who. But God did. He would take care of them. Of this, I was confident. I, myself, grew evermore rejuvenated and strengthened with the words that were prayed. I continued to pray in the Spirit in a language foreign to me but known entirely by God, my Spiritual prayer language.

I felt an urgency come over me as I prayed. An urgency of something coming soon that required preparation and an awareness of my surroundings. There was a deep-set sense of a need to stay alert and vigilant in my studies. I did not know what for. I did not know when. But God did. He would take care of that, too. Of this, I was also confident. There was a protective warmth I could feel come round-about me, and a joyful outburst came from my lips, suddenly! My heartbeat had quickened. The feeling of great victory had physically come forth in the vocal celebration of an "Amen!" and a "Thank You, Lord!"

I dwelled upon the silence and His calm presence that filled the room afterward. "What Great Love! What great strength! What a Mighty God I serve!!" I exclaimed, praising Him. The remaining time I invested in prayer was a combination of things. There were many praises and thanks to Him given. It all came from a place in my heart that was overflowing with an outpouring of gratefulness. They brought me both joy and tears of awe and amazement. Prayer continued in the Spirit. Only God knew what was being petitioned and interceded for. However, a few of the subjects He blessed me with His understanding. The interpretation and revelation came quickly with those things.

There were moments of battle that I could feel within my spirit as I prayed. I physically braced myself for them, standing firm and steadfast. I half-expected the enemy to try to knock me down, for real! It was like wading out into the water, waist-deep, and suddenly seeing a huge wave come barreling forward at you. You have nowhere to go and nothing to do to escape. You can only brace yourself for the impact and hope to God you don't get taken down!! "Thank God, hope in Him does not disappoint! Jesus has already conquered this world! No weapon formed against me shall stand in the authority and name of Jesus Christ!" I had confirmed after the last battle moment had subsided.

There were moments of repentance that I came to, with utter surrender and uncontrollable tears. God bringing things to light within me that I did not even know about was always a tearful account. Those moments caught me off-guard when they came; but, oh the relief that came from them! I did not desire to grieve the Holy Spirit within me in any way at all! I desired to please God in all my ways – not just some. Behaviors and choices that I did not even realize I was doing that were hurtful and rooted within me were shown to me. I did not want them. I knew that they would not be corrected if they were not brought to light. It was, more often than not, in this Spiritual prayer time that God would gently show me these areas. It wasn't easy, but I needed them.

There were moments of pure, indescribable, overflowing joy that would lead to these beautiful moments of worshipping Him in the Spirit. I cannot describe the love and complete fulfillment that is found within those moments! They just are….. and I just…am loved and fulfilled within them. The worship part of my Spiritual prayer time with the Lord is intimate and genuine. It is edifying, encouraging, strengthening, sharpening, and always fulfilling. It answers every need, every time in all my many seasons.

Every single time I pray Spiritually, in full submission and surrender, His love washes over me. When I turn off my fleshly mind to just *Be* and speak with my Father in the Spirit, His love answers. I refuse to even attempt to try with my own feeble words to describe it. I know that I would not come close to doing it justice in my own efforts and thinking. The way He has with my heart and soul during prayer in the Spirit is so precious! It brings me to worship and praise in spiritual songs with great joy! Petitioning and interceding for others in and outside

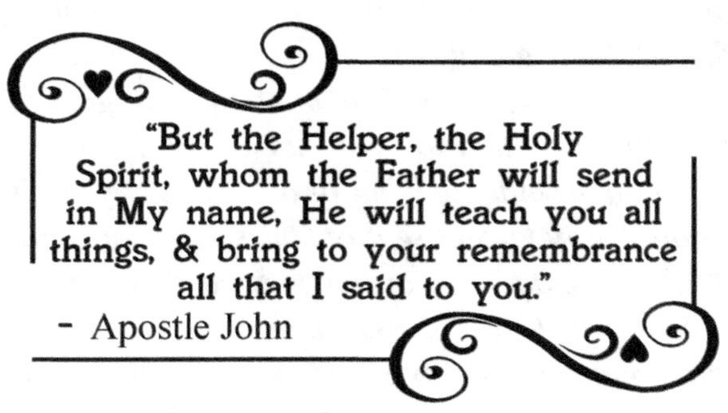

of the body of Christ…it is an unspeakable honor. "I can't describe the measure of beauty, vulnerability, and intimacy found within those moments!" I said.

I thought about how I could explain such a time as this to another person. It would be difficult. It was, after all, one of many mysteries of a walk with God. It was like understanding in complete fullness all the many moving parts of *Spiritual Gifts* or even a full understanding of the *Holy Trinity*. It wasn't achievable by man. Only a prideful person would say they know everything about such things or say that their way of understanding is the only way. "God forbid I ever come to such a state of belief as that!" I pleaded. "Spiritual prayer language may be thought of crazy by the world, but even Paul writes about how those he would teach about Jesus thought him to be crazy. He was ok with it, and so am I. I don't mind being crazy for You, God." I thought to myself. Paul's response to it was, *"For, if we are out of our mind, it is for God."*

The scripture had come quickly to my remembrance. With that, I opened my Bible to read the full context. 2nd Corinthians, chapter 5 is where I found the passage. Paul was writing about the temporal and the eternal differences and he was trying to convey the ministry of reconciliation that we have while we are here on this earth to share the gospel of Jesus Christ with others to be reconciled back to God. It said, *"Now He who prepared us for this very purpose is God, who gave to us the Spirit as a pledge. Therefore, being always of good courage, and knowing that while we are at home in the body we are absent from the Lord—for we walk by faith, not by sight— we are of good courage, I say, and prefer rather to be absent from the body and to be at home with the Lord. Therefore, we also have as our ambition, whether at home or absent, to be pleasing to Him. For we must all appear before the judgment seat of Christ, so that each one may be recompensed for his deeds in the body, according to what he has done, whether good or bad. Therefore, knowing the fear of the Lord, we persuade men, but we are made manifest to God; and I hope that we are made manifest also in your consciences.*

We are not again commending ourselves to you but are giving you an occasion to be proud of us, so that you will have an answer for those who take pride in appearance and not in heart. For if we are beside ourselves, it is for God;

if we are of sound mind, it is for you. For the Love of Christ controls us, having concluded this, that one died for all, therefore all died; and He died for all, so that they who live might no longer live for themselves, but for Him who died and rose again on their behalf. Therefore, from now on we recognize no one according to the flesh; even though we have known Christ according to the flesh, yet now we know Him in this way no longer. Therefore, if anyone is in Christ, he is a new creature; the old things passed away; behold, new things have come. Now all these things are from God, who reconciled us to Himself through Christ and gave us the ministry of reconciliation, namely, that God was in Christ reconciling the world to Himself, not counting their trespasses against them, and He has committed to us the word of reconciliation. Therefore, we are ambassadors for Christ, as though God were making an appeal through us; we beg you on behalf of Christ, be reconciled to God. He made Him who knew no sin to be sin on our behalf, so that we might become the righteousness of God in Him."

I meditated on this scripture for some time. Reflecting on the question at hand of how someone could go about explaining praying in the Spirit. I, of course, came up with nada! It wasn't for me to explain. "That's in the conversation-between-them-and-God bucket, silly," I corrected myself. "That's right, child, that's My job." I heard the confirmation from the Holy Spirit gently follow. "The world will reject the message and dismiss it, of course. Rejection from the world comes, regardless. They rejected Me. They will reject you. It is still My job to teach them," He said.

My mind contemplated the word *rejection* for a moment. Even those within Jesus' very family and hometown rejected Him being the Messiah. I imagine they were thinking something like, "How could this possibly be the case!?!" in their disbelief of someone they grew up knowing, saying He was the Savior of the world. Jesus even gave encouragement to His disciples by telling them, *"If the world hates you, you know that it has hated Me before it hated you. If you were of the world, the world would love its own; but because you are not of the world, but I chose you out of the world, because of this the world hates you."* "Yes, Lord. I always find encouragement in that passage, as well." I agreed.

"Yet, I know *nothing can separate me from the love You have for me,*

God, that is in Christ Jesus, not even rejection from this world or anyone in it!" I said. With that conclusion, I looked over at the clock and checked the time. It was getting close to the time we would need to leave to make sure my daughter arrived at the Community Center for her practice that she was so excited to attend. I braced my hands upon the edge of the bed and lifted myself up to begin to get around. I walked through the house and gave my daughter a quick reminder that the time to leave was drawing near. I told her that she would need to come to a stopping point on what she was doing. With a mixture of emotions, she replied. I heard reluctance in her voice from needing to stop and get ready. She began by responding hesitantly, "Ok……..", with a drawn-out pause, following. Yet, as the renewed excitement for leaving for her play practice returned, her voice shifted into that of high anticipation as she said, "Yes, ma'am!"

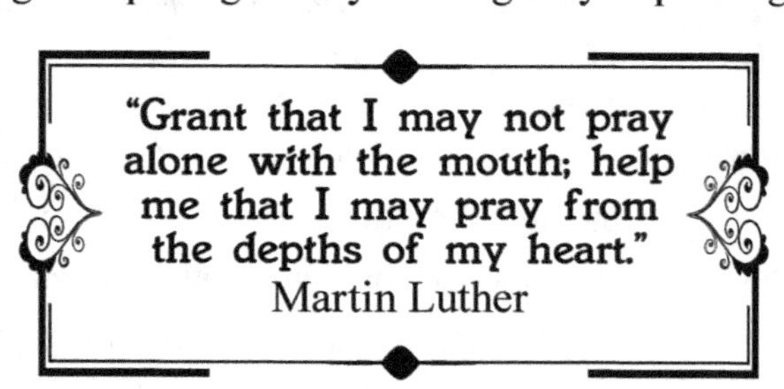

We both gathered ourselves together to leave for her practice. Between her excitement to conquer the day and my well-invested time of renewal and strengthening in the Spirit – we were ready for whatever was ahead of us! We prayed together for God's provision and protection. We invited Him to be with us in all that was before us. Closing our prayer with an 'Amen', we pulled out of the driveway and out onto the road. We had finally embarked upon the highly anticipated journey that awaited us within this new day! We were both filled with excitement and surrounded by His love. It was going to be a terrific day!

<u>MEMORY VERSE</u>

Rejoice in the Lord always;
again I will say, rejoice!
Let your gentle spirit be known to all men.
The Lord is near.
Be anxious for nothing, but in everything
by prayer and supplication with thanksgiving
let your requests be made known to God.
Philippians 4:4-6

Chapter Nine

Indescribable Joy

*I will extol You, O Lord, for You have
lifted me up, and have not let my
enemies rejoice over me. O Lord my God,
I cried to You for help, and You healed me.
O Lord, You have brought up my soul
from Sheol; You have kept me alive,
that I would not go down to the pit.
Sing praise to the Lord, you His godly ones,
and give thanks to His holy name.
For His anger is but for a moment,
His favor is for a lifetime;
Weeping may last for the night,
But a shout of joy comes in the morning!*
Psalm 30:1-5

"Oh My God, My Heart!" I exclaimed with an avidly keen awareness of a sudden resounding aching from within that made me buckle at the knees. Moments that bring me to my knees in such a way as this are rare. However, this was, most assuredly, one of those very moments! It hit me like a ton of bricks falling atop of me from a twenty-foot tall skyscraper and crashing into the center of my chest. I couldn't breathe! I desperately grasped for any grip I could possibly grasp of the edge of the bed, to no avail! I missed it and found myself collapsed on the carpeted floor within a sudden blink of the eye. My heart ached deeply within my chest. I was in such disarray that I felt that the world would surely begin spinning from my very next blink! Thankfully, my eyes blinked, and the world stayed put. "But, Oh my heart!" I shakily said as I tried to focus. The heartbeat was so profound that I could hear it inside my ears and even feel the rhythm of its repetitive drumbeat throbbing throughout my head and neck! My alertness to it was so sharp that even the veins in my wrist seemed to be visibly pounding! They throbbed in unison with every bass kick of this thunderous drumming from within my chest. Bam… Bam-Bam…BAM…my heart loudly spoke within and throughout every cell of my body! At least, it sure felt like that! I could have, would have, or should have moved if I had known the moment the bricks had first begun to fall from such a tall height! There would have been plenty of time to dodge and scurry to safety before they came crashing down upon me. I could have been just like a squirrel that bobs and weaves out from under the impending doom of speeding car tires. Yet, I didn't have the opportunity. I didn't even see it coming! Before I knew it, I was squashed like a bug being slammed against the bullet of a car windshield. "Oh My God, dear Lord, how it did happen!" I thought.

It all started with the previous day. It had been an incredible blessing of time with my not-so-little-anymore teenage daughter. She was full of delight that shone so very brightly! Her bliss was like diamonds in blinding sunlight casting rainbows of joy all about her! It filled every conversation she had with others and every interaction with those around her. The joyful spirit she had overflowed from her. It was like a surging river that overflows with an unrequited passion over the riverbanks after a flood-worthy rainfall. Her joy poured into the unsuspecting fields and land all around her. You could see from the responses of those she engaged in conversation and interacted with that it was like a refreshing drink of sweet water for their tired and weary desert-bound vagabond souls.

They reminded me of what the Israelites must have looked like and the expressions that must have prevailed among those wandering about the desert with Moses right before they came to Marah. The Israelites were tired, thirsty, hungry, and weary. They were grumbling and complaining. Yet, in all of God's goodness, He still Provided for their needs. They still received the blessing of provision for their thirst. The bitter water was turned into sweet water to drink and quench the parched lips of the Israelites. They still received the blessing of provision for their hunger, too, in the form of manna and quail for their weary, tired bodies. They still were provided with rest and rejuvenation in the middle of the long journey they were on. In all God's goodness, and only by it, this was done for them, as the Word recounts. Yes, it was because of nothing of their own doing, but that of God's incredible love for His people.

The joy that my child spread about through the day that God gave us was just that! It was not received because of anything the people she shared it with had done. The joy was not a reward for some action they had taken. It was because she allowed it to flow through her to them that they received the blessing of the contagious, overflowing joy. Yes, God had given a measure of joy for her to share that day. She, herself,

> "Shout joyfully to the Lord, all the earth. Serve the Lord with gladness; Come before Him with joyful singing. Know that the Lord Himself is God; it is He who has made us, & not we ourselves; we are His people & the sheep of His pasture."
>
> King David

didn't even receive it because of anything she had done! God blessed her with that measure of joy because He chose to do so. It was according to His riches and glory, and it was beautiful to see!

Some of those she shared it with…. well, most, actually… looked so sad, so despondent and void of hope. I was grateful that I had the privilege and honor given me by my Heavenly Father to witness how her joy had impacted others. It spread like wildfire within the entire day all around us: joy here, joy there, joy everywhere! It was fascinating and such a blessing to have that glimpse. "Oh, that is what it looks like to impact those around us with what God blesses us with! Letting joy flow through like that is honoring God! I definitely want to do so in what I choose to do, say, and think about, for sure!" I thought as I watched my daughter impact all the people we met. She had truly invested her time, even without knowing it, to be a blessing to others. At least, I thought she may not know it in its fullness, given her youth in spirit, still yet. "Oh God, how thankful I am to see it for what it is - honor to You! Thank You for letting me see it clearly - in all its glory! Thank You for working through her and in her, Lord!" I said, with great appreciation. Yes, indeed! Yesterday's events had brought much joy and encouragement to my heart to be a part of and witness!

This morning had come with an immediate splash of remembrance of that joy. It had come crashing into my mind, even before I arose from the bed! With it came a scripture. *"And though you have not seen Me, you love Me, and though you do not see Me now, but believe in Me, you greatly rejoice with joy inexpressible and full of glory,* remember?" I felt the words, deeply, as the Holy Spirit reminded me of the Word I had meditated on the day before. "Yes, the joy of the Lord is mighty and powerful," I confirmed, in agreement. "It is a place of strength and glory from the Lord," I said. The Holy Spirit continued in His teaching, saying, "Yes, just like the man that found the hidden treasure in the field and had joy over it, so he went and sold all he had just to purchase the land with the treasure – *the Kingdom of Heaven brings great joy when it is found.* It is that pureness of joy that brings light to those in the darkness. It is that immovable joy found in the hope of the glory to come when we are called home that breathes new life into those who are hopeless. Sharing and showing the joy within your heart, vulnerably and transparently as she did, spreads the love of Jesus without even knowing it, sometimes!" The Holy Spirit's words were felt deeply.

I admitted to myself, "How many times I have hidden the treasure I have found, allowing it to be covered up and not sharing it…for whatever reason..." I allowed the candid confession to linger in the air for a moment. My day today had started with remembering my daughter's impact. I was over-filled with such thoughts concerning this great joy given her. I had already stepped into an arena of dwelling upon it. "What did the joy of the Lord look like in action?" I pondered. "Well, that demonstration yesterday is certainly a close second, if not a first-place winner in answering that question," I quickly responded to my query. Thinking about it again, I admitted, "It is glorious to see Your glory working in my daughter like that, Lord!"

I had been through quite a bit this last few weeks and had felt exhausted from it all - spiritually, emotionally, physically, and mentally. Yes, I was exhausted in all the '-ally' departments. This morning, my mind was in recounting mode. My daughter's practice had lasted 2 hours. That did not include the visiting time before-hand and afterward. So, I had plenty of time to share all my woes and recount the many events of the last few weeks. Thankfully, I was able to do so with a dear Sister-in-Christ. We had been friends for over a decade. She knew me quite well. I was so very relieved that she was there for me to visit. Her company had brought me great joy, also. With it, there was great comfort yesterday.

She was an elder in spirit to me by quite a few seasons of training. As a result, she was a good listener – her training was that of the advanced level in the *"slow to speak, quick to listen"* department. When she spoke, the words that came from her lips were that of pure honey. 98 percent of the time, she only allows those words that are Good to flow out of her mouth. Words that are for encouragement, exhortation, admonishment, edification, strengthening, accountability, sharpening, and the like were her focus. They were fruitful words she chose to speak with me and others. There was not many a time…if any, actually, that I heard her speak loosely, with quick or unwise words. At this point in her walk, she never spoke with corrupt talk. Over the years I had known her, she had proven to be of good character, high morals, modest, strong in the Word, chock-full of wisdom, and submissive unto the Lord in the humblest of ways. She intentionally walked with a gentle spirit that was so very kind, loving, and sincere. I did love my friend so! Her walk was a walk that I aspired to! She walked carefully with the Lord and reveled in His presence. She truly, truly did love the Lord with all her heart and soul and mind and strength, as the Word calls us to do. Thinking about our friendship today brought with it such gratitude!

Oh, don't get me wrong, I had seen her in some really rough times. Times that made my last week look like a happy carnival day full of children's rides of great enjoyment. Times - as the saying goes, that I would not wish upon anyone - that she had endured. "Yes, she did! And with what grace and resolve, she did endure them!" I said admirably of my friend. I witnessed, first-hand, how her hope was placed immediately in the Lord. I saw how she dug her heels in and prayed and fought, unrelentingly. I could account for how she trusted the Lord with every last piece of it, every step of the way. I observed her choices to be at peace during those times. She continued to praise His name for it and through it all! I looked up to her quite a bit because of the Good example she set.

In the middle of the strongest storms that I have ever seen anyone go through, I saw her thrive in His love! AND, on top of her own dire-straight caliber of circumstances, she was still sharing the gospel of Jesus Christ. She was still spreading encouragement to others, praying for others, sharing proclamations of His love and goodness, giving of her time and money cheerfully and without hesitation, and…..the

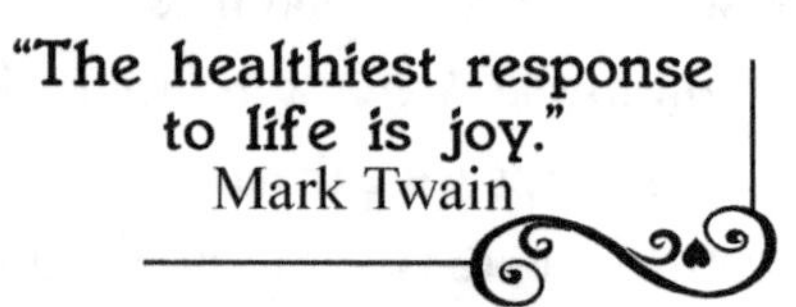

list went on. She never once strayed from the Good path. I remembered many a time that she would say to me, *"The joy of the Lord is my strength."* Recounting her affirmation now, I thought to myself, "She has been such an encouragement to me, Lord! Thank You for her friendship! It has been a terrific example of the caliber of heart and devotion I want to have in my walk with You, God!"

Rewinding in my thoughts by roughly a decade, I thought to myself this morning, "During that season of my life, I had no clue what the joy of the Lord meant. How could anyone find joy in the circumstances she was dealing with, let alone be in such a calm state of peace!?" A smile crossed my lips as I dwelled upon this recollection of my confounded response to her confident response in Him at the time. I was perplexed because I was still a baby Christian in that season. I was still going through basic training with milk as my food, and I had a minimal understanding of the vastness that was God's power, love, and faithfulness. However, she didn't. She knew Him well, and her devotion to Him was inspiring, to say the very least!

I would have easily caved within a day or two of having to endure such hardships! Giving myself a bit more credit, though, I said, "Well, I might have made it a few weeks; but she had to endure that particular trial for well over 2 years!" Her endurance had been admirable and encouraging more than she probably ever would know. I had attempted to commend her efforts in the past, to no avail. She was far too humble to admit she had anything to do with it. Again, that response was something that I did not quite understand back then. Through those conversations, she had taught me the best way to give someone a compliment

> **"Joy is not in things;
> it is in us."**
> Richard Wagner

was to always point to Him. Her typical response was, "Thank You, but it is not me. It is Christ in me." Eventually, I got to the point of saying things like: *"I just wanted to tell you, that was a great job of allowing God to work through you!"* ... *"Your submission in that situation to let God handle things was awesome!"* ... *"I could see God in you with what you just did, and I just wanted to encourage you to continue in what you are doing."* It was a different way of commending her, but she knew I was doing so to lift her up and be an encouragement to her in her walk. Plus, it made it easy for her to agree, because it honored God and gave Him the glory in her life. Yes, indeed, she was an elder in spirit – a true warrior – a bold and faithful Daughter of God – a woman with a heart for God! I jokingly agreed with that, saying, "Yes, back then, she was the type of woman that I wanted to be when I grew up!"

I highly respected my friend. I intentionally chose to be aligned with her and be around her, often. Learning from her and being held accountable by her has helped me grow in my walk. She was in my inner circle - a tiny group of people that I could divulge anything to that were brothers and sisters in Christ. I admitted with a smile, "Yes, but she is my favorite." Ours was an intimate friendship. One that was transparent and vulnerable. There was no concealment. It was all laid out there, completely bare and square. I confirmed in thought, "That is how a good relationship is supposed to be." There is No withholding or leaving things out, No missing details or almost-truths, No negative speak or lies, No conceit or selfishness, No walls or unforgiveness with grudges, No assuming cynical or corrupt motives from the other, No confidence breaking or only taking from the other, No manipulating or word-twisting, No old wounds hindering our sharing, No reasons are given not to trust one another – none of those type of things exist in a good relationship. No, indeed! I thought about the list of things that had gone through my mind. Then, concluded with ease, "No, there is nothing like that at all in our friendship. There is just full transparency with *the whole Truth and nothing but the Truth.*" I pondered the many times I had bared my soul and she to me. "Yep! There is full vulnerability between us with nothing left to give because it all has been shared!"

She was a true friend that I had complete confidence in. Over time, we had both been that way with one another – completely honest and true. We both appreciated our friendship and protected it dearly. Because of our unity in Spirit as sisters in Christ, we had many battles against the enemy. There were many times we had to join together as a united front. We were and still are bound and determined to not allow the enemy to hinder our friendship. Things come up, and situations of deceit and gossip arise, but we have each other's back. With each area considered, my heart grew more and more grateful this morning.

It is our priority to ensure that we are both grounded in the Word. Nothing outside of the walls of our friendship is allowed through that gate to harm either of our hearts. I pondered on this truth in our relationship. I thought to myself, "It is good to have her as a friend. I can easily come to her with insecurities instigated by the enemy. I can address attacks from him that have twisted stuff around without any hesitation. She does everything she can think of to put a stop to it immediately. She gives no room for an attack of doubt or fear or anything of the like!" Her tactic, which I mirror now, is to obliterate even the slightest hint of dishonesty or negativity that could hurt our friendship. My response is the same, although she does not come to me near as often as I do to her. She knows that trust in our friendship is the bond that keeps it at the deeper level it is. She told me very bluntly that she is not willing to sacrifice it for anything or anyone. So, when things have come up, and the enemy tries to use other people to attack our friendship, she shuts it down, and so do I. Hurting or losing our relationship is not an option. Especially over some person she hardly knows, visits with from time-to-time, or works with, etc. that is trying to start drama.

We both felt that way, protective of one another and caring for one another more than worldly people with their opinions and worldly ways. We both had a few other friends that were allowed in our individual circles and our mutual circle that were good friends and Christian women. Yet, that level of confidence and intimacy was only prevalent in the friendship between her and me. "We are besties, for sure," I said. She also is an excellent example of what a *Woman of God* looked like in action, word, and deeds: consistent, trustworthy, and dependable. Yes, the relationship we have shared over the last fifteen years of our lives is a priority to both of us. "I would much rather lose every single worldly person I know in my other distant circles than lose our friendship!" I admitted. I held it far above the things and people of the world that desired the world and its ways. "I would drop those other folks in a heartbeat!" I said with great determination. I knew she felt the same exact way! At the thought of how much her Good example and friendship had impacted me, I began to thank God for the divine appointment He had established to meet her. "Thank You, God, for bringing such a woman across my path to draw me closer to You! You are wonderful and all- knowing, and she definitely has been a way for me to see You and Your *philia* kind of love clearer through this friendship!" I said with great joy and an outpouring of gratitude.

My day of thoughtful recollection of yesterday's great joy that was widespread by my daughter and my divinely appointed friendship continued to progress with such delight and goodness! I was tremendously aware of the Holy Spirit and His presence every single step of the way through my day! I couldn't begin to describe it to anyone that would have asked me. No words could explain the light in my eyes and the smile upon my face. If they had asked about it, I would have stumbled over my words! His joy was upon my heart and outwardly evident all throughout the day. Yet, I couldn't describe it! If it was dependent solely on my abilities to speak to what was overflowing my heart and resonating through my entire being, my attempt would have fallen short. "How can I describe it?!" I asked.

> "Always hold fast to the present. Every situation, indeed every moment, is of infinite value, for it is the representative of a whole eternity."
> Johann Wolfgang von Goethe

There was a building up of my soul, of my heart, of my mind….my body felt light as if walking upon the steps of clouds in the heavens that I felt surrounded me. A veil of unspeakable peace and joy enveloped me with the warmest of loving tenderness! Inspired by these thoughts of my sweet daughter and dear friend, I asked God to bring to my remembrance moments of provision and great joy that I had found in Him. I desired to be reminded of those moments in my walk with Him. I also asked Him to show me things even before I had known Him! With my thoughts resting upon the blessed assurance found in the parable of the fig tree, I asked this *In faith*, because I knew He would provide. I said, "Dear Jesus, I know You said that *if I have faith and do not doubt that I will not only do what was done to the fig tree when it withered at a spoken word of Yours but also do even greater*! You said that *when I say to this mountain, Be taken up and cast into the sea, it will happen*! Oh, those mountains that are in front of me and obstructing my view of You are so big!" Thinking about the mountains, my eyes grew big. However, I continued, "They may try to block all You have laid ahead of me to see and be, but You are bigger! Yes, most assuredly, this parable is a promise of Yours to me, and Your promises are true! Yes, You said that *all things* I ask in prayer, *believing, I will receive them*! So, I come to You and ask this in a prayer of faith in You. My hope of Your grace-filled and love-centered provision is full! I know my good is in Your hands, and Your wonderful glory is in my heart, Lord. Bring to my remembrance all the many times in my life that You have been there for me, Lord. Show me when You provided during times that I did not see the way. Remind me how You have given me Your Good gifts, Lord. Recount to my heart how You have shown up in ways I could have never imagined! Yes, show me all the many moments in my life even before I knew You! Please let me see with Your eyes what You have done in every part of my life, Lord," I prayed. It was something my heart desired in excess today. I could feel the Holy Spirit's presence as I spoke to Him. I concluded my petition by saying, "I ask for the *enlightenment of the eyes my heart*, today, to remember Your marvelous glory, Oh, My God - my dear, sweet, loving, merciful Father!!! Thank You, Lord!"

Yes, this is what I prayed. I just didn't know *how much* God would bring to my remembrance through His Spirit! I wasn't prepared for *how much* He would provide throughout the entirety of the day! He had quite the movie of recollection laid ahead of me to walk with Him in! At the thought, I said, "Yes, *some* prayers we should enter into carefully, especially if we are not ready to be brought to our knees at that very moment!" Some prayers are answered immediately! I recalled telling a friend about this about a month ago, actually. I had said, "I would advise anyone to wait when praying such powerful, and awe-inspiring prayers while, say, driving down the road. You will have to pull over from the overwhelming power of His presence pouring into that car, my friend! It's like the crashing water of the Niagara Falls as it shoots out its cloud of water below! It permeates across the entire surface upon impact when it crashes down from such a height! Just like that, you gotta be prepared! His presence fills the whole place! It overwhelms and permeates through all your senses! Driving is not advised, for sure!"

A song came to mind as I closed my prayers. It is called *Holy Spirit* and is sang by Kim Walker Smith. The lyrics are something I incorporate into my prayers during congregation worship at my church. I purposefully invite the Holy Spirit into the worship service. I ask Him to wash over the entire congregation and overcome each person's heart with His beautiful presence & love. I also pray for God's protection of the group as He gives these sweet moments of intimacy with Him through worship. I ask Him to be there as that intimacy is entered into

> "Through Him then, let us continually offer up a sacrifice of praise to God, that is, the fruit of lips that give thanks to His name. And do not neglect doing good & sharing, for with such sacrifices God is pleased."
>
> book of Hebrews

through the assistance of voices lifted on high to Him. With that protection request, I sing sweetly in prayer the words of the song from my heart as the musicians play on stage and sing other songs to the congregation. That same song came to my heart as I thanked Him.

Yet, this afternoon, as I found myself missing the grasp for the bed and falling onto the soft, carpeted floor in complete surrender upon my knees; the words of this song came without hesitation. They welled up from deep within my very being! But not before I had exclaimed, *"Oh My God, My Heart!"* My heartbeat seemed to keep the rhythm as the words poured out of my lips. They felt as if they were from the deepest recesses of my soul! I finished the chorus, and another song came. In a state of absolute unrelenting submission to the movement of the Holy Spirit within me at the mention of the invitation within that song, I sang it as well. It was called *Set a Fire*. Over and over again, I repeated the lyrical lines for this song. It was a song I had heard many times on the radio by Jesus Culture. It just flowed out along with the tears of joy found in my submissive state.

The surrender and peace I found within His presence that came in like a flood was overwhelming! Out of my mouth came words fueled by that joy-filled surrender. I said, "Oh, My God! My sweet, sweet Lord! *Oh, My God, My Heart!* My heart is Yours, always. I love You so much! Thank You for loving me the way You have loved me. Yes, even before I was born, You knew me and loved me and called me Yours! You are what I long for! You are what my heart desires! I want to know You more. Lord, have Your way in me! Not my will, but Yours, Lord! Yes, Your will, Lord! Lead me and direct my path! *Search me, Oh God, and know my heart; Try me and know my anxious thoughts; and see if there be any hurtful way in me and Lead me in the everlasting way!* Forever and ever Amen and Amen, Lord." There was so very much joy that completely bound my heart within the confines of His great love.

The day ended in pure peace and was filled with the joy of the Lord. With every beat of my heart saying, "I love You, oh how I love Thee, Lord!" Bam… Bam-Bam…BAM. Yes, my heartbeat resounded in the declarations of love I had for my Heavenly Father. I felt a peace with this keen insight as He watched over my family and me that evening. Before I fell asleep, I was left with these final thoughts to myself: "There is a tremendous difference between the world's definition of needing to be happy and God's definition of joy. In all circumstances, good or bad, there is a joyful contentment found within the peace that God provides. The more I grow, the more I know this to be true! It is that very contentment which brings me an indescribable joy – even amid terrible storms and distress! There is always, always, always a reason to be joyful when I focus upon the Lord." Scripture was brought to my remembrance with this. His

Spirit said, "Yes, there is a time for everything, but do not grieve, do not lose heart - *for the Joy of the Lord is your Strength…*" A yawn escaped me as I tried to finish my thoughts. Rest was knocking on my door, and I could feel it with every flutter of my eyes as I fought to keep them open. I said, "Lord, if You are willing that I have one, of course, help me to remember that tomorr….." The words softly blended into the good rest that awaited my tired body. My awareness of His presence continued far into the night of rest He provided. It found its way beyond that into my dreams.

<u>MEMORY VERSE</u>

But let all who take refuge in You be glad,
Let them ever sing for joy;
And may You shelter them,
That those who love Your name may exult in You.
For it is You who blesses the righteous man, O Lord,
You surround him with favor as with a shield.
Psalm 5:11-12

Chapter Ten

Confessing To Freedom

*Oh, the depth of the riches
both of the wisdom and knowledge of God!
How unsearchable are His judgments
and unfathomable His ways!
For who has known the mind of the Lord,
or who became His counselor?
Or who has first given to Him
that it might be paid back to him again?
For from Him and through Him
and to Him are all things.
To Him be the glory forever. Amen.*
Romans 11:33-36

The new dawn had come with all its new mercies and in all its artful majesty. There was so much beauty of life reverberating in the landscape that I was blessed to admire. As I gazed upon it through the window, seeing it dimly through the steam above the rim of my morning coffee cup, I let out a sigh of satisfaction and awe. It was a morning of overwhelming gratitude for the day that preceded and for this new day that I was in. "God, Your goodness is *so* great, even when I do not see it. It is still *so very* great, just as You are, my Lord!" I testified. I slowly breathed in, letting the air fill my lungs.

I felt my chest rise with the inflow of new oxygen. I sat there, soaking up a moment of appreciation. I thought to myself, "What a blessing to merely be able to take another breath!" I took another one, held it in, and paused before releasing it into another sigh. The sigh was faint, but it was still there. It wasn't a sigh of heartache or dismay. It wasn't a sigh of relief or one released amid the fervor of stress. Neither was it a sigh of exhaustion or grief. There wasn't any frustration attached to it. It didn't remind me in the slightest of a sigh that is shoved out in a moment of being fed up. No…quite the contrary, actually. It was a sigh of gratitude and heartfelt praise. "Yes, it has been a few days since last I sighed like this," I admonished myself. I thought of the many other kinds of sighs that seemed to escape my lips more often than gratefulness. Thinking about the time between again, I said, "It has been a few months, probably." I pondered on this for a moment further. I agreed with myself, stating with blatant exaggeration, "So often so, that people would think the gratefulness sigh was altogether extinct!" Of course, that was not the case. Yet, it was humorous to add a bit of exaggeration every once in a great while. I found it amusing but did not overuse it, by any means. When I did use it, it was as if I was playing the role of quite the melodramatic actor. I entertained this thought for a moment. I pictured myself standing upon a stage full of other comically engaged actors who also were exaggerating their lines just enough to rally mild laughter from among the audience viewers. "You're not on a stage, silly!" I said to myself. I heard the standing ovation that I imagined I would get fading off into the distance of my playful mind this morning. It made me smile. My gratefulness and joy had brought out my inclinations to be just a tad bit silly this morning.

I agreed with my corrective self, of course. It was getting close to the time I liked to invest in studying God's Word. I needed to reign in my focus a bit. Distractions of the entertaining kind were a mild weakness of mine, at times. After all, it was one of my top priorities in the morning to give my time to Him. Over the years, the *Put God first* instructional line that I heard when I was a young lady in Bible Study, was taken quite literally. There were many years that God had *not* been a priority in my life. He was more like a backup plan, or a second thought. I used to dislike admitting to this because of the taste of disappointment in myself that it would leave. Yet, it was the truth, nonetheless.

In hindsight, I knew that the disappointment part was a condemnation attack from the enemy. One of the things he liked and *still* likes to do is try to weasel his way into my days. That was precisely what the enemy was doing back then when those feelings used to come about. However,

> "You are from God, little children, & have overcome them; because greater is He Who is in you *than* he who is in the world."
> Apostle John

it wasn't going to work now. They were quickly dismissed, through identification in discernment. "Yes, now I just call it out for what it is - a lie." The Holy Spirit's confirmation echoed my thoughts with scripture. He said, *"Submit therefore to God. Resist the enemy, and he will flee from you."* It was another one of my go-to's in battle. I stood on that scripture quite often! "Yes, Lord! There are no *ands, ifs,* or *buts* about it! That promise ends in a solid, matter-of-fact period. You're right!" I agreed.

There was a process I had learned years ago that had become standard practice in my walk, now. My response to any attacks of the devil in this season of my life was grounded in truth. When the enemy came at me, I simply practiced *standing firm & bold* in the understanding and awareness that I *am* a child of God. Learning and more in-depth training in *who I am in Jesus Christ* and *Whose I am in Jesus Christ* has taken some time, but it has been worth it! All that time that I invested in getting to where I am today has made all the difference! My walk with God has been tremendously more fruitful through my obedience to practice *standing firm* in my identity. "Yet, I know I *still* have the ability to go *even deeper* in that understanding. Even after many

> "We never know how high we are till we are called to rise; & then, if we are true to plan, our statures touch the skies."
> — Emily Dickinson

years of sharpening, crushing, refining, and growing - I'm just getting started! I haven't even scratched the surface of *how high, how deep, how wide, and how long Your Love for me is in Christ Jesus,* Father!" I excitedly declared as my mind continued in this thought.

Although there is plenty more for me to learn, I know enough that I can cast out the enemy when he attacks, for sure! The Holy Spirit had reiterated the enemy's existence quite early on in my life. My Grandmother fought the enemy, often. She was a Prayer Warrior and Intercessor on behalf of others daily. I remember her instructing me once as she quoted scripture. She said, *"For it is not flesh and blood that we struggle against,* the Word says. No, it is a battle we face that is *against the spiritual attacks of the evil kind* and *the world forces of this darkness.* I know the devil's schemes are no match for God and His awesome power! So, I *stand firm and boldly* in this knowledge when he tries to come at me and mine. You, too, will need to know this when you get older, young lady. There <u>will be</u> spiritual warfare. You gotta be ready *when* it comes. It is not *if* it comes - but *when.*"

She taught me this process of *Claiming Authority* in Jesus Christ. I have built on the foundation she laid so many years ago, as God has drawn me closer to Him. He has called me to intercede for others more and more these last few years, just like He did with Grandma. This is what I have learned, so far - *AND* I use it, without hesitation, on the daily. Staying s*ober-minded* and on a*lert* has been vital in obedience to His Word concerning this spiritual battle. This is a brief summary of *claiming the authority* given to me by Jesus Christ over the enemy within primary areas of my daily life. Temptations come in many forms and attempt to attack me. I *boldy and firmly stand* in *authority* over the following:

my flesh – primarily, my body – lusts & passions not of God
my thoughts – what I am dwelling on, identifying what I am allowing to set up house in my mind that is of the world
my words – both in speech and writing that contradict the Word of God.
my feelings – emotions and reactions that are a result of the temptation, and the desires that go along with being ruled by feelings
my sight - perspective and focus; as well as, literally, what I allow before my eyes through different media types

I immediately declare that I am bringing them each under the *Obedience of Jesus Christ.* I call out the enemy by name & *boldly resist* his attacks of deception and lies. I tell the enemy, "Devil, you have no authority here. That authority is mine as a child of God through Christ. You must leave in the Name of Jesus!" I state this in full assurance of faith as a *co-heir with Christ* and a *redeemed child of God.* I follow this by speaking the truth of the scriptures from the Word to dismiss those attacks, answering each temptation with the truth of God that replaces it. Then, I *stand firmly* on the knowledge of God within me, written on my heart, of that truth in scripture. The enemy is a liar. God *is* truth. It's that simple, and there is no gray area. Finally, I shift my focus back to *Jesus Christ, the author & perfecter of my faith,* with the understanding that He intercedes on my behalf in full victory over the enemy and the world. "Yes, victory is found in Jesus Christ! It is important for me to continue to practice focusing on Jesus with my mind, my heart, my soul, and my body - with all my strength and dedication that I know to focus with," I reminded myself. I echoed this thought with confirmation, saying, "Yes, it is! Thank You, God, for filling the gap in the areas I do not know and *fighting those battles for me*! Your power is mighty and *above all other names*!"

Although that is what I do now, it was not always the case. In this deeper season of my life, I actively desire a more intimate, personal, moment-by-moment caliber of relationship with God. It feels a little bit surreal to think about my life b*efore* this desire. I allowed my mind to drift back to previous seasons. "Oh, how much of a beautiful mess I was!" I softly chuckled at the exaggerated thought. The fondness of my naivety was at the forefront of my mind. So, I allowed it to stay for a bit. I had been through many twists and turns that led down wide, well-traveled roads. They were roads I would have passed by and ignored had I known God like I do now. But, alas, I went gallivanting down them, none-the-wiser, like the naïve young lady I was back then. "Man, oh, man! What trouble I got myself into! What traps and snares I stepped on down those roads!" I thought to myself. This time, my thoughts did not have much humor. It was bad! Like *really* bad, in my view, now. Of course, I took a moment to give myself the grace and compassion that He, too, has given me.

Nope! I did not know God like I do now. I was easily swayed…*very* easily swayed. "Yeah! *And* I could justify with the best of them the many things I did," I continued, reflectively. It was so easy to do something I thought or knew I probably shouldn't be doing and make TOTAL sense as to why it was ok to do. I would say things like,

"It is No big deal."
"It's not really that bad."
"God is totally ok with this because He really doesn't care what I do."

I was an easy target for the enemy. My lack of the knowledge of God made me so. I didn't know Him well enough to disqualify those justifying attacks of thought that would come at me. I didn't have a personal walk with Him like I do now. I didn't desire full accountability to the Word. *AND* I definitely wasn't seeking Him with all I had!

Actually, I wasn't consistently seeking Him, either. It was better described as a seeking of the *sporadic* kind. Easter and Christmas visits to Church were a given. Sunday mornings - when it was convenient for me and my schedule - were a maybe. If I were to be *really* honest with myself in this reflection, I would have to say I was going to Church *just to go to Church*. I had no purpose apart from it was something I was *supposed to do*. "Yet, in all Your goodness, Father, You never left me and continued to pursue after my heart!" I gratefully acknowledged. Thinking about it now, I said, "There were so many things that took precedence over time with You, God!" Oh, I had been baptized and received Jesus as my Savior. Yes, I knew the stories about Jesus from the Gospels shared on Sundays. I knew that He came to

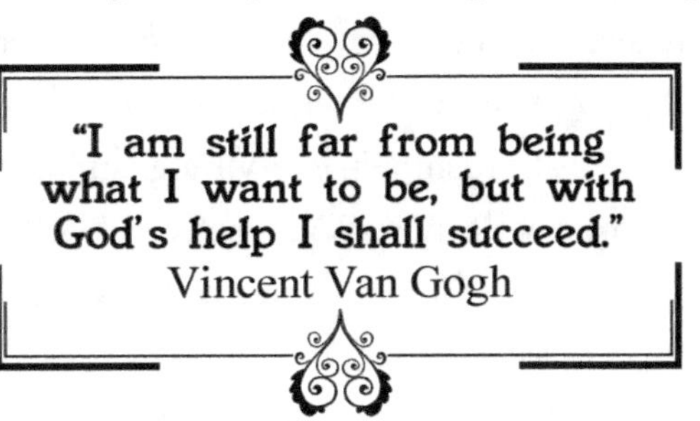

save the world from sin...He died on the cross for the sins of the world...He rose on the 3rd day...yada, yada, yada...BUT I didn't truly know Him like the Word defines <u>*Knowing*</u> Him.

On top of this lack of knowledge, I had not accepted Jesus as my *Lord*. I recall asking one of my non-Christian friends at the time, "What is the point of spending time with someone I don't really know, who may or may not really care? He is God of the *entire* world! There are *billions* of people in the world. Why would He be concerned about me?" It didn't make sense to me, then. So, I simply did what I was *supposed to do*. I went to Church. I was baptized. I was behaving like a good kid would. At the time, that was pretty much my understanding of the requirements to be a Christian, in a nutshell. I know, now, that there is a *HUGE* difference between knowing *about* God and knowing God.

I also know there is a difference between *baptism by water* and *baptism by the Spirit*. In one, you just get wet with water. That's it. Dirt returns, over and over, because it is done in the flesh. You choose to be baptized for the benefit of the on-lookers. There is no genuine, intimate relationship established with the Lord. It merely is surface deep. The understanding as to why the choice is made is missing, as well. It is done *just because I am supposed to* or *only because it is expected of me*. In the latter, being *baptized by the Spirit*, it is a completely immersive experience for the mind, body, heart, and soul. You get washed and purified by the *Blood of The Lamb*, Jesus Christ. You are wholly redeemed and are a *New Creation in Christ*. You have this fire lit in the depths of your soul that awakens this overwhelming desire to seek after God, the Father, with *every* fiber of your being. You intentionally *choose & commit* to surrender and submit yourself unto His Lordship, in everything, and in all your ways – daily saying, "not my will, but Your will, Lord." You actively yield to the guidance and teaching of *the Holy Spirit, whom God has given you, as a newly adopted child of His and co-heir with Jesus Christ.*

I considered these steps in great detail this morning in my grateful recollections. I thought about the ways I had applied them in my walk over the years. "Yes, there *is* a big difference between the two, and you did not know any better in those days, My child. Remember to be on guard against any potential attacks of condemnation as you think upon past seasons," came the cautionary guidance from the Spirit. "You are right, Lord. You have promised that there is *a sufficient amount of grace given to each of us* to cover the sinful nature like I once walked in," I somberly acknowledged. "Condemnation has no place here. I will stay on guard, Lord," I confirmed.

It was challenging to think that I once walked in all those things, as I looked back. In the light of considering who I had grown to be, now, it made it even more so! The differences were so stark that I thought to myself, "It's like *The-Me-Then* and *The-Me-Now* are two different people!!" Before I could add to this thought, the understanding in my heart came to the forefront. I replied, "No," with a slight pause of contemplation concerning scriptures that came to mind, "It is EXACTLY like that!" I let the thought of blessed assurance sink in a bit. Monday's study time dawned on me suddenly. With it, a strengthening was present. "*Therefore if anyone is in Christ, he is a new creature; the old things passed away; behold, new things have come."* The scripture reminder helped me to *guard my heart and mind in Christ Jesus* as I moved forward down this road of recollection. It was a benefit of the sharpening kind for me to venture down this road, from time to time. As long as I did so, intentionally, it was very therapeutic to dwell on the many ways God had provided opportunities for me to *grow in the Knowledge of His Love.* Recalling the many ways God had saved me from *The-Me-Then* brought about strengthening and encouragement.

Remembering such things was like my own version of the production of *A Christmas Carol* by Charles Dickens. The main character, Mr. Scrooge, found new enlightenment in his forced perception change. He saw how his past choices and ways had impacted others *and* himself when he was taken down memory lane to his past. In the trip back to the present, he witnessed what was happening around him. The 2nd ghost showed him how his choices of behavior were hurting others. Fast forward through the story, of course, and that's when the real change occurred! The final ghost brought about a fear of what awaited him at the end of his life if he continued in his choices. That fear of the reality that would befall him if he did not change was what eventually spurred his *change of heart to gratitude and good works.* Like his epiphany, I had already had a *change of heart.* Through my surrender to the Lordship of Jesus Christ, I was changed. He changed the course of my life in that one decision of submission to servanthood in Jesus. God's process of renewal had started that very day! Just then, the Holy Spirit brought to my remembrance the new heart scripture. I agreed, saying, "Yes, God has done in my life just as He promised to Israel in the book of Ezekiel. *He has given me a new heart and put His Spirit within me.* Glory be to God!"

With the thought about the scripture, I walked into the other room to retrieve my Bible. "It has been a while since I last read Ezekiel. What else did God say through His prophet, "I asked? Curious to reread it, I sat down and opened my Bible to chapter 36. I skimmed through the section and found the passage that I had recounted. Written were these words: *"For I will take you from the nations, gather you from all the lands and bring you into your own land. Then I will sprinkle clean water on you, and you will be clean; I will cleanse you from all your filthiness and from all your idols. Moreover, I will give you a new heart and put a new spirit within you; and I will remove the heart of stone from your flesh and give you a heart of flesh. I will put My Spirit within you and cause you to walk in My statutes, and you will be careful to observe My ordinances. You will live in the land that I gave to your forefathers; so you will be My people, and I will be your God. Moreover, I will save you from all your uncleanness; and I will call for the grain and multiply it, and I will not bring a famine on you. I will multiply the fruit of the tree and the produce of the field, so that you will not receive again the disgrace of famine among the nations. Then you will remember your evil ways and your deeds that were not good, and you will loathe yourselves in your own sight for your iniquities and your abominations. I am not doing this for your sake,"* declares the Lord God, *"let it be known to you. Be ashamed and confounded for your ways, O house of Israel!"* As I read the words, I admitted to the Father, "It is such a beautiful promise of renewal and restoral back to You, God. It is a powerful message of *knowing* that You...Yes! You, alone, are God! What great and mighty things You do, Father, to bring Your children back home to walk in Your presence daily! There is no denying how good and merciful You are with all that You have done and *still* promise to do to reconcile Your children back to You!" I rested in the peace that came from that admittance to Him. It was good.

I let time move along a bit more before I thought upon things once more. These set aside times I take to focus on the things of my past are done with a specific objective. The end goal is to *grow in the knowledge of His love.* Even before I allow the thought process, I know that they will, ultimately, lead me directly to deeper accountability in my walk and a thankful heart for where I am today. They always do. I am confident that it is because

I *only* chose to look back *while* walking hand-in-hand *with* the Holy Spirit. I was not about to walk down those old roads without His guidance. "No way! I know better. Look at what happened just a few days ago when you were being empathetic toward . You had a bit of time not getting sucked in, because you walked hand-in-hand with temptation, at first," I said. I shook my head, despondently. Answering that attack of discouragement, immediately, I replied, "Yes, but I know in God's presence, I am safe and secure in my understanding of *Whose I am in Jesus Christ*. Without the Holy Spirit, it is a total fail! It opens me up to quite the onslaught of attacks from the enemy, for sure!" It was something that I could easily admit. Without God, the efforts were frivolous, at best.

"Yes, trying to remember such things on *my own*, in the flesh, is an entirely different story. It was just a bad idea. Period." I affirmed. That lesson was one I learned the hard way. Talk about sitting around in a depressed, *I-am-totally-worthless* mindset! *AND* talk about being surrounded by old temptations just waiting for an entry point to attack! Yes, I had wound up there quite a number of times, due to my own lack of understanding concerning how the enemy works. Dwelling on the past without the Holy Spirit's leading and protection is not safe at all! I've learned that the best defense is to *just not be there* without the Holy Spirit. Shame, guilt, condemnation, judgment, doubt, insecurities, second-guessing, truth-twisting, temptations of old ways *…you name it….*the twists of the knife were brutal and not protected against early on in my walk with God. I didn't know how to protect against such things; or even *what* I was doing. I wasn't

> "**And not only this, but we also exult in our tribulations, knowing that tribulation brings about perseverance; & perseverance, proven character; & proven character, hope;** *and hope does not disappoint,* **because the love of God has been poured out within our hearts through the Holy Spirit who was given to us.**"
> Apostle Paul

aware that they were even attacks. My knowledge of spiritual warfare was highly limited in that early season. "Yes, it is something that has taken years to develop training and understanding in even with my Grandmother's sound counsel on the subject early on," I said, perceptively.

This morning, it was ok for me to venture down this path of recollection because He was with me. So, I shifted my focus back over to *the history of me*. It was quite a thing! I had walked down many paths that were not acceptable to speak of, in general conversation. They were difficult subjects to even bring up in public, let alone to bring up in Church, due to the judgment that would, most assuredly, befall me. "Oh, *but* I did admit to it all before You, Lord," I thought in my attempts to justify I was doing *something* right, at least. "Yes. And that was good. Yet, you had not *confessed it* to anyone else, as my Word has instructed," the Holy Spirit responded. "You are right, Lord. Initially, I had not done as the book of James teaches us to do. As a result, I left the door wide-open for condemnation to come in and set up shop…and it did, for a while." I conceded.

Eventually, I had admitted to my struggles with condemnation, guilt, and shame to the Pastor of my Church. Yes, 'eventually' I had sought prayer against the condemnation that I was struggling with on *my own*. It took me a while; but, 'eventually' I did. I didn't know how to fight against it and was tired - *so very* worn out! I knew the Pastor did, though. Well, at least, I sure hoped he did!! He was spiritually and biblically my elder by many years. It was a step I felt in my spirit that was needed.

Funny enough, *confession* was even taught in a Bible Study of the book of James a few months before. The teachers had shared with us James' instruction. He said, "In the book of James, it says, to *confess your sins to one another and pray for each other so that you may be healed.*" I recall the conviction that I felt in my heart that evening. It was pretty heavy! "Oh, but I sure did put it off, Lord, didn't I?!" I rhetorically asked. I did not expect a reply to the well-known fact of *just how long* I put it off. Trusted sound counsel was what I needed, even if I didn't really know what that was, at the time. Yet, I wasn't ready to confess, at first. Thankfully, I knew 'the basics' enough to 'eventually' listen to the beckoning in my heart.

Thinking about it now, I said, "Yes, I knew to *listen to that still, small voice,* even if my hearing was intermittent." 'Intermittent hearing' was *still* hearing. Although, in my case, it was exceptionally limited at the time.

My mind continued to rest on the topic of my confession back then. That morning had been quite the experience! Completely-transparent-confession was not something that I wanted to do in the flesh, by any means! Yet, God was calling me to do so. He placed a heavy conviction upon my spirit. Then, He showed me the command to do so in His Word through a weekly Bible Study. Did I want to? No. However, He was preparing me to confess it all, whether I thought I wanted to or not. He knew best for me and desired for me to be near to Him. So, He called me closer. I thought about the other scripture in Hebrews that had come up right after the Bible Study through conversation with a friend of mine. It, too, was a reassurance and held its own weighted conviction within my heart. She had sent me one of those out-of-the-blue messages with a verse she said to read. Her text read, "Read Hebrews 4:11-16". I had put it off for about a week until God decided to remind me through the radio with the same exact passage! The preacher had cut into the music on the commercial time with the "minute of hope" segment. He read it word-for-word! *"Therefore let us be diligent to enter that rest, so that no one will fall, through following the same example of disobedience. For the word of God is living and active and sharper than any two-edged sword, and piercing as far as the division of soul and spirit, of both joints and marrow, and able to judge the thoughts and intentions of the heart. And there is no creature hidden from His sight, but all things are open and laid bare to the eyes of Him with whom we have to do. Therefore, since we have a great high priest who has passed through the heavens, Jesus the Son of God, let us hold fast our confession. For we do not have a high priest who cannot sympathize with our weaknesses, but One who has been tempted in all things as we are, yet*

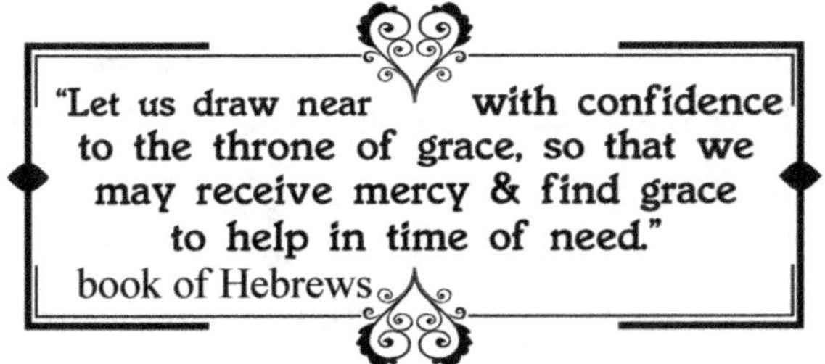

without sin. Therefore let us draw near with confidence to the throne of grace, so that we may receive mercy and find grace to help in time of need." I made sure to read it when I arrived home. I wanted to see it for myself. I remembered being in a state of disbelief at the time, saying out loud in the car, "Did that preacher just say what I think he said!?... Wait! Wasn't that the verse she shared with me?... Oh my goodness! It *is* the verse she shared with me! No way! I've got to see this for myself!" So, I did. As I recalled it now, it was simple to see how much He was pursuing me at the time. Yet, then… I had not a clue what He was calling me to do and just how much it would mean in my walk that weekend!

It happened a few Sundays following the Bible Study. I had responded with submission to the draw to come to the altar for prayer, but it was with great difficulty! I was staring into the vicious face of smothering, paralyzing fear! My feet were frozen - for what seemed like days. The fear of the potential for me to be disgraced and punished and judged by my peers left me feeling incapacitated. I was struck by a devastating blow of doubt from fear, too. I doubted that God would provide after I confessed. I doubted the *new creation* bit of scripture. I doubted that people would see me through God's perspective. Those doubts brought about a fear of losing those I had come to know in the Church body as my Church family. After all, if they knew *all* that I had done, they would never look at me the same, right?! I knew that my admittance to the struggle with condemnation to the Pastor, ultimately, <u>required</u> my admittance of the reasons *Why* I felt condemned. "What are you feeling condemned about?" would most definitely be one of the *very* first questions I would get from him!

I remembered all those thoughts that bombarded me within that moment of confession. As I recalled the event, I pictured it. It was like I was there all over again! Even now, I could feel the sick-to-my-stomach reaction from doubt and fear. I could feel the battle against the enemy. I had walked smack-dab in the middle of a war and didn't even know it! I was being tormented *while* trying to make a decision to be prayed for. What was intended to be a few easy steps when I walked into the Church that morning had turned into this suffocating battle!

I felt like I was either going to take a *giant* leap of faith toward God and His healing grace, or I was going to stay bound in the death grips of condemnation. I didn't want it anymore! I couldn't bear it one more second! The weight was too heavy, and I was tired of feeling beat up. I was tired of feeling ashamed about *everything* I had done to myself and others before I was saved. Yet, I was still stuck in the clutches of fear as I stood in the multitude of people that only seemed to grow. It felt like *thousands* of people were there! Yet, if I had been rationally thinking, I knew the congregation was usually only a few hundred on a good day. My legs were like gelatin, though. My feet felt frozen to the ground, unwilling to engage in steps.

I tried to continue to play out the scenario in my memory this morning. However, I was interrupted by an attack of disappointment at my weakness as I looked back at *the-me-then*. It tried to creep into my mind and convince me that I should be disappointed in myself. It whispered, "You couldn't even walk up to the Pastor! What kind of Christian are you? You were just weak! You must not have had very much faith, if any! So much for you being a good Christian..." I dismissed it immediately with a sharp, "No! None of that is true," spoken aloud. The disappointment scurried quickly back into the darkness from which it came.

I returned back to my thoughts about the pivotal event that had changed my life for the better. I knew the end result was where I was today, and that was assurance enough. "I am so thankful for the strength You gave me that morning, Lord! I could not have done it without You!" I said as I took a moment to give Him praise. It had been challenging to get through, indeed! Taking steps should have been easy. Walking should have been super simple. However, it most certainly was not that morning!

It was with great dismay and frantic thoughts of hysteria that I finally started to walk to the front of the room to where the Pastor was standing that Sunday. Every single step was like I had cinder blocks tied to my feet. I felt bound and cast over the side of the dock, drowning with no way to get any air! My heart was racing, and I was in full-on *fight or flight* mode with every foot gained of forward-movement!! Oh, how I wanted to fly right on out of there!! "It's not too late to turn back!" I remembered the words screaming in my mind. "Run now, while you still have a chance! Make an excuse that you had to go to the bathroom, then get in your car and leave! By this time next week, no one will remember you even got out of your seat!" Tons and tons of thoughts came flooding in as I neared the front. The loudest of these was at the very end right before I spoke. It was like a pleading demand and threat - all wrapped up into one. It said, "No! Don't you dare say anything! You are going to regret this! You will never live this down! You will lose everything if you do this! I promise you!" Those thoughts had made it difficult to think clearly. My mind felt like rubbish tossed about in pure chaos!

I began to reflect on the words that I spoke to the Pastor that morning. I thought about how they wouldn't come, at first. I could picture in my mind the questioning look the Pastor gave me. His eyes sought the truth. I could see it! It felt like knives piercing through my soul! It was like bullets penetrating through the so-called bullet-proof vest I had worn for so very long. I wore that vest for a reason. I didn't want anyone to get too close to me. In my experience, that meant emotional suicide! Just like bullets would have,

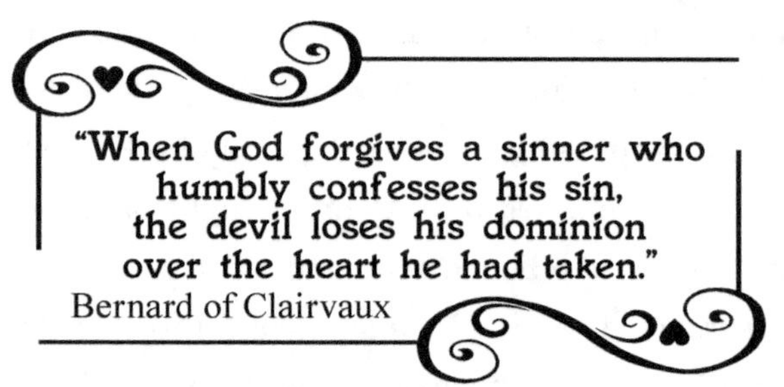

his piercing look slammed into my chest like a freight train!!

This morning, I recalled how the heat rose to my cheeks almost immediately. The redness flushed my skin from the feeling of embarrassment and humiliation. I felt overwhelmed as I stood in front of a gazillion people...or so the thoughts tried to convince me there were that many! "Don't do it! Don't do it! No one has to know!" they yelled. With one straggly, deep breath, I managed to think over the thoughts and ask in desperation and surrender, "Lord, Help me, please!" It was like a rush of calm came upon me instantly! I was filled with this strange, foreign sense that said, "You are going to be ok." I couldn't explain it, but, somehow, I knew it was ok.

My eyes had dropped to the floor as I shifted my feet back and forth awkwardly. With this newfound reassurance, though, I lifted them back to the Pastor and met his gaze. I stumbled over the first few sentences. The fluster of humiliation was quite profound at that moment! However, with each sentence shared, I felt a strengthening and a sense of confident resolve. That feeling was something that I had not known before. Soon, the words began to pour out of my mouth, smoothly and without hesitation. In quite the elevated sense of suspense, I had said to myself, "There is no going back from here! Whether I like it or not, I am all in!" At that point, I was committed to seeing this through. This whole confessing-it-all choice of mine was going to be successful. Whether I liked it, or not...whether it ruined me, or not...whether I never spoked to another person at that Church again, or not...I was going to see it through!

I told that Pastor every last thing! And, I mean, _everything_. It was one of the most difficult, embarrassing, revealing, vulnerable, awkward, scary, emotionally draining, pressure-filled, honest, humiliating-in-the-humbling sense, and freeing _real things_ that I had ever done, but I did it. _Only_ with God's help, I did it. "It's been Your way, _not mine_, ever since, Lord," I said, with a smile, as I looked out at the vibrant blue sky dappled with stratus clouds. I recalled what the Pastor had told me that day. His sound counsel has remained with me ever since! He had said to me, "Your Story and God's Presence is all you need to make a difference! So, share your testimony!" I blurted out my response without thinking. I said, "Well, that's scary! I don't like being vulnerable!" He replied, "Don't be afraid to be vulnerable. You never know who may need to hear only some of it and who may need to hear all of it. But God sure does! Listen to His prompting on your heart. He will be there with you when He calls you to share your story, I promise you this." He paused in thoughtful consideration and added, "Did you know that the Bible tells us to *Fear Not!* 365 different times?" Incredulously I replied, "Really!? Wow! That's a scripture a day! That's cool!" He continued, "Yes, fear is a tactic of the enemy. It's actually a spiritual attack. We don't have to accept it as our truth, ever! His Word says that *there is no fear in love, but perfect love casts out fear.* You can stand on that simple promise the next time fear comes against you." I didn't say anything further. I just nodded. I had thought at the time, "Man, no more fear would be awesome! I have some practice ahead of me, for sure! I deal with tons of fear attacks right now. The enemy sucks!"

Recalling our conversation now made my heart fill with joy. Regardless of all the nail-clawing attempts of the enemy to deter me, I had succeeded in admitting it all. I gave an entirely transparent confession to the Pastor that day! I continued in my acknowledgment this morning of what that day had meant. "That was the day that I learned what it meant to submit to Your Lordship and break the bonds of sin that were still holding me back. That was the day that I found a closer walk with You, God. That was the day my trust in You grew. From that day's experience, I was shown another level of how I could trust Your voice; so, I began to practice listening for it. Not only that, but I learned that submission meant being obedient to Your leading, and I learned that You have my best interest at heart, always! It was one of the best trust-exercises I have shared with You, God. I could trust You, then, with it all. When I have continued to trust You - You have not failed me once! I will trust You, now, My Lord."

With that final thought, I bowed my head and gave Him some time in prayerful thanksgiving and praise of all He had done, and of all He is. The memory of how wonderful it was to confess every last detail stayed with me throughout the remainder. The good and the bad was confessed, no longer could the enemy use it against me. The ugly, uglier, and ugliest had been out in the open since that day, and there was absolutely nothing the enemy could do about it! *I was no longer a slave, but a child of God and co-heir through Jesus Christ.* I was not a slave to the enemy and most certainly not to the world and its corrupt ways. That day forever changed me. I became totally free in Him. Confession and complete surrender to Jesus as my Lord had provided that freedom. One of my favorite scriptures came to mind through the Holy Spirit at this thought. He said, *"So if the Son makes you free, you will be free indeed."* That is one promise that I have held onto ever since that day! Thinking about it this morning, I knew, in my heart, that the rest of the day ahead would be, most assuredly, a day full of worship... "Yes, because I am *still* and *always* will be *free indeed*!" I said as a glorious smile lit up my eyes. I imagined His light shing through me and broadcasting out into the world around me – displaying for everyone to see His great love for me. *"Letting your light shine before men in such a way that they may see your good works, and glorify your Father who is in heaven,"* confirmed the Holy Spirit. I gratefully replied, "Yes, this light will shine for You, Lord. Because of You, I am *free indeed*! Thank You, Father!"

MEMORY VERSE

But flee from these things, you man {children} of God, and pursue righteousness, godliness, faith, love, perseverance and gentleness.

**Fight the good fight of faith;
take hold of the eternal life to which you were called,
and you made the good confession
in the presence of many witnesses.**

*I charge you in the presence of God, Who gives life to all things,
and of Christ Jesus, Who testified the good confession
before Pontius Pilate, that you keep the commandment
without stain or reproach until the appearing of our Lord Jesus Christ,
which He will bring about at the proper time—
He who is the blessed and only Sovereign,
the King of kings and Lord of lords,
Who alone possesses immortality and dwells in unapproachable light,
Whom no man has seen or can see.*

To Him be honor and eternal dominion! Amen.

1 Timothy 6:11-16

Chapter Eleven

Wait! Stop Right There!

> *1 The Lord is my light and my salvation;*
> *Whom shall I fear?*
> *The Lord is the defense of my life;*
> *Whom shall I dread?*
>
> *4 One thing I have asked from the Lord,*
> *that I shall seek: that I may dwell in the house of*
> *the Lord all the days of my life,*
> *to behold the beauty of the Lord and to meditate in His temple.*
>
> *8 When You said, "Seek My face,"*
> *my heart said to You, "Your face, O Lord, I shall seek."*
>
> **14 Wait for the Lord;**
> **Be strong and let your heart take courage;**
> **Yes, wait for the Lord.**
>
> Psalm 27:1, 4, 8, 14

There it was – the knock on the door I had been waiting for f-o-r-e-v-e-r. Thursday's anticipated delivery had come, at last! "Finally! It's here!" I shrieked in excitement. "At least, I sure hope it is this time!" I said. I had waited for quite some time on this delivery. Almost enough time had passed that I was considering getting on a plane, flying across the country, and giving those folks at the main manufacturing plant a piece of my mind. "Hehe, yeah, right!" I laughed at myself. The pieces I would have given were that of frustration and impatience. I could just imagine how foolish that would make me out to be. I pictured this ridiculously high-strung person coming up to me, full of drama about some undelivered item *while* I was on the job working, minding my own business, and going about my daily routine. How absurd I would think that person to be, at that moment! And, yet, that would be me after such a long flight!

There I would be, traipsing around the country, half-lost and half-exhausted. Finding the directions *and* a ride from the airport to the plant, let alone also locating the right person to speak to, was all a nightmare-in-waiting! "No, thank you!" I exclaimed in my imaginative thoughts. In my defense (what little ground I had to stand on, given my impatience), the package was *supposed to be* delivered 6 months ago. I had waited half a year for a package that could have probably been picked up at a nearby specialty store…or, at least, substituted for something else that would have done the trick, just as well. "6 months! Goodness! That is a lot of time waiting, for sure!" I thought. Of course, it was a special-order item. I had thought long and hard about what I wanted to get my husband for our upcoming anniversary before deciding to go this route. Thankfully, I am not the procrastinating type when it comes to gifts like this. I had placed the order and sent in the information 7 months prior to the due date. Thinking about it now, I admitted, "God, You definitely provided for what You knew was already coming – a huge delay of delivery!" He had placed it on my heart to go ahead and order the gift with plenty of time to get it here. It didn't make much sense to order it so soon, at the time. Normally, I would have only ordered a few months ahead. After-all, I understood that it had to be designed to the specs I provided as the customer. Although it didn't make much sense at the time, I listened to the beckoning of that still, small voice of His. Six months later, here I was with one month to spare. "Give me a break! A few weeks, maybe even a month – but surely it isn't supposed to take 6 months!" I thought again to myself. He had definitely provided even when I didn't ask Him to do so. How could I have? I would have never guessed it would take that long and require so much waiting!

Waiting was definitely one of the more difficult things for me to learn over the years. "Did you *learn* to wait...or *grow* in the understanding of waiting?" I inquired of myself. I pondered on this potential sharpening. I allowed my mind to briefly contemplate the difference between the two *very* similar words. "There is a scripture about patiently *waiting* and losing heart," I said to myself, "How does it go, again, Lord?" I paused, *waiting* for a response. The Holy Spirit brought it to my remembrance, saying, "*Let us not lose heart in doing good, for in due time we will reap if we do not grow weary.*" He continued, "*So then, while we have opportunity, let us do good to all people, and especially to those who are of the household of the faith.*"

> "But love your enemies, & do good, & lend, expecting nothing in return; & your reward will be great, *and you will be children* of the Most High; for He Himself is kind to ungrateful & evil men."
> Jesus Christ

I thought about the scripture I had recounted to memory. "For just a few lines, there sure is a lot being said, Lord!" Then, somewhat abruptly, I interrupted the train of thought and said, "Nope! That one's too deep for right now. You've got stuff to do. Put it back in the box," I told myself. So, I placed the topic back in the box, closed the lid, and put it up on my *This Is For Later* shelf. It had to be done, or else I would be chasing that rascally rabbit *right* down its hole! The pattern of my thoughts would be of the curious kind and lead me to waste a ton of time that

I could not afford to lose. Today was not the day to be doing that. "No, not at all. Today is *not* the day, at least for now." I agreed as I shifted my attention to the tasks at hand.

It was mid-morning, already, and the time for fun and games was over! It was game-time…go-time…THE time to be on-the-ball and movin'-to-the-groovin'. I had multiple meetings lined up. Those clients were waiting for their reserved time from me. It was daunting if I looked at it from the perspective of the <u>whole</u> day. It looked like a *giant* mountain when it was all compounded together!! On days like this, it suited me best to focus on smaller, more tangible goals *within* the day instead of the day as a *whole*. While thinking about my tasks, an old saying came to mind this morning. The words of it came to the forefront of my focus. *"How do you eat an elephant….one bite at a time."* It applied, but I never really understood why anyone would want to eat an elephant, in the first place. "Seriously, who does that, nowadays?!" I thought. "Did You inspire writings about elephants in the Bible, God?" I asked curiously.

I didn't *wait* for a response. Instead, I came to a simple conclusion. I surmised, "On the other hand, an elephant is definitely a *very* large animal to be eating, and this day is a *very* large day to be conquering. So, the two have that in common." The *largeness* aspect did apply, regardless of the silliness of the turn of phrase. I did not really have the energy or time to be trying to research it. My norm would have been to investigate why someone came up with that phrase, the historical references behind it, the usages throughout history, etc., etc. Yes, that was my norm. If it was not for the day's jam-packed schedule, I would have found out all about this peculiar turn of phrase. My natural sponge-like curiosity to odd tidbits of trivia like that would have suckered me into *ALL* the research. I smiled at this personal awareness – it was the truth. I enjoyed learning all sorts of new things! This was simply not the day to do so, though.

Instead, I delved into my first two meetings that were scheduled before noon. Thankfully, they were remote conference calls. This stage of my day would be in the *easy-peasy* category had it not been for the unfinished report for the 3rd client I had to wrap up. 75% done was not 100% done, *by far*! Even though I was not a huge fan of multi-tasking, it had to be done like that today. My view of multi-tasking was simple: Multi-tasking is just *one* person with *one* brain that's focus is stretched *too far* apart doing *multiple* jobs. The end result of multi-tasking: *One* person doing *multiple* jobs, <u>poorly</u>. Ideally, I preferred single-tasking. The end result of focusing on one single task at a time: *One* person doing *one* job, <u>superbly</u>! My productivity and success were never more stellar than when I was *focused entirely* on *just one thing* – the single task at hand. I was good at the job God had provided for me, as long as I stayed focused, of course.

I could accomplish much in the things that I set my mind to. An onlooker who knows me well could say, "She excels at what she puts her mind to." "Don't we all have that ability, though?" I questioned the thought. The question lingered as I was waiting for the client to return to the line. He was waiting, as well. His secretary was retrieving some forms for him, and he had placed me on hold during the wait. "I have to make another call, do you mind waiting on hold for a bit," he had asked? "I don't mind at all," I responded, "go right ahead!" With the window of opportunity beckoning me, I dove into the other 25% of work that needed to be completed for the 3rd client of the day. The hold music was the typical *make-you-fall-asleep* elevator music. I turned it down to focus more on the work in front of me. So much so, that I almost missed the 1st client's return to the call! Thankfully, I found the mute button after the second request of, "Are you still on the line?" In relief, I thought to myself, "Man, that was close! An unhappy customer, you will not be today, sir!"

It was not much longer before I was on the phone with the 2nd client. The 1st client's conference was wrapped up, all nice and neat with a bow, like a present under a Christmas tree. Time slot 2 was well underway. Much to my surprise, I found myself waiting on hold again! "Thank You, Lord! Maybe I can get this done!" I said. With only a few more items left to the 100% goal for client number

3, I finished it up just in time for client number 2 to come back on the line. "Phew!" I thought to myself, "That was close, too!"

She remained on the line for the next 20 minutes to discuss the matters that were important to her business and how she felt I could assist her with those goals. I listened attentively. My mind was *in-the-zone*. My replies went like this: *"Yes, Ma'am."*... *"That's Right, I agree."*... *"I like that idea, but what if you did this, too?"*... *"No, Ma'am."*... *"What date would you like to have this accomplished?"*... *"Who did you have in mind for this project?"*... *"This is what I am hearing from what you are saying. Is that correct?"* Repeating, clarifying, reasoning, brainstorming, candid feedback, respect, consideration of her values, and addressing the business needs… It was a *home-run* kind of day, and it was not even noon yet! I was excited to be helping in these new steps for both client number 1 and client number 2. Both conversations went very well and were *exactly* what I expected from two *very* independent, improvement-driven entrepreneurs. *"Better is the ending,"* I said with a sigh. "Yes, it is!" I agreed. I, of course, had simply paraphrased the passage of scripture that had come to my heart. I felt a great sense of completion from the work I had completed. The achievement brought about a good feeling. I smiled as I thought about the passage. Solomon was contrasting wisdom and folly in Chapter 7 of Ecclesiastes. He wrote, *"the end of a matter is better than its beginning; patience of spirit is better than haughtiness of spirit."* I replied, "Yes. Patience is better, indeed!"

The majority of my clients had similar stories of success to tell, but these two were a few of my favorites to work with. They had both started from nothing: Scratch and more scratch. They built the foundations of these two exceptionally successful companies from a zero beginning point. Yet, they had grown tremendously! They achieved this with transparency and truth *every step of the way*. That, in and of itself, had drawn me to say, "Yes," and take them on as clients. There was no deceit or manipulation in their business tactics. Their moral compasses were pointed directly North, and they were both ethical in their focus. I admired their passion and zeal for what they did.

I did not desire to do what they did, of course, but I did appreciate the genuine *behind-the-scenes* goals for their individual companies. They lived-to-serve and worked-to-live. Thinking about this, I pulled up the scripture on my computer. I knew that in the book of Hebrews, the writer discusses working unto others. I found it in Chapter 6. *"For God is not unjust so as to forget your work and the love which you have shown toward His name, in having ministered and in still ministering to the saints. And we desire that each one of you show the same diligence so as to realize the full assurance of hope until the end, so that you will not be sluggish, but imitators of those who through faith and patience inherit the promises."* I considered this as it pertained to my two favorite clients. I thought to myself, "Well, neither of those two can be counted as *sluggish*, for sure! They are quite *diligent* in all that they work toward. They definitely are *ministering* on the daily!" I thought about it for just a moment longer, then concluded, "Yes, they both have such good hearts behind what they do!"

The Holy Spirit added another scripture, saying, "They also demonstrate servanthood well. Remember in 1st Samuel, it is written, *Only fear the Lord and serve Him in truth with all your heart; for consider what great things He has done for you.* In more than one place, God inspired the writers to direct His children to *continue to acknowledge Him and do unto Him in all they do*. That is what you are called to do just as they were called to do." Yes, my two fav clients had good hearts behind it all. Their actions spoke for themselves. "I am grateful for these divine appointments in the work I put my hands to, Lord," I acknowledged.

Their motivations came to the forefront of my mind with that reminder. I said, "The *why* behind it all is what I value about these two clients." Yes, they made money. As I mentioned, these two clients both ran very successful companies. Yet, that was not their focus – it was just a happy byproduct. They cared about having satisfied customers. They also understood that their employees and other businesses were customers, too. As such, they were successful at achieving big-picture, quality customer service on all levels. This, in turn, helped their companies thrive financially. Yet, the investment of their time to honestly care for all types of customers meant more than the money. They were investing in sharing the Word of God with others. To them that was far more important than their checkbook and bottom line. God's Word is the bottom line that they stand on. Thinking about this again, I said, "Thank You, Lord."

Considering the two clients further, I agreed with myself, "No. It is not really the profitability that draws me to them, although they are quite profitable! It is the *motivations behind* the businesses." Each, by their own merit, had end goals that had nothing to do with profitability, in the worldly sense. They were *storing treasures up in heaven* with the real work that they did. The principal business effort of each was purely in secular industries. That was true. However, the real effort in their endeavors was what sold me on bringing them on as clients. They had enormous

> "The afflicted will eat & be satisfied; those who seek Him will praise the Lord. Let your heart live forever!"
> King David

goals for servanthood! There were many facets of serving that each company was grounded in. That work is what had drawn me in, 100%! "Man, oh, man! It is awesome to see!" I exclaimed in my reflection.

Both companies actually paid their employees to go out into the community to help and serve. Their employees serve *while* on the job! This isn't just once or twice a year, though. It's almost every single week! In addition to this, the two companies also give back in monetary contributions. Both companies gave above 30% of all their profits each month to local community projects. "They do so, joyfully, too, just as scripture instructs to do," I added. I continued, saying, "Yes, that's right! Paul tells the Corinthians, *Now this I say, he who sows sparingly will also reap sparingly, and he who sows bountifully will also reap bountifully. Each one must do just as he has purposed in his heart, not grudgingly or under compulsion, for God loves a cheerful giver."* They definitely gave *cheerfully* and *bountifully*!

That wasn't the only way they were committed to giving, though. No, it didn't stop there. There were *many, many, many* instances where they went beyond that! When they heard about a need in the communities around their businesses, both clients would stop, drop, and roll. They would: *Stop* what they were doing, *Drop* the funds necessary to help, and *Roll* out the reinforcements of on-the-clock manpower. "It is so great to help these clients with their businesses!" I said, with great joy. They didn't do it for personal gain or personal glory. In fact, not many people even knew about the servant side of the work. Unless they asked or were on the receiving end, most were none the wiser! Yes, they were *storing treasures in heaven*! With this thought, my excitement grew. I said, "It's just like it teaches in Your Word, Lord! *Do not let your left hand know what your right hand is doing so that your giving will be in secret, and your Father who sees what is done in secret will reward you.* I know the rewards they are storing up are great, indeed! Thank You for providing this example of *charity* through working with them, God!"

I just knew that the better they did with their routine, day-to-day operations, the more the community and people benefited. Yes, I knew that the better they did, the more people would hear God's Word from their lips and those of their employees. That was my role in their work: To help them *be more* successful so they could *help more* of the community for the glory of God. "I am very thankful to help those who help others, Lord. Especially when their number one priority in that help is to share the Gospel. Look at all the Bibles they dispersed just last week! It's awesome! What about the Christian music concerts and the Biblical teaching seminars and the..." I continued to list the lengthy amount of outreach events that they did just this last few months.

I thought about those events that I had attended and how these two business owners were always on-site, shaking hands, and speaking God's Word with others. I had walked up on one of them, once, and she was in mid-sentence. She had been visiting with a young woman who had two little children in tow. I approached to say hello but did not want to interrupt. So, I stood to the side, patiently waiting for her to finish her conversation with the lady. She asked the woman simply, "Has anyone ever told you about Jesus?" That young woman went from having this look of resilience, to utter brokenness. Tears began to fall upon her youthful cheeks. Her heart had been breaking, and no one could tell. No one except God working through those hearts like that of my God-fearing client that is! Right then and there, she invited the young woman to go sit down and visit more about Jesus. I could hear the woman now, as I

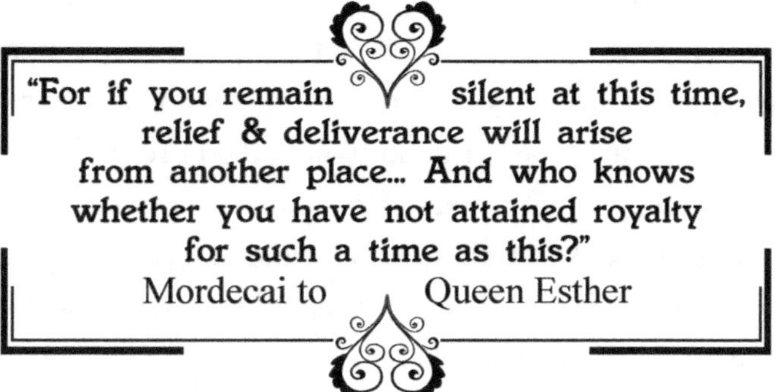

recalled this memory, saying, "I cannot thank you enough! I was at my wit's end. You don't know how much your kindness has meant to me. Thank you, thank you, thank you!"

My client wasn't there for publicity or appearance's sake. She wasn't there to get her name out there or network with people for more business. She was there to share Jesus. Later that afternoon, when I did finally have the opportunity to visit with her, she had said with great joy, "I am so glad you are here! Another sister-in-Christ is needed, for sure! God has brought so many people here that do not know Jesus! I have been so busy sharing Jesus and praying with people to accept Him into their hearts! I haven't even had time to eat yet! Wanna go grab a bite, real quick? Maybe someone else will be at the table, too!" Her brilliant smile and fire in her eyes were enough to get an in-kind, passionate commitment out of me! Just as she had hoped, we ended up praying together and leading four other young ladies to Jesus, right there at that long table over a quick bite! Thinking about it now, I once again gratefully said, "It was glorious for You, God! It always is with those two! They talk about You far more than they ever talk about their business. And yet, with every event, You provide them with more and more customers! Thank

You for letting me be part of it. Thank You for the opportunity, Lord."

Smiling at the fondness of this all, I gathered the rest of the paperwork for my 3rd client. I had a 45-minute drive ahead of me and *no clue* of what traffic awaited me, mid-day, or the waiting that may be ahead. My mind was still dwelling upon my favorite clients. I thought to myself, "Hands and feet working together in unity, that is what my role in partnering with these two clients reminds me of." We were working together in unity unto the Lord. As I walked out the door, the Holy Spirit brought another scripture to the forefront of my thoughts. He said, "Before you leave, look at Ephesians 4." I didn't have my Bible, so I pulled it up through the browser on my phone. He pointed out a few verses, confirming with a response as I read, saying, "that one, that one, and that one right there." He pointed out:

Therefore I, the prisoner of the Lord, implore you to walk in a manner worthy of the calling with which you have been called, with all humility and gentleness, with patience, showing tolerance for one another in love, being diligent to preserve the unity of the Spirit in the bond of peace. There is one body and one Spirit, just as also you were called in one hope of your calling; one Lord, one faith, one baptism, one God and Father of all who is over all and through all and in all.

...for the equipping of the saints for the work of service, to the building up of the body of Christ; until we all attain to the unity of the faith, and of the knowledge of the Son of God, to a mature man, to the measure of the stature which belongs to the fullness of Christ.

As a result, we are no longer to be children, tossed here and there by waves and carried about by every wind of doctrine, by the trickery of men, by craftiness in deceitful scheming; but speaking the truth in love, we are to grow up in all aspects into Him who is the head, even Christ, from whom the whole body, being fitted and held together by what every joint supplies, according to the proper working of each individual part, causes the growth of the body for the building up of itself in love.

The passages were about maintaining *unity* to do the work that God's children are called to do - not as individuals, alone, but as a whole team - as a body, together, as one. As I began to drive, I thought about the waiting I had endured over the last 6 months. The day, itself, also had a theme of *waiting* that had developed. I was curious about what such an ever-present topic would mean for the remainder. The drive provided plenty of time to dwell on the subject of waiting. "I spent a ridiculous amount of time waiting on that package!" I stated in thought to myself. The impatience came suddenly, flashing into my mind like a neon sign. "Let it go already!" I told my self-focused flesh sharply. Waiting was not near as difficult as it once was, but I still had a max capacity that would boil over from time to time.

My tipping point on *this* particular waiting period for *this* package was around day 20 of month 5! "Month 5! Who waits 5 months for the delivery of something!?" I asked out loud, incredulously. "Enough already!" I scolded the incoming thoughts of temptation to be impatient that were *oh-so-appealing* to my flesh. If it had not been for the fact it was my anniversary gift to my husband, I probably would have stayed in that irritated mind-set a bit longer. The reason behind the package was more important than enduring the waiting I went through to get it, for sure! Love is the best reason to wait! "Things happen that are out of my control. God is the one who is in control of all things. He dictates the very existence of that which makes up the atoms of the entire universe, the very dust and particles that make-up all the stars in the sky – yet, He knows every single one of them by name!" I followed up the scolding with much fortitude in my words. "I don't see the big picture from His view. Never have, never will. No, not until He calls me home will I see the big picture. I rest in the peace of that fact. I don't need to know every last detail of every single thing going on in the universe, because I know that God does. I know that He knows best. Impatience, you have no place here and must leave – in the name of Jesus depart from me. Now," I boldly proclaimed.

> **"Adversity is the diamond dust heaven polishes its jewels with."**
> Robert Leighton

I felt like a principal who just fired an uncaring, ill-equipped substitute teacher. First, was the scolding. Then, came an attempt to reason and educate the substitute on the importance of knowing. *What you are doing* and *Why you are doing it* were important, indeed! Finally, after a blatant disregard for care was demonstrated, and no evidence of desiring to change for the better was seen, the *unqualified-to-work-as-a-teacher* substitute was told to get out. I said, "I am what I feed myself, and I am not about to feed my mind and heart the substitute teacher of impatience! No sirree, or ma'am! Not today! My feeding for my heart and mind is coming from *The Real Teacher* today! Yep!" Seldom were the times that impatience would be invited in for dinner and win, nowadays. However, I do still remember the days when that was not the case.

As I pulled up to the stop sign before rolling into town, I asked myself, "Remember those times of impatience with driving? There were three speeding tickets in a row!? They were all within a couple of months!" I shook my head at this *out-of-the-blue* thought, then questioned, "...or was it all in <u>one</u> month!!??" I couldn't remember the time frame, exactly, but I *did* remember the tickets. I was a bit shocked and did not expect this memory today while waiting at a stop sign. "*Not once* did the officer let me off with a warning. I was held accountable - to the letter of the law, every time," I said. Of course, my teenage view on it was: *that is so unfair!* After all, there were plenty of people that drove faster than the speed limit signs. They would zoom by or even creep on by, ...but they *still would* pass me by when I drove within the speed limit. It was the majority of people, too. So, of course, since everyone was doing it – it was totally unfair that I would get busted, and they got off the hook like that, all the time! "It wasn't, though. It was exactly fair," I said in my stern correction tone.

Regardless of what others did or did not do, I had disregarded the speed limit signs. I disobeyed the law of the land and received the just consequences that came as a result of my disobedience. The Holy Spirit brought to my remembrance the passage in Romans of obeying authority. *Every person is to be in subjection to the governing authorities. For there is no authority except from God, and those which exist are established by God. Therefore whoever resists authority has opposed the ordinance of God; and they who have opposed will receive condemnation upon themselves.* It was stern but true. Yes, it would have been the same if I was only driving 5 mph over the limit. It would *still* be me choosing to operate my vehicle at a speed that was over the speed limit and disobeying a very clearly stated law.

With a shake of my head, I responded to myself, slightly irritated, "Oh, yes! I remember. It was within one month!" It was the summer after I turned 16. I was fresh out of school for the break. It was a 45-minute drive to the closest town that had actual job openings. Monday through Friday, I was driving back and forth to my new summer job. Keep in mind, I was also a teenager who tended to lean toward procrastination when getting out the door on time. After all, I had to look the part. It was a *welcome face* position at my uncle's law office. A receptionist to a law firm had to fix her hair and dress presentably, *at the very least*. That took a bit of time, given my other teenage tendency to second-guess what I had done with said hair, outfit, or both!

Just then, I saw a speed limit sign and looked down at my speedometer to double-check my speed. With all this talk about old speeding tickets, I was keenly focused and aware of my responsibility to obey the law on my drive this afternoon. My mind went back to those incidences. I had a reason behind every single one of them…well, I had an *excusing* reason at the time. Each choice to speed was justified with one of those reasons. I remembered saying, *"That ridiculous train! I have to get there, on time, or I will be fired, for sure! I was just blowing off steam! … That stupid clock didn't go off, and now I'm leaving late!… I can't believe that guy just cut me off! I'll show him! Watch this!"* I was busted every… single… time. What did all three of those offenses have in common: *Waiting.* I did not know how to be patient and wait. I did not know how to wait for the emotions to level out and respond, instead of reply with a knee-jerk reaction. So, within a month, I had received 3 separate speeding tickets.

A month later, I found myself standing in front of a judge in the local county courthouse. I thought to myself as I watched the median lines pass by on the road ahead, "16 years old and without a clue, that was me!" The day before my court appearance, my parents had both advised me concerning my courtroom behavior and conduct when interacting with the Judge. They said, "Keep your mouth shut. *Only* speak when spoken to. The Judge's name is Your Honor. <u>*Do not*</u> call him or her any other name. Eye contact and honesty are *essential.* Make them a requirement in your head, kid. Be accountable & willing to accept the consequences: *Don't try to justify it. Don't give*

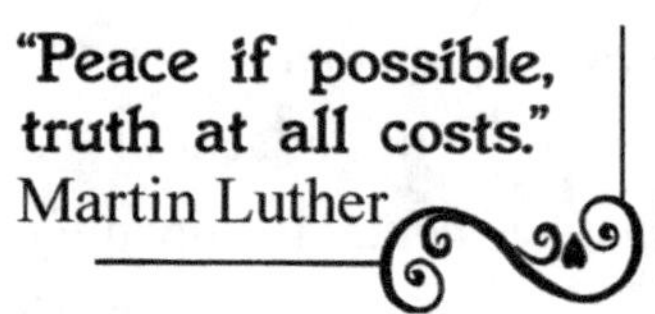

excuses. You did what you did. *Don't lie.* Ask to talk to the District Attorney to discuss probation instead of conviction. Be respectful. Pleading Guilty goes on your record, kid. Don't do that. Plead No Contest and see if they will work with you..."

I was wide-eyed and freaking out! For me, that whole situation was crazy to be in! I was a good kid and focused on doing well...never been in trouble with the law...strived to do well in school with grades...and obeyed those in authority (with a few exceptions to this, of course…I clashed with a few teachers). Yet, here I was, going to go to prison for the rest of my life! At least, that was what the thoughts said. The ones of anxiety and fear that I was dealing with that day and the entire week before that!

I winced at the flood of those feelings that invaded my quiet space in the car. My grip tightened on the steering wheel with every recollection, it seemed! I was on the 2-lane highway going into the city now. A gentleman in the lane next to me sped by. I said, "Man! He is passing me like I am standing still! What in the world?! Lord, please keep that man safe." I watched intently as the back of his taillights disappeared on the stretch of road ahead of me. I very much desired that man to stay safe, for his own well-being and that of everyone else on the road, too!

I shook my head solemnly. The gravity of the situation began weighing heavily upon my heart. I still had plenty of windshield-time with God for *Our Talk* to continue a bit longer. I said to Him, "That is why I don't speed anymore.

Well, I mean, that's why I try super-hard *NOT* to! I would much rather be safe than sorry. Every once in a while, I may get there a bit late, but *at least I get there!* <u>That's what matters</u>: to get there safely." A gentle, "Yes, your safety matters," was whispered to my heart. I smiled from His words. They gave such reassurance! "Besides, this whole driving thing is like riding in a two-ton-speeding bullet," I observed, continuing my review of the subject's seriousness. It was, indeed, a massive bullet that could hurt someone else, or worse, kill someone else! At this thought, my heart sank instantaneously. I concluded in quite the matter-of-fact tone, "I've seen too many wrecks in my lifetime to be the one pulling the trigger like that guy! Not gonna be me! Please be with that man and convict his heart to obey the law and drive safely, as You have done for me, Lord. Keep him an others around him safe, please."

My mind went back to the sound counsel I was given that day at court as a teenager. With a smile, I rhetorically stated, "The Judge was definitely right, wasn't he, Lord?" I picked up my reminiscing, responding to my windshield as if it was talking to me, "That's right, I was at the super anxious part!" That lobby was not pleasant to be in. If anything, the fancy marble tiles, grand entrance, and looming pillars just made it worse. The appearance alone seemed to validate that this was, *100 percent*, no laughing matter! "I am in so much trouble," I remember thinking as I shifted my weight back and forth in the lobby. I had to wait…for what seemed forever, then, too!

Entering the courtroom did not help the feeling go away. Neither did sitting down. The *wait* was still there and the *weight* of the situation, too. They called the names of us *perpetrators* (what I had referred to myself as), alphabetically. Guilt and shame were playing a hand in that *perpetrator* self-imposed labeling bit. Many of those thoughts kind of thoughts were running rampant in my mind throughout the experience. They had plenty of time to run rampant, given my name was toward the end of the alphabet! When *my* name was finally called, my heart jumped up into my throat. I felt a tightening in my esophagus; and, momentarily, freaked out a bit.

"What if I get up there and can't even speak," came the worrying fear. My heart was racing super-fast! "This is crazy! What am I doing here!?" I asked myself with every step to the front. I remember trying to control my heartbeat. How I was going to do so, I didn't know, but I sure was attempting it with all might! I was trying to control it because I feared that they may hear it and accuse me of being *Guilty*, immediately!

I thought to myself as I saw another speed limit sign ahead, "My racing heartbeat would probably have synchronized perfectly with all that racing I was doing on the roads to get those tickets in the first place!" In the middle of it all, I feared that they would, undoubtedly, drag me to a cell, lock the door, and throw away the key if they heard how fast my heart was racing! I had so much anxiety and fear during the proceedings. I felt like I was going in front of a firing squad! All the drama in my mind I was experiencing made it feel like precisely that! "Attacks of the enemy. That's all they were," I acknowledged to myself, in recollection. At that time, I knew of spiritual attacks, but did not know what spiritual attacks were, in operation…let alone that those attacks of fear and anxiety were not *my* truth. They were *thoughts to be taken captive and brought under the obedience of Christ*, but I didn't know that then! All I knew was that they felt *Real*! I was beside myself in a state of worry! I said to the blur of trees along the road, "Yes, that was all I knew…and…it was all truth…in my mind. I had allowed it to convince me that it was *my* truth, although it was not. Thank You, Lord, for providing freedom through Your Son's sacrifice from such attacks!"

The simple reality of the situation was that I could lose my license. If I couldn't make arrangements for a driver, I would lose my job. That was the worst-case scenario on the table. Try telling me that, then, though! "Yeah, I

> *"Amazing Grace!*
> **How sweet the sound**
> **that saved a wretch like me!**
> **I once was lost but now am**
> **found, was blind but now I see."**
> John Newton

wouldn't have listened. I would have *still* been frantically responding in fear and anxiety, just like I was!" I was 16 and had never stepped foot into a courtroom as a convicted lawbreaker with 3 separate offenses…one after the other!!! In that state of mind, I had thought, "I am going to be taken to the cleaners, for sure! I'm gonna be thrown in the slammer for the rest of my life!!! There is going to be some horribly cruel chick that beats me up and steals my lunches every day! I may just starve because of never eating again! If I stand up to her, though, I might get shanked...spend weeks in the infirmary after she beats the living bejeebies outta me. They could throw me in solitary...and I end up alone, making friends with a rat that I start talking to and calling Fred!!!"

My mind was a mess as I sat there waiting in that courtroom for my name to be called. I had sat there and witnessed the honorable Judge dish out sentence after sentence. All of which were unfavorable and full of punishment. He showed *no* mercy...*no grace*!! It sure looked like the book was being thrown at everyone...and that *everyone* included me! Over and over again, he said, "The court finds you Guilty..."

...You will serve 3 months in jail, no chance of parole.
**gavel slam* Next!*
...You will serve 6 months in jail, then probation.
**gavel slam* Next!*
...That's 3 years in jail, don't even think about asking for parole, and don't let me see you back in my courtroom, young man!
**gavel slam* Next!*

I didn't want to go to jail!! By the time it was my turn, fear levels were in the red…full throttle…running wide-open! I paused in my thoughts to focus keenly on the car that had pulled off the road ahead of me. It was about a mile away, but I began signaling to move over to the left lane. After 4 blinks, I was out of the way with *plenty* of distance to spare that gave them *plenty* of space if needed. "Safety first," I said. After passing with no incident, I signaled again and returned safely back to the right lane of this 2-lane highway. I was getting closer to my destination in the city. The drive seemed longer than usual. "It's probably all this reminiscing you are doing," I said, replying to myself. I nodded in agreement. The event was not one of excellence in my lifetime, for sure.

> **"Wisdom is the right use of knowledge. To know is not to be wise. Many men know a great deal, & are all the greater fools for it. There is no fool so great a fool as a knowing fool. But to know how to use knowledge is to have wisdom."**
> Charles Spurgeon

"The look on the Judge's face, though…" I said. "Yep! It was one for the record books! I will never forget that look!" When the Judge finally called my name, he had the *most* severe look on his face that I had *ever seen!* He held me accountable for the choices I had made to break the speed limit law. In my replies, my voice cracked at first. I stumbled over words, left and right! I agreed that I was in the wrong, just as my parents had advised. I knew I had broken the law and regretted doing so tremendously! When it came to pleading time, I went full-on truth! I admitted my ignorance in understanding how a court system worked. I told him I was very sorry and had no intention of doing it again. I told him that my parents had given me advice on what to do, and I had no idea what I was supposed to do. I told him *everything*. A few tears of fear and anxiety accompanied this admittance. I couldn't help it and felt so very embarrassed by their sudden, unexpected appearance. I wiped them away quickly, hoping no one noticed. Thankfully, the Judge didn't see. He was looking down at the paper reports from the officers and all my tickets.

Then it came… the inevitable question: "How do you plead?" I paused and took a deep breath. A ton of words came out, again, fueled by all the nervousness just under the surface. I told him, "I don't know. My parents told me to plead No Contest and ask to speak to the District Attorney to see if there is a way to get on probation or something. I have no idea what I am doing. What do you normally do?" It was then that I saw a softening in that stern stone face of his. If I wasn't in such a state of dismay, I probably would have noticed the smile that crept up in the corner of his eyes. His crow's feet were only *slightly* visible, but they were there. "Young lady. Do you plan on doing this again? I take speeding quite seriously, and you have 3 tickets here. This is not a light thing you have done. Speeding can lead to very terrible wrecks and injuries, even death," he said. His words of chastisement

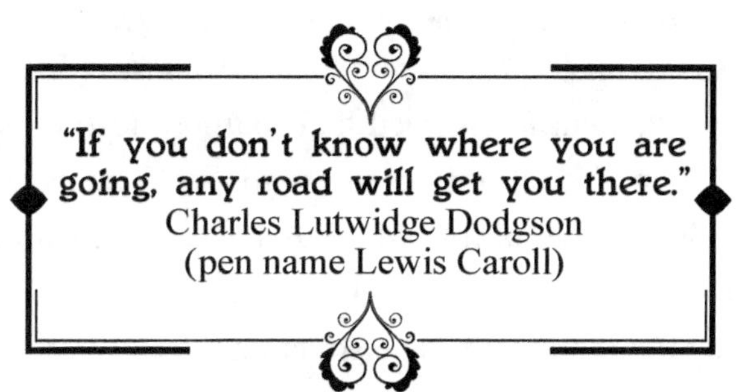

continued for a few more minutes. They were stern, sharp, and direct, but they were true and unwavering. The tick of the clock on the wall was deafening. It was a lecture of correction and advice that I deserved, but it made the waiting for the verdict even longer! Scripture came to the forefront, interrupting my thoughts as I turned the steering slightly. I guided the car smoothly around the corner as His Spirit reminded me of another truth. He said, "the Hebrew author writes, *All discipline for the moment seems not to be joyful, but sorrowful; yet to those who have been trained by it, afterwards it yields the peaceful fruit of righteousness.* Look at the fruit it has yielded to be disciplined by the judge concerning your disobedience, child. *The rod and reproof always give wisdom.* You will do well to remember this." I sighed and echoed my agreement, "Yes, Lord. I will do well to remember this."

Even at my youthfully ignorant age, I knew that I needed to hear the weight of every word of his lecture if I was going to succeed at adjusting the behavior. I didn't want to be in that courtroom again, EVER! It was wisdom from someone who knew every letter of the law. I took every word to heart as he explained the seriousness of the responsibilities I had to others and myself while driving a car.

"Proverbs is full of passages like this," I said to myself. My eyes were keenly alert to the lines on the road as I considered the Word that came to mind. I had recently delved into studying further about *Discipline* after a conversation with my mother. We had discussed the world's view versus the Bible. They were fresh on my mind - ripe for the picking. *"Foolishness is bound up in the heart of a child; the rod of discipline will remove it far from him."... "Whoever loves discipline loves knowledge, but he who hates reproof is stupid."... and, finally, "He whose ear listens to the life-giving reproof will dwell among the wise. He who neglects discipline despises himself, but he who listens to reproof acquires understanding. The fear of the Lord is the instruction for wisdom, and before honor comes humility."* There were plenty more, but these were sufficient and served their purpose to remind me: *Discipline* is good. It just is. "Thank You, Lord, for this reminder. It helps me to not give in to the temptation to be ungrateful toward the Judge as I remember all he taught me that day. It puts a stop at the door of my heart that does not allow pride in with its temptation to take offense to that wise instruction," I said.

When the Judge finally finished with his sound counsel and orders of correcting my behavior, I said, "Yes, Your Honor. I mean! No, Your Honor! I don't plan on doing this again. And, Yes, I understand, I meant." The heat from my flushed cheeks was avidly warm already. I was johnny-on-the-spot and the center-of-attention to an entire courtroom full of people! The embarrassment of stumbling over my response in front of everyone did not help matters. It deepened the already red coloring that was most assuredly all over my face, by now, and increased my temperature even more! I thought to myself, "He is gonna toss me in and throw away the key!" My head hung low as I waited for his verdict. Remembering my parent's advice to keep eye contact, though, I fought the feelings of disgrace and raised my gaze to meet his. There was a strange, out-of-place softness behind his eyes. He looked at me, looked at the papers, looked across the courtroom, looked back at me, and sighed. Then, he said, "Go see the DA for discussion. Then, come back to me for sentencing." Shocked, but out of knee-jerk obedience, I immediately said, "Yes, Your Honor." I felt a bit of doom and gloom at the last word he said: *Sentencing*. I thought as I walked across the room and through the corridor to the office door that read DISTRICT ATTORNEY, "Yes, I am definitely going to jail! My life is officially over!"

The District Attorney's disposition had been the exact opposite of the Judge's. He was just as firm but had a lightness about him. The conversation was very educational. He explained to me the different options anyone in my situation has. He told me all the rights I had and the ways I could plead. Like the Judge, he invested quite the time in making sure he gave me a further lecture on speeding. I didn't complain, though; I just listened because I knew it was needed. Finally, he gave me an offer. 6 months probationary period with no more speeding tickets; 2 Saturdays spent in a driver's safety course; and I could keep my license. If I did that, the speeding tickets would be removed from my record, and I would be able to put this all behind me. I sat there for a moment in a state of surprise. I didn't question it, though. I felt like I just won a million bucks! "You mean I don't have to go to jail," I remember asking him, incredulously and with a tinge of distress in my voice that was still present. His smile brightened up the room and was associated with an unexpected outburst of laughter. His deep laugh resounded off the silent walls around us. He replied, "No. You are not going to jail today, young lady. We believe in second-chances around here." He paused for a moment and reached in his pocket for a handkerchief. He wiped away the tears that had gently rolled down his cheek from the laughter I had inadvertently triggered. Then, he said, "I don't know if you know this, but God is all about grace and mercy. The Judge and I have been friends for a long time. We agree on this. There is a passage in the Bible that says, *Therefore let us draw near with confidence to the throne of grace, so that we may receive mercy and find grace to help in time of need.* This is grace in your time of need, young lady." I nodded. I didn't really understand what he meant. I just knew they were not going to be throwing me into the slammer that day.

My time on the highway was coming to a close, soon, up ahead. I signaled far in advance that I was getting off the road to anyone that was behind me. "Courtesy and kindness are always important," I said to the passenger seat, pretending to have a traveling companion. "You do have a traveling companion, though," I told myself in the rearview mirror, adding a wink. "Yes. Yes, I do," I replied in complete confidence that God's presence rides shotgun with me every time I travel. I thought about the conversation with the DA. I said, "Yes, but thinking about it now, it was wonderful to go through all that waiting and correction! Look at all you've learned from it!" If he only knew the relief that he had given me that day! "That was an active demonstration of mercy and grace being provided to you," I told myself, again through the rearview. Agreeing, I said, "Yes, that was a *tremendous* amount of mercy and grace given to me, back then - for sure!"

The looming *Sentencing* from the Judge was not anywhere as bad as I thought. He kept it rather simple and to the point and asked the DA if we had worked something out. The DA said, "Yes, here it is, Your Honor." Then, the DA gave him the paper I had signed earlier. The Judge simply read the terms, asked if I understood them, and said, "Do you agree to these terms, young lady?" All I had to do was confirm the agreement. It was that easy! I said, "Yes, Your Honor, I do. Thank you." He had replied, "You're welcome." Then, with a bit of twinkle behind his stern gaze, he added, "Don't let me see you in my courtroom again." I had immediately replied, "Yes, sir...I mean, Your honor."

It was over. They let me leave a free person! No jail time for this young lady! Nope, indeed! Boy, was I ever grateful! "I even had to wait passed that point, though!" I thought to myself with a sudden realization! "Yes, actually, it was 6 months of waiting, then too!" I exclaimed with some humor. Looking at my reflection again, I said to myself, "Come on, that's funny. You know it is." I didn't care too much for the similarity of *waiting* 6 months to get off probation and 6 months of *waiting* on that package, but it was a little funny. It might have been a little too soon, but it was funny, nonetheless. "At least you don't speed race in cars anymore," I told myself, reflecting on the benefits of that process.

It did seem like quite a long time of waiting, especially as a teenager.

Acknowledging my feelings then, I said, "Those months seemed like they lasted ages!" To have something looming over my head for that long wasn't a fun experience, in the least! Fear had been rampant then, as well. I was fearful that someone would find out, and it would cause some horrible results in my job, in my life, etc. "But you learned so much through that experience," I told myself encouragingly. Yes. I had learned quite a bit in the waiting from the consequences for my actions. Daily, I would keep a sharp eye on that speedometer of mine. The required safety classes taught me the difference between defensive and offensive safe driving. They were exceptionally beneficial! "I still use almost all of those lessons today," I admitted in agreement.

I paused to take in the memories of lessons learned through those mistakes. I thought about the mistakes I did not make *because of* those lessons, as well. There had been many, many paths I did not choose because of what I learned from that entire experience. "*Waiting* is worth it," I concluded. "*Waiting* on Me is worth it," came the interjection of the Holy Spirit into my thoughts. "Yes, Lord, it is," I responded in agreement. I was almost to my destination for the 3rd client. I noticed familiar buildings and knew that I was, roughly, about ten minutes out.

> "The flower that follows the sun does so even in cloudy days."
> — Robert Leighton

"Yes, Lord. *Waiting* on You is worth it. What I choose to do *during the waiting* and how I choose to behave *in the waiting* is essential to my walk with You," I solemnly agreed. I knew it to be true. A preacher had told me once that it is essential to still continue, "Praising God through the circumstances and being content in all of them - whether good or bad." Some days are harder than some, but I try to practice contentment daily. "Yes, even when it is hard… practice, I will," I said. With my submission to practice, the Holy Spirit reminded me of a passage in Hebrews. He said, "*Make sure that your character is free from the love of money, being content with what you have; for He Himself has said, "I will never desert you, nor will I ever forsake you," so that we confidently say, "The Lord is my helper, I will not be afraid. What will man do to me?"* I replied, "Yes! What can this world *ever* do to me when my Father watches out for me and is always there for me? Nothing! Absolutely Nothing! Father, You say that You will never, never...No, *Never* leave me! I place my trust in You. Help me to not fear when dire circumstances come at me, especially those that require great endurance and long, long, long waiting periods! Thank You, Lord!"

Intentionally, I took this time to focus on His goodness and provisions after times of waiting. He had not failed me once when I called to Him and turned away from following after my own ways. But Man! That was a hard lesson to learn...that I still learn more about each day! How often, I recalled wanting my own way and taking forever to turn to Him! A preacher on television said, once, "Patience is not something we are born with. It is a part of the fruit of the Spirit. It is not of our own doing, but given to us by the Holy Spirit, as a gift to operate in." Thinking about that teaching now, I asked, "Lord, is it the same as faith? Your Word says that my faith is perfected in Jesus Christ. It says that He is, also, the author of *that very same* faith. The fruit of the Spirit is all the same. I learn it and grow in it *by* walking *in* it <u>with You,</u> Lord. It stands to reason, then, that I could easily say that patience is perfected in You, also. After all, You are the author of *all* the parts of the fruit of the Spirit. You put new desires in my heart that line up with walking in them, in all fullness," I said to Him. A smile came upon my lips. It was all truth. I knew it to be true in the depths of my soul. In my own life, I could *quite easily* see the distinct difference between walking *with* Him and walking *without* Him; as well as, *abiding in* Him and *not abiding in* Him. "Night and Day difference, they are!" I acknowledged wholeheartedly.

There is much to be learned in the waiting seasons of my life. I know this to be certain with a massive emphasis on the *MUCH*. There is a Lewis Carroll quote that states, "You're not the same as you were before…You were much more …muchier…you've lost your muchness." My heart pondered this as I pulled in to park my car in front of the client's office. I took a moment to pray to God. "I never want to lose this *Muchness* that I have found in You, Lord! In You, I am much more…*muchier*…that is, indeed, true! Lord, help me to be ok *in the waiting*. Thank You for giving me the strength I need to endure *through the waiting*, providing the peace *while I'm waiting*, teaching me to focus on You *as I'm waiting*, and walking with me *before, during,* and *after the waiting*. Help me to *wait* as You *wait*. Help me to demonstrate through my choices and actions, in all I say and think, the fruit of the Spirit in fullness. Draw me near and…and, please, splash me with some water or make a loud noise to get my attention back to You when You call me to wait. You and I both know that temptations try to tempt me to focus on my surroundings. Thank You for showing me the difference between *Your Truth* in the circumstances and the *enemy's lie* about the circumstances. My Faith is in You, Lord! I want to place all of the faith You've given to me completely in You, always! Strengthen My Faith in You and help me fight against this unbelief in these waiting seasons! Help me to understand there IS a reason in the waiting. That reason will always lead me back to You and Your goodness for me. In Jesus' Name. Amen. Love Ya, Dad! Gotta Go!"

With that final statement, I hurried into the client's office – not late… But <u>*right on time*</u>…with 10 minutes to spare! Even after the long wait of the driving, and other clients to tend to, my patience was still intact. "Thank You, Lord, for Your protection and provision for this safe arrival. Thank You for being with me, every inch of the way!" Pausing my thoughts to unzip my binder, I looked up at the receptionist as I waited to be called back. She was very welcoming, but even if she wasn't, I was still going to smile back! With that, I told God in my thoughts one more quick thank you. I thought, "Oh, Yes! And Thank You for showing me how to praise You *in the waiting* and praise You *in everything*, even the bad stuff, Lord... even the bad, You are teaching me how to be content in them all. Thank You!"

<u>MEMORY VERSE</u>

*But do not let this **one fact** escape your notice,*
beloved, that with the Lord
one day is like a thousand years,
and a thousand years like one day.
The Lord is not slow about His promise,
as some count slowness,
but is patient toward you,
not wishing for any to perish
but for all to come to repentance.
2 Peter 3:8-9

Chapter Twelve

Expecting the Unexpected

> **Therefore I urge you, brethren, by
> the mercies of God,**
> *to present your bodies a living
> and holy sacrifice, acceptable to God,
> which is your spiritual service of worship.
> And do not be conformed to this world,
> but be transformed by the renewing of your mind,*
> **so that you may prove what the will of God is,
> that which is good and acceptable and perfect.**
> *For through the grace given to me I say to
> everyone among you not to think more highly
> of himself than he ought to think; but to think
> so as to have sound judgment, as God has
> allotted to each a measure of faith.*
> Romans 12:1-3

I woke up on a Friday to something strange and unexpected. It caught everyone by complete surprise! No one predicted it, and then, BAM!! Here it came, right out of left-field! News crews were out, in full force, all over the state! It was crazy to witness! Each station was trying to get the best perspective on the situation and communicate it to the residents. Some might say it put people at ease to hear the news folks covering it as detailed as they did. That was us – we were the 'people' in that. For my family, it sure did add ease to the situation! To see our local go-to guru on the matter providing constant updates brought quite the relief! It was nice to be *in the know* in situations like this. Everyone in the state was impacted, and our local news guy and his team were doing their part, just like the other stations, to ensure the public knew what was going on. At first, there were *definitely* a few emotions, to say the least, that the local community had experienced because of it. Shock - was a big one! Panic – another. Amazement - a close tie. Saturday and Sunday, it continued to happen. By Monday, it seemed there was no end in sight! This morning, as I stood at the window, I looked outside in wonder. There had already been so many days and days of this! Surely, it would end soon, right?!

"How could there possibly be this much?! And, since when does it *snow* like this…and… in the Spring, no less!?! Tornado season just recently settled down! Besides, we haven't even had snow *like this* during the Winter season in my lifetime! A Blizzard?! Here?!?!" I thought. I was amazed. My thoughts in the silence of the early morning were interrupted by our local and trusted weather meteorologist's voice. I turned to watch the television and see what the most recent news was on this crazy, unexpected, and unpredicted white, fluffy stuff covering *everything*! Reluctantly, he said, "I know it's been quite rough out there. Everyone is trying to get a handle on how long this will last. I still have the same to report, though: Nothing new yet. The high for today will still be low, folks. The freezing temperatures we are in are estimated to stay that way for the next few days…Snow drifts have reached heights of 10 feet or more in some areas. If you must go outside, please be careful out there…." He continued covering the forecast and wind patterns that carried in even more snow. Then, he said, "For all of you that planned to plant gardens for this season and are still germinating indoors – my wife agrees that you all caught a break this year. Thank you for your time. Now, back to your regularly scheduled program. We will keep you up-to-date as the day goes on." It was an apparent attempt at cheering up his audience from all the unwanted *more snow* he just reported on, but it seemed to soften the blow a bit.

I walked over to the kitchen in disappointment. I had hoped to hear that this was going away soon. "Apparently, our meteorologist begs to differ," I thought. I had shifted all my clients to remote video conferences because of all this mess. It was the next best thing to being there, in person. "Well, frankly, it was the *only* next thing," I admitted. There was *no way* we were getting out in this storm! The state had declared this to be an emergency. This morning, our governor had announced the start of negotiations for federal disaster funds, as well. It was *that* bad! My husband agreed, saying, "There are a lot of farmers and ranchers that are going to be *hit hard* by this snow. You know the guy 5 places down that has all that pastureland for crops…well, he was planting just a few weeks ago! The weather report said the ground temps have dropped below freezing again. I'm not a farmer, but that doesn't sound like something a seed is going to like!" I nodded my head at his observation. Regardless of the accuracy of his conclusion, he was right.

On the first day of the snowfall, there were many interviews. One of the news channels had one with a representative from the Department of Agriculture. She had warned that farmers and ranchers were going to be in the crosshairs of this shift to colder temps. She had said, "We have to just hope for the best…and pray that God takes care of it." That was the main reason I recalled her interview. She had pointed to God in the middle of all this. It was good to hear from someone in the public eye. I appreciated it and agreed with her on behalf

> "Everything that is done in this world is done by hope."
> Martin Luther

of those that were in the middle of, possibly, having their livelihood taken away by unexpected weather. "You just never know, do you?! It can happen so quickly! Everything can get wiped out in a matter of a few days, like this…or worse…in just a moment!"

My heart ached for those landowners who were struggling all over the state. Other people were struggling, as well. Missing person reports were coming in, consistently, in the nightly news. People venturing out in this stuff, *thinking* that they could make it to wherever they *thought* they needed to go, and finding themselves stranded for hours in their car and covered in thick snow!!! Volunteer firefighters, Department of Transportation road crews, county and state workers, unpaid reserve officers, off-duty police, search-and-rescue personnel, emergency responders, and good, ole-fashioned community hand-lifters were out trying to find these silly people. The goal: to return them safely home. I *was not* about to be one of them! The state had really pulled together to try to battle through this unexpected storm and help one another. It brought joy and sadness to my heart. There was a sense of joy to see *that they had* risen above *in Unity.* However, there was also a sadness *that they had to* rise above because of the situation. I prayed for those folks, too.

With the venturing out, came many injuries from car accidents. There was also the chance of illness… and, even, death! The report had said that a young man died because of a choice to drive in the weather. He took a turn too fast. Yes, that is all it took! I prayed for all the families that were impacted by all of it. Nope! There's *no way* I was about to get out and drive in this nonsense! Work *was not* that important to me. My husband agreed. "We are not getting out in this, Babe. It's not safe," He told me firmly when Monday had shown no letting up of the blaring flurries of snow coming down. Unbeknownst to him, I had already come to that conclusion early on. I was more determined now, especially after all the incidents that the news had reported on. "Why even chance it?" I had thought. He had also arranged to work remotely. After a brief call with the owner of the company that he worked for, he switched to working from home until this snow mess cleared up. The owner had agreed with my husband's point. He told him, "Sir, I can easily *still* do the majority of my office work without coming into the actual office. Besides, *no one* in this industry is going to be doing outside work in this mess! No one." It didn't take much convincing. They were both on the same page within a few minutes. After-all, this storm was in the category of unprecedented kind of stuff for our state! No one was prepared. Only a handful knew what to do, and they were doing all they could.

There was definitely a shortage of manpower in the **know-how** department. That, of course, had led to many rescue folks going without any rest! They were the ones who knew how to help, but that group was a small one! They were pushing through this for the good of the public, in its time of need. Some of those guys were going on 1-2 hours of sleep - if that! A reporter had interviewed a group of our local firemen yesterday. The 5 men looked ragged and worn-out. The chief had looked directly into the camera and said with a certain conviction, "It's our job. We will continue to be out as long as we are

> **"Not in achievement, but in endurance, of the human soul, does it show its divine grandeur & its alliance with the infinite."**
> Edwin Hubbel Chapin

needed." His team had silently agreed, nodding whole-heartedly. I could see the fire in their eyes to persevere through to the end. It brought a sense of pride in our community to my heart. My husband was watching the report with me and said, "That's awesome! Those guys are just awesome!" I agreed. They were. They had the grit to keep going. It was inspiring! Thinking back to the interview this morning, I said, "4 days up with very little sleep…Man, they are dedicated to the cause, for sure! God, continue to be with them!"

I walked over to the back door and grabbed my boots to put them on. The aroma of coffee was beginning to saturate the kitchen. My husband and daughter would be up soon. The fire was dwindling down in the fireplace. The pile of wood was tall just the day before, but, now, it only had a few, small logs left. "Time to restock," I said. I pulled on my boots and grabbed my heavy winter coat and work gloves. Zipped up and ready to go, I opened the door. "Brace for impact!" I said, trying to find humor in the dread of going outside. As anticipated, a blast of cold wind hit me suddenly. Although I thought I was prepared for it, I wasn't. I jumped up and down, stomping my feet in an attempt to make my body create a heat shield. In my mind, it could've worked...*ya know*...if I was a cartoon character. It was to no avail, though! "It's freezing cold out here! How can anyone be out in this today!?" I asked to the air. The outdoor thermometer had icicles hanging from it, but I could still see the reading. "15 degrees!?! Man, the windchill with this wind blowing like it is has got to be *at least* 10 if not 15 degrees *below* that!" I exclaimed. "Zero degrees!??! Oh, my goodness!!" I said, incredulously. I hurriedly gathered an arm full of logs and quickly made my way back inside. "Oh, thank God!" I praised aloud. I bent down to place the logs in the pile neatly.

As I raised up, I looked over to the door with great reluctance. Yes, I was *foot-dragging*, as my grandfather used to say. "Lord, I *really* don't want to do this...3 more times," I admitted. I knew someone had to, and I did not want my husband or daughter out in it...so, I went outside...again. However, it felt colder this time than it did the first! "What?! Did you decide to drop a few degrees while I was inside?!" I told the air. My hands had begun to shake with the shivers as I placed the logs in my arms as quickly as I could manage. Again, I hurried back in to find the warmth that was *most definitely NOT* to be found outside! I added to the pile and stepped back. I evaluated the size of the new stack as I glanced back and forth to the door, doing the math. "Ok, so...over the last two days, we've used roughly that much wood...so...for just one day ...we will use..." my math added up far too quickly! "Ah, man!! We need more than this." I concluded with a whine. "Lord, I *really, really* don't want to do this...again," I stated. Again, I reminded myself that I didn't want my husband or daughter out in this. I'd rather it be me. I could handle it.

It took a minute, but I managed to pump myself back up enough to walk out that door. I was in full regret mode the moment I crossed the threshold. "What is your problem?!?!" I exclaimed. "I was only in there a few minutes, at best! And…noooooooowwww…you decide to kick up the speed! What did I ever do to you?! Here I am, minding my own business, just trying to get wood piled up for my family, and you want to blow harder – making it even colder?!?! Why?!" I muttered to the harsh wind as I collected more wood. Debating the wind seemed to help me get through the situation. Although, the real culprit wasn't the wind. I was really battling myself. One part of me wanted to stay comfortable. The other part of me wanted to do what was right and good for my family. I was in the middle of a battle between self-servanthood and self-sacrifice. Self-sacrifice was winning, but self-servanthood was *definitely not* happy about it. Again, I hurried back into the warmth.

I stood there looking at the stack of wood that I had accumulated after the 3rd trip. I knew there was one more trip needed. "Let's get this over with," I said with a bit of an attitude. I turned to walk toward the door. "How about we change that attitude, first, kiddo," the Holy Spirit said. "But God, I don't wanna! *This sucks*! Can You, at least, calm the wind down this time?!" I begged. Then, came the simple question, "What does my Word say?" I was not happy at all. I did not want to reply… *or comply*, for that matter!

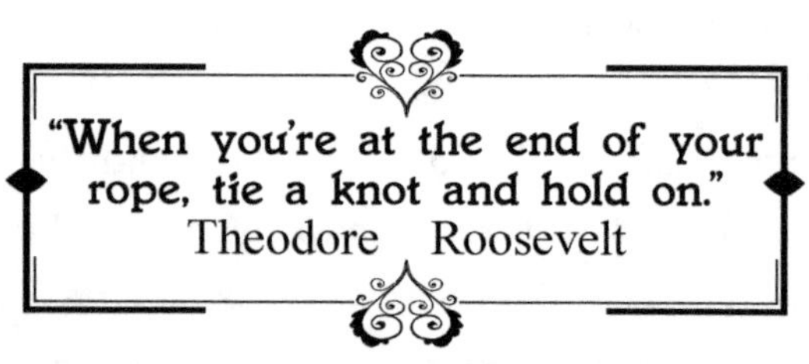

I was still cold from being outside in the freezing air. My fingers tingled, my irritation level was raised, and I had just jammed my toe as I turned to walk away from that silly wood holder! I was forcing myself to go out and be uncomfortable for the sake of others. I definitely was not doing it joyfully, as a cheerful giver would do. Yes, I can assure you; I was acting like a bit of a child. Throwing a fit in that moment was a description that fit me well! I didn't want to think about the Word. As if I was some whipped little dog, I answered, "I know. I know. But…" I didn't finish the statement. I knew better than to rebel. With a sigh, I let the words fade into the background. It was no use arguing with Him. He was right. I needed to fix my attitude and do this work correctly.

I let out a sigh in my physical attempts to shake off the leach of negativity and grumbling that I had allowed to take hold of me so early this morning. Its development was quick and had only taken 15 minutes to reach the frustrated state it had escalated to. "Yes, God. That did, indeed, escalate quickly! Ok, Lord. Please forgive my selfishness. You are on the throne, still and always. I want Your way, still and always," I acknowledged. "It's Colossians, right?" I asked rhetorically. I knew it was. I pulled my gloves off and grabbed my Bible. I turned to the chapter, now, in humble obedience. "There it is," I said and began reading. *Whatever you do in word or deed, do all in the name of the Lord Jesus, giving thanks through Him to God the Father…* and, again, a few verses after…*Whatever you do, do your work heartily, as for the Lord rather than for men, knowing that from the Lord you will receive the reward of the inheritance. It is the Lord Christ whom you serve.* "Yes," I said, "it is You that I serve." With quite the solemn demeanor, I read the remainder, *"For he who does wrong will receive the consequences of the wrong which he has done, and that without partiality."* With a wince, I sat down at the table, reflecting on this passage.

"There is another in Titus," the Holy Spirit directed. I turned to the book of Titus, meekly. I wasn't quite sure where this one was, so I began by skimming through the first chapter. "Nope. That's not it," I said. "Not it…nope…nope…" I said as I finished my browsing of chapter one. Then, shortly into the second chapter, I saw it. "Aha! There it is!" I said with a smile of accomplishment. It was as if I had found some hidden chest on a treasure hunt. Reading aloud, I said, *"In all things show yourself to be an example of good deeds, with purity in doctrine, dignified, sound in speech which is beyond reproach, so that the opponent will be put to shame, having nothing bad to say about us.*" It was a passage directed at the elder in spirit men to demonstrate to the younger men how they were to be. The guidance was for mentors to follow - those who were spiritually grown up in the Word of God. The Holy Spirit added His sound counsel to further reiterate to me this critical point. "Yes, let it *all* - in *everything* you do - reflect the great love that you have for My Word and the truth found within it. Let it all be *pleasing to the Lord*

> "Do you not know that you are a temple of God and that the Spirit of God dwells in you?"
> Apostle Paul

and demonstrate His great love through you." I nodded in somber agreement.

With a fresh perspective, I put my gloves back on. I had shifted my thoughts back to a higher level of focus on God and His goodness. I could physically feel the weight lift off my shoulders! There was a lightness back in my step. "There it is!! I lost it for a moment, there. Thank You, God, for showing me how to get Your joy back," I said. I was motivated in the Word and encouraged to go forth and conquer this enemy of coldness! Fortitude was going to win this one! Endurance was going to happen! "Stuff just got *real*! It's gonna happen, Captain!" I told the air. Continuing my proclamation as I stepped outside into the battle arena of frigid winds and fleshly tendencies tempting me, I said, "God's got my back, today and always. I will get through and get this done because I do it *for* Him. I walk *with* Him. I choose to do *all* things as *unto* Him as if He is right there beside me! <u>And He is</u>! *Nothing* can stop me with God by my side…most certainly not little, puny cold temperatures. He's got this covered like He does *everything* and *anything* else that comes at me! He calms the winds and silences the storms!" With that last proclamation of faith, I shut the door behind me. I had spoken truth the entire time of collecting wood and didn't even feel the bitterness of the cold! The warmth encircled me, once more, and I found myself to be quite elated! "*Next time*, I am going to talk to You **first**, Lord! It didn't even phase me that last time! How awesome You are!!" I praised aloud. "You never cease to amaze me with Your provision and covering of protection! Even when I *don't* come to You **first**, Lord – You *still* show up! Thank You," I said. "Yes. Just think what it would be like if you *did* come to me **first**," The Counselor replied. "Yes," I agreed, pondering the thought and letting it sink down to my heart, "it makes all the difference."

I had pulled a chair up to the fireplace and sat down to soak up the heat from the reignited flames. "Reignited," I said, "hmmmmm, that's a *good* word!" I had felt like I had just been reignited, too. The dwindling coals were still burning and red when blown on, but they were not ablaze like this fire. At the observation, I stated, "Neither was I, during my little fleshly attitude I was touting around with. I went in and out of the house for firewood with only barely embers of a burning flame for Him." I opened my eyes a little wider as I stared into the flames picturing it all. "Yep! A lump of dwindling coal...that was me in all that," I admitted, shaking my head at myself as I gazed longer into the dancing flames. Having the flames within my heart reignited in His Word was always so fulfilling! It did not disappoint, ever! "I'm not sure why it takes me a bit, sometimes, like this. I don't know why the circumstances hit me so harshly…or why I let them, Lord," I said to Him. "I don't want that to be the case: And, I definitely don't desire that to be the case, at all, God! You know my heart when it comes to You. I love You so very much and desire to please You in all I do *and* think *and* say *and*…well, *everything*. I want nothing more than to have You tell me at the end of my days, *Well, done good and faithful servant*." With this admittance, warm tears began to roll down my cheeks – splashing upon my jeans and leaving evidence of my heart in stains of tears upon the woven fabric.

I imagined what it might look like to come before the Father at the end of my days. I sat there in front of the fire in silence, allowing any walls I had up to simply fall. I desired to be *in* the moment *with* Him. My heart desired this intimacy

> **"But seek first His kingdom and His righteousness, and all these things will be added to you."**
> **Apostle** Matthew

with my Abba, Father, so very much! What would I say? What *could* I say? Would I even be able to say anything *at all*?! Or would I just fall to my knees and be so overwhelmed that all I would be able to do is raise my hands and weep with joy? Would I praise Him, shout for joy, or remain silent in a state of pure reverence and awe? What would that be like? Would I be able to contain my heart as it overflowed in great abundance of the outpouring of love from the nearness of His presence?! He *is* Love. So, what would it be like to be so close to Love itself? What would it feel like to be at the core of Love? What would I even do at the very epicenter of the existence of such Love?! Would He say to me, *"Well done, good and faithful servant?"* I had no idea.

Sitting there, I looked over at the table, then out the window. There was no grass, just white, glistening snow covering any hint of green. With certainty, I knew that my future experience with the Lord was just as hidden as the grass. It was there. It existed, but the mystery had not been revealed yet. Reluctantly but with high expectations, I thought, "Nope. I don't know if He will say that, but I sure want Him to! I'm going to do what I am called to do unto Him and submit to His will for me." I looked around and took in the physical emptiness in the room. The time was passing slowly, but every moment felt like such a huge gift of contents in His presence that it seemed as if I had been there all day! Yet, no one else in the house was even awake. In spite of the coffee floating through the air and the assorted scents of the breakfast I had going on the stove beginning to pour out from the bounds of the kitchen, no one had joined me yet. I glanced at the clock and thought to myself, "Yes, it is still quite early…I haven't been awake that long, myself. I will let them sleep until breakfast is done."

My eyes shifted back to the kitchen table. The Bible was laying there still open from earlier as if it was beckoning me back to it. I rose from the chair to retrieve it. A few steps there and a few steps back, found me right back where I started, in front of the warming fire. I pondered with this simple physical action, "Sometimes, all it takes is a few simple steps to come back to Him to find the warmth again." I answered in full agreement and admission, "Yep! Repentance and turning away... completely...from the world...in my case this morning - that means not choosing my foolish fleshly focus." In an immediate response, I added, "Well, that takes faith, for sure! Hebrews 11 is where all those *by faith* passages are." I flipped the Bible open to the chapter and began reading. "*Now, faith is the assurance of things hoped for, the conviction of things not seen. For by it the men of old gained approval.*" There were many *by faith* passages throughout this particular chapter.

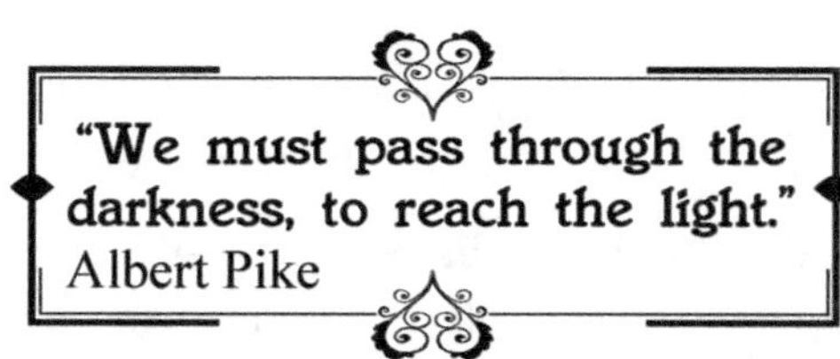

The author of Hebrews had been inspired to write 'example after example' of what was accomplished *by faith*, adding, *"And without faith, it is impossible to please Him, for he who comes to God must believe that He is and that He is a rewarder of those who seek Him."* Reading it now brought a significant warmth to my soul. "Yes, returning to You and Your Word, does indeed bring me warmth, Father!" I agreed with the thoughtful acknowledgement.

Suddenly, a song came to my heart that brought more tears. It was one of those "*undoing of one's self in all reverence and submission*" kind of songs. Kim Walker-Smith is the artist that sings it but also co-wrote the song with 3 other songwriters. It may have taken a team to write such a song, but it successfully spoke to the spirit and heart and soul of me as it came to my remembrance. Its title, *The Throne Room,* is so very fitting for the imagery that occurs when I listen to it. I thought, "God, You call us each to do great things as a part of the body of Christ. You call me to walk in the unity of the Spirit *with* You. You never leave my side, Father. Your love is always there, Lord! This song is a testament to that." I began to sing the words of the song. In broken surrender to Him, I praised His Name and gratefully honored Him with my heart's worship. His wave of wonder and love had washed over me with great force, unexpectedly. Then, slowly, it was drawn back into His ocean, leaving a peaceful stillness that stretched into the horizon. God's peace was immeasurable and unending. His love – the same. The flames of the fire were a direct reflection of the burning flames within me. He had washed over the barely burning embers with the purifying fire of His Word, and I felt renewed.

The comprehension of the vastness of Him cannot be obtained – I know that. He is from everlasting to everlasting! I, for one, am not about to pretend I know how to define that or understand the extent of unendingness. Thinking about His peace and love, I said, "And, yet, in all my silliness, He still gives them both to me. In my unwillingness to cooperate in times like these, He still shows up! He is always there," I said with immense joy resounding in my words. His grace, mercy, & forgiveness – each and all - holding the same characteristics…it was all…just…unfathomable to me! Yet, I was so very grateful for all of it within this moment with Him! "Lord, help me battle this unbelief, and strengthen me in the faith You've given me. Teach me to *walk by faith* in *all* things – not by sight. Help me to look to You **first**, in *all* I do and in *all* I go through," I prayed.

My mind lingered upon the topic at hand. There were more times than I could count that I had allowed my circumstances to dictate how I would walk, talk, think, behave, respond, share, choose, dwell upon, etc.… And *that* is only <u>since</u> I have been saved! I *didn't even include* in my thoughts the time <u>before</u> I was saved! "My oh My! Could you imagine *how many* that would be?!?" I asked myself. Without missing a beat, I replied, "Well, I might not be able to – BUT, I know God can imagine it! He knows everything about me, *even* <u>before</u> I was born! That is *way* <u>before</u> I was saved!" I nodded in full agreement. It is true. He knows me even better than I know myself. There are days I have walked in self-deceit, yet He knew all along the truth-of-the-matter. He knew then and knows now…every last intent and reason why behind all I do and have done. With that, I said, "Thank You, Lord, for holding me accountable with my attitude today! It was wrong and grieved Your Spirit within me. I know. I felt its heaviness upon my soul. Thank You for Your mercy and grace when I stumble and struggle against the flesh like I did this morning."

I continued to dwell on His knowledge of me in detail (mainly for strengthening purposes). I admitted, "Yes, He's seen it all - *every single* trial in my life. He's witnessed *every single* heartache and loss. He's known *every single* thought I've ever held onto. He's observed me at my weakest when I didn't choose to ask Him for His strength…trying to do it all on my own. He's watched me try to find my way and stumble around in the darkness. He's examined the deepest parts of my heart and found some that are still cold or hardened that I haven't faced yet…some I may subconsciously be avoiding even now! Yes! Who knows, but Him!?!" At this train of thought, I said, "Yes, Lord, You see me. You know me. And, You *STILL* call me Yours – You *STILL* love me and meet me where I am. You take my hand and direct my path right back to Yours when I lose sight of the right direction. You continue to pursue me with zealousness abounding! You continue to pursue my heart with great fervor and passion! Where can I begin to

> "I sought the Lord, & He answered me, & delivered me from all my fears…they who seek the Lord shall not be in want of any good thing…Come, you children, listen to me; I will teach you the fear of the Lord…Many are the afflictions of the righteous, but the Lord delivers him out of them all."
> — King David

thank You for Your perseverance and great patience?! I have grown and gained wisdom and knowledge in Your love, Father…but, Oh, *how long* You have waited and endured for me to get to this point?! And *how much more* I *STILL* have to learn about Your love!?! What great forbearance You have shown! What great mercy & grace You have given me! What vast amount of forgiveness you have blessed me with! Where can I begin to praise You for the goodness You've demonstrated to me *every single* moment of my life?!" I asked this in wonder and awe.

There was no answer to how I was supposed to repay His love. There was no explanation to the extent of the reach that His great love had. The amount of debt that was erased on the cross by Jesus that day of Calvary was incomprehensible. It would take an eternity to learn it all! "That is probably why He gave you *eternal* life," I said to myself, jokingly, "It's going to take *that long* to learn all about His love." Of course, this was me just being silly in rhetoric to myself. I knew that there was no such thing as repaying Him for *that kind* of gift. Jesus was the *Ultimate Gift*. My thoughts turned to The gift of Jesus Christ, and I allowed them to stay there, saying, "He gave His life to wipe away the sins of those before me and those to come…*and* me. It was finished in His one act of sacrificial agape love. He chose that path, although not one of us was righteous on our own accord – not one of us did anything to deserve such grace. Even now, there is no way for me to earn such a gift of compassion & mercy. He gave it *to me* and did it *for me* out of pure love. It was according to His will and for His purpose." A fresh stream of tears came from within my grateful heart, up to my eyes, overflowing. They rolled down my cheeks once more. "I cannot begin to thank You enough, Lord, for what You have meant to this heart of mine," I said.

In my state of wonderment and attempted comprehension, I felt a peace within the brokenness and surrender. My gratefulness shined through the tears as a smile graced my lips at the thought of God's great love for me, His daughter. I desired to accept it. Yes, I desired to soak it in as my full truth. I took a moment and claimed it over myself, my husband, my daughter, my family, my friends, and the world in my heart. Thinking back to the joking reference to eternity, I said, "Singing His praises and thanking Him in true worship…every day…for the rest of eternity…well, that sure sounds terrific to me!" I paused, a moment. "After all that You have done for me, God, I will be honored to have the privilege to do so!" I concluded with high expectations partnered with excitement. Scripture came to my heart, and I turned my attention back to the Bible that was laying on my lap. I wanted to see it for myself and speak it, exactly.

The first one was in John 14. I breezed over the chapter, then eagerly returned to the start to soak it in, sincerely. In it, I had speedily read about Jesus speaking to His disciples in an attempt to comfort them with the blessed assurance of the hope to come. "Well, that's precisely what I have been dwelling on this morning," I said with a huge smile of appreciation, "the blessed assurance to come! Amen!" I reread the passage to let it soak in more. He said, *"Do not let your heart be troubled; believe in God, believe also in Me. In My Father's house are many dwelling places; if it were not so, I would have told you; for I go to prepare a place for you. If I go and prepare a place for you, I will come again and receive you to Myself, that where I am, there you may be also. And you know the way where I am going." Thomas said to Him, "Lord, we do not know where You are going, how do we know the way?" Jesus said to him, "I am the way, and the truth, and the life; no one comes to the Father but through Me."* It was so very comforting to my heart.

"Yes, I come to You, Lord, in full surrender and submission…in full gratefulness and wonder of all You have done for me! Thank You for being the middleman to intercede on my behalf to the Father. Thank You for washing away all my sins, Jesus. Thank You for this pure and white-as-snow robe of righteousness that You have given me! Thank You for preparing a place for me…I will continue to strive to do all I can to honor and bring glory to

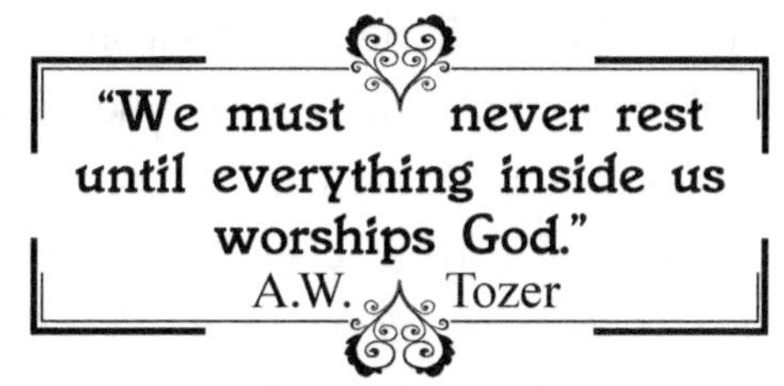

God…not to try to earn anything, but simply because my heart desires to choose You **First**," I said with *much* esteem and love beating in my heart. "I cherish and adore You, Lord!" I admitted before moving to the next passage.

The second scripture the Holy Spirit brought to my remembrance was Psalm 84. His soothing words flowed over me gently, saying, *"For a day in Your courts is better than a thousand outside."* I responded, "Oh, how I love the Psalms – such beautiful, eloquent writing…there is so much passion and heart behind every line of words!" I paused in the jubilant thought. Continuing, I said, "And, to think, they were written for someone to sing!! Wow!" I thought about this briefly and surmised to myself, "Most are for someone to just be still and worship Him, I bet…I do know they were inspired to point to Him in all circumstances...and there are 150 of them!! That's a lot of praise and worship time, right there!" I thought in amazement. "Goodness! What does that say about the time one should allocate to Worship?! Our set-list for the choir isn't *nearly* <u>that many</u>. Look how long it has taken for me to recount those to memory! That's a lot of time!" I said. With a bit of corrective thinking, I added, "Oh, but I am supposed to recount the scriptures to memory and write them on the tablet of my heart! How long those would, surely, take…one hundred and fifty…." I let the thought trail off as I considered all of them. I paused to think about the time that would be needed. Memorizing such a large amount of songs would be a significant investment for sure, but oh so worth it!

Continuing in my thoughts, I replied, "…Now *that* is true Worship, right there! It's a *sacrifice* of my time *to invest* it into building a stronger relationship with the Father through heart tablet writing." I smiled at my humorous wordplay. "heart tablet writing…silly but true." I said to myself, shaking my head. Returning my thoughts to Psalm 84, I opened the pages and found it, quickly enough. The passage began, *How lovely are Your dwelling places, O Lord of hosts! My soul longed and even yearned for the courts of the Lord; my heart and my flesh sing for joy to the living God.* "Yes, yes, it does, God!" I agreed. I read the remainder of the passage. Then, quietly sat there and let the words soak in again. After some time, I looked over at the clock. A half-hour had passed since I had started the coffee. I knew the breakfast I was preparing was almost finished. I stayed a moment longer, though, not desiring to leave this present of time that He had given me - this gift of fellowship. "So magnificent, Lord…You inspired words that are so very beautiful!" I declared, with much certainty and conviction of truth.

I arose from the chair and walked over to the window after checking on the food. I could feel the freezing chill seeping through it, although the windowpane was trying its best to hold it at bay. After all, that was its job – to keep out the cold or hot air. It was responsible for protecting the inside of the house from the outside of the house. "That's what I do, kiddo," the Holy Spirit confirmed to my heart. I thought about the many ways that statement was, indeed, valid! He had protected all of me – my mind, my heart, my soul, and my body. He had shielded me from the enemy and his ploys to attack me in all of those areas, just like the window shielded me from the cold air.

I also thought about the many times I wasn't protected – not because God didn't want to protect me, of course…No. It was more like I didn't desire to be protected by Him. I had rejected His protection. At the thought, I wrinkled my nose a bit. "Yes, it might be a catchy turn of phrase - *rejecting His protection* - maybe even lyrical or poetry-worthy, but I don't like the thought of it at all!" During those times, I didn't want to be *under the shelter of His wings.* I didn't want to go to Him to be *my strong fortress and shield.* I wasn't interested in His protection, on the regular. I wanted His love and all the benefits that came with it – but I wasn't willing to submit or surrender my will and replace it for His good and perfect Will for me as His child. Nope. That required me to put down *my* wants…and, frankly, I didn't want to in those early seasons of my life, even after finding Him. I didn't want to give up the supposed control that I thought I had. After-all, the flesh in me said I could do it on *my* own.

With that truth brought to my memory, I said, "Oh, how stubborn and pig-headed I was! I was under this silly misconception that I learned from the world. I was under the impression that I could control things. Such a joke!" I exclaimed as I recalled the point that I was able to make as I saw through the self-deception that I had fallen into. "I can't control anything, let alone circumstances around - when it rains…or it snows *like this*; people around me and what they do to me or say about me; things that happen to people around me; events that happen in the world…" I let the thoughts trail off. There are too many things to list of ***things I can't control.*** I know that. With a firm resolution, I said, "The only person I can control is myself. That's it. Even that, though, I cannot do alone. No, not on my own! One of the parts of the Fruit of the Spirit *is* Self-Control. It is a gift given from God." I let this sink in for a minute. "*Abide in Me and I in you,*" said the Helper. "Ok, I probably need to pull that one up, too, huh," I responded.

Before I did, though, I turned the stovetop off and set up the counter with hot pads to place the pans and pots on for breakfast. Satisfied that everything was done and ready to go, I sat down one more time. It was in John 15. *"I am the true vine, and My Father is the vinedresser. Every branch in Me that does not bear fruit, He takes away; and every branch that bears fruit, He prunes it so that it may bear more fruit. You are already clean because of the word which I have spoken to you. Abide in Me, and I in you. As the branch cannot bear fruit of itself unless it abides in the vine, so neither can you unless you abide in Me. I am the vine, you are the branches; he who abides in Me and I in him, he bears much fruit, for apart from Me you can do nothing. If anyone does not abide in Me, he is thrown away as a branch and dries up; and they gather them and cast them into the fire, and they are burned. If you abide in Me, and My words abide in you, ask whatever you wish, and it will be done for you. My Father is glorified by this, that you bear much fruit, and so prove to be My disciples. Just as the Father has loved Me, I have also loved you; abide in My love. If you keep My commandments, you will abide in My love; just as I have kept My Father's commandments and abide in His love. These things I have spoken to you so that My joy may be in you, and that your joy may be made full."* "Full," I said, allowing the word to dangle in the air, suspended in the depth of my thoughts. "Yes, *made* full," I replied to myself, emphasizing the word *made*. "I cannot be *made* into anything, let alone the fullness of all God has for me, if I do not surrender and submit to His Will for me in this life," I told myself in edification. I thought about how I had been walking through a renewal and transformation process for many years now. It was challenging and sometimes painful to do, but the goal was right in front of me, identified in that very passage. I heard it again from the Counselor, *"Abide in Me and I in you."* I want to bear fruit abundantly and for His glory. It requires this *Abiding*. With that acknowledgment, I confirmed to myself, "Exactly! That is what I want to do, to honor You, Lord… in all I do – I desire to honor You."

I sat there for another moment, pondering His goodness and my admitted heart's desire. I bowed my head in reverence of His presence and awe of His splendor and majesty. The words of conviction and strength soon followed. I prayed and praised Him. I couldn't help it. The moment called for it to the depths of my soul! "I will set my eyes on You, God, and not my circumstances. I will praise you in the trenches! You will hear my war cry in songs of jubilation and victory that come from my heart! I will speak words of victory over my situations and not allow appearances to deceive me. I will seek Your counsel and listen to what You have to say about the matter in Your Word. I will hold to Your promises and claim Authority against the enemy. I will place my faith in You, for I know hope in You

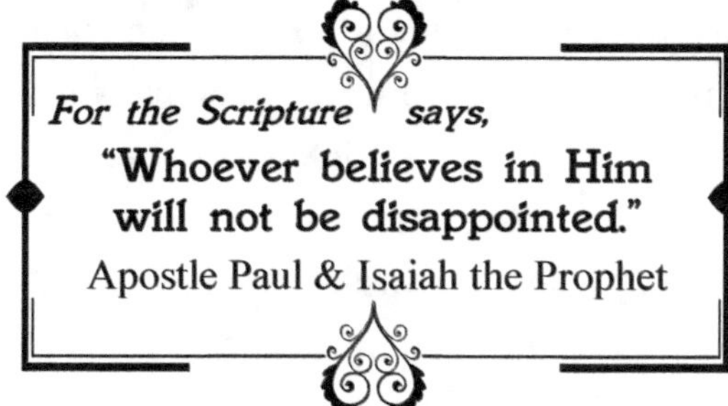

does not disappoint! I will do all of this – with Your help and Your strength, of course…not my own. Thank You for helping me and teaching me how to do so, Lord. And Thank You for Your patience with me as I learn

how to, deeply and daily." I allowed the words I had spoken to edify my soul and strengthen my resolve for a few more silent minutes. Then, I told my Heavenly Father, "I love You! It is in Jesus' name that I come to You, Father. Thank You for all You are *and* all You do *and* all the Love You have for me, as Your daughter. Amen."

I walked to my daughter's bedroom and woke her up for breakfast. Her sleepy smile was enough to tell me she had already caught the smell of coffee in the air. She said tiredly, "Ok mom, it smells good…is the fire going? My blankets are warm. Is it warm in there?" I smiled at her hesitation to venture out of the warmth and comfort of her bed. "Yes, kiddo. The fire has been stoked and restocked. It is warm in here and breakfast is ready to be enjoyed. You ready to get this day started?" She was still smiling as she looked at me, then, took a deep breath before tossing the covers to the side. She said, "Yes, ma'am. What's for breakfast?" I replied teasingly to her inquiry, "I guess you will just have to come and see for yourself. It smells good, though, huh? I've gotta go wake up the other sleepy head in the house. I will be right back. Go ahead and get you a plate, kiddo." With that said, I went to wake up my husband.

His response was quite similar to that of our daughter. He asked, "Did you start the fire, yet, babe?" I replied to his question with the same encouragement to leave the bed as I did with her, saying, "Yes, I did. It has warmed up the kitchen and living room already, and it should fill up the bedrooms and the rest of the house, soon enough." He smiled at my reassurance, but still eased out of the covers as if expecting some unseen cold wind to come rushing in. His caution made me shake my head. It didn't matter how reassuring anyone was, he definitely did not like the cold. Not one bit and it showed! It wasn't that he didn't trust me. Nope. It was simple – he didn't trust the cold. "You are just too silly, sir," I told him with a smile. He looked at me with an innocent, "Who me," written upon his face. "Oh, you know what you are doing, cautiously creeping out of bed like the cold is going to get you if you don't sneak well enough." His laughter and twinkle in his eyes said enough. He was busted and he knew it. He was caught in the act of trying to be a ninja to avoid a non-existent cold attack. There was no use denying it. Changing the subject quickly, he replied, "So, that breakfast sure smells delicious, babe. What did you cook?" I said teasingly back, "Yes, it does smell good. I will tell you like I told our daughter, though, you are just going to have to come see for yourself, sir." He replied with added over-exaggeration and teasing, "Yes, ma'am. I would be glad to do so! Serve me up some of that awesome food. I'm starving!" We shared a smile as we both walked into the kitchen to join our daughter who was waiting patiently with plate in hand. He said, "Let's pray so we can get this day started off right, sound good?" It was a rhetorical question. My daughter and I knew it didn't require an answer. We joined hands, bowed our heads, and prayed together over the day ahead. It was going to be a great day, indeed!

<u>MEMORY VERSE</u>

But God demonstrates His own love toward us,
in that while we were yet sinners,
Christ died for us.
Much more then,
having now been justified by His blood,
we shall be saved from the wrath of God through Him.
For if while we were enemies
we were reconciled to God through the death of His Son,
much more, having been reconciled,
we shall be saved by His life.
And not only this,
ut we also exult in God through our Lord Jesus Christ,
through whom we have now received the reconciliation.
Romans 5:8-11

Chapter Thirteen
Part One

New Beginnings:
Sound Counsel Needed

**The Lord is near to the brokenhearted
and saves those who are crushed in spirit.**
Psalm 34:18

**He heals the brokenhearted
and binds up their wounds.**
Psalm 147:3

Yesterday, I didn't have any meetings. Most of the clients that I had spoken with wanted to reschedule until after the Blizzard had passed. There were a few on my schedule, of course, but they were not for yesterday…or today. Again, the day ahead of me was wide open! My husband had slept in this morning. He had said last night, "I don't really have a lot to do tomorrow. I may just sleep in." And, he had done just that! By the time he woke up, it was well beyond a few hours passed his norm. "Man, he must've been pretty tired," I had thought to myself, as I drank the rest of my cup of coffee. Just then, he tiredly walked into the living room where I was sitting by the fire. Bending down, he kissed my forehead and said, "Good morning, Sweetheart." "Good Morning, Honey," I replied.

"Is our *teenager* out of bed, yet?" he inquired, lightheartedly. I smiled at his melodramatic usage of the word teenager. "She is up, *but not* out of bed. I think she is still working on her school assignments," I told him, "but I haven't checked back in on her this last hour or so. You can go check on her if you would like." He nodded and walked through the house to her room. I heard him knock on the door. Her reply, "Come in," was distant, but still audible enough for me to make it out. A few minutes passed by, and he came back toward the living room. He stopped, though, right at the edge of the carpet from the kitchen and said, "Yep, she's up and working. She said she is almost done??" He spoke the last word as a question. So, I replied, "Yes, that sounds about right. She only had a few assignments to do today." I could see the relief on his face as the temporary confusion disappeared, and his wrinkled forehead smoothed. "Coffee?" he asked. "Sure! That would be great! One more cup may just keep me warm for a bit longer," I said.

He brought me a cup, mixed the way I like it. I told him, "Thank you, Babe!" "You're welcome, Sweetheart," he replied, then said, "I guess…I am going to get started on some work." I answered, "Sounds good. I've got a few things I wanted to do today, while I have some free time." I appreciated the polite way we were with one another. We both made it a point to *intentionally* and *actively* infuse our conversations, no matter how short or small, with politeness and courtesy.

There was something about him being respectful *and* considerate *and* appreciative of the little things that always warmed my heart. He felt the same way. That's why we did so for one another – to show that extra love and care. It was just...good. "Yes, a little gentleness…a little kindness…a bit of sweetness…some politeness…a lot of mutual respect…all that kind of stuff goes *a loooong ways* in keeping a firm foundation in our marriage," I thought to myself.

A fond smile rested upon my lips as I watched my husband set up his work laptop and binder of notes. In my mind, I surmised, "I guess he is going to use the kitchen table, today, instead of the couch." He looked over at me to see the smile I still had as I looked at him. He smiled back. Then, as if he was reading my mind, he said, "The day before last, I must have been *too* comfortable," he paused, then finished his thought, "thank you, by the way, for waking me up when I fell asleep. Maybe this will help me stay alert." I laughed and said, "You're welcome. *Any* time, Babe – You can count on me to wake you up." He smiled and shook his head at my humorously exaggerated retort. I walked over to him, flattened down the shaggy bed-hair that he had not combed, yet; and kissed the top of his head. "I'll letchya get to it, then. Love You," I said as I made my way to check on our kiddo before getting started on my projects. "Love you, too, Gorgeous," he replied.

I turned the corner to where our daughter's bedroom was. Popping my head in, briefly, I asked her, "You doing ok, kiddo?" She replied, "Yes, ma'am." Following up to get to my point better, I asked further, "Need any help, or do you think you got it?" She wrinkled her nose and tilted her head to the side, slightly. "Ummmmm…," she hesitantly said, "...I *think* I've got it…but maybe just be on standby, k?" she requested. "Sure thing," I told her. Her smile said it all, but she kindly responded, "Thanks, Mom." "You're welcome, Honey," I said. "Yes. Kindness goes *a loooong ways* in <u>all</u> relationships," I thought to myself with a grateful heart. Our home was *definitely* full of mutual respect, kindness, and consideration for one another. Stepping back a few steps, I asked both of them, "Are you guys ready for breakfast yet?" My husband said, "That sounds good, Babe." My daughter hesitated and looked a bit confused. She looked at me with that puzzled look, and I asked, "What's wrong, Honey?" Before she could say anything, my husband looked up from his computer and replied with a bit of a shocked face, "Nothing's wrong, what do you mean?" This odd triangle conversation made me laugh. Recovering from the humor I found in it all, I said, "I was talking to our kiddo, Babe. I know nothing is wrong with you." He smiled back, relieved that we were on the same page. "I guess I gotta watch that *Honey* usage when you are here, huh, Honey?" I asked. He nodded in agreement. "Yep! That's what it was," he replied. Turning back to my daughter and her still-perplexed state that was written all over her face, I asked, "Soooo…what's wrong, kiddo?" "Well," she said, "I'm not sure if I'm hungry or just reeeeaaallly nauseous." A little confused now, myself, I hesitantly responded, "Oh!...ooo…k…soooo…is that a *no* on breakfast…oooorrrr…???" I let the question linger. She thought about it. Then, she replied with an odd mixture of certainty and maybe-ish confirmation, "No, I'm *Definitely*, probably, hungry!" With this response, my husband chuckled, too. Again, I eased into my next reply, "Oooookaaayyyyy," I said, drawing it out a bit. "Are you sure it's a go

> **"But through love serve one another."**
> Apostle Paul

for food?" I asked her, just to double-check before I delved into *fixin'* breakfast for everyone. Her simple response sealed the deal, this time. She said, "Yes, ma'am! I'm sure."

I walked over to the refrigerator and began to gather up ingredients for scrambled eggs, bacon, and homemade drop biscuits. As I prepared the meal, my mind thought upon the goodness and kindness that had filled my morning so far. It is nice to have those good, healthy dynamics and positive communication in my life, now. There was a time in my life when that *was not* the case. Maybe that is why I appreciate it so very much: I know what it is like to *not* have *good* and *healthy* in the environment around me. "It is such a fulfilling blessing from God to have that provided in my days with the people I love," I thought. "Yes, it is a nice thing, indeed!" I agreed with myself.

I delivered the plates of food around the house. One to my husband, at his makeshift workspace in the kitchen at the table. One to my daughter, at her workspace in her bedroom at her desk. One to myself, at my workspace in the office at my desk. My husband paused and said a blessing over breakfast after I had served everyone their plate of *awesome food*. That is, of course, in my head, it was *awesome*. However, I always do a follow-up question to both of my taste-testers to confirm whether or not it is actually *awesome*. I simply ask, "So, on a 1-to-10 scale, what's the score?" I had done this since our daughter had been about 3. It started as a way to get her to try new things. I would set the question up with a sense of high anticipation, then show her how much I valued her thoughts on the matter. She would hesitate with some things that looked "*really* weird," of course. With a little coaxing, though, she would try it. So, it became *a thing* for our family.

Yes, food rating was an established family tradition. 1-2 was a *no way* on her rating scale. A 3-4 was *tolerable*. A 5-7 was a HUGE win and added into the mixture of go-to recipes. An 8-9 became favorites in her book. She would request those, quite often! After all these years, though, I had only received a 10 from her once. It was my lasagna. Once he started joining her in the rating, my husband stayed in line with her valuation system. I did, as well, so that everyone was on the same page…ya know…to keep it sweetly simple. At first, my husband had thought that there was *no way* this approach was going to work. "Boy, was he ever surprised!" I thought with a smile. "It's been over a decade now, and it's *still* a thing for us," I said. I remember the look on his face after the first time of her diving right into her plate to provide her *expert* rating as a newbie food critic to mama's cooking. He was shocked. It had been a bit difficult to get her to eat different foods before that. Fast forward to now, and he participates just like she does! I laughed at this development of a family tradition we had unintentionally established. "It came about all because of trying to find a solution to her pickiness with food," I thought, shaking my head. It was simple; yet, it has been a part of our entire dynamic, ever since. I received a well-rounded 7 this morning from my daughter and an 8 from my husband.

They both enjoyed my cooking this morning, and *"really, really"* liked the drop biscuits I made, they said. The recipe probably went back further than just Grandma – but I knew them as *Grandma's and Mom's* biscuits growing up. I recalled the moment I had pulled the biscuits out of the oven this very morning. The responses said it all! "Deliciousness!" I said to myself when I pulled them out of the oven. The smell was definitely that! "Those smell great, Honey!" My husband said, looking up from his work. "Yes, they do!" echoed my daughter from her room. Yes, the responses said it all! After the prayer and all of the *'Thank You for cooking'* comments of appreciation and my *'You're very welcome'* replies, I delved into my work.

I looked at the blank page before me. There it was – a college-ruled, blank, loose-leafed piece of paper to write on – and I had *nothing*. I had pulled a sheet out to write a few things down. My earlier thoughts from yesterday about God's Love had brought my attention to two words: *Perseverance* and *Endurance*. They had remained on my mind throughout the day until this morning. Between the fireplace wood restocking fiasco, yesterday, and the interview with the fire chief that had come to my remembrance, I was curious. So, this morning, I had made up my mind. "I'm going to just write it all down! There is a reason why they are stuck in my thoughts. Writing it down may just be the ticket to getting it all out!" I told myself. Yes, I was curious to see *just how many* situations I could recall in which *much* endurance and perseverance had been required. I also was curious to see *in how many of those* I had focused on God and *at what point* I had chosen to do so.

I knew there *was much* to improve on in this area. I also knew that God was *not* <u>the first</u> that I turned to…very often, back then. I sternly told myself, "I need to re-train my brain in this part of my walk. I *don't want* to practice *old* habits <u>anymore</u>. I want God to be my <u>First</u> choice - not my *last* or my *middle-of-the-issues* choice. I *don't want* to choose *old* patterns of behavior like I did yesterday morning with the firewood; and, then, come to God when I have run out of options. I *want* God to be my <u>First Go-To</u>, always." I sat there for a moment, then concluded, "That's going to take intentional re-training, on my part, and me staying focused, focused, focused…on Him, *consistently*."

This idea of writing things down had formed earlier as I listened to the flames crackling in the fireplace this morning. Yes, I had made up my mind. However,

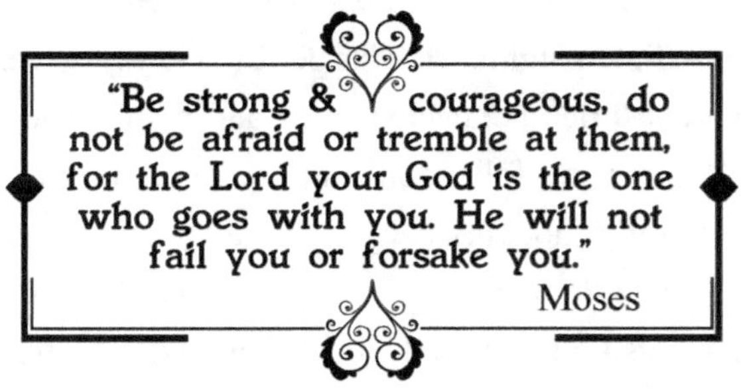

now that I had *actually* sat down to write, I was frozen. "What is my deal?!" I asked myself, rhetorically. I knew what my deal was. I knew because this was quite the *familiar* state of response that I was in. "Avoidance, that's your deal," I answered back. I was right. The first question wasn't anywhere close to being valid. It didn't need to be asked. I knew what was causing the hesitation. *Rehashing* this stuff…or *reevaluating* it...*whatever* I wanted to call it…it was going to be some massively heavy stuff! Yes, circumstances that required *much* endurance and perseverance were all difficult to think upon, let alone write it down! I knew that. This wasn't rocket surgery, after all, as I liked to say. (and, no, that isn't a *real* thing) I smiled as I recalled the conversation that this little phrase of mine had developed from. A while back, a friend and I were debating *rocket science* and *brain surgery* as the most common cliché response people use for things that are supposed to be easy. I had said, "I've got one better – what about *all* those things people talk about that are *beyond* easy…or should be, that is. Ya know…the kind of things that shouldn't even exist! The ones that it's a shame that things like that even happen?" I had waited for the acknowledgment and then delivered the final blow. I said, "Now, *those* things need a special name –

They should call that *rocket surgery*." My friend had burst out laughing. Maybe it was the sold-out look on my face, or the twinkle in my eye through the seriousness I was demonstrating...whatever it was, the resolute delivery was a hit. From then on, I had used that phrase in place of both those other responses. It was one of those phrases that seemed to be a 50/50 shot with any given audience, of course. Over the years, I had received one of two responses from it. Either, "I don't get it," or "I see what you just did there!" The first was, typically, associated with a confused look and a quick *breeze right over and ignore it* reply. The second was almost always followed by immediate laughter or a smile. Either way, it was funny to me. Life was meant to have a little unexpected spice and humor added to it, I had always thought. "It's ok that some folks don't like it. I do, and that's enough," I said with a smile. I shifted my thoughts back to my avoidance...that I was, literally, avoiding with this reflection on *rocket surgery*. "What?!" I asked myself. "It's easier to avoid. Plus...it was funny to think about that, instead...for a second...*before* I faced all this stuff," I said in my own defense.

I was in a state of self-preservation of the unhealthier kind. I recognized that. Avoidance was a coping mechanism I used to use *quite often*. In all respect and consideration – Avoidance used to be my Go-To response. It was usually dappled or covered with humor and deflection. I would just *smoothly* make a joke to distract someone and break the focus off of me. Then, I would, immediately, dangle a carrot of an *entirely different* subject...<u>or two</u>, if that's what it took... until, they chased it. At that reflection, I agreed, "Yes, avoidance and diversions go hand-in-hand." It was hard to debate the obvious, so I did not try. Instead, I admitted to myself, "Yes, they do! And, man, was I good at both of them!" Yes, I remembered how easily and swiftly, I was able to pull those off.

Avoidance is not a healthy coping mechanism, though. I know that. Many a counselor and I had discussed that *very* thing after I chose to end my first marriage. "You are a Master of Avoidance!" one counselor had told me once. In his defense, I had been *foot-dragging* then, too - exceptionally bad. I was not in any hurry to confront any of it. I was in the middle of divorce proceedings, and the wounds were deep and fresh, still. It was a *very* traumatic topic that he was pushing me to discuss, and I wasn't ready to discuss it. Needless to say, I didn't keep that counselor for too much longer after that. "No. Good counselors don't slam your face into a subject like he tried to do with me," I said, recalling his pushiness and impatience with me. "A Good counselor *leads you* by the hand and walks *with you* through major life traumas into healing and empowerment to overcome. They definitely do not get you to the cliff and then push you off of it in hopes you will *just get over it*." I shook my head as I recalled how abrasive that man had been. In comparison with the one I had finally found, he was a mess. Most counselors have other counselors they discuss their own life stuff with…that guy needed, *at least*, 10 more counselors…but *didn't have a one*! "Now, you are exaggerating a bit," I corrected myself. "10 is a bit much, don't ya think?" I

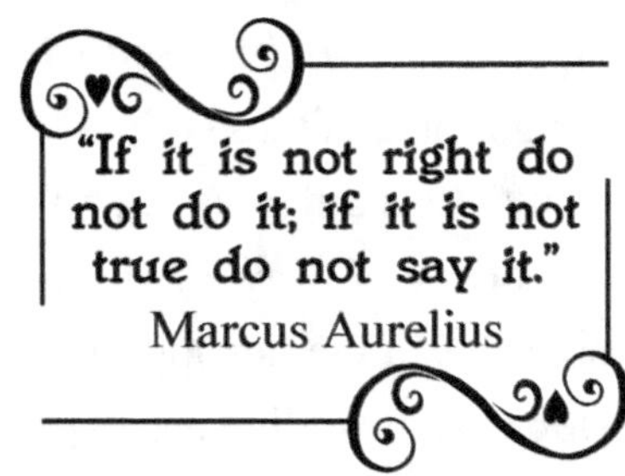

asked. I gave it a second thought but wasn't sure if it was or not. S, I didn't reply and left the idea hanging there, unanswered. "I just know that he *thought he knew* it all, already," I concluded.

Looking back, it was easy to identify the arrogance and self-centeredness he had been walking in at the time. However, given the state I was in, I had been blind to it all during those sessions. At first, I even felt as if there was something wrong with me because of how harshly he handled my counseling sessions. It was not a healthy, safe environment for me to be in. I was glad that God had provided another option in the *finding-a-good-counselor* department. After the move to a nearby suburb, I had been given a referral from a friend. "What a divine appointment, that was!" I thought. God had opened the door to a Christian counselor that *actually* listened and didn't *talk over* me or *tell* me what I was feeling or what I *should be* feeling. It was a nice change.

With my exaggerated usage of the word *should*, came a memory. I laughed as I recalled another turn of phrase used by another counselor that I had visited with, shortly. He had said, "Whatever you do, don't *should* all over yourself." I remember being shocked by the word usage and the emphasis he placed on it. At first, it had sounded like an inappropriate, cursing phrase of old. I was a bit appalled until he explained himself. It must have been written all over my face because he jumped quickly into doing so. He said, "What I mean is this: You're stuck in that mentality of *shoulda, coulda, woulda.*" The relief was prevalent as I responded with a bit of laughter behind the words, "Oh! I see!" He just meant that changing the words I used when I was *talking about things* would help me *work through* some of those things. If I would simply work on just replacing those words, I would see a difference in my perspective. He said, "Removing words like *should have* or *could have* or *would have* will also assist in the healing process and put a stop to some of the internalizing you are doing." He was so very correct! At the time, I was internalizing and placing the

> **"Whatever you do, don't should all over yourself."**
> Anonymous Counselor

blame for every single thing all upon myself. Condemnation and regret riddled my shares in counseling sessions with him. I learned later how someone in an abusive relationship like I was in will, inevitably, begin to do that – internalize everything. Going through the learning process, however...well, that was another story!

There were many things that I would use those phrases with, too. Thankfully, that counselor had recognized the consistency in it with all of my conversation shares very quickly. So quickly, in fact, that he had addressed it within my 4th visit with him! "Funny, the timing that he delivered that line," I thought to myself. "It sure was a great delivery, though...he had only just built enough rapport to lay the foundation for open sharing with me after the 3rd visit. Relationship building in counseling is pivotal to the process, for sure! But, he definitely shocked me with that!" I said, laughing a bit at the unexpected line of advice again. I thought about the many areas I had shared with him about my previous relationship. I found myself talking about stuff like:

Apologizing for everything because the other person is flying off the rails in anger at the slightest drop of a pin. (God forbid I actually dropped a pin and made a noise!) *There he was yelling and going off on me again...*

Constantly, second-guessing myself because of daily undermining and manipulation that he would use to twist things around and control the situation... whatever it might be - *it didn't matter. After a couple years of that, I wasn't sure what was real...*

Feeling worthless because I was made to believe I was an unwanted and undesired burden. Being told that I was only good to have around because of all the things I did *for* that man that benefited him only. *Mind games, galore, were in this bucket...and name-calling and berating, of course– believe you, me – I was convinced I was no good...*

Not making decisions or speaking my opinion because of fear of the immediate attack or recourse that would follow if it rubbed him the wrong way on any given day. *Eggshells were everywhere! It was easier to not say or do anything...it was less hostile...and...safer...sorta...but not really...*

Existing for years in solitude – not by choice, mind you, but because after 5 years I had given up on fighting after *every single* time I would go spend time with friends, family...my parents...anyone. It was a slow fade into the oblivion of loneliness. One that I didn't notice until after the fact...*what was the point? I was tired and didn't want to fight about it...just do what he says – do what he wants...maybe it will help...or maybe not...I didn't want the added drama if I could help it...*

Thinking '*if only*' I do such and such…or '*if only*' I say such and such…it will change, it will be better…because this is all my fault, that's what he says...every single day…it must be true, …right?…yes, it's true…this is all my fault! *At least, I think it is…isn't it?!...*

…and many other similar areas of damage that had been done…some worse. Yes, *much* worse… "I don't want to dwell on those. The bruises are gone from every last part of it all. I am in a safe place. The healing that God has provided in all those many different areas has been awesome! I am blessed beyond measure and greatly loved by Him. That's what matters now…Not all that nonsense. Nope, not that," I told myself.

I shifted my focus back to the present and this list. "I need to practice new habits, just like I did with the *should* word," I reaffirmed. The Holy Spirit said, "Yes, child, *the things you have learned and received and heard and seen in Me, practice these things, and the God of peace will be with you.*" I nodded in agreement. I had practiced the word replacement for a few months after that session until it became my constant, new habit. It was a good thing, too. Now, I could easily see what the counselor had meant with it all, in the clarity of hindsight. There was a vast, looming mixture of feelings tied to that. Regret, disappointment in myself, devaluation of my worth, guilt, condemnation, and the like were allowed into my thought life and heart with just that one word – *Should*. At first, I really couldn't believe the shift in my perspective! It was a leap of significant improvement, for sure!

Shortly after I had begun working with him, he received a promotion. I had *dove* right in, too. Only to be left with trying to find yet another counselor. It wasn't intentional, though. He was offered a job as a site supervisor – no more clients. The only gig he had was to manage all the counselors at the facility. "He was a pretty smart cat," I thought to myself as I recalled the few months of sessions that I had with him. "Yep," I added, "that is why he was promoted, probably." So, I went in search of another one, and another one, until I found the right one for me. Just like doctors, not all counselors are made equal. Book knowledge and life knowledge and Bible knowledge are all in their very own bucket of experience and capabilities.

Healing from the divorce and the abuse that had been endured for 14 years was essential to me. If I had not been focused on healing – it would have impacted how I interacted with my daughter, my husband, and…well, everyone, really. I wanted to be the best mom, wife, friend, and family member I could be. Although I had restarted from scratch, I did not let that deter me or discourage me. Some days were far easier than others trudging through the muck of it all, but it had to be done! I was on a mission to start renewing me. I didn't like the way I was as the *abused* version of me. I knew that. I also knew that I did not want to be a *victim* any longer. I had survived that mess! If anything, I was a *survivor*, not a victim. I did not want to live in fear anymore like that. I did not want it or the many after-effects of being in such an environment to hinder my present. I was self-aware enough to see some of it. However, I didn't know how to get out of *that way* of existing...of daily operating *as if* I needed to still be in that constant hypervigilant state of being. I was tired of it. I wanted something better for my life, for my daughter, for my future. A scripture came to my remembrance as I thought upon this desire for change. The Holy Spirit said to my heart, *"For everyone who does evil hates the Light, and does not come to the Light for fear that his deeds will be exposed. But he who practices the truth comes to the Light, so that his deeds may be manifested as having been wrought in God."* I desired to come to the Light. I desired to practice the truth and find my truth. I didn't want the lies that I had known, that were familiar to my soul, that had surrounded me. I wanted the darkness of the abusive environment that I had been living in obliterated from my existence! So, with that decision of renewal, counseling came up as a possible solution.

> "Make me know Your ways, O Lord; teach me Your paths. Lead me in Your truth & teach me, for You are the God of my salvation; for You I wait all the day."
> — King David

I remember telling my mother, "I don't know how to fix what's been broken in me. I just know it isn't right. It isn't the real me." Of course, she had readily agreed. "Why don't you go visit with a counselor about some of this stuff you are feeling?" she had suggested, gently. She knew 'the me' before and 'the me' during. She had witnessed most of the changes, even from a distance, in the later years. She had continued to encourage me *for years* to get out of the situation. I let my mind go back for a moment to that first month after I, *finally*, took her advice. I had called her and said, "I just wanted to call and tell you *Thank you so very much* for continuing to be there for me – before it, during it, and after it. *Thank You.*" If not for her, I'm not sure how long it would have taken me before I visited with a counselor. Yes, hindsight was always a 20/20 thing. It seemed so surreal to me now, as I looked at the piece of paper. It was still in front of me – still blank.

I continued with my memories. I recalled how desperately I wanted to figure out who the real me was, again. "I didn't even know how I liked my eggs! Just like that chick in that silly movie!" I said to myself as I shook my head, remembering my lack of understanding of who I was. I needed to figure it out for myself, for my child that I wanted to raise well, for the man that God would send me, eventually, after all this was cleared up, and for everyone that I would come into contact with from here on out! I knew that I *needed to* heal - I just didn't know *how to* heal. So, I sought help.

However, I *did not* share that I was going to a counselor, back then. "Nope! Nope! Nope!" I remembered thinking. There was a fear of judgment and a considerable measure of embarrassment that was tied to *going to counseling.* Needless to say, not many people knew about it for the first year or so. During that season of my life, I was also struggling with attacks of shame. Although, I didn't know they were attacks, then. They are easy enough to identify now, though. "Yes, attacks of shame were exactly what I was enduring through at that time," I confirmed to myself with a nod.

It was a vicious cycle that would start when thinking about sharing with those close to me about my counseling sessions. Fear, anxiety, insecurity, doubt, shame, disappointment, depression, guilt, condemnation, and a variety of unsultry characters would come knocking on my door. I wasn't *that* prepared, spiritually, to identify those for the attacks they were. I was in a season of self, still. I couldn't see beyond myself to see anything else. I knew about discernment, but definitely wasn't walking in it. Thinking about it now, I said, "I was like a 10,000-piece puzzle with all the pieces scattered about and the box missing in action. The front of the box was gone. The image that it is supposed to be after it's put back together was nowhere to be seen! I had *no clue* what pieces went where or how to even begin identifying them all for what they were!" The enemy was succeeding, quite well, in his deception tactics. Even with my lack of discernment skills at the time, I still knew it wasn't right...it wasn't in the 'good' bucket. So, I would pray – in my despair - for God to help me in my time of need. There wasn't much success with that, though, that I could see in my circumstances. It wasn't until later that I learned more about this whole prayer process thing. I laughed, fondly, at myself, "Oh, what a mess I was!" I knew I was. That's why I was going to counseling. I couldn't see beyond myself in the chaos and aftermath of all the trauma.

Eventually, though, I was able to build up some coping skills and learn some hard truths that helped me get out of that mindset. Eventually, I was able to get over the fear of rejection from sharing that I was even in counseling. I told a few of my friends, and they stuck around – go figure! No judgment. Eventually, I was able to find the box and see the image to put the puzzle back together – a real *breaking of the unbreaking* kind of healing, mind you. I concluded, "Yes, Eventually. It had taken time invested. It was a process, and I walked through it - every pain-staking, heartbreaking step of the way! Thank God that I did! Thank God for His help!"

Within a year of counseling, I was wide-open about the subject. I thought, "And, wouldn't you know it...Confessing did it! Letting people know that I was actually *in counseling* was the key to freedom. That was all it took to break free from those jerk-face attacks!" I continued by adding, "See, God! There's another time that would have been easier to endure, if I would've come to you First, Lord." His soothing words came to my heart, "Lessons learned, kiddo. Lessons learned." My mind focused back on the counseling that I still go to today. "This new counselor is a Godsend, for sure," I said to myself. "She even makes it a point to invest time to pray with me during sessions!"

At the thought, I admitted, "It is terrific to have such an elder in spirit to seek sound counsel from *as* my person-counselor." I gave credit to God for this, telling Him in my heart, "God, You did well with that divine appointment. Thank You! And, yes…I know You are <u>The</u> Ultimate Counselor." I thought about this with a grateful heart. How much help and sound counsel the Holy Spirit gives me! How much encouragement

> "Consider it all joy, my brethren, when you encounter various trials, knowing that the testing of your faith produces endurance. And let endurance have its perfect result, so that you may be perfect & complete, lacking in nothing."
> James - Jesus' brother

and accountability the Helper provides to me! How much teaching and guidance and leading and directing the Counselor administers, on the daily! How much of a minister to my soul His Spirit is! Yes, He is <u>The</u> Ultimate Counselor! "It is pretty neat how much I have grown through His Counsel and that of my Christian counselor I have spent years with," I said, in conclusion to this. Sometimes, the conversations were lighter than others, but most times – they were spiritually charged with much depth in the Word of God running through each of them, nowadays. I sought her counsel, in this season, for strengthening of the *iron-sharpens-iron* kind, edification in the Word, and accountability in my walk with Christ. I had learned a great deal within that first year, let alone the intentional, continued visits of accountability that I maintain *still* today.

My daughter and husband had both found counselors, as well. Personal growth and development are so important in my walk with God. I was delighted to see that they both desired the same level of growth and learning. As far as *my family* is concerned, counseling is a way to increase our personal arsenals to maintain our mental, emotional, spiritual, and physical focus on God, Almighty. Through it, my family is better able to defend against the attacks of the enemy;

especially, with <u>all</u> of our counselors being Christian counselors. Not one of them would hesitate to apply scripture and look at the circumstances in an objective, biblical way. "That makes all the difference, right there!" I declared. We were definitely blessed in that department. My daughter had a full toolbox, after the first 6 months for her arsenal of coping mechanisms. After the next 6 months had passed, she had learned how to apply biblical perspectives *while* implementing those coping mechanisms. I definitely *did not* have the same when I was her age. It has helped her tremendously! She is learning how to cope through the many moving parts in her life, as a middle-schooler. The counselor guides her through this, all while showing her how to keep her focus on God. "Pretty cool!" I thought to myself. "And, boy! Have those been a lot! Young girls *and* young boys are full of some drama nowadays!" I asserted.

Changing my focus back to my husband, I thought of what he had said to me after his first 3 visits. He said, "Babe, I was super hesitant to do this whole *counseling* thing. To be honest, I really didn't want to…at all! I have been so impressed with this man, though! He is a man of God, for sure! He listens, and what he says is…just…*right on*! Did you know he prayed with me today?!" I casually replied, "Really! No. I did not know that, Honey. That's great! I'm glad you like him." I didn't want to be overly excited and seem like I was pushing *for* the counseling, given his opening line of hesitation that he shared.

I wanted him to figure it out on his own how awesome and beneficial it is. I was confident that it would sell itself without me saying a word. I remembered his smile lighting up at the small bit of encouragement I gave. He continued with a bit more enthusiasm, "Oh! And he sent me home with a bunch of things to practice that can help me get through some things I… might… well… maaaaaybe… sorta… had on a shelf for a *long* time…By the way, I'm sorry. *But* I don't want to tell you right now what for." He let the statement hang in the air a bit. I wasn't sure if he was expecting me to respond, or what, exactly. I didn't move. I wasn't about to put a stop to his avid sharing moment. Frozen like a deer in the headlights, I just stood there, soaking up the moment. It was far too cool!

He picked up where he left off, "First! I want to work through those things *and then* explain them to ya later...*ya know*...after they aren't there anymore." After this statement, his expression told me this time he wanted a response. However, I hesitated and scrunched up my nose, wrinkling my brow in confusion and uncertainty. I didn't really know how to respond and stumbled over some words, "Oh...ok...well...I'm not sure what that all means, but...I guess... ummmmm...I accept your apology?" I said with a questioning ending. His smile of a reply was littered with signs of relief and fortitude - there was newfound courage weighing in his words and demeanor. It was as if *that simple acceptance* had helped him make up his mind, for some reason. Either way, I tried to show him that I was *for* him, not against him. I wanted him to know I supported him and whatever physical, mental, emotional, and spiritual house-cleaning he wanted to pursue! No matter how small or big – I wanted him to know that I was *for it*...even if I was clueless to *what it* was!

As a result, his sharing continued. He said, "Oh yeah! *Aaaannd*...I have *already* handed out the counselor's business cards to a few of my coworkers this week, too!" They had shared with him about struggling in their walk. He recounted what he said to them. "I just asked them – straight-up - Have you ever thought about seeing a counselor?" With sheer shock mixed with pride all over my face, I said, "That was very bold of you, Honey. That's awesome!" I told him. He explained that his question had been rhetorical to them. He said, "Yeah. I didn't even give them a chance to respond! I immediately went right into my next sentence." He smiled a bit before sharing what he had told them. "I just said I've been going this last month, and it's really great to have someone to talk to about this stuff. Then, I said – Here, take this. It's my counselor's card. He's a good Christian guy and knows his stuff about the Bible. And, then, I told them about how he actually prayed with me this last time! Each of 'em was floored," he said excitedly. I smiled and said with encouragement and sincerity, "That's great, Babe! I am very proud of you!" I don't know if my husband heard me whisper after he left the room, but if he did, he would have heard me say, with a smile, "That's cool!"

As I sat in the office, looking at my now-scribbled-on-with-doodles-of-all-kinds paper…I recalled the day that he had shared this with me. He was elated to have helped break that stigmata about counseling with those guys. Out of the guys he gave the cards to, 3 out of the 4 had gone to see his counselor. He knew that because they had come to thank him for the referral and had shared the same good report that he had shared with them. I could tell he was quite encouraged by the results of the seeds he had planted so quickly! It was edifying and encouraging to hear about this success from my husband. I was glad that he had shared it with me. Little, daily achievements like that were just as significant as the big ones, to me. He was definitely experiencing quite a few of both in my eyes. I was proud - in the elated-and-joyful sense - of the Good work that God was doing in and through my husband. It was good to be the wife of a husband that was choosing to grow and learn more about God and unroot things of old that are hindering that close, intimate walk with Him. It was even better to see that he was sharing that pursuit of God with those other men. I smiled for a moment as I thought about the leader he was growing into under Christ's supervision. He is trying his best each day to practice submission and surrender. That, in

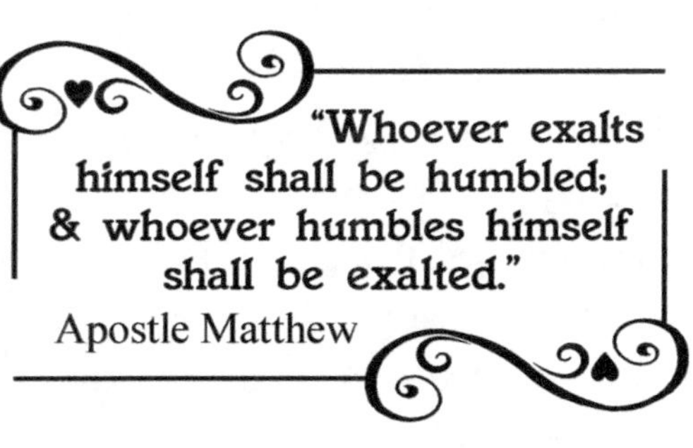

and of itself, was absolutely breathtaking and melted my heart. Humility is such a precious and beautiful thing to witness! Such strength and courage is required to do so! It was one of many scripturally founded reasons I was attracted to my husband. "I am so thankful for what You are doing in my husband's heart, Lord! Thank You!" I said in great appreciation and wonder.

My thoughts went back to reflecting on both of them – my daughter and my husband. They are both seeking after more knowledge and wisdom in Who they are in Jesus Christ and Whose they are in Jesus Christ. It was beautiful to see! A gentle reminder came to me, though, with this thought. The Holy Spirit said, "This kind of seeking leads to deeper prayer time needed in the intercession you are called to do, kiddo." I acknowledged in all seriousness, "I know, Lord. I know. That has been prevalent in the last few years. It hasn't been easy. Thank you for the reminder to continue as I have been doing." There had been times that spiritual attacks against my daughter…or my husband…had felt like an onslaught of a gazillion arrows being shot, all at once! I had spent weeks and weeks in prayer over a few topics. There were temptations and stumbling blocks in those topics that had come to the forefront of their walks. They couldn't see it clearly, but boy, oh boy, could I ever! Intercessory Prayer is not for the faint of heart, but it is a calling nonetheless, and obey the call I must!

Thinking about it now, I admitted, "Yes, there is even one particular subject that I am still in prayer for, after 4 years! God's provision is what I am waiting upon. And I will not simply just *wait*. No! I will *wait in confident-trust* of His Love and His Promises. He will provide," I encouraged myself before the enemy had a chance to discourage me in this. However, the trenches seemed unending during some days – ya know…on the days that I was wearier than on others. "Praise You, in the trenches, though…That is what I am supposed to do," I said, knowingly, "and that is what I am going to continue to do! Back to the *Persevere* and *endure* focus! God, I know Your timing is perfect. I will trust that You know best in this, too, as in all things!" I let the moment linger in stillness.

I looked at the still-void-of-written-words, scribble-riddled page before me. A sigh escaped my frowned lips. With great strain, I began to write down some areas God had shown me regarding what it meant to *endure* and *persevere*. I didn't make them very specific – just wrote a few notes like this:

Loss...(oh, how many kinds of this I had endured! "Where to begin?" came the overwhelming thought. I reset my focus and affirmed, "No. I am just going to list it as a title, for now.")

Divorce…**Recovery** from it all! (I can't even begin to explain the complexity of this decade-plus dosage of a slow-fade of trauma after trauma. Needless to say, recovery was a feat of exceptional, pain-staking perseverance.)

Heartbreak…**Restoral** of missing pieces back to one heart…for God. (that one was a long learning process that required much endurance & fortitude!)

Provision of Healing…physical ailments over the years had come and gone (some had taken longer than others, a few still lingered – I was persevering through it in hope, still)

Financial Provision…there was a time I didn't have funds to buy groceries or make rent. I had to make do with what I had…still yet, even a few times that I had to ask for help (endurance had been challenging to do in this one, for sure! Finding out just how much of the Ultimate Provider He is in *all* things…that one took a bit to accept as my truth.)

Betrayal… "This one's staying as just a title, too," I told myself, moving on as quickly as I could!

Loneliness…starting over in a new place without knowing anyone…but, mostly, feeling alone in a crowded room…(It took a lot of knocking on my heart's door before I opened it for God – persevering through on my own was definitely harder than persevering through *with* Him.)

… … … …

I put the pencil down. Turning my head toward the window, I looked outside at the glistening snow. My eyes looked from one side of the landscape to the other, soaking in all the many details. Then, I said, "Lord, You have known me. You know my heart. You know my ways. This conviction You place upon my heart about these ways of mine that need to be renewed and transformed – Lord, it always leads me to a deeper understanding of Your Love. I know this, and, yet, I find myself hesitating yet again." I let the awareness of my avoidance and hesitation rest in the air. I likened this hinderance they caused that I was feeling to a freshly hung curtain blocking the view of this gorgeous landscape of a window. "Why would I ever want to remove such beauty from my sight?!" I thought. The absurdity of it all was just that…quite absurd.

Then, His voice came. He said, "My child, your faith is found in Me. It grows only in My Presence. There is an *abiding*…an alignment that grows *in depth*, in vastness, *in height, in width, in length, in knowledge* and *wisdom* as you come to Me. *Abiding in Me* is the key that you seek. I am your *all in all – the fullness* in *everything*. I am the fullness of the eternal kind – of depths you cannot fathom." There was a boldness of great certainty that could not be shaken or moved in the truth of those words. They washed over me and surrounded me in confidence of Who He was. With that thought of remembrance, a rush of excitement hit my heart and I acknowledged, "Yes, it is a confidence through Christ toward God! I desire all the fullness You have for my heart, Lord!" I let the words sink in a bit more amid within the intimate silence I was sharing with Him. Opportunities, such as these, to bask in the Light of His truth are always time-well-invested for my heart. I know this to be true! My heart rested in this.

MEMORY VERSE

*In this you greatly rejoice,
even though now for a little while, if necessary,
you have been distressed by various trials,
so that the proof of your faith,
being more precious than gold which is perishable,
even though tested by fire,
may be found to result in praise and glory and honor
at the revelation of Jesus Christ;
and though you have not seen Him, you love Him,
and though you do not see Him now, but believe in Him,
you greatly rejoice with joy inexpressible and full of glory,
obtaining as the outcome of your faith the salvation of your souls.*
1 Peter 1:6-9

Chapter Thirteen
Part Two

New Beginnings:
Abiding

> *Yours, O Lord, is the greatness*
> *and the power and the glory and the victory*
> *and the majesty, indeed everything that is*
> *in the heavens and the earth;*
> *Yours is the dominion,*
> *O Lord, and You exalt Yourself as head over all.*
> *Both riches and honor come from You,*
> *and You rule over all, and in Your hand*
> *is power and might; and it lies in Your hand*
> *to make great and to strengthen everyone.*
> *Now therefore, our God, we thank You,*
> *and praise Your glorious name.*
> 1 Chronicles 29:11-13

My eyes were focused upon a small tree in the pasture, now. It was covered in glistening snow with icicles pulling the fragile limbs down. His words came again. He said, "My love is Great – incomprehensibly so! Each day I give you will be an opportunity for you to come closer to Me – continuing to *abide in Me*. It is an invitation that I provide every single day! *From glory to glory* was written for a reason, My child. This is the sanctification that you will endure and persevere through. It is a transformation into the image of the Lord. There is a glory found in the Spirit that abounds in greatness! When a person turns to the Lord, this glory is seen in *all fullness*!" My heart was lifted up in joy, and there was a sense of fullness of His love at the words He shared with me. I knew this scripture. It was one that I had felt drawn to over the last few months. "God, Your Word promises there is freedom…liberty where the Spirit of the Lord is. I choose You <u>First</u>, God. Thank You for sending Your Son. Thank You for sending the Holy Spirit to testify about You, just as Jesus did." I could feel my heart and mind resting in the gratefulness they felt for His Love. "Lord, I am so very grateful for all You are to me...for all You do that I don't even know about! It is just…so very much to be grateful for!" I stated

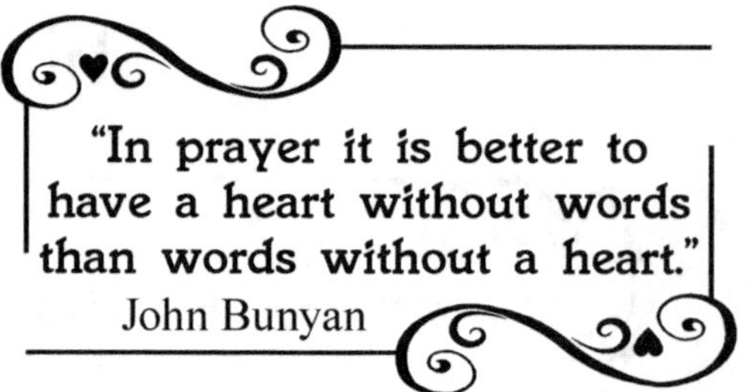

with certainty. I closed my eyes and breathed in, deeply. Yes. There was just *so much*!

I arose from my chair and walked into the bedroom to find my Bible. The Vinedresser passage was what I desired to read again from His prompting to my heart. I began to flip through the pages to the book of John and found chapter 15. I read what was written in the passage. It was such an encouragement to my heart of His love. I softly spoke these parts out loud. *Abide in Me and I in you…Just as the Father has loved me, I love you, abide in My love… if you keep My commandments, you will abide in My love… I have spoken this so that My joy may be in you, and your joy may be made full.* I sat there on the edge of the bed in the calm. I turned the

Bible to Ephesians 3 for the prayer that I enjoyed reading that spoke to the vastness of His great love to encourage my heart further in this moment. *For this reason I bow my knees before the Father, from whom every family in heaven and on earth derives its name, that He would grant you, according to the riches of His glory, to be strengthened with power through His Spirit in the inner man, so that Christ may dwell in your hearts through faith; and that you, being rooted and grounded in love, may be able to comprehend with all the saints what is the breadth and length and height and depth, and to know the love of Christ which surpasses knowledge, that you may be filled up to all the fullness of God. Now to Him who is able to do far more abundantly beyond all that we ask or think, according to the power that works within us, to Him be the glory in the church and in Christ Jesus to all generations forever and ever. Amen.* I felt such peace come over my heart and humbly admitted, "Yes, Father, I gladly and with full joy made complete in Jesus Christ bow my knees before You!"

All morning I had been tap-dancing around this truth. It wasn't that I was doing wrong by wanting to do right. No. It was more like I was focused more on correcting the habit, rather than I was on *abiding in Him* and His great love for me. I had a tendency to do that, of course. I would lean into my own self before I would lean into God. Even still, today, it was something I had to intentionally hold myself accountable on. I desired to lean into Him, though. I told myself, "Yes, indeed I do! Practicing changing out my ways of addressing things for His ways of addressing things is how I am going to do precisely that! Yes, submitting before Him in it all and shouting from the rooftops – Not My Will, Lord, BUT Yours Be Done…That is what I am going to do!" My heart felt encouraged in this admittance of surrender.

I continued to think about this struggle of flesh and spirit. Imagery that I did not care too much for came to my thoughts as I recalled a study that I had read, once. There was said to be a ritual in Tarsus, the Apostle Paul's hometown, that was reserved for those who convicted crimes of the murdering kind. The person committing the crime was sentenced to have a dead corpse bound to their back and would spend the rest of their days with that decaying body wherever they went. If caught removing the corpse, they would be killed. Either way, death not only awaited them, but it enveloped and saturated their very person, their very existence until the end of their days! In that study, the ritual was said to be what Paul may have been referring to when he wrote the letter to the Romans in chapter seven. This chapter was part of his lengthy internal testimony of his own struggle of the flesh and spirit. He proclaimed in his writing, *"Wretched man that I am! Who will set me free from the body of this death?"* Ever since reading about that possible meaning behind verse 24, the visualization of the consequences of carrying around a dead body in reference to choosing sin has been quite the deterrent! It pains me to know I grieve the Holy Spirit in such choices of the flesh – yet, to add to that pain and breaking of my heart that desires to please Him with such vivid demise and torture… it leaves my heart with even more of a motivation to not walk in the flesh! I shook my head at the thought. I didn't care to have the imagery hanging around any longer than a moment! "I don't want a disgusting dead corpse hanging off my back! No thank you!" I thought to myself with quite the firm stance! Some days, the empathy felt in my heart when placing myself in Paul's descriptive circumstances was far too much for my heart to bear! I replied, immediately, "Yes, BUT! I know it is good for strengthening and edification in the warfare that I must face!" A nod followed as I agreed with this understanding.

I thought about the passages that followed such a description. This was the part of his letter prior to telling the church, *"Therefore there is now no condemnation for those who are in Christ Jesus. For the law of the Spirit of life in Christ Jesus has set you free from the law of sin and of death."* A daily struggle of the flesh and spirit, it was, most assuredly! Paul was right in that, indeed! My mind questioned the simplicity of this dilemma, asking, "Isn't it *ever-so* easier to lean into something tangible and able to be seen like the flesh, rather than something intangible and unable to be seen like the spirit?" I knew that it was. I responded to this thought with much confidence, saying, "Yes, but that is where my faith comes in…well…I mean, that is when Jesus has another opportunity to build up *the faith He has given* to me. He is the *author and perfecter* of it, after-all!" Even in his letter to the Romans he made sure that even amidst these battles of internal struggle- flesh against spirit – there is much hope! Jesus Christ is the answer to freedom from it all! "Yes, He most assuredly is! Amen!" I exclaimed in agreement with Paul's letter.

I sat there, solemnly and meekly, thinking about the deeper lessons I had learned with *enduring* and *persevering* through the days of sharpening. I said in acknowledgement, "All of it simply takes time… Yes, it is a building-up-of-faith process that takes time to go through. It takes seasons of fire and flames, storms and struggle, crushing and purifying, and the like to build such faith in Him." My mind was hit with two thoughts. I started to recount a very encouraging line that helps me in this kind of daily choosing. But, also, acknowledge that this pursuit of God must be chosen by me every day, intentionally and completely. Interrupting one for the other of my own thoughts, I admitted, "Yes, I could easily choose to remain in avoidance...or ignorance, I suppose. Either of those ways leave me spinning my wheels in the mud. Stuck. I don't want to be stuck. I want to continue to grow. I want to continue to move forward and become all that I can be in Christ. I want to be what I have been called to be, in all the fullness that is found in Him!" As I pondered the consequences of what it would mean to choose to **not** *abide in Him*, my heart grew in gratefulness of all that *abiding in Him* meant. Then, I returned my thoughts back to the encouraging line that was spoken by a friend of mine some time ago. She said, "I know it's hard to do so, but practice makes permanent, girl. Practice makes permanent." She was referring to reading my Bible, consistently and 'on-the-daily'. However, little did she know, I would use that phrase for years to come with many things! As I walked out my faith in Him, I used it as a reminder that old habits do, indeed, die very hard - BUT! with God on my side, all it takes is practicing His ways that He teaches and convicts my heart about. That's it! It just takes simple, focused-on-Him practice to make permanent For-His-Glory, from-glory-to-glory caliber of changes. Again, I said, "Amen!"

"<u>First</u> Him – *Then* everything else falls into place," I acknowledged to myself. It just has, in my experience. *Every single* time – it just has! Those new ways of doing, talking, thinking, behaving, walking, sharing…just existing… being still with Him…*all of it* – It all becomes the new permanent my heart has a desire for. It's funny, though. Looking back over the practicing seasons, I can still recall the moments each new desire was put there in my heart. It was like a breath of fresh air – this new awareness of a better way to be…or kinder way; or gentler way; or more loving way…or more compassionate, empathetic, bold, honorable, chivalrous, sincere, honest, vulnerable, transparent, open, trusting, stronger, confident, able, consistent, long-suffering, patient, joyful, content, faithful…oh, the list goes on and on! The areas He has called me to grow in over the years have been immense and I love Him even more with each level of growth! Yes, looking back, it is clear. There are many things that I have accepted His way for me in, instead of my own. In pure fascination, I admitted, "Yet, there is still so very much understanding to grow in!"

I remember joking…pridefully, of course…early on in my walk… it was with a friend much older in spirit than I, by far! I had said, "I don't know what that preacher could possibly teach me that I don't know about God. I've already heard all the Bible, practically, from all the other preachers and teachers. I've been going to church for years!" She had just smiled and shaken her head at my ignorance and fleshly speech, saying gently, "My dear, you are so very loved by God. I cannot wait to see what He does today…and tomorrow…and the next day, in your life! Each new day is an opportunity to learn a little bit more about Who He is and for Him to teach you a little bit more about Who you are…in Him. You have a calling on your life – a purpose of a most glorious kind! *From glory to glory*, He will call you closer to Him…each new day." Of course, I had no idea what she was talking about. Riddles were in her words. My puzzled look said as much, and she just said, "Trust me. You will see. However, submission and surrender are required. You've got to stay on alert – pride is a very tricky cat! The enemy weasels his way in from the oddest areas in our life…some we don't even know about. Just make sure to stay in His Word. The Holy Spirit will teach you all you need to know about this and even more! Much more than I can share with you, for sure!" Her words had hit me hard. I dwelled on them for days and days after that conversation. There were many times that God brought this particular conversation up to my remembrance, although I didn't know it at the time. I pondered in thought of this to myself, "When He wants me to learn something, He certainly finds a way! He has used friends, family, and even the radio station…Oh! And that ridiculous billboard with the donkey on it, of all things! Seriously!" I smiled at the memory.

There were so many of those moments, though, precisely like that! God uses so many ways to speak to the heart of the matter. In my times of need and in my days, He finds a way to reach my heart. He is so very good to me – such a good Father – such a good Friend and Loved One to me. "Truly, truly, Lord. I do not know what I would do and where I would be and…all of it – without You! Your Love has been the greatest gift I have ever received or will *ever* receive. It has changed my life! Of all those who live, You know this the most…the deepest…the greatest! Yes, You know me…more!" My heart was full and overflowing with love for my Heavenly Father. I reflected on the many ways that He has been there for me and *all* that He is to me. I told Him, "There are so many ways You have infiltrated the walls

and barriers surrounding my heart, Lord. I know there are plenty more areas that I do not even know of…and that is ok. I trust You, Lord…I place my hope, my faith, my trust, my love – I place it all in Your loving and

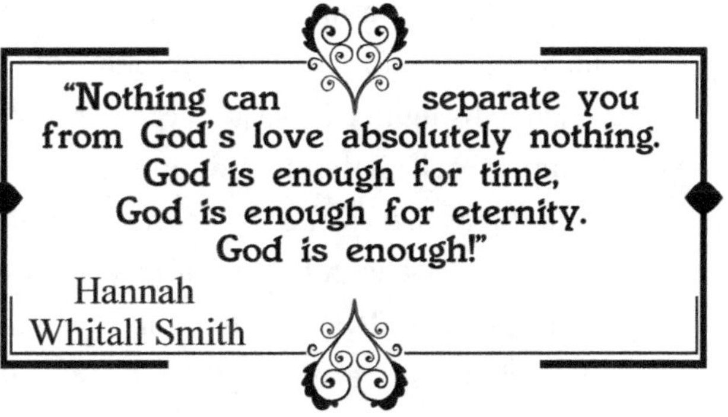

protecting hands. You are my God, and I will pursue You in all the days You give me…in all the ways I know how to…in all the times of endurance training You call me to…*from glory to glory*, Lord…Yes! *From glory to glory*, my heart will continue to pursue Your love! *Not my will*, Lord. No – Never my will! Holy Spirit *bring to my remembrance* this decision, this desire…every new day I am given! Not mine, but Your will be done in this heart of mine…forever and ever, Amen!" It was always so very cleansing and refreshing to *Talk* to Him like this. Vulnerability always had a way of filling and overfilling my heart, especially in those tempted-to-accept-empty days. "There is no emptiness with God!" I retorted. The weight of the world that sneaks its way to resting upon my shoulders over time - it evaporates before my very eyes…every…single…time that I come to Him!

It never ceases to amaze me how quickly His love washes over me in times such as these. I know everything will be alright, the moment I seek Him like this. I just know! He takes care of whatever it is. It doesn't matter. He just does! I can't explain it, and I can't deny it. It is just the simple truth – a matter of a very true fact in my days. I thought upon the reverent and undoubtable truth of it all as I let my eyes settle at looking outside again. I had pulled the curtain back, earlier, to use the natural sunlight for reading, rather than the light on the ceiling. It was prettier, in my opinion, and felt real…not fake. And, oh, how I desired 'real' today…well, most if not all days, actually. All sunlight felt like that, to me, though. I really looked forward to the Spring coming each year. Not just for the beauty of new growth and symbolism of renewal it brought with it, but also for the fresh, warm light it brought. His light, His masterpiece of beauty found in the seasons is just… so Good! I throw back all the curtains, flip open those window locks, and lift those puppies as far up as they will go! The fresh Spring breeze and beautiful sunshine coming in – Yes, oh, what a feeling of renewal and fresh new beginnings Spring brings with it! There is always such beauty and newness all around in that season!

I thought upon the topics of the day in comparison to the feelings Spring brought with it each year. The prevalent results of Spring were just like after the *growing-and-learning* seasons I go through with God. After it is all said and done…after those seasons have finished rolling in and making their changes in me…there is a newness that comes with it and a striking Beauty in my soul that

I…I really can't explain. "It just *is*," I concluded. His kind Spirit agreed, saying to me, "Yes, kiddo. It *just is*. You will find that to be true every time when You come to me <u>First</u>. Just keep it sweetly simple, My child. <u>First</u>, Me – *then*, everything else…and remember…just as I am, always - be gentle with your heart as you learn from Me. You will fall, you will fail, and you will stumble. I sent My Son to be The Perfect One because no one was. It is *in Him* that you will find the you that I have called you to be, little one. It will *only* be *in Him*. So, again I say, <u>First</u>, Me – *then*, everything else." I smiled in understanding. His words felt like a cool drink of water, rejuvenating my soul and filling me up to the brim with His Love. It never failed. They just always do feel that way!

With a quickening of remembrance, I said, "Oh! P.S. If You didn't hear it between the lines, which I am sure You did…" I paused with a twinkle in my eye as I looked out into the sky from the bedroom window. The crystal-like snow caught my attention for a moment, mid-delivery. They sparkled from the sunbeams pouring down upon them – glistening like a sea of diamonds to the end of the horizon. It was beautiful, just like this sweet moment with Him. "…just to be clear and consistent, Lord…I just wanted to say… Thank You, God…Oh, my God, my heart…is and always will be Yours!

> "Teach me Your way, O Lord; I will walk in Your truth; unite my heart to fear Your name. I will give thanks to You, O Lord my God, with all my heart, & will glorify Your name forever."
> - King David

I love You so very much! Thank You for loving me, too!" I breathed in, slowly, still looking out the window at the crystal beauty He had painted and prepared…for reasons unknown to me, but for whatever reasons that He saw fit to do so. I looked, and I sighed, taking in the scenery with wonderment filling my heart. It was just so beautiful…although quite a devastating blizzard…there was just so much beauty in it! A faint smile kissed my lips as the sun did the same to my cheeks. Even with this bitter cold of an unexpected Blizzard Winter covering my Spring that I so cherished and looked forward to each year – I could still feel warmth in the midst of it! I may be confined to the quarters of this house during this long period of time because of it, **BUT** I could still smile during it! I could still appreciate the beauty within it! Yes. With Him, I can still…I can, still. The list that I had started, stared back at me in the pause of my thoughts of appreciation. "Speaking of *still*, there is work to be done… still," I said with a deeper awareness than I had when I began this morning. Instead of discouragement, though, I felt greatly encouraged at this new awareness. Another new beginning was ahead of me and I felt excitement flowing through my soul at the thought! I desired the work ahead, even though I knew it would be difficult. It had to be done. I desired to be transformed into the fullness of His image. I desired to participate in the purification, refining, and sanctification processes ahead of me. I desired renewal and complete restoral in Him. Those steps had to be taken. They just had to! With all my heart and

> **"We Love Because He First Loved Us."**
> John the Evangelist, an Apostle

everything in me, I desired to pursue Him and His great love for me. I bowed my head once more and said, "Thank You, Lord. Forever, Thank You! I choose to *Abide in You*! Prune me and make me into all that You are calling me to be, Father. I Love You, Amen…again…and still."

MEMORY VERSE

*We give thanks to God, the Father of our Lord Jesus Christ, praying
always for you, since we heard of
your faith in Christ Jesus and the love which you have
for all the saints; because of the hope laid up for you in heaven,
of which you previously heard in the word of truth,
the gospel which has come to you, just as in all the world also
it is constantly bearing fruit and increasing,
even as it has been doing in you also since the day you heard of it and
understood the grace of God in truth...*

*.... For this reason also, since the day we heard of it,
we have not ceased to pray for you and to ask that
you may be filled with the knowledge of His will in
all spiritual wisdom and understanding, so that you will
walk in a manner worthy of the Lord, to please Him in all respects,
bearing fruit in every good work and increasing in the knowledge of
God; strengthened with all power, according to
His glorious might, for the attaining of all steadfastness and patience;
joyously giving thanks to the Father, who has qualified us to share
in the inheritance of the saints in Light.*
Colossians 1:3-6, 9-12

To You

Dear Heart,

Your story is precious to the heart of God. He loves you, greatly! His Love is unending, reaching from everlasting to everlasting. He promises to never leave you, never forsake you, never abandon you, never lie or hurt you. He is close to the broken-hearted and is there for you every step of the way! Jesus Christ is the same yesterday and today and forever! He is in a fervent pursuit of *your* heart, even as you are reading these very words! God is as close to you as your <u>*very next breath*</u>! Jesus says, "Come to Me all who are weary and heavy-laden, and I will give you rest. Take My yoke upon you and learn from Me, for I am gentle and humble in heart, and you will find rest for your souls. For My yoke is easy and My burden is light." Yes, Indeed! He says come to Him, dear heart! He will give you rest when you lay it all down at the feet of Jesus! God desires for you to bring it all to Him. His heart beckons to *yours*. Do you hear it? *You* are not alone. <u>Every moment</u> of your life, <u>every single</u> intricate detail of *your* heart, *your* mind, *your* soul - Yes, *your* entire being - <u>every part</u> that He wonderfully made, every part of *you* and *your* heart is precious in His sight and to His heart! **Know this.** God made *you* and He <u>***does not***</u> make mistakes. You are wonderfully made by a Father who Loves you so very much! I encourage you to seek Him, pursue Him as He pursues you!

I encourage you to strive to make Your Story - His Story,
each new day He gifts to you!

<u>GOD LOVES YOU</u>

Closing Prayer

Father,

Let me hear Your lovingkindness in the morning; for I trust in You; Yes, I confidently place my trust in You and know that in peace I will both lie down and sleep, for You alone, O Lord, make me to dwell in safety. Teach me the way in which I should walk; for to You I lift up my soul. Teach me how to love You with all my heart, all my soul, all my mind, and all my strength. Yes, Father, show me how to acknowledge You in all my ways so that Your glory be shown in and through my thoughts, my words, my deeds, and the deepest parts of my heart. Cleanse and Sanctify me, Purify and Renew me, Transform and Guide me...Yes, Lord, search me and know my heart, try me and know these anxious thoughts, if there be any hurtful way found in me, show me and lead me in Your everlasting way. Here I am, God, send me - use me for Your will and glory! I submit to Your calling, I desire Your path. It is in You that I take refuge. Teach me to do Your will, for You are my God; let Your good Spirit lead me on level ground. For the sake of Your name, O Lord, revive me and draw my heart ever-near to Yours! Oh God of peace, who brought up from the dead the great Shepherd of the sheep through the blood of the eternal covenant, even Jesus our Lord, equip me in every good thing to do Your will, working in me that which is pleasing in Your sight, Father, through Jesus Christ, to whom be the glory forever and ever. Yes, Oh God of my hope fill me with all the joy and peace in believing so that I will abound in hope by the power of the Holy Spirit. Fill my heart with all the fullness of Your Great Love for me, Lord! Grant me, Father, according to the riches of Your glory, to be strengthened with power through Your Spirit in my inner being, so that Christ may dwell in my heart through faith. Yes, indeed, the very faith that Jesus has given and is perfecting in me. Lord, give me a spirit of Wisdom and of revelation in the knowledge of You and in what You have called me to do. Enlighten the eyes of my heart, Father, so

Closing Prayer

I will know what is the hope of Your calling and I, being rooted and grounded in love, may be able to comprehend with all the saints what is the breadth and length and height and depth of Your Great Love! Yes, I desire to know the love of Christ which surpasses knowledge, so that I and this heart of mine may be filled up to all the fullness of You, Oh My God! Yes, my heart is Yours, Father! Now to You who is able to do far more abundantly beyond all that we ask or think, according to the power that works within us, to You, God, be the glory in the church and in Christ Jesus to all generations forever and ever.

Your Will Be Done, Father!

Amen

Scripture Reference

Scripture Reference